CAMPBELL ARMSTRONG

THE BAD FIRE

HarperCollins*Publishers*

HarperCollins*Publishers*
77–85 Fulham Palace Road,
Hammersmith, London W6 8JB

www.**fire**and**water**.com

This paperback edition 2002
1 3 5 7 9 8 6 4 2

First published in Great Britain by
HarperCollins*Publishers* 2001

A catalogue record for this book
is available from the British Library

ISBN 0 00 651497 9

Typeset in Palatino by Palimpsest Book Production Limited,
Polmont, Stirlingshire

Printed and bound in Great Britain by
Omnia Books, Glasgow

The Bad Fire

Campbell Armstrong was born in Glasgow and educated at Sussex University. After living in the USA for twenty years, he and his family now live in Ireland. He has been in the front rank of modern thriller writers for many years, and his bestselling novels include the acclaimed *Jig* series. His recent heartbreaking memoir, *All That Really Matters*, was also a remarkable success, particularly in Scotland and Ireland, where it was a No 1 bestseller.

'*The Bad Fire* strips bare a world in which bent coppers, vicious hitmen and sectarian powerbrokers clash, and family loyalties are stretched beyond breaking point. Enormous fun.'   *The List*

'An engaging mystery thriller. Armstrong creates a powerful sense of place.'   *Dublin Evening Herald*

'A thrilling, complex plot with characters that bring the city of Glasgow to life.'   *Newcastle Upon Tyne Journal*

'An excellent thriller filled with mystery and suspense and peopled by gritty, full-bodied characters, some of them truly menacing. A real page-turning plot, lush with rich Glasgow dialogue and dark humour, liberally peppered with ruthless violence. In short, a sure-fire bestseller.'   *Aberdeen Evening Express*

BY CAMPBELL ARMSTRONG

AUTHOR WEBSITE

www.campbellarmstrong.com

The people who bring Glasgow to life for me:
Annie Spiers, Erl and Ann Wilkie, Kevin and Susan
McCarra, Nigel Clark, Brenda Harris. Thanks.

1

On a hot Monday night in early summer Jackie Mallon went on a leisurely pub crawl. Dressed in a black suit and black shirt and a slim silver tie with a wide ostentatious knot, he allowed himself only one drink, Cutty Sark and water, in each bar he visited. A dandy at sixty-eight, thin hair held back with gel and dyed the colour of crow, his dentures vanilla-ice-cream white, he wore ruby cuff-links and his cuffs hung exactly half an inch from each sleeve. His movement was economical, his manner careful; he might have been walking barefoot on a surface of shaved glass.

He surveyed the customers in each pub, winking at the gilded girls who pierced their lips and eyebrows with safety pins and hooks, girls who knew nothing of his reputation as a ladies' man in the old days, a knight of nooky. He nodded at friends and acquaintances who waved and called out his name cordially and wanted to ply him with drinks or just be seen sharing a joke with him because of his rep, because it did no harm to say you knew Jackie Mallon, you even *drank* with him.

He was also conscious of the young turks who drifted

in from the outlying housing schemes and were looking to make their mark. These neds sometimes caught his gaze directly, and he felt a hostile challenge in the way they stared at him. *Who the fuck does this old tosser think he is? High time he was put out to grass.*

Jackie thought: Snottery wee boys. Couldn't lick my black suede shoes. I'll be retired soon enough, lads. One last deal and I'm off into the big red yonder.

He rode from pub to pub in the back seat of his pale blue Mazda, chauffeured by Matty Bones, a former jockey with a pallbearer's face and a Smith & Wesson 4006 in the glove compartment. Bones drove him to the New Monaco Bar, where he bought everyone a drink. Next, they went to the Three Cheers and then the Clutha Vaults in Stockwell Street.

This was Jackie Mallon's terrain. This was where he'd been born and brought up, and where he felt secure. He had this part of Glasgow in his back pocket. He knew the tenements, the people, their feuds and marriages and divorces, their kids. His cocoon was an area bounded by the Duke Street abattoir, the Necropolis and the Gallowgate – a parish of tenements and tombstones and elaborate crosses that made eerie patterns on the Necropolis skyline. His territory encompassed Glasgow Cathedral and the spine of the Tolbooth tower where centuries before the heads of executed criminals were impaled on spikes for public enlightenment.

Jackie Mallon, who'd left school at the age of eleven, remembered Luftwaffe bombs falling on the shipyards, demobilized sailors and soldiers flooding the streets at the war's end, horny and high-spirited, government-issue orange juice that looked like neon chemical goo, old Granny Mallon's rabbit stews on Tuesday nights at the flat in Bathgate Street – but the city's true antiquity was a shuttered house to him.

He sat in the back seat of his car and surveyed the streets with proprietary affection. My town.

'Where to now, chief?' Bones asked.

Jackie Mallon wondered if he wanted another drink. He considered going back to his terraced house a few blocks north of Duke Street. He pictured Senga painting her nails flamingo or scarlet, and drinking Crossbow in front of the TV. He heard her big merry laugh and saw her fleshy underarms tremble. If she'd drunk enough cider she might be listening to a CD of Eagles songs and looking melancholic, and she'd say: O do you still fancy me, Jackie? Say you do. I'm in the mood to feel wanted.

Eagles, he thought. 'Crying Eyes.' Electric cowboy shite. He was very fond of Senga, but her taste in music gave him the willies. He liked Sinatra. Elvis. 'All Shook Up' was an anthem to him.

He peered from the window. Bones was driving down Bell Street, close to the old Fruitmarket, now a venue for musical events. A lot of the old city had been stripped down and tarted up. Jackie Mallon preferred things the way they'd been before the developers came hurrying in with their big blueprints and their wrecking balls and their frantic greed.

It's changing, he thought, and I'm changing too. I don't look at crumpet the way I used to. And they don't look at me. The ashes in the grate grow cold.

For the first time in a long time, Jackie Mallon felt a touch of nervousness. He wasn't sure why. The last bit of business was going fine. The pieces fitted nicely, thank you. He'd go into the sunset with a small fortune. So. Was it the idea of retirement that upset him? What to

3

do with his time? How to fill the days? Or was it because this job was a Big Score and he wasn't sure if he still had the goolies for that kind of action any more?

'Blackfriars next?' Bones asked.

'I don't know if I feel like another drink, Matty.'

'You usually finish off your night at Blackfriars . . .'

Jackie Mallon was quiet a moment before he said, 'Right, right, I'll have one last wee drink. You've twisted my arm.'

'Easy arm to twist, eh,' Matty Bones said, and smiled, showing a mouth filled with the stumps of old teeth. He parked, opened the back door for Jackie Mallon.

Mallon clapped the little man on the shoulder with affection.

'Righty-o. I'll drive down there and wait for you,' and Bones gestured towards an area of wasteland about a hundred yards away.

'You'll not join me for one?' Mallon asked.

Matty Bones rubbed his stomach. 'Ulcer's playing up.'

'Milk of magnesia,' Jackie Mallon said.

'That stuff doesn't work for me,' Matty Bones said.

Jackie Mallon paused outside Blackfriars pub. He looked up. Starlings and swallows flew in the darkening blue sky over the city. Soon streetlamps would come on.

Blackfriars was dark and comfortable. He ordered a Cutty, added water from a jug, looked the place over – students arguing about an Italian film, and a couple of familiar faces from a local TV news show trying to look conspicuously incognito. He tossed back his drink, stood at the bar for a few minutes, eyed a flame-haired barmaid, then he went outside and walked towards the patch of wasteland where he could see the Mazda parked among other cars. The driver's door was open. A figure sat behind the wheel. Bones.

Cigarette smoke drifted out of the car towards a nearby streetlamp where thousands of moths created a frantic blizzard. Jackie opened the rear door. He got in and looked at the back of Bones's head.

'I thought you'd quit smoking, Matty. Had a relapse, eh?'

The man turned his thin face. He wasn't Matty Bones.

'What the fuck's this?' Jackie Mallon said. 'Where's Bones?'

The man had a smile that was a sneer, upper lip drawn way over the top teeth. The look was camel-like. He tossed his cigarette away. 'He had to leave.'

Jackie Mallon said, 'Bones wouldn't leave.'

The man had a thin moustache. His breath smelled of alcohol. He was twenty-five, maybe, and had a small silver stud in his right nostril, which was inflamed by a yellow cushion of pus. He wore a transparent plastic raincoat buttoned to the neck. Jackie Mallon knew him, and considered him scum.

'Are you ready to talk, Mallon?'

Mallon sighed. 'Take this back to your boss. I've got nothing to tell. I've said it before, I'll say it again. And I'll keep saying it.'

'Oh my. That's going to depress him.'

'My heart aches.'

'Is that your last word, Mallon?'

'Aye.'

'The boss hates bad news.'

'Tough shite.'

The man's gloved hand rose to where Jackie Mallon had an unimpeded view of a gun, the barrel of which was pointed at his face. The gun was Bones's Smith & Wesson. This troubled Jackie, because Bones wouldn't let anybody – especially this scruff – touch his weapon.

Which meant.

Jackie Mallon didn't like to think what it meant. He didn't like to think what a plastic raincoat on a hot dry night meant either, although he knew.

I took my eye off the fucking ball. Complacency, the curse of old age. He stared directly into the gun, then the man's face. The man had a look in his eye Jackie Mallon had seen before, fear pretending to be bravado, terror masquerading as cool.

'That's a very dangerous weapon, sonny,' he said.

'I know.'

'Think. Think carefully.'

'Haggs doesn't pay me to think,' the young man said.

Mallon looked at the gun again. I'm an endangered species, he thought. Cold skin, hot night. He shivered. Mibbe I'm coming down with something. He heard moths buzz with the intensity of locusts under the streetlight and he had a sense of his life dwindling until he was no more than a fly-sized speck that might fit inside the barrel of the Smith & Wesson.

'Tell Haggs to go fuck himself,' he said.

2

The telephone rang and Eddie Mallon opened one eye: the bedside digital clock read 3:22 a.m. He was tempted to let the answering machine pick up and go back to sleep and see if he could reboard the train of his dream, which had been taking him on a pleasant ride through smooth green countryside that looked exactly like the land where the Jolly Green Giant lived, a place where peas were quick-frozen for freshness at the moment of picking. But he knew the locomotive would have gone from the station by now, and so he reached reluctantly for the handset and hauled himself into the real world.

The room was humid even with the window open; the dark was dead and heavy, the rasp of crickets somnolent and slow. He said his name into the mouthpiece, his voice thick.

'Eddie?' The woman sounded distant and nervous.

Mallon recognized his sister's voice at once. 'Weird time of day to be calling, Joyce. It's almost half past three here.'

'In the morning?'

'You got it,' he said. What was *wrong* with her? 'That makes it – what? About eight thirty a.m. where you are.'

'I'm not wearing a watch,' Joyce said.

Eddie's wife Claire woke and reached for the bedside lamp. The sudden pale light made Eddie blink.

'Who's calling?' Claire asked.

Eddie covered the mouthpiece. 'Joyce,' he said.

She looked surprised. 'Is she calling from Scotland?'

'I guess,' Eddie said. He spoke into the handset. 'Are you in Glasgow, Joyce?'

'Yes,' Joyce said.

'Something's wrong. I hear it in your voice. Talk to me.'

'I need you to come home, Eddie.'

'I *am* home. Queens is where I live, Joyce. Remember? Give me one good reason I should drop everything and come over there.'

'Because I bloody need you,' she said. 'Sometimes a sister needs her big brother.'

Joyce had never said such a thing before. She didn't even sound like herself, her voice was small and hurt, and she wasn't in the habit of calling him at this or any other time of day to ask him to go back to Glasgow.

A moment's silence on the line. He wondered if this call travelled through a cable on the dark Atlantic seabed, where no light had ever penetrated. He felt a touch of sorrow, thinking of the ocean's black width and the tourniquet of family and how tightly it was knotted even if you thought it had worked loose over the years.

He heard Joyce take a deep breath. 'It's Jackie, Eddie. Oh Christ, why is it so damn hard to say? He's dead. Jackie's dead.'

Something he couldn't identify turned over inside Eddie Mallon and dropped like a stone falling from a great height. A heartbeat skipped, an irregularity, a valve

8

malfunctioning. He had a feeling of a screw being drilled through his chest. *'Dead?* How? How did it happen?'

'He didn't die in bed, Eddie. There was no gentle into that good night shite.'

'I don't understand what you're saying, Joyce.'

Joyce told him in a single spare ugly sentence.

He was surprised by the heft of loss. There was a weight inside him, an iron pendulum creaking back and forth. His eyes smarted. He had difficulty swallowing. He felt himself splinter. He walked with the phone to the window and pressed his forehead to the warm pane and looked down into the darkened back yard. He listened to the heavy silence of the house. A beam of light extended from the bedroom window into the yard, illuminating a narrow patch of grass. He looked beyond the light to a place where blackness concealed beech trees and he had the other-worldly sensation that the ghost of his father was out there beneath the thick limbs and silent leaves. *I'm leaving, Eddie. I wanted to say my last goodbye.*

'What is it?' Claire asked. 'What's going on?'

Joyce asked, 'Eddie? You still there? Hello hello?'

Eddie Mallon felt as if he'd floated from this room, transported back to a Glasgow street in the early 1960s, a little boy on a kerb with his small hand in his father's big palm, and tramcars clattering past on their iron tracks and sometimes in the rain an overhead wire sparking and the air smelling scorched.

Never cross until the way is clear, Eddie. Look left, look right, look left, make sure nothing's coming. Don't you forget that, Eddie.

Okay, Dad. Left, right, left again.

Good boy.

You're dead and I don't understand why, Dad. I loved you, yes, I did, no matter what.

He felt tiny and scared a moment, no longer an adult in an adult world.

Claire asked, 'Who's dead, Eddie? Who is it?'

Mallon didn't hear his wife. His head was racing. Questions crowded his mind. Professional habit. What kind of weapon had been used? Had he been alone at the time of his murder? Had a motive been established? He imagined the old man's pain, or maybe there was no pain, maybe it was all over in a fraction of time too tiny to calculate. 'Have you phoned mother?'

'That's your side of the world,' Joyce said.

Eddie pushed the thought of his mother from his mind; he'd return to it soon enough.

Joyce said, 'The funeral's Friday. The pathologist says he's finished with the body . . . I can't deal with this alone, Eddie.'

Claire was out of bed now, standing at Eddie's shoulder. 'It's Jackie, isn't it? It's Jackie who's dead . . .'

Eddie Mallon touched the side of his wife's face gently and nodded his head.

She said, 'Oh God, I'm sorry, Eddie,' and he held her against his shoulder, grateful for her comfort even as he was miles away in that place where he could still sense his hand wrapped in his father's spectral grasp. The past could ambush you. Like the way he smelled his dad at that moment, so *real*, so *close* – tobacco clinging to a woollen overcoat, damp socks drying in front of a coal fire, a whiff of Cutty Sark, these things bushwhacked you.

'I'm sorry, really I am,' Claire said. She had a genuine heart. In her world all setbacks were opportunities in disguise; deaths weren't doors that slammed shut.

They were openings into other spaces, worlds we knew nothing about.

He spoke quietly into the handset. 'I'll call you back in a couple of hours, Joyce.'

'I'm feeling fragile, Eddie.'

'I'll arrange something. I promise you.'

'I'll be waiting right here by the phone,' Joyce said.

Eddie Mallon put the handset down.

'Sit beside me,' Claire said.

Eddie sat on the edge of the bed. Claire held his hand. He stroked her skin, which was damp. Eddie gazed at his wife's face. Once thin and delicate, a delightful skeletal construct, it had been made puffy by the mischief of time, the lines around the mouth deepening. But he still saw the beauty of a young woman in her. She was still the girl he'd fallen in love with more than twenty years ago. He wondered how much *he'd* changed from her perspective. His black hair, dense and curled, was streaked with grey, and he carried about fifteen pounds more than when they'd married, and some mornings he woke feeling the mass of forty-five years pressing down on him, and it was an effort to face another day.

The really *good* mornings, when you leapt out of bed, when you felt like a god who could overcome any crud the day threw in your face – a flat tyre, a cup of bad coffee, even a sniper in a tower with a scoped rifle and a bad attitude – were diminishing yearly. *I love you, Claire*, he thought. We're just not the people we used to be, those bright smiling kids in the old wedding photographs on the dressing table.

She said, 'You have to go.'

He heard her, but her words might have been filtered through muslin. He said, 'He was always talking about

11

coming over here. Always wanted to see his grandson. When we spoke on the phone last New Year's Day he told me this was the year he'd finally make the trip. I don't know if he meant it. You might as well take a goldfish out of a bowl as the old man out of Glasgow.'

He thought of his son, Mark, fifteen years old, asleep in the bedroom down the hall. Mark had never seen Jackie Mallon. And now he never would.

Claire said, 'You could get a flight today. Joyce is going to need support.'

He hadn't seen his sister in five years, the time of her last American trip, when her marriage to the irredeemable Harry Haskell – a permanently unemployed freeloader – had just ended. She'd dressed in black clothes during her stay, jeans, T-shirts, sneakers, impenetrable sunglasses. She projected an attitude of mystery and cool. She looked as if she were wandering, in a distracted fashion, some Left Bank of her imagination.

But he couldn't bring to mind her features clearly, and this bothered him. He knew what it was: the world was out of focus all of a sudden, and his memory with it. 'There's a bit I haven't told you.'

'I'm listening,' Claire said.

He heard a pulse in his skull. It was like the sound of a cork in water slapping time after time against the struts of a pier. 'I haven't told you how he died.'

3

At ten a.m. Charles McWhinnie drove his Rover south across Kingston Bridge. The heat haze had already burned out of the sky above Glasgow. It was going to be one of those days when light rose shimmeringly from pavements and tar surfaces melted. The headlines in the *Evening Times* would invariably read, TEMPERATURES SOAR, CITY SWELTERS.

McWhinnie, born and brought up north of the river, didn't like the Southside. The city seemed alien over there. Even the neighbourhood names struck him as strange. Crossmyloof. Strathbungo. Ibrox – which he thought sounded like a veterinary ointment for chafed cow udders. *A jar of Eyebrox lotion, please.*

He glanced at the narrow motionless river as he crossed the bridge. He saw the tall cranes that serviced the Govan Yard, and the George V Docks, but where these huge constructions had once crowded the skyline, they were few now – skeletal souvenirs of the shipbuilding that years before had been the city's most vibrant industry.

It had been a time, McWhinnie thought, when people took a pride in their work. What did you have nowadays? Social Security and welfare fraud and chancrous housing estates where kids bought and sold drugs with brazen abandon and fried their brains on lethal concoctions; any stray traveller in such places might have thought himself in a suburb of Beirut.

Collar undone, tie loose, he parked his car in a narrow street of black tenements a quarter of a mile from the drabness of Govan Cross Shopping Centre. Govan had always been a shipyard burgh, a company town, vibrant and cocky. Now shops were barricaded behind steel shutters, and graffiti had been spray-painted everywhere, most of it cryptic save for the occasional sectarian slogan. *IRA Rules*. Bigotry had never truly died here, no matter what claims to the contrary certain civic leaders and flash media guys might make. It was still simmering in segregated schools and uneasy mixed marriages. Prods and Tims. McWhinnie despised this divide, this moronic anachronism in a city alleged to be surging into a glossy European future.

He took a big paper bag from his Rover, then locked the car. He entered one of the tenements, passing a group of very young kids who were smoking cigarettes. The kids glared at him with tribal hostility as he made his way into the building and walked the length of the close, which was dark and clammy, to the stairs.

He climbed. On the first landing he unlocked a door whose nameplate read: *A Factor*. He slipped inside quickly, nudging the door shut behind him.

'I want in and out of here as fast as humanly possible,' he said.

The little man who sat in the room and gazed at the TV said, 'Aye, I don't blame you. This place . . . I wasn't expecting the fucking Ritz, granted, but this is a bloody slum.'

'We'll deal with your accommodation at the appropriate time,' McWhinnie said. He tried very hard to be non-specific in his utterances. When you were precise, you often found yourself compromised.

He looked round the one-room flat; claustrophobic, faded daffodil paint, a window so grubby it was opaque, a rag of a curtain, a cracked porcelain sink. A single bed faced the window. On paper, the premises belonged to a certain Arthur Factor, who was non-existent.

McWhinnie put the bag on the table and watched the little man open it hurriedly. It contained a loaf of white bread, a packet of bacon, six small eggs, three apples, three oranges, a carton of milk, a box of tea bags, a paperback sci-fi saga entitled *Planet of Ice*, Tagamet capsules and a bottle of cheap blended whisky.

The little man looked at the label on the bottle with slight disgust, then surveyed the items on the table. 'How long am I staying here?'

'I can't say.'

'A rough idea.'

'A week,' McWhinnie said vaguely. He didn't have a clue.

'A week? Christ's sake. The telly's shite. You can't expect me to sit here and go blind looking at a picture as bad as that,' and the little man pointed at the TV, where a fat woman with big hair, blurred by snowy interference, wept in front of Jerry Springer. The caption on the screen read: *MaryLou Says Her Husband Made Love To Her Mother*.

Bones picked up the paperback. 'A science-fiction book. Beam me the fuck up, Scotty.' He looked at McWhinnie. 'This isn't my kind of thing, squire. I like anything by Dick Francis.'

'Your literary taste is noted. I'll send round a horsy selection,' McWhinnie said. 'And I'll find somebody to adjust the bloody TV. Do you have any more complaints? Or are we finished now?'

'You didn't bring a newspaper. I like the *Record*. I told you that. In a pinch, I'll read the *Sun*.'

'Tabloids tend to slip my mind. I'll arrange it.'

'White bread. I'm supposed to live on this?'

'Think of it as a starter kit. The duck à l'orange with potatoes au gratin and baby carrots comes later.'

'You're a card, son. People would pay to hear you. See, I've always watched my diet. I've sat hours in sweatboxes to lose a few pounds. And white bread is just not fucking *on*. As for bacon . . . fat clogs arteries fastern twenty rats stuck in a drainpipe.'

McWhinnie ran a hand over his straw-coloured hair. He had the look of a sprinter only a year or so past his prime. Women warmed to him instantly, but somehow prolonged relationships failed to happen. He was never sure why. Maybe women thought he was too committed to the job, too anxious to be accepted into the bloodstream of the Force.

'Right, finished here,' he said. 'I'm offsky.'

'Just a minute, son. What school did you go to?'

'Beg pardon?'

'A toff's school, was it? A fee-paying school, eh? Your accent is posh Glasgow. Not like mine. 'Course, I only went to the local eedjit school with all the other toerags. I wasn't privileged, you understand. No silver spoon in my gub.'

'Get this straight. My name, my background – off limits to you. Think of them as protected by live high-voltage wires. Go near them, they barbecue you like a sausage on a hot grill. Is that clear?'

'You're a tough guy, eh? I'll tell you something, sahib. You don't have the stuff for this work. I can hear it in your voice.'

'I'll be sure to keep your opinion in mind,' McWhinnie said. 'One last thing. Don't even think about leaving here and wandering around. You understand me? It's in your own interests to stay indoors.'

The little man said, 'Your wish is my command,' and opened the bottle of scotch. 'You'll have one for the road?'

'On a cold day in hell,' said McWhinnie. It was insufferably hot in this room, and the trapped air irritated him, and he didn't like this little fart he had to deal with. In fact, this kind of thing wasn't in his job description. Nowhere. Buying bloody groceries for scum. How did he get into this? What did this have to do with law and order? He hadn't signed on as an errand boy.

Somewhat dejected, he stepped towards the door. *You don't have the stuff for this work.* The little man's observation rolled through his head.

'A wee minute, squire. Did you take care of that, ah, business matter?'

McWhinnie removed a plain brown envelope from his pocket and tossed it to the little man, who caught it.

'Twenty-six hundred all squared away,' McWhinnie said.

The little man looked inside the envelope. It was filled with slips of paper. Each was marked *Paid In Full.* Twenty-six hundred and ninety-seven quid of debts to bookies all taken care of in one swoop.

McWhinnie said, 'I'll leave you to your purgatory.'

'You might have put in a bloody phone,' the little man said.

'You don't get phones in purgatory, Bones. It's a place of solitude where you contemplate your sins.'

McWhinnie shut the door and went down the stairs two at a time, relieved to be making his exit. Outside, the smoking kids had gone, the front doors of the Rover lay open and where the expensive tape deck had been there was only a black slot, like an unsmiling mouth.

Those little fuckers, he thought.

Those bloody monsters. He clenched his fists and looked up. The bright sky over Govan turned angry black-red in his vision.

From the window of his dreich one-room cell, the little man looked down at the sight of the well-spoken prat in the bright white shirt striding in a spluttering rage around his shiny car, kicking at useless tyres, *fuming*.

Funny stuff. Ho ha.

He opened the scotch, poured a measure into a cup and sniffed it. Granted, nobody was obliged to provide him with liquor. But if they were going to, why did they have to donate sewage?

Bones took whisky into his mouth and swirled it for a time. *Purgatory*, he thought. So this is what good Catholics fear.

The waiting room. Where you find out if you're getting a ticket for the onward journey.

I know where I'm going, he thought.

He stared at the gloomy walls. The faded yellow. The crap TV. The single bed with what looked like an Army-issue blanket, rough as a bear's arse. It wouldn't take long before this place spooked the daylights out of him, and then the sheer force of the terrible thing he'd done would kick him, like the hoof of an angry horse, straight in the soft core of his heart.

4

Eddie Mallon arrived at his mother's house in Stony Brook on Long Island at dawn; a red sky, a frail arrangement of still clouds tinted by thin sunlight. He parked his Cherokee, then walked up on to the porch. He could hear the 24-hour radio station his mother favoured, big-band stuff of the 1940s, Glenn Miller, Artie Shaw. 'Stars Fell on Alabama.'

He opened the front door and called out, 'Hello?' and Flora appeared in the kitchen doorway. She rose every morning of her life at daybreak and set about pruning, clipping, planting. Her garden was no mild hobby. It was serious business, an escape to a fragrant world of petal, stamen, pollination.

She was a small white-haired woman with pale red cheeks and rounded features. She looked, Eddie sometimes thought, like the Universal Grandmother. She stood on tiptoe to kiss her son.

'Surprise surprise, a dawn visitor,' she said. 'Tea?'

Eddie shook his head. 'I'd prefer coffee.' Then he remembered she'd quit drinking caffeine. He wondered how to approach the matter of his father. Direct. Say what you have to, then deal with the consequences.

'I can do you a herbal tea,' she said.

'How about plain old water, Ma?' He followed her inside the kitchen.

'Just passing, did you say? You're so *transparent*, Eddie. I've been expecting you.' She flipped the switch of an electric kettle.

'You heard . . . ?' He wondered if Joyce had called after all.

'Rennie phoned from Glasgow to tell me.'

'Rennie?'

'A cousin of mine. She was married to Nick.'

Who the hell were Rennie and Nick? There were so many relatives in the old country, uncles, aunts, cousins, second cousins, people Eddie Mallon knew nothing about, strangers' faces in hefty photo-albums Flora dragged out whenever she'd had more than two glasses of vodka. *This is Sammy, my sister Sally's husband in Pollokshaws. Here's Willie and Anne at their silver wedding at the Grosvenor.*

'How are you taking it? How are you feeling?' he asked.

Flora said, 'It was like I'd been struck on the head . . . I'm not sure I believe he's dead yet.'

Eddie drank his water, then set his empty glass in the sink. The kettle boiled, switched itself off. Flora dumped a tea bag into a mug decorated with a toadstool. The tea smelled of raspberry.

Flora said, 'I turned the radio on a minute ago and the band was playing "Moonlight in Vermont", and I thought of your father, and I remembered we danced together at the Barrowlands Ballroom in Glasgow and that was one of the tunes they played. He loved to dance. He was so nimble.' She looked at Eddie. 'Did he ever tell you he wanted to be a soccer player?'

'No. I knew he enjoyed the game. He took me to a couple of matches, I remember.'

'When he was eighteen he had a trial for a team called Third Lanark. The coach wasn't impressed. Jackie was so *disappointed*. He wanted to be a football hero, get his face on a cigarette card, newspaper clippings. "Mallon scores winning goal in the last minute." His whole life might have gone in another direction if he'd played well that day.'

Eddie touched the back of his mother's hand and thought: she seems to be taking it well. But why shouldn't she? She hadn't seen Jackie Mallon for thirty years, and so far as Eddie knew hadn't spoken to him in all that time. She'd loved him enough to marry him, but after so long a separation even the strongest of loves would surely deteriorate into a series of small regrets and smudged memories.

Eddie said, 'So he never became a football hero.'

'He didn't become any kind of hero.'

'We can't all be hotshots. Most of us make compromises with our ambitions, Ma. Dad made them. He quit dreaming and went into business.'

Flora looked at her son. '*Business?* Is that what you call it? Fireplaces and doors ripped out of old houses, fancy ironwork, lead guttering. He had that warehouse in Bluevale Street crammed with mountains of absolute junk piled up with no sense or order.'

Eddie Mallon remembered the warehouse, and how it smelled of rust and damp and paraffin. It was a wonderland of the used and discarded, busted statues and skewed sundials and rusted iron radiators, ancient Singer sewing machines and old Underwood typewriters and valve radios from the 1930s and '40s. Jackie always had a nightwatchman around in case of thieves, and warehousemen in grey coats who had pencils stuck behind their ears and smoked Woodbines all day long. At night guard dogs were left behind to roam the premises, fierce beasts with fangs.

Flora said, 'I always thought he could have done much better than become a glorified junk man.'

'Ma –' But Eddie wasn't sure how he wanted to continue. He was no junk collector, Ma. Let's give him some dignity: call him what he called himself, an architectural salvage dealer. When an old house was about to be demolished, he was there, studying, picking, assessing.

Flora smiled a little sadly. She spoke as if to herself. 'He was a beautiful man to look at. And charm? In *abundance*. He could talk the moon out of a cloudy sky. Sometimes we'd be walking along Alexandra Parade and all the girls would turn their heads when we strolled past, and I was the one on his arm. I was so *proud*. Other women wanted him and they'd do anything underhand to get him. And your father was easily led, Eddie. He had the ego of a film star. He couldn't pass a shop window without glancing at himself.' *Couldnae pass* . . . She'd shed most of her native accent; but when she spoke of the past she sometimes slipped into Glasgow dialect. 'And then I think of that time in Largs and how sweet life was in the beginning.'

Whenever Flora spoke of Jackie Mallon, the coastal town of Largs invariably arose and her expression became glazed: she had a golden memory of Largs where she'd honeymooned with Jackie. Eddie wondered why she'd never found a new husband, or even a lover. She'd buried herself in teaching grade school and then when she retired she'd hit the horticultural books vigorously. And suddenly this little house in Stony Brook overflowed with plants; a greenhouse out back was crammed with growing things. Flora worked at her gardening with the zeal of a Victorian botanist.

She said, 'I confronted him a couple of times about his . . . amorous misadventures. He always looked so ashamed. It would never happen again, he'd say. But it did. Then after you were born my priorities shifted – I just wanted to keep a nice house and raise my family. Jackie could have had a harem for all I cared. I wanted respectability.'

She blew her nose into a tissue she plucked from a box on the table. '*Salvage*,' she said, as if the failure of the marriage could be crystallized in this one word she obviously found so distasteful that it seemed to stick, like some bitter tablet, at the back of her throat.

Eddie moved close to her, placing a hand on her shoulder. 'Joyce wants me to attend the funeral.'

'Jackie was your father, Eddie. If you want to see him buried, that's perfectly natural.'

Eddie Mallon was a little uncomfortable. He wondered if he was being disloyal to his mother. No, I'm not betraying her, I'm going to help bury my father, it's what a son does, even if his parents have been estranged for years, even if he's lived with his mother in the United States and he hasn't seen his father since 1969 in Glasgow. Taking sides doesn't come into it.

Death negates the need for diplomacy.

He wondered if Flora knew about the letters and birthday cards that had started to arrive from Jackie seven or eight years ago or the phone calls Jackie made a couple of times a year, or the fact Eddie had phoned his father from Queens. Eddie could still remember how that first letter had begun: *Dear Eddie, It would be unnatural if you didn't think bad of me.* Christmas packages had begun to arrive later, gifts of Scottish origin, tartan scarves, fruit-cake, McCowan's toffee and Edinburgh rock for Mark.

During one of his phone calls Jackie had said, *What I did was a big mistake,* and there was the dolorous note in his voice of a man who'd drunk just enough to be honest. *Hacking the family apart like that was a bloody selfish cruelty, Eddie. Now I wish I'd told your mother to keep you and your sister together. But no, no, I knew better, I chose another way.*

If Flora knew about any of this, she never said so.

'Does anyone have any idea who killed him?' Flora asked.

'Joyce didn't say,' Eddie remarked.

'Killers always go to the Bad Fire,' she said.

He was surprised to hear her utter this phrase from childhood, and even more surprised by the fact she hadn't used it with any flippancy. She'd said it seriously. It was where sinners were sent in Glasgow. *You'll go to the Bad Fire if you steal, if you lie, if you cheat, if you swear . . .* Parents told kids that. Eddie would lie awake in Granny Mallon's third-floor flat in Bathgate Street and see flames created by streetlights in the folds of the blinds. He believed the Bad Fire lay in the street below and if he went to the window at night he'd see the pavement explode and people coming home from the pubs get sucked through a slit into the inferno.

'I stopped believing in the Bad Fire long ago,' he said.

'Not me,' she said. She stepped towards Eddie and held him a moment and he thought he detected a shiver run through her, as if she were suppressing an emotion. 'He must have had enemies, Eddie.'

Eddie shrugged. 'You don't know that. He might have

been shot by somebody who didn't know him. A random slaying. A robbery. We don't have the facts.'

'That time he went to jail,' she said, then she paused.

Jail . . . Eddie remembered how he'd constructed a fiction in which Jackie hadn't been incarcerated for eight weeks in Barlinnie, that austere fortress in the far eastern reaches of Glasgow. No, Jackie was secretly working for the government in an unspecified country overseas, fighting in something called the Cold War, which Eddie always imagined took place in the Arctic, tanks camouflaged white, soldiers with frostbitten noses.

He wanted to be proud of his dad. He wanted to adore him.

Flora said, 'He was never quite the same after jail. He was harder under the surface.'

Eddie had to ransack his memory. What crime had Jackie allegedly committed anyway? It came back to him in a flash, a little nugget of recall. Possession of stolen goods.

Flora continued: 'He met men in jail who didn't think twice about violence. Hard men. And Jackie had never been a violent person. He never once raised a hand to me all the time I knew him. But after Barlinnie, nobody could ever convince me he was the same man. I don't mean he started beating us up or anything like that –'

'He was angry with the system, Ma. He was embittered. He always said he was innocent. He was adamant about that. I remember he kept saying he'd done nothing wrong.'

Flora wasn't listening to him. 'He became withdrawn and furtive and he'd vanish for days at a time. He had a look on his face that said, *Don't ask me where I've been, woman. Just don't ask.* So I never did. He came and he went . . . And then out of the blue we moved up in the world, from Granny Mallon's flat in Bathgate Street to a house in Onslow Drive, and I didn't know how Jackie could afford a place like that on the money he made selling junk out of that bloody warehouse.'

She sat down at the table. She was reflected in the polished wood like somebody drowning in brown water. Eddie Mallon remembered moving house. Less than a mile separated Bathgate Street from Onslow Drive, but the houses in Onslow Drive weren't decrepit tenements, they were smart terraced properties, your own garden front and back. People living there belonged to a class that enjoyed a certain genteel prosperity.

'Obviously he made some good business deals,' Eddie said.

'Is that what you really believe?'

'Why not? What are you trying to say – he sometimes walked on the wrong side of the street? He ran some scams, broke some laws? How can you be absolutely sure of that?' He thought of Jackie Mallon saying: *I was never a criminal, son. Remember that. If anybody says anything against me at your school, learn to ignore it. I was the victim of spiteful men. That's the truth.*

The victim of spiteful men.

You don't know anything about him, Eddie, do you? You don't know how the man lived his life. You remember him the way a small kid might remember the scent and texture of a long-lost security blanket or a favourite teddy bear. You wanted more than that. All through the years of separation you longed for reconciliation.

Flora patted the side of her son's face. 'Oh, Eddie. He's stone-cold dead, but he's still got you thinking good things about him. What a bloody great talent it is to get the benefit of the doubt – even after you're gone.'

Eddie Mallon said, 'I missed him when I was growing up, so okay – maybe I idealized him a little. A kid misses his dad.'

Flora said, 'If you go to Glasgow you'll get to meet the mysterious Senga.'

'Is she so mysterious?' Eddie asked.

'I don't know the first thing about her. Admittedly, I haven't inquired too closely. She's been with Jackie for what – twenty years? Just think. If he'd married her she'd be your stepmother. There's a thought for you, Eddie.'

Flora sagged suddenly; she hunched over the table.

'You okay, Ma?'

'Just a little breathless. It'll pass. My days are usually more humdrum. This is . . .'

'Are you sure that's all?'

'I'm sure.'

He stood over her. He noticed her hair was thinning, her pink scalp faintly visible on the crown of her head through a white lattice-work of strands. He imagined her growing infirm and still somehow managing to hobble out to the greenhouse, watering can trembling in her hand. He wondered if Senga looked the same age as Flora, and if she had that same grandmotherly vibe about her – then he remembered Joyce had described her as red-haired and tall and flamboyant, a vibrant character. My stepmother, he thought. But Jackie hadn't taken the conjugal route with Senga, who had the status of a common-law wife.

He said, 'I have to make some travel arrangements. You sure you're okay?'

'I'm fine, fine.' She walked with him to the door. She held his elbow tightly. Stepping on to the porch, Eddie saw distress on his mother's face. 'I missed him too,' she said.

5

Flora watched Eddie walk to his vehicle and thought: he looks the way his father used to. He moves the same way, that measured step, like a man afraid of standing on something unpleasant. He's taller than his father, and better built, but not as handsome as Jackie; he doesn't have that same flighty charm. But more dependable than his father.

He has more heart. Or maybe less camouflage around it.

She saw the Cherokee back out of the drive. The lights blinked on and off a couple of times, Eddie's goodbye signal. Then the vehicle swung out of sight.

He's going to Glasgow to bury Jackie, she thought. I'll never see Glasgow again. Bellahouston Park. The Botanic Gardens. A saunter down Buchanan Street, a left turn along busy Argyle Street. She wondered if there was still that awful smelly zoo in Oswald Street where they kept a couple of mangy lions caged.

It was all lost to her.

She went inside the kitchen and opened the refrigerator. She removed a bottle of Absolut from the freezer. The glass was cold and adhered to her hand. She poured a little, drank it down quickly, filled the glass again. What is happening to you, lady? Two small shots at dawn. Strolling down Stumblebum Street. You shouldn't be doing this.

The radio was playing 'What A Little Moonlight Can Do'.

Oh aye. Oh yes. A little moonlight. Jackie's dead and there's a sharp stick in my heart and I remember what a little moonlight can do.

The honeymoon in Largs, the hotel room with the sea view, the big brass bed. Jackie was an energetic lover. He exhausted her. She loved that fatigue and the deep ache of it all. She recalled how it rained all week, but it didn't matter, because they never left their room. Jackie took the bedsheets and hung them between chairs, making them into a kind of tent, just for laughs. *I'm the sheikh*, he said. *Come inside my desert hideaway, Flower*. He often called her 'Flower'. Flora my flower, he used to say.

She picked up her glass and entered the greenhouse. She was a little out of breath: age, she thought, the system on the blink. She loved this glass room at dawn. The tranquillity, the quiet force of greenery, the subtle modifications of colour.

Flora my flower. What had replaced her? Senga my sunshine? Senga –

She remembered The Raid suddenly, the day she'd come home to the house in Onslow Drive from shopping and found it crowded with policemen, some uniformed, others in suits, and they'd yanked floorboards up, hauled drawers open, strewn clothing all over the place, dragged books from shelves and tossed them around, ripped open cushions and pillows – a mad intrusion, a crazy nightmare of vandalism.

This was when she'd first met a young policeman called Caskie. He had an easy manner. He'd taken her to one side and said, 'We have a warrant, Mrs Mallon,' and he flashed paper in front of her, but she pushed his hand away and raced from room to room, shouting at the policemen, throwing punches, and then Caskie had tried to calm her down, leading her gently into the back yard where he lit a cigarette for her and opened an umbrella to keep her dry from rain that had just begun to fall. She wanted to scratch Caskie's eyes out of his head.

But it wasn't Caskie's fault. He had a bloody warrant. He was doing his job.

Jackie was the cause of this. It was something Jackie had done.

She'd been expecting the sky to collapse ever since he'd come out of jail for possession of three 19th-century statues stolen from a country house in Ayrshire. He swore he'd bought them in all innocence from a dealer. She'd been dragging a sense of impending catastrophe around for more than a year.

And now this. Whatever this was.

She listened to the wreckage inside the house. Nails pulled out of wood, screeching. A closet ripped apart. 'What in God's name do you expect to find?' And she was shaking with rage, sucking smoke as deeply into her lungs as she could.

Caskie said, 'Read the warrant, Mrs Mallon.'

'Fuck the warrant,' she said. 'Just tell me.'

'We believe there are certain items in the house –'

'What items?'

Caskie, who wore a dark blue suit that was a little too baggy for him, looked like a young man who'd been promoted beyond his experience. This situation was obviously awkward for him. In other circumstances, she might have been touched by his immaturity.

He said, 'Specimens of counterfeit money.'

She laughed in disbelief. 'Counterfeit *money*?'

Caskie had pleasing blue eyes, a detail she remembered only later. And he had a hard time looking at her.

'And you have to tear my whole bloody house *apart* to search for this alleged counterfeit money?'

'Some of the men are a little . . .' and Caskie hesitated.

'They're brutes, Caskie. They're *enjoying* themselves, for God's sake!'

'I admit they're over-enthusiastic –'

'*Over-enthusiastic?* Who do I sue for damages if you don't find this alleged counterfeit money?'

'We try to leave things the way we found them.'

'And I sailed up the Clyde on a water biscuit. How do you put back broken vases and a broken mirror?'

'You'd be reimbursed for that kind of thing.'

'And my peace of mind – do I get reimbursed for that?'

Caskie touched her arm. 'We go through a rigorous process to get warrants like this, Mrs Caskie. They're not handed out lightly. Usually we get them only when we're sure.'

'And you're sure, are you?'

'I'm not enjoying this.'

'Somehow I believe you,' she said. She flicked her cigarette into the rain. 'At least my children are at school and don't have to see this demolition.'

A uniformed policeman stepped out into the yard and

gestured to Caskie. Caskie placed the umbrella in Flora's hand and said, 'Excuse me,' and then he disappeared inside the house. She smoked another cigarette, listened to rain drum on the taut black skin of the umbrella. She cursed Jackie Mallon. She cursed him for bringing these men into her home.

Counterfeit money. No. Stolen goods maybe, just maybe; she didn't think he was beyond doing a dodgy deal concerning paintings, statues, antique jewels. But fake money was something else altogether, big-time crime against the financial structure of the country, against the bloody government. Serious business. Serious punishment.

Caskie came back. 'We found what we were looking for,' he said quietly.

Flora was dizzy, lost her balance, slipped against Caskie, who had to catch and hold her. She stood with her face pressed into his shoulder while he talked quietly and reassuringly about how his men were making the place tidy again, it wouldn't be one hundred per cent but it wouldn't look too bad.

She stopped listening to his individual words. She liked the soothing sound of his voice.

'Do you know where your husband is?' Caskie asked.

She said she didn't. It was true. He'd been gone for the last two days.

'Myself and another officer will wait for him,' Caskie said. 'And you can tell the children we're here to investigate the break-in.'

Jackie came home the evening of The Raid. He was arrested before he could enter the house. Cuffed on the street and tossed into the back of a car and driven away quickly; the kids didn't see it happen. No charges were ever brought against him. His lawyer argued that the counterfeit notes had been planted by police officers who had long-standing grudges against Mallon because they suspected him of crimes they could never prove. The only charge they'd ever been able to make stick was the business of the stolen statues – and that case, the lawyer contended, was so thin as to be downright transparent. Besides, the evidence of involvement in a counterfeit scheme was circumstantial at best.

Flora didn't believe Jackie was innocent. He'd brought illicit material into the house and he'd threatened the security of the only things she cared for, home and family. How could he have put everything at risk? She didn't doubt he loved her after his fashion, and she never questioned his love of the children. But the marriage had turned cold.

Flora. My flower. Flower of ice, she thought. Petals dipped in frost.

I gave you my heart, Jackie Mallon. And you dropped it.

Three weeks after The Raid, weeks of arguments followed by fragile truces and promises of future good behaviour, weeks of madness and acrimony, she and Eddie had flown to America.

Without Joyce.

Flora had made a deal with the devil and she'd never stopped regretting it. Not in all the years since she'd left Scotland.

She wandered through the greenhouse with the half-drunk shot of Absolut in her hand. She wondered what Christopher Caskie looked like now. They'd corresponded a dozen or more times through the years. His letters were usually in response to her inquiries about Joyce: was she doing all right? In his last letter Caskie had written that his wife had died of cancer.

A blackbird flew over the greenhouse and was briefly reflected in sunlit glass. From inside the house the radio played Artie Shaw's rendition of 'There's A Small Hotel'.

6

Captain Zeke 'Marvel' Stock, Eddie's superior, was so big and wide that some of the men in his command referred to him as the Eclipse. He weighed an imposing three hundred pounds plus, much of it solid muscle. Eddie sometimes thought of the captain as an African tribal chief, a man you expected to arrive at a crime scene held aloft by a congregation of bearers.

Presently, Marvel was motionless under a traffic signal, and the red stop light gave the impression that his face was smeared with the bloody innards of a goat sacrificed in his honour moments before.

Eddie gazed at the dead man in an expensive overcoat who lay face-down in the middle of the street.

Marvel twisted his huge neck and scanned the grey edifice of a twelve-storey office building. 'A jumper,' he said.

'He's sidewalk salsa all right,' Bobby Figaro said. Figaro was Marvel's right-hand, yes-man and all-round gofer.

'Anyone got his name?' Marvel asked.

Figaro had it, of course. Figaro always had the scoop. 'John Boscoe Bentley, an address on East 32nd. According to what was in his wallet, he worked down on Wall Street for a brokerage firm called Something Somebody and Something Else Incorporated. I gather from a preliminary inquiry – to wit, a phone call to the company CEO – he was something of a player. How he came to be on the ledge of this particular building,' and Figaro shrugged.

'Coulda been pushed,' Marvel said.

'All possibilities will be explored, Captain,' said Figaro, with his ever-ready halogen-bright smile.

Detectives and uniforms were already inside the building, knocking on doors, asking questions; because it was only seven a.m., the building was largely unoccupied save for custodians and a cleaning crew, also a few lonesome workaholics, some of them demented guys who'd been in the place all night trying to balance ledgers or make sense out of spreadsheets.

Mallon stared at the corpse and wondered about a life terminated this way – whether he jumped or was pushed, it was a hell of a place for a guy to die; the hard pavement of a city street. He thought of his father and realized how few details he had about the old man's death. Was he gunned down in the street? At home? Were there witnesses? What calibre weapon? The questions buzzed him like gnats.

He watched Marvel yawn. It was an awesome sight; the mouth opened like a giant oyster about to yield a pearl. Gold fillings flashed in his mouth, which became one vast maw. 'I need coffee,' Marvel said. 'Somebody be good enough to get the captain a shot of strong java, huh?'

'There's a joint round the corner,' Figaro said. 'I'll go.'

Figaro disappeared. Brown-nose Figaro. Marvel looked at Eddie Mallon.

'Say, this ain't your shift, is it, Mallon?' Marvel said. 'Come to that, it ain't my shift either. So why have I dragged my sorry ass downtown at this time of day, you ask? Lemme tell you. Because I ain't been home, Eddie. I been struggling with paperwork. I been wrestling figures. Budgets. City Hall needs numbers to crunch.'

'Way over my head,' Eddie said.

'Way over mine too.' The captain lit a small brown-papered cigarette and stared at the corpse. 'My brain feels like a punchbag. I just stepped out for some air and take a look at this body we got here. What brings you out?'

'I need to talk with you,' Eddie said. 'I want some leave.'

'You got vacation time coming to you?'

'This would be leave of absence. Family reasons.'

'Somebody sick?'

Mallon saw lights go on in the upper floors of the building. He imagined the dead man, John Boscoe Bentley, falling through space, through darkness: what did you think as you dropped? You knew you were going to hit ground hard, and you'd break, so what went through your mind in those few seconds? Nothing? Everything? Or was it all just one blind deep-red searing panic? And at the end – what? A fraction of acceptance? A microsecond of tranquillity? Maybe you just blacked out, or your heart exploded out of fright halfway down.

'My father died.' Eddie turned to look at Marvel.

'Say. Sorry to hear that. Real sorry. How did it happen? Was he sick?'

Eddie said, 'He was shot.'

'*Shot*. Jesus Christ.'

'I don't know the circumstances.'

'Shot. Fuck. Fucking world we live in.' Marvel sucked on his cigarette and stared into the lit end a second. 'You got any heavy cases on your desk as of now?'

39

Eddie said, 'There's the dead girl we found in the empty brownstone . . .'

'That junkie kid nobody can ID?'

'Yeah,' Eddie said. He pondered the mystery of the missing teenage girl, a runaway from somewhere, and the fact her identity hadn't yet been established. Somebody must be missing her, waiting up for her, insomniac parents in a small backwater township in a faraway state.

'Tom Collins can deal with that,' Marvel said.

Tom Collins was Eddie's partner, a dark-jawed second-generation Irishman.

Eddie said, 'Apart from the girl, it's stuff that can wait.'

'Stuff that can wait, huh? I never heard of stuff like that before,' Marvel said, and smiled. 'Must be new on the market. I gotta grab myself some of that good shit. You take the time you need, Eddie. You want any help, you know where to turn.'

'I appreciate that,' Eddie said.

Marvel dismissed the gratitude with a quick motion of his hand and was already moving away, drawn towards the door of the building by the sight of Figaro, who was clutching a cardboard cup of coffee.

An ambulance appeared, lights whirling. Eddie Mallon watched the paramedics emerge. He saw them surround the body. And he felt weirdly lonely, out of touch with this world of his, as if he'd already left it, and was airborne, flying back to a place he barely remembered.

Glasgow, a city seen through a rainy mist, a fuzzy sketch in damp charcoal.

7

In the doorway of his parents' bedroom Mark Mallon asked, 'How long will you be gone, Dad?'

'A couple of days,' Eddie said. He marvelled at how tall his son had become; magically, he'd stretched from five feet to just under six in the space of a year. He was almost as tall as Eddie himself. Facially, he resembled his mother; he had a delicacy about him that gave him an androgynous look. Girls loved it. They worshipped the way his long hair lay against his shoulders. They telephoned him constantly. High-pitched little voices filled with squeaky hope: *Is Mark home?*

Claire was packing. She took special care with Eddie's best suit, a navy blue number for the funeral. It wasn't too late to change his mind, he thought. Cancel the airline ticket. But he'd already phoned Joyce and given her his arrival time, and she'd yelped with excitement at the idea of seeing him, and he felt good he'd been able to give her this much pleasure just by buying an airline ticket and rearranging his life for four days or so.

'Did somebody really shoot Gramps?' Mark asked.

'It seems that way.'

'Boy,' Mark said. 'You know why?'

'I don't know anything yet,' Eddie said. He flipped the pages of his passport, saw a picture of himself taken seven years earlier. Black hair, no grey. Face leaner. He thought he looked passably attractive in this picture, but gravity hadn't given him jowls back then.

'Was he, you know, like a crook?' Mark asked.

'A crook? What makes you ask that?'

'Something Granma once said. He was in jail for a while.'

'Sixty days. It was nothing, a mistake,' Eddie said.

'Why didn't he ever come visit?'

Eddie shrugged. 'He never got around to it, that's all. He was perfectly happy to stay home. He didn't like travel.'

'So why didn't *we* visit *him*?' Mark asked.

Good question, and Eddie Mallon had no easy answer; only excuses. He'd graduated high school, gone to the Police Academy, got married, bought a house in Queens, settled down, raised a kid, took his vacations in places as far away from any city as he could get, isolated cabins in Idaho or Montana, National Parks in Tennessee or Kentucky. A life went rushing past and it preoccupied you, and suddenly you realized you were never going to read *War and Peace* or sit drinking blood-orange juice at a sidewalk café in Florence or sail the Greek islands for a month. And all you could say to your son when he asked why the family had never visited Glasgow was, 'Somehow we just never found the time, Mark,' which wasn't a good explanation but close to the truth.

Thirty years of life. A bubble in the wind, drifting.

He touched his wife's hand. 'I wish you were coming with me.'

Claire zipped his case, smiled at him. 'It's only a few days. Anyhow, somebody's got to hold down the fort here.'

'Hey, I could do that,' Mark suggested. He was suddenly eager.

'Why does that offer make alarm bells ring in my head?' Claire asked.

'You think I'd throw all-nighters, big parties, invite hundreds of kids,' he said.

'Did I say that?' Claire asked.

'You don't have to,' Mark said. 'But it's what you think.'

Eddie stuck his passport in a hip pocket of his black jeans. He put his airline ticket in the inside pocket of his pale grey linen jacket, patted the place as if to reassure himself of something.

He looked at Claire. He was about to say it a second time: *you could still come with me.* Claire and Jackie Mallon had never met; the old man had always existed on the periphery of her life. Once or twice they'd talked on the phone and he'd made her laugh, but that was it. He was a dead stranger who'd spoken in a funny accent she sometimes didn't understand.

'If you're ready, I'd better get you to JFK.' She glanced at her watch, rattled car keys in her hand.

He gazed round the room in the manner of a man taking his leave of a place he'll never see again. Why did this departure from wife and son make him feel so goddam *melancholy*? He'd be back before they knew he'd even gone. They had lives of their own. Mark had friends, girls, serious hanging-out to do. Claire had a part-time job with Century 21 and every Wednesday and Friday she went to a health club where she rode an exercise bike and checked her pulse rate and blood pressure, then drank lo-cal fruit smoothies with her pals in a health-food bar.

'Ready,' he said.

8

Sun burned fiercely on the mouth of the Clyde. A launch, a thirty-footer, was anchored about a quarter of a mile from shore. Christopher Caskie stood unsteadily on deck and watched small boats sail towards Ardrossan, Ayr, the Isle of Arran. Sails dazzled yellow and white in the hard light.

Caskie was a card-carrying landlubber. The sea affected his stomach. The rise and fall of water was gentle but it made him queasy anyway, and he had to sit down. He closed his eyes, felt the sun on his eyelids. His short white beard was warm.

He heard footsteps on the stair that led from the lower deck. The man who appeared was six feet six inches tall. He had a tubercular appearance, circles the colour of grape juice under his eyes. His pear-shaped face was too small for the rest of his body. He wore a black silk shirt and white slacks. He farted quietly, sighed with pleasure, then sat down beside Caskie.

'There's nothing in the world as satisfying as a good healthy expulsion of gas,' the man said. His name was Roddy Haggs.

Caskie said, 'I suppose that depends on your priorities.'

'Ah. Are bodily functions off-putting to you? Note to self: do not discuss gases with Caskie.' Haggs studied other boats in the vicinity with his binoculars. 'Look at that. *Look* at that. Fuck me. I know what I'd like to do to her. Ooo.'

The object of Haggs's lust was a tanned blonde teenage girl in a neon lime bikini who dived from a small yacht about three hundred yards away. She vanished underwater, then surfaced laughing. She climbed back into the boat. She had a melodic laugh. Her water-flattened hair was pressed to her skull.

'Very nice,' Caskie said. He felt Haggs expected an appropriate response. They were members of the same club: men of the world. But different worlds.

'*Nice?* Show some enthusiasm, Caskie. She's completely shaggable. What they call a *babe*. Don't tell me you wouldn't fancy a poke at that crumpet.'

A high-powered speedboat passed, sending waves towards the launch, which trembled a little. Caskie felt his stomach tighten.

'Beer?' Haggs asked.

'I'll pass.'

Haggs popped a lager and slurped it. 'I'm fascinated by the idea of squeezing out whatever deep secrets the former jockey knows about good old Jackie's mysterious enterprise. I'll pop him like a bloody flea. Talk to me about the daughter.'

Caskie shrugged. 'Divorced. Intelligent. She had a fondness for amphetamine a few years back but she kicked it. I seriously doubt she knows anything. She was close to her father. But I don't imagine for a moment he discussed his business with her.'

Haggs said, 'Which leaves Senga.'

'Senga's a good-hearted sort, but probably hard as bloody nails if you step on her toes the wrong way. I don't think she's privy to anything either . . . I'll tell you one thing, Haggs. Her heart may be good, but it's broken right now.'

Haggs was silent for a time, cracking his knuckles. Caskie wondered if the silence was some form of sympathy, then decided it was more likely that Roddy Haggs didn't have a clue what to say about grief. He just wasn't good with little sounds of commiseration, the *so sorrys* and the *oh dears* that were the basic currency of response to human tragedy.

'I bet she kept her ears open,' Haggs said eventually. 'I bet she knew Jackie's business.'

'Even if she did, which I doubt, it doesn't mean she'd be willing to repeat anything she heard,' Caskie said. He stroked his white beard. He thought it made him look almost nautical, like an admiral. How ironic.

'Sod it,' Haggs said. 'It doesn't matter who tells us what. We'll get it in the end anyway. There's just too much buzz vibrating along the grapevine for this to be a bag of hot air. That old tosspot Mallon was up to something, and it was big, and I'm not being left out in the fucking cold. Nothing passes me by.'

Loose talk in the criminal fraternity, Caskie thought; but enough to convince Haggs something profitable was in the wind. Caskie decided to risk standing up. He leaned carefully against the handrail and looked down into the water. Reflected light hit his sunglasses. His mouth filled with sticky saliva. He was going to throw up. His moment of courage passed and he made his way shakily back to his seat. I'll never be a seagoing man. No life on the ocean wave for me.

Haggs said, 'Jackie Mallon left Glasgow last Wednesday from Central Station. You any idea where he went?'

'It's news to me,' Caskie said.

'My man saw him enter the station, then he was gone in a flash.'

'Maybe he didn't go anywhere. Maybe he was playing games with your man.'

'He was seen buying a ticket,' Haggs said.

'And then your man lost him? Downright careless.'

'You know nothing about this jaunt?'

'Nothing. Anything else on the agenda, Haggs?'

Haggs gestured loosely. 'We're almost finished.' He ticked off the names on his fingertips. 'Matty Bones. Joyce. Senga Craig. I'll deal with Matty when he's had a few more hours to sweat. You can cope amiably with Joyce. And Senga – do you want me to leave her to you?'

'Yes,' Caskie said.

'You're the expert on the Mallon family, after all. You're the authority. You're the historian.'

'Up to a point,' Caskie said.

'What you don't know about the family isn't worth knowing.' Haggs stretched his long arms until his elbow joints cracked. He smiled. The expression made him appear ugly and unwanted, like the solitary bruised Comice left in a greengrocer's display after all the others have been sold. 'It's a bloody shame Jackie was such a stubborn fucker –'

'I don't think he'd have told you anything in a million years,' Caskie said. 'He was never easily intimidated. If he didn't want to tell you something, that was the end of it. You could pull out his fingernails one by one, he still wouldn't tell you if he didn't want to.'

Caskie remembered Jackie Mallon the last time he'd seen him – Jackie's ruined looks, the glossy hair, the sunken cheeks that might have belonged to an old trumpeter. A chance encounter on Argyle Street on a busy Saturday afternoon last Christmas, the shops festooned with tinsel and light, an army of Santas everywhere, a kiddy choir singing 'O Little Town of Bethlehem', and Jackie walking one way, Caskie the other, and they'd collided. They shook hands vigorously, men who tolerated, perhaps even liked each other, despite the fact they worked different sides of the street.

What are you up to these days, you old rogue? Caskie asked.

All I do with my time is play dominoes in the senior citizens' centre. You didn't hear this from me, but we actually play for money. It's illegal, I know, I know. But where's the harm in gambling for a few quid, eh? Such are the innocent pleasures of sorry old men. I was never a reprobate. Jackie had smiled then, the easy-going smile that made you feel he was sharing an enormous confidence.

Caskie laughed. *And I believe in Santa.*

Aye, everybody should believe in Santa. Where's the spirit of Christmas if you don't believe in the gaffer?

They wished each other seasonal greetings. Jackie Mallon had patted Caskie's arm and walked away, bent forward a little against the wind that came rushing up from the Clyde and shook the decorations in the streets. Caskie thought he had a quality few rogues possess; he could make you believe he was incapable of the lawlessness attributed to him. He had about him an unsettling air of innocence. Charm, Caskie thought. All charm.

He blinked against savage sunlight. Unsteady as the

launch shivered again, he wanted to tell Haggs – look, we didn't need to meet on this boat, we could have talked over a glass of wine somewhere nice and private outside the city; but no, you have to drag me out to this bloody vessel *because you know I don't have the stomach for water*. Haggs had a mean-bastard streak and enjoyed other people's discomfort.

'There's a son,' Caskie said.

'He lives overseas. So I hear.'

'In New York,' Caskie said. 'He may come back for the funeral. He's a cop, incidentally.'

Haggs did another stretching thing with his arms. He looked like a figure made out of pipe-cleaners twisted by a child. 'So what? Is this a cause for concern or something? An American cop, is that supposed to worry me?'

'I mention it in passing,' Caskie said. He thought of Flora Mallon. Had the years been good to her? When he first met her he'd been more than a little smitten by her beauty; she had the kind of presence that would turn heads at parties, the rich black hair and the square jawline that suggested pride and self-assurance and an element of ferocity, the mouth that defied you to kiss it, the dark chocolate eyes that saw straight through you. He'd felt clumsy and inadequate in her presence, he remembered. But he'd been kind to her at a time when she needed somebody.

How was she taking the news of Jackie's murder? Had she ever stopped loving Mallon? Her notes never made any mention of him. The last time she'd written it was to say how very sad she was to hear of Caskie's wife Meg dying. Meg had been sick for a very long time, clinging to an existence that seemed worthless to Caskie. Slow death had been a lonely experience for her. And for him too.

That pathetic solitude. You sit in a room and hold the sick woman's hand but you might be the only person on the planet. You want her to die. You pray for it.

Then you wonder if you want her to die for all the wrong reasons.

Haggs scrutinized Caskie for a moment. 'You don't like this, do you, Caskie? You and me involved in this. It makes you feel dirty. You think I'm a fucking lout, don't you? Beneath your station in life. You've always looked down your fucking nose at me. For years you've made me feel like a turd.'

'I'm cooperating with you,' Caskie said. 'Isn't that all you've ever needed? Feelings don't enter into it.'

'I could buy and sell you and it wouldn't make a fucking dent in my bank account,' Haggs said. 'In one month I probably go through more than your entire net worth. You know what this boat cost me? You any idea what I paid for my house in Rouken Glen? Did you know I have a villa in Lanzarote with a swimming pool?'

Caskie said, 'I'm deeply impressed, Haggs.'

'Fuck you. I have a real estate company that covers the entire city. I own six full-service garages and a car-rental firm with a fleet of forty. So don't turn your nose up at me, mister. Don't talk to me like I'm slime. What have *you* got, Caskie? Let me tell you. Qualms, right? You've got qualms.'

'I certainly don't have a fleet of damn taxis,' Caskie said.

'Qualms, for fuck's sake,' Haggs said. 'I never trust a word that doesn't sound the way it looks.'

'Can we go ashore now?' Caskie asked.

Roddy Haggs said, 'Why? Don't like the water?'

'I get seasick, Haggs.'

Haggs said, 'Note to self: Mr Caskie does not like sailing. Don't ask him again. It makes him want to vomit.'

Caskie stared at the shore. He thought: I have one year until retirement. I've never looked forward to it before now. One year and then I'm beyond Haggs's reach. Gone. All this will be a dream hurriedly dissolving: *you hope.* He couldn't wait a year. He didn't have that kind of patience. He sucked sea air into his lungs as if to cleanse them and thought, I need to get Haggs out of my life soon. Today. Tomorrow. The day after. First chance I get. He'd had dreams of killing Haggs. In one, he dropped Haggs from a great height into a vat of acid and Haggs, screaming, was skinned within seconds. In another he'd strangled Haggs with an old bicycle chain. These dreams always left him drained.

Roddy Haggs unlocked a small cabinet and took out a plastic Tesco bag which had been rolled over and wrapped with very thick rubber bands. He thrust the bag into Caskie's arms and said, 'Before I forget. Evidence for the prosecution.'

Caskie, whose heart thumped, and who felt gluey saliva rise again in his throat, took the bag with great reluctance. What have I done? he wondered. What in God's name?

9

Eddie Mallon sat in the sky, hunched forward in his seat while he waited for that moment when the wheels struck the runway and the aircraft with all its great weight roared to an unlikely halt. A time he always found tense and scary. All bets with gravity were off. You could die in an instant of fire.

When the cloud cover was blown away and he saw the city appear, he forgot his alarm. He found himself looking out at a mazy profusion of orange streetlamps burning in the night, the lights of cars on long ribbons of motorway, and in the west beyond the limits of Glasgow the outline of hills. He couldn't recollect the city having been so bright before. It didn't square with his boyhood memory. He recalled a grubby place, more shadow than streetlamp. A soot-cloaked city, darkness at noon, black buildings.

'Your table, sir.'

The young woman who wore the sombre blue uniform of the airline chided him for his failure to put his table in the regulation upright position. He did as he was told; only on planes was he so readily obedient. This high off the ground he had no control over anything, no choice but to defer to people cloistered in a cockpit, men and women who understood instrument panels, radar, all the rest of it.

His nervousness wasn't entirely founded in this life-long dumb-ass fear of flying. He was also thinking of what he'd encounter when he landed. He was thinking of his sister and wondering how she'd handle her father's funeral. He was thinking about the old man's long-time live-in companion, Senga Craig. *What you see is what you get with Senga,* Joyce had said. *She's sentimental and she'll weep at the sight of a dead budgie in a cage, then out of the blue she'll hit you with a hard opinion or a tough insight you never saw coming. Under that pile of red hair there's a sharp brain.*

The prospect of finally meeting Senga made him a little uneasy; maybe it was the idea of seeing another woman in a house he'd only ever associated with his mother. Now somebody else slept in Jackie's bed. Somebody else controlled the household, chose the furniture, all the things Flora had done. *Jackie loves her,* Joyce had said. *And she's devoted to him. They're happy.*

He heard the thud of the undercarriage, a noise that always distressed him. The plane was four hundred feet, three, then two hundred, above the runway. And now, his nerves leaping like doomed kittens in a canvas sack on their way to a river, he watched the runway rush up to make contact. It was always easier when Claire flew with him; he had her hand to squeeze.

Landing. Touchdown. The wheels whined on the run-way. Eddie clutched the handrest until he was certain everything was safe, then he sat back in his seat, relieved, as the craft taxied. Why the fuck was he scared in planes?

It had always been so, starting with the first flight he

ever took, and that was the day he'd fled Glasgow with his mother, and he'd locked himself in the toilet and trembled, just stood there looking at himself in the mirror and *shaking*, not really knowing where he was flying to or why, except it was the end of the world as he understood it. Easy for a shrink to make something out of that, Eddie. You associate flying with upheaval. With change and the fear of change. *You can get off the couch now, Mr Mallon. That'll be two hundred bucks.*

He unbuckled his seatbelt. He stepped into the aisle, opened the overhead compartment, hauled down the leather bag Claire had packed for him. This was the only luggage he had, which meant he didn't have to waste time at the baggage carousel.

He checked the inside pocket of his jacket, made sure his wallet was in place, then moved along the aisle towards the exit. In the terminal he stood in the Immigration line reserved for non-Europeans. He was a naturalized American. Stuck in this slow-motion throng, he wished he had dual citizenship, because people with European Community passports were streaming through other channels unimpeded. He shuffled in stages towards an official in a glass booth, a rotund individual with no neck and Coke-bottle glasses.

Eddie handed his passport to the official, whose name-tag identified him as Arthur Dudgeon. He checked Eddie's photograph against the real man, then said, 'Somebody wants to talk to you, Mr Mallon,' and he nodded in the direction of a man who was standing, hands in the pockets of a pin-striped suit, twenty yards away.

'Is there a problem?' Eddie asked.

Dudgeon said, 'It's a formality, I'm sure.'

You couldn't argue with passport-control officials. It

was a waste of time the world over. These guys dreamed in their sleep of the Ultimate Rubber Stamp, the imprimatur of Total Authority. You possessed that, you had World Domination.

Eddie took his passport, picked up his bag, then walked towards the man in the suit, who shook Eddie's hand firmly; he was somewhere in his thirties and had thin ginger hair and a pleasantly bland face.

'Sorry to inconvenience you, Mr Mallon. I'm Detective-Inspector Scullion, Strathclyde Police. Will you follow me, please? We need just a wee minute of your time. Good flight?'

Eddie said, 'We didn't fall out of the sky or anything drastic.'

Scullion smiled. 'Ha. Indeed indeed.'

Eddie tracked Scullion along a narrow corridor to a room that was little more than a partitioned space with a desk and three chairs and a single metal filing cabinet and a neon strip in the ceiling.

'Sit down if you like,' Scullion said.

Eddie did so.

Two men entered the room. One, big and square-headed and business-like, had a build and complexion that reminded Eddie of cinderblock. He sat behind the desk. His suit was charcoal, his jacket buttoned tight across his midriff. The other man, who stood slouched, wore an unfashionable brown suit with a two-slash back flap, and thick-framed black glasses. He had a pale pink patch over his left eye and short silver hair cut in the fashion of a marine butchered by a half-blind barber. Hard to tell his age. Middle fifties, but he looked older.

'I'm Detective-Superintendent Tay,' the big man said. He shook Eddie's hand firmly and then gestured to the man with the eyepatch. 'This is Detective-Sergeant Perlman.'

Eddie nodded at Perlman who smiled and adjusted his glasses. Eddie wondered about the purpose of the patch under the lens. Perlman had the look of a man whose tailor had expired in the mid-1970s.

'You're here for your father's funeral, I suppose,' Tay said.

Eddie said, 'Your grapevine's working.'

'We like to keep our feelers out,' Tay said. He smiled now, but without enthusiasm. He had a small mouth and tiny teeth. His hands were granite things, enormous, like industrial sculptures. He had the watchful eyes of a prizefighter. 'I'm in charge of your father's murder investigation.'

Interested suddenly, Eddie leaned forward, elbows on knees. 'How far along are you? Have you identified the shooter –'

'So far,' Tay said, 'no, no shooter. All I can tell you is your father was killed by a person unknown using a forty-calibre handgun. He was sitting in the back seat of his car – a 1998 Mazda – when he was shot. We've ruled out robbery. Your father's wallet was in his pocket. He had a wad of money. Eight hundred and twenty pounds, give or take. The man who was his driver, a longtime acquaintance by the name of Matthew Bones, AKA Matty, has vanished. Nobody knows where. He hasn't been seen.'

'Is he a suspect?' Eddie asked.

'He'd been in your father's company for several hours before the murder, and now he's disappeared, so let's just say we'd like to talk to him.' Tay spoke slowly. He appeared to weigh his sentences for possible ambiguities. His pauses were finely calibrated.

Perlman spoke now. His voice was gruff but sympathetic, although his accent was thick and hard for Eddie to follow. 'We're looking for him, Mr Mallon. You may be sure. We're checking all his usual haunts.' *Aw his yewshall hawntz.*

Matty Bones: Eddie Mallon searched his memory. He thought he saw a shadow more than thirty years old, that of a very small man with callused hands – had he encountered Bones in the company of his father a couple of times? But so many men had drifted into his father's orbit, men who drank bottled beer in the sitting room of the house in Onslow Drive and filled the room with laughter and cigarette smoke. Bones could have been one of those men.

Tay said, 'You're a policeman in Manhattan.'

Eddie said yes, he was.

Tay looked at Scullion. 'The Big Apple, Scullion. Kojak and such. I was there once. Didn't like the place. New Yorkers think they live at the centre of the universe. Everything else in the world is crude and unsophisticated. Including police activity. Let me say this. We don't get as much gun-play in this country as you do. So we do our policing a wee bit different here, Mallon.'

'I'm sure you do,' Eddie said. Three cops, he thought. Quite a welcoming committee.

Tay said, 'Some people in your situation – especially in your occupation – might fly into Glasgow gung-ho about finding their father's killer. That kind of stuff makes it hard for me to stay focused. And so I get cranky. Right, Sandy?'

Scullion, Tay's foil, said, 'Very. Worse than cranky.'

Tay said, 'So let's understand each other, shall we?'

'I don't intend to make a nuisance of myself,' Eddie said. 'All I ask is you keep me posted if anything develops.'

Tay said, 'No problem. We'll keep you up to date. A simple courtesy.'

Eddie said thanks, but he wasn't sure how deep the sincerity ran here. This could be the soft-shoe brush-off, the old we'll-call-you routine.

Tay asked, 'When are you leaving?'

'After the funeral.'

'And the funeral's . . . ?'

'Friday,' Eddie said. The subtext here was unspoken, but it wasn't subtle, he thought. Finding Jackie Mallon's killer isn't your concern, Eddie, old chap. It's the business of the Strathclyde Police. No outsiders need apply.

Tay consulted a typewritten paper on the desk. 'You're staying with your sister Joyce in Ingleby Drive, Dennistoun. So if I need you for anything, I know where to find you. Sandy will walk you out.'

Eddie moved to the door. 'I hope you find the killer.'

'I'm confident,' Tay said. 'I'm always confident . . .'

Perlman rubbed his hands briskly. 'Nice to meet you, Eddie. Sorry about your father. Really I am.'

'Thanks.' Eddie nodded at Perlman, then picked up his bag and walked with Scullion back the way they'd come.

Scullion said, 'Tay's an excellent policeman, Mr Mallon.'

'I'm sure.'

'Dealing with the public isn't his forte. He's brusque at times.' Scullion paused, smiled at Eddie in a forlorn way. 'I just wish you had a better reason for visiting our fair city, Mr Mallon.'

'So do I,' Eddie said.

'Anyhow,' Scullion said, spreading his hands in a gesture intended to suggest that the city might be surprisingly bounteous just the same, 'welcome to Glasgow.'

10

Joyce was waiting for him in the Arrivals lounge.

She'd changed her appearance since he'd seen her last. She'd shed the black clothes and the aura of existentialist gloom in favour of faded old blue jeans, an oversized T-shirt with a camouflage pattern, tan sneakers with yellow-and-brown striped laces. She still wore shades, but the lenses were royal blue and tiny, not big and black. Her hair had been cropped short and dyed blonde. The style gave her oval face an undernourished quality. She threw herself at him energetically, clutching him hard.

'Eddie Eddie, oh Eddie.'

He held her tightly. He had a sense of love, like oxygen flowing to his head; it surprised him how easy it was to love her, because he often imagined absence and distance would eventually erode his feelings, and hers too, but that hadn't come about. And now all at once he was goddam tearful. It was what happened as you got older, he'd noticed. You sniffled more readily at things, choked up at reunions and soft-hearted movie sequences and farewells. One day you'd be a sentimental old fart in an armchair crying into a Kleenex during *It's A Wonderful Life*.

'I'm just so damned *glad* you came. Hold me and don't let go, Eddie.'

She felt thin, fragile. He wondered how her life had been lived in the five years since he'd seen her. They were neither of them letter writers. They spoke a couple of times a year by phone, and that was it. In New York he thought about her, missed her – but then, like everyone else, he got immersed in the currents of his own life and the promises he made to himself about calling Joyce more often were pushed to a backburner where they simmered. And that was sad, because the years were rolling inexorably away.

Then he was thinking of how far he'd drifted from Jackie Mallon too, and he wanted to say something to Joyce about him, but he was groping for words. Jackie floated before him, the thick eyebrows and the upright walk that was almost military at times, the cheeky dazzle of the smile and the habit the old man had of cupping a cigarette as he smoked, as if he were afraid of a wind blowing it away. It might have been a mannerism born in the drab post-war years, when cigarettes were precious.

I didn't have enough time with him, Eddie thought, I invented him from memories. And he was suddenly consumed by anger. Somebody had killed the old man, and that fucker, whoever he was, would goddam have to pay in the end –

He caught himself in mid-rage, breathed a couple of times deeply, sought calm. Don't go off the deep end. The police are looking for the killer. They'll find him.

Joyce said, 'I'm all cried out. Talk to me about the living, Eddie. Talk to me about Claire. Tell me about my gorgeous wee nephew.'

He spoke about Claire. He brought her up to date on

61

Mark and the girls who chased him. She linked her arm in his and they walked across the terminal, which was new and shiny, a gilded palace that corresponded to nothing in his memory of how it had been years ago, a drab matchbox where you half-expected the only craft permitted to land would be 1940s Spitfires in need of fuel to continue the war against Jerry.

They went outside. It was dark and the night air warm, almost tropical. 'It feels like Miami,' Eddie said. Any subject but their father.

'We're having an extremely rare heatwave, Eddie. Enjoy it while it lasts. It'll probably be pishing rain again in a day or so. My car's over there,' and she pointed to her left.

The conversational transition from murder to the weather; it was wonderful comfort. How would people live their lives without a vocabulary of weather?

He said, 'You look . . . different. You were all dark last time. Your clothes, hair . . .'

'Oh, that was my black self. My tragic period. The troubled divorcee, et cetera. You think this haircut's too flashy for a woman almost forty? Too *gallus*?'

'Gallus?'

'Have you forgotten your Glasgow patois, Eddie?'

'Gallus,' he said, remembering. 'Wait. Brazen, swaggering.'

'See, it's like riding a bike. You never forget.' She led him across the car park. 'I love you, Eddie. We're too careless, the way we let ourselves drift.'

'I know, I know.'

She gripped his hand. He had a strange disorienting moment, as if he'd come to a city where he'd never been, and was talking with a woman he'd never met in his life

– and then this web of illusion blew away and he was himself again, except for the fact that he had no idea of time, neither day nor date. Was it still Wednesday? Was it only this morning at 3.30 US Eastern time when Joyce had phoned him in New York? Time zones, loss of hours. He tried to calculate, but gave up.

Joyce unlocked a car, an old dark blue Mini. 'Just stick your bag in the back.'

He got inside. The space was small and his knees were jammed against the glove compartment. Joyce drove out of the lot to the freeway. *Motorway*: he corrected himself. He looked at the blue signs pointing to Glasgow. He couldn't recollect a motorway linking the airport to the city. It was new. So were the bright tidy sub-urbs he saw from the window. And light. So much light.

'When did they do all this?' he asked, nodding at the housing estates.

'Who knows? Glasgow's a constant work in progress, Eddie.'

What had he expected? Everything the same, pre-served in aspic? He thought: I don't recognize the city of my birth.

'We're right up there these days with the high-flyers,' Joyce said. 'Milan. Paris. We're dead cosmopolitan now, Eddie. No more soggy tomato sandwiches washed down with cups of nasty instant Nescafé. We've crossed into the promised land of croissants and cappuccino. We're Europe, Eddie.'

'And you – you're still educating the young?' he asked.

'What else would I do?'

Joyce, like Flora had done, taught school; she drummed Romantic poetry into the heads of fourteen-year-olds in a school in the Southside of the city. Once, Eddie remembered, she'd announced that the work was too exhausting for a mere human. These kids to whom she force-fed Wordsworth had enough problems understanding the lyrics of fucking *Boyzone*, for Christ's sake.

She drove in silence for a couple of miles.

'Did you know I identified him, Eddie? At least what was left of him. Did I tell you that?'

'I didn't know. I'm sorry.'

'Who needs more raw material for bad dreams? I've got some already.' She flicked her cigarette into the night and it was whipped away in a quick riot of sparks.

Eddie Mallon had seen the violent dead too many times, the faces of clerks shotgunned in robberies, the heads of people blown off for chump-change in filling stations. He touched his sister's hand and wondered why anyone had asked *her*, the stricken daughter, to ID the corpse. They might have been tactful and asked one of Jackie's friends, somebody hardened by the streets. But no. In their insensitivity or haste they'd turned to the daughter.

Is this your dad? Is this mess you see before you Jackie Mallon?

'Did the cops tell you anything?' he asked. 'Do you know if they have any ideas about who killed him, or why?'

'I just remember they asked me to look at the body. There were so many people drifting in and out, suits, uniforms, I was hysterical in a kind of slow-motion way. I remember a guy drove me home after I'd been to the morgue. He was nice. He asked me if I wanted to go for a drink with him any time I felt the need to talk.'

'He's a master of timing, this character,' Eddie said. 'What did you tell him?'

'I said call me in a month or two. But secretly I was flattered because he was drop-dead in a kind of little-boy-lost way. Any other time I would have said yes without thinking.'

'The last time you said yes without thinking you ended up marrying the guy,' Eddie said.

'Just as I'd forgotten all about Harry Haskell, you go and remind me. I wish you could do something about that American accent.'

'Am I supposed to sound like a guy who's been selling newspapers outside –' and he fumbled for a location '– St Enoch Station all his life?'

'Sorry to tell you this, Eddie, but there's no such station any more. Shut down long ago . . .'

A streetlight illuminated her face a second. She lit another cigarette. She looked, he thought, very young. A person too young to have her kind of history – a family hewn apart, a marriage that had been disastrous from the beginning, a murdered father.

'You wanna hear my American?' she asked.

Eddie Mallon said, 'I have a choice?'

'Hey, it's your loss, buddy.'

'That's bad, Joyce.'

'Bad as in good?'

'As in terrible.'

They'd slipped into banter, he thought. Steer clear of the real subject. Digress. He looked at his watch but the damn thing had stopped. 'I need to call Claire. She worries when I have to fly.'

'Phone from my place,' Joyce said. 'I just remembered the man's name.'

'What man?'

'The one that drove me home from the morgue. McWhinnie. Charles, I think. Detective-Sergeant. Posh Glasgow accent. He said yes instead of aye and didn't drop his gs at the end of -ing words. Classy, eh?'

'Very,' he said.

The car left the motorway and headed into the east end of the city, where Eddie had been born and raised; suddenly streets were darker, tenements overbearing and the occasional streetlamp was missing, presumed vandalized. Stores were shuttered, bars closed. The only place open was a fish and chip shop. Eddie saw a fat man behind the counter toss a chip in the air and, like a trained sea-lion, catch it in his mouth on the way down.

Joyce turned the car into Onslow Drive and parked outside the house that had been the Mallon family home in another lifetime.

Eddie said, 'I thought we were going to your flat. Why are we stopping here?'

'I want to see how Senga's bearing up,' Joyce said, and stepped out of the car.

Eddie didn't move.

He gazed at the garden, which was a tangle, a jungle of shrub. He stared at the windows, half-expecting to see a curtain drawn back and his mother's face appear there, or the shadow of his father pass in front of a pane. He imagined Flora calling, *You finished your homework, Eddie*? Or the sound of Joyce practising scales she could never master on the old upright piano in the living room. Doh ray me fah *clunk*, the lid slammed down in frustration and Joyce running upstairs to her room and Jackie shouting after her, *You won't learn to play the bloody piano by hiding in your room, young lady.*

I don't want to get out of the car and go inside the house, he thought. Jackie's *Daily Express* would be lying on the kitchen table and Flora might be peeling onions under running water and maybe some of Jackie's friends would be in the sitting room, laughing at a joke or talking in a low masculine rumble Eddie found impenetrable. And Flora would say, *If you're looking for your dad he's in the front room with his business associates, so-called.*

The dead walk this house.

Ghosts. Including the spectre of young Eddie Mallon.

'Come on, Eddie,' Joyce called. 'You'll like her. Don't look so worried.'

It wasn't the prospect of Senga that troubled him here. He stepped from the car. Joyce was inserting a key into the front-door lock and turning it; then she ushered him ahead of her into the hallway where the first thing he saw was the coat-rack where Flora had always told him to hang his blazer or raincoat after school. He looked down and yes, *Jesus*, it was *still* there after all these years – the same goddam doormat, he was sure of it, worn to nothing except a few flat bristles. *Wipe your feet, Eddie. That mat's not there for decoration, you know.* This house didn't exist in the present tense.

Joyce called out: 'Senga? Are you there?'

Music was playing very quietly from somewhere. The Eagles: 'Lying Eyes'.

11

Matty Bones, who'd finished his whisky a while ago, shut his left eye and surveyed Haggs through the bleary slit of his right. 'Did you bring me drink? Eh? I need more booze.'

Haggs turned away from Matty Bones and looked at the third man in the room. His name was John Twiddie. He wore a black leather jacket and gloves, and had a ring through one nostril and a wad of pus where metal punctured skin.

A plook, Matty Bones thought. That was the word for that kind of inflammation. A big fucking golden *plook*. If it grew any more it would be like an extra nose. This guy looked familiar but Matty Bones was lost in a boozy mist and all links with the world were tenuous.

There was also a young woman Bones had never seen before. Face like a dented medieval battle helmet, scar on her neck, tattooed knuckles, black hair combed upright and held in position by a complex arrangement of pins and metal clasps. She also wore gloves.

'You there,' Bones said.

'You pointing at me, jim?' she asked. A snarl.

'Aye, you. You bring me any drink, dear?'

'Don't point your bloody finger at me. I hate when anybody does that.'

'Oh, you're a toughie, eh? A hard case.' Bones laughed.

The girl turned one hand into a heavy fist and punched Bones in the face and he slipped and clattered into a chair before he fell. Anaesthetized by booze, he felt nothing. He lay on the floor and continued to laugh. He'd fallen from too many nags and no-hopers in his day to let this stumble worry him. He was known around the Scottish flat-racing circuit, Hamilton, Lanark, Ayr, as resilient. You fall off, you get back in the saddle.

Roddy Haggs said, 'Christ's sake, put a clamp on that temper, Rita.'

'Well, I'm sorry, but this fucking wee dwarf annoys me,' she said. She had an expression of permanent rage about her. Whenever Haggs was obliged to look at her, which wasn't often, he thought of somebody who dragged around her own private tempest in which all manner of wild emotions were tossed willy-nilly.

'Give me the booze, Twiddie,' Haggs said.

John Twiddie, who had a sorry thin moustache such as an adolescent might achieve, took a half-bottle of scotch from a pocket of his jacket. He passed it to Haggs, who opened it, then leaned down over Matty Bones and let some of the alcohol slide into the old jockey's open mouth. Haggs had a good view of the interior of Matty's gob; a dentist's nightmare. You could send down a hundred technicians with the latest in laser dento-technology and they'd pronounce this mouth condemned.

Matty Bones said, 'Aye, great, keep it coming, keep the stuff coming, Haggs.'

Haggs quit pouring. 'A question or two first, Matty.'

'Ask away. I'm your man.'

'Jackie Mallon,' Haggs said.

'Jackie and me. Best mates. Peas in a pod. You know that.' Bones felt a momentary sobriety. A shudder. He didn't like the world in clarity. Something bad had happened to Jackie.

Twiddie said, 'Fuck the talk. Just let me stick the boot in, Roddy.'

Haggs frowned at John Twiddie and his girlfriend Rita. They had hair-trigger brains. They were always on the edge, pissed off by the smallest inconvenience. Pierced like tailor's dummies, they were also embroidered with tattoos of flowers and guns. Roddy Haggs didn't want to be in the same room as them, but in this world you had to have your enforcers. And since Twiddie liked to work with Rita, they came as a pair. Lovebirds. Ugly ones.

Haggs grabbed the old guy's hand and squeezed hard. 'Listen, Matty. This is important. What was Jackie Mallon up to? What was he planning?'

'Up to? Oh, this and that. You could never keep track of Jackie. Too fast on his feet.' Matty reached for the bottle and Haggs drew it away with his free hand.

'Matty, you were his driver. You took him everywhere.'

'Pubs, here and there.'

'No, not just pubs, Matty. Other places you took him. Who did he see?'

'Now how the hell would I know, Haggs?'

Haggs crushed the little man's hand as if it were the dried carcass of a squab. Matty Bones moaned. The feel of bone crunching penetrated the armour of booze. He stared at his broken hand. It dangled strangely. Red and green lights jitterbugged in his vision.

'Where did you take him and who did he see?' Haggs asked.

Bones had tears in his eyes. He shoved the broken hand into his mouth, thinking saliva might help ease the agony.

Haggs made a signal to Twiddie, who launched his metal-tipped boot into the little man's scrotum. Matty Bones went at once into a fetal position and his face lost all colour. Aw God, this is a bad fall, he thought. Right bad. He heard his horse gallop away. Hoofbeats on frosty earth. He was paralysed. Red Cross would be coming any minute. The morphine wagon.

He wanted scotch. He nodded his head at the bottle.

Haggs held the whisky high over Matty's face. 'Make it easy on yourself, Matty. Tell us what you know and you get to keep the booze, and we leave you in peace.'

Flat on his back, Matty Bones stared up at the ceiling. He had an image of Jackie Mallon stepping inside Blackfriars pub. It was clear as a photograph. Bones didn't like the picture at all. It brought stuff back he didn't want to look at. 'You said you wouldn't hurt him.'

'I say a lot of things,' Haggs remarked. 'Most of it unbelievable.'

'You fucking *snuffed* him. You said you just wanted to ask a couple of questions and you wouldn't hurt him but you bastards shot him.' Bones wept softly; a drunk man's black guilt. I loved you, Jackie. Really loved you. Honest to God I did.

Haggs said, 'Let's not sob like some wee lassie whose ballerina dreams have just been binned because she's got knock-knees. Let's keep on track here. Who did he see?'

'I drove him to Hyndland a couple of times to meet Billy McQueen.' Bones drew his cuff across his eyes.

'Wan-Fittit McQueen?'

'Right, the Stump –'

'And what were they scheming, Matty?'

'I sat outside in the car. I never joined in. I wasn't asked. Wait in the car, Bones. Take a walk, Bones. Here's a tenner for a fish supper and a pint, Bones.' Bones's voice was wheezy. His broken hand felt five times its usual size and still swelling.

Haggs asked again. 'What were they scheming, Matty?'

'Swear to God, I don't know. Jackie didn't tell me anything.'

'Right. Try this one. Where did Mallon go when he left Glasgow last week?'

'I never knew he left Glasgow,' Bones said.

'I'm to believe that?'

'It's the truth,' Bones said.

'His woman took him to the train station last Wednesday morning.'

'I never knew,' Bones said.

Haggs shrugged and looked at Twiddie. 'Do it,' he said. 'Just do it.'

Twiddie and the girl dragged Matty Bones across the floor and out of the flat and hauled him down the stairs by his ankles, and his head struck the edge of each stone step in a synchronized way. He was sobbing and pleading, *I've telt ye everything I know, I swear on my mother's grave, I swear to God*, but nobody was listening, God especially.

He was yanked out of the tenement and across the pavement and dumped in the back of an ancient Transit van. Haggs got behind the wheel and drove. Twiddie and his girl stayed in the back with Bones. They took turns kicking him, ribs, mouth, belly, skull, it didn't matter, anywhere they could land their boots. Bones curled up like a dying armadillo, and after a while he just stopped feeling anything. He drifted into a dreamy place where

72

faces shimmered, visions of people he might or might not have known.

Jackie was there, hands folded behind his back like a stern schoolmaster. Let this be a lesson, Matthew Bones. Don't betray your pals, wee man.

Haggs drove along Edmiston Drive, heading west past the redbrick monolith of the Glasgow Rangers football stadium. For a couple of miles he listened to Bones whimper. In the back, the girl was smoking a cigarette. Haggs could hear her suck smoke deep into her lungs. Twiddie lit a cigarette too. Thugs on a tobacco break.

'He's a tough wee cunt,' Twiddie said.

'He's had enough,' Haggs said.

'I'm no finished with him.' Twiddie blew a long stream of smoke.

'Enough's enough,' Haggs said.

'He's still breathing,' the girl said.

'I want him out of the damn van,' Haggs said. 'I want the bugger dumped.'

He drove west until he came to a dim-lit street of houses which gave way after a half-mile or so to a path dense with trees and weeds. Then he parked. A stretch of water called the White Cart flowed sluggishly nearby.

'Don't forget the shovel,' Haggs said.

Twiddie grabbed the tool, opened the door and pushed Bones out, then he jumped down and hauled the little man by the collar and dragged him between trees and through bushes and nettles to a slope in the land. Twiddie set the spade aside and took a spool of piano wire from the pocket of his jeans. He unravelled a length of it and wrapped it round Matty Bones's neck and pulled.

I'll fuckin' finish you here an' now, Bones, Twiddie thought.

Bones raised a hand to the place where the wire touched flesh. His eyes popped and he gasped, *No please no let me go, I'll say nothing to a single soul about what I know*, and Twiddie said, *You don't know fuck all anyway, you ignorant old git*. Blood fountained high from Matty Bones's throat when thin razor-edged steel sliced vein. Then Twiddie grunted and tugged harder, his knuckles sharp and almost luminously white, until Bones's head rolled to one side and blood was everywhere, over Bones's face and neck and clothing, as well as Twiddie's hands and shirt and face.

Bones slid over on his side and he thought he saw his dead ma at the finishing line at Ayr races in July 1967 when he brought home a high-strung no-hope gelding called Isaac's Lad at 33-1, and his ma waved, one pale hand raised in the air, and rain was falling on her flowery umbrella and the grass smelled good. He wanted to wave back but he had the reins in his hands, and then somehow they just slipped from his fingers and the horse quit and that was it, the book closed, and Twiddie rolled the body down the earthen incline to the place where, that morning, he'd dug a hole four feet deep.

One I prepared earlier, he thought.

With his foot he nudged Bones into the damp shallow pit, and the dead man's face was visible for a while. Then Twiddie took the shovel and heaped soft earth into the hole and after a few minutes he couldn't see Bones any more.

Breathing hard, he hurried back to the van. He climbed inside, and the girl pulled the door shut.

Haggs drove away quickly. He told himself: I don't need to be here, doing shite like this. I could pay somebody else to drive Weird Twiddie and the Deranged

Bimbo back and forth. So why didn't he stick a driver on the payroll? Why was *he* behind the wheel of this clapped-out old van, running risks, instead of sipping aged brandy in the sunken living room of that expensive house in Rouken Glen with the marble Jacuzzi and the gold taps and the handprinted wallpaper and the murals?

Be honest, Roddy. You like the buzz of this, the action, how your blood races. You like the sport of it, rough company, dark alleys, doling out some pain now and then. Cracking the old jockey's frail hand. *Kerrunch.*

You like the wild side.

Girls. Gambling. Yachts. Deals. Making more and more dosh – all that was banal. But this, driving the night streets with murderous scum as your passengers – you can't go inside a fancy showroom and buy this. You can't get anything like this kick from the rat-a-tat-tat click of a steel ball rolling round a roulette wheel. You can't get it sitting in the Rogano or the Corinthian, sipping a Campari and smoking a fat Cuban. And you can't even get it between the velveteen thighs of some long-legged call-girl with big cow eyes who licks your ear and whispers, *Come for me, Roddy, oh oh shoot your wad, big man.*

This is the life.

You couldn't live in a world like Caskie's, say, a horrible wee cardboard box of law and order. Regulations and requisitions, screw all that shite. Hypocrite.

Haggs thought that Jackie Mallon, for all his cunning, his sly secrecy and stubborn ways, had been a more admirable human being than Caskie could ever be. In fact, in his own off-centre manner, he'd liked Jackie Mallon, and the decision to put him away hadn't been easy. But a time came when you had to make the move, establish your supremacy, plant your own flag on Mallon's moon.

And that's what he'd done. Or tried to.

What had he learned about Jackie's scheme?

Sweet Fanny Adams.

He thought of bloodstains inside the vehicle. 'We'll need to torch this bloody van, Twiddie.'

'I want to be the one to do it,' the girl said.

'Aye, Rita likes fires,' Twiddie said.

Haggs said, 'Why am I not astounded.'

Twiddie said, 'She likes playing with matches.'

'I was a Girl Guide once,' Rita said. 'Building bonfires was the only thing I liked. All the rest was crap. Crap games and stupid badges. Dykes running about giving you orders.'

'Make sure you do the job right.' Haggs glanced in the rearview mirror. Twiddie and his girl were kissing in the back. Twiddie covered in blood. *Kissing* his girl. Her T-shirt was up round her neck. Twiddie had one wet red glove on a bare tit. Haggs stared straight ahead. Note to self, he thought: love brings some very weird customers together.

12

Senga Craig, early fifties, a big tornado of a woman in a bright gold blouse and black slacks, somebody just a little larger than life, loomed in the open doorway to the sitting room. Her red hair was piled up and a long gold pin stuck through it. Her eyelids were swollen from crying. She seized and hugged Joyce and said, 'My darling, oh my wee darling,' and then she looked past Joyce at Eddie. Before he could speak, Eddie was clutched in an embrace so strong he felt almost faint, crushed like a man trapped in the forward surge of a mob. He smelled Senga's pungent scent and gin on her breath. Her arms were bare. She emitted raw energy; this wasn't a woman who'd waste away in grief for ever. She'd fight it and in time she'd win.

'Eddie,' she said. 'Oh, jeez, you're the spitting image. Isn't he the spitting image, Joyce? Oh my God.' She put a hand over her open mouth.

'There's a resemblance all right,' Joyce said.

'You're Jackie Mallon's boy,' Senga said. 'God in heaven, I can't get over it.'

She dragged Eddie inside the room. The music was issuing from a CD player, the Eagles singing 'Cheating Side of Town'.

Senga said, 'Jackie's favourite group, I was listening to them because I'm a silly old cow and I've had one gin too many and gin does funny things to me . . .' She somehow managed to get both Joyce and Eddie into a single hug now; three bodies pressed together, three heads in contact. 'If I can't have Jackie, then I can have his kids. Right? Right? I deserve some kind of consolation, don't I? I loved that man. Loved him.'

Eddie was vaguely conscious of the room beyond the tight limits of Senga's embrace. Years ago the walls had been covered with red and purple floral wallpaper. Now they were painted a flat grey colour and hung with black and white photographs of Scottish scenery in silver frames. The furniture was black leather. The effect was a little austere; Eddie couldn't imagine that Jackie, who liked clutter and wasn't the kind of man who'd give a damn about decor, had any say in decorating this room.

He tried to disentangle himself from Senga, but she was persistent and strong, and seized him harder, holding him in such a way that his cheek adhered to hers, which was fleshy and damp. Joyce, he noticed, had escaped from the communal squeeze, and was lighting a cigarette as she moved to a chair in the corner where a man with a white beard sat.

Eddie hadn't noticed the bearded man before. Joyce gripped the guy's hand, fingers locking for a moment. Then she embraced him, and he closed his eyes as she leaned down to press her face to his shoulder.

'Let me get you a drink, Eddie,' Senga said.

'A beer would be fine,' Eddie said. He observed a small tattoo on Senga's upper left arm, a half-inch below the oval mark of a smallpox inoculation. He thought the tattoo looked familiar, but it eluded him.

'I'm not sure we have beer.' Senga took a Kleenex from a pocket of her slacks and dabbed her damp eyes with it. 'I'm not sure what we've got in the kitchen . . .'

Joyce said, 'Senga, I'll look in the fridge; you stay where you are,' and she left the room.

The man with the white beard rose. He wore a blue double-breasted suit and a black tie. He shook Eddie's hand and said, 'Chris Caskie. We met before you went to America. You couldn't possibly remember me. You were about thirteen years of age and we saw each other two or three times at most.'

'You look vaguely familiar,' Eddie said. He wasn't sure if that was a truth or something he imagined. He felt weary, and sad. This house burdened him. Echoes of family and old songs.

'It would have to be a very *vague* memory,' Caskie said. He sipped from a glass of sherry. 'I was a friend of your mother.'

'She never mentioned you by name, as far as I can recall,' Eddie said.

Senga said, 'Chris has been close to this family for years. Haven't you, Chris?'

'Close enough.'

'Joyce has always been his favourite,' Senga said. 'After Flora, of course.'

'Senga, you know I don't play favourites,' Caskie said. 'I corresponded with Flora now and then over the years.' He turned to face Eddie again. 'How is she taking . . .'

'I'm not sure,' Eddie said. 'Shocked. But we're talking about thirty years of separation, so it's the kind of shock with a long slow fuse. It might burn out tamely.'

Senga filled a glass with gin and looked at Eddie, then linked an arm through his. 'I sympathize with Flora, I do,

79

I really do, it's just, well, I'm trying not to think, just hold myself together, it's like I've misplaced something except I don't know what the hell it is, but if I keep looking I'll remember . . . I'm sorry, sorry, I'm just talking a pile of gibberish. Forgive me, the both of you. But I keep expecting Jackie'll walk through the door at any moment. Hello, my great big beautiful doll, he'll say. And I'll say, Tell me you love me, Mallon . . . Oh my heart's wrecked.'

She sniffed, tried to force out a little smile of fortitude, but it didn't work. She looked, Eddie Mallon thought, out of focus, a badly taken snapshot. The stark grief of this stranger his father had apparently loved – it was odd to him, it lacked a framework into which he could place it. She and Jackie had built a life together. He needed to absorb this fact, and accept it.

Caskie said, 'You've lost somebody you loved, Senga. You're entitled to your sorrow.' He passed her a handkerchief, a neat square of folded linen he took from his jacket.

Senga blew her nose, then walked across the room. She sat down, balanced her gin on the arm of the sofa. She'd raised her spirits enough to welcome Eddie, she'd worked at seeming sober, but the effort had been too much, and now she'd lapsed into a place of silence and melancholy.

Alone in the corner of the room with Caskie, Eddie asked, 'How well did you know my father?'

'I tried to arrest him a couple of times,' Caskie said, and smiled.

'Arrest? You're a cop?'

'Just like you,' Caskie said. He looked a little amused. 'The truth is, I used to have a young man's crush on your mother – all totally innocent, I assure you – and when she left for America she asked me to keep an eye on your sister. You obviously didn't know about this, did you?'

Eddie Mallon shook his head. He was sure Flora had never mentioned Caskie. Or it had escaped him. It wasn't important. He could easily imagine somebody having what Caskie quaintly called a 'crush' on Flora, because once upon a time she'd been beautiful in a way men might find both haughty and challenging, as if her sexuality were a minefield you crossed at your own peril; and somewhere along the graph of time the colour had gone out of her rich black hair and she'd begun the decline into the little white-haired lady who spent most of her life stooped over potted plants.

Caskie said, 'I'd phone Joyce every three or four months. Sometimes we'd meet for a drink when she'd reached the legal age,' and he smiled here, raising one eyebrow as if the word 'legal' had a meaning only cops understood. 'Sometimes we had dinner. How are you doing, what's happening, anything new – that kind of thing. I'd run into your father every so often too . . . but I could never pin a damn thing on him. Either he lived a life of total innocence or he was the most clever man I ever met.'

'Which do you think it was?' Eddie asked. He was remembering what his mother had said: *He's stone cold dead, but he's still got you thinking good things about him.* Yes, yes, I want to believe that. Apart from one godawful error in his life, he was basically a decent guy. What was so wrong in needing a little faith?

Caskie shrugged. 'I believe he kept some bad company. And maybe his business ledgers wouldn't have survived microscopic scrutiny.' He drank a little sherry. 'I don't think this is the time or the place, Eddie, to dissect your father's life.'

'I'd like to know more about him –'

'That's perfectly natural, but I'm not sure I'm the best person to help.'

Joyce came back into the room on the tail-end of the conversation. She handed Eddie a chilled bottle of Amstel and asked, 'Help with what, Chris?'

'Your brother's curiosity,' Caskie said. He moved back towards the sofa and sat down beside Senga, whose eyes were shut.

Joyce said, 'What are you curious about, bro?'

Eddie swallowed some beer. 'Just Jackie in general.'

'I knew him better than anyone, except maybe Senga. You have questions, Eddie, ask me.'

Before Eddie could respond, Senga got up from the sofa and approached him. For a tall big-chested woman she looked fragile; she weaved from side to side as she walked, like somebody trying to cross a tricky bridge in a fun-house. Caskie moved behind her in an attentive way, to catch her if she lost her balance.

'This has all the feel of a bloody dreeeeary wake,' Senga said. 'Och, Jackie would've hated this. He'd already be looking for the side door so he could sneak away. When I die, he used to say, play some happy music and drink yourself into a stupor. So I'm changing this . . .' She went to the stack of CDs – two steps to the side, one forward – and she found what she was looking for. She ejected the Eagles.

Suddenly the room was filled with Scottish dance music of a kind Eddie hadn't heard since they'd all lived in Granny Mallon's flat in Bathgate Street. Accordion and fiddle, diddley-dum-dee, jigs and reels, foot-tapping stuff.

Senga hooked an arm through his and said, 'Dance, Eddie. Come on. Dance the sadness away.'

'*Dance?*'

'You heard me, laddie. Dance!'

It was weird. Inappropriate. Maybe it was the deranged way grief made some people act. Eddie found himself spun in a reckless circle by the big-boned woman whose red hair had fallen down the sides of her face. Round and round. She whooped. The ceiling rotated. Eddie felt dizzy. Senga threw her head back and stamped her feet as she moved and the floor shook. This was her house, her stage, her performance. She dominated all the space around her.

'Dance dance *dance*, Eddie,' she roared, and tears slid down her face, and she placed an arm above her head in the curved manner of a Highland Fling, and held it aloft while she swung Eddie ever faster. She was strong, fired with the crude energy of grief. He saw the black-and-white photographs rush past like scenery glimpsed from the window of a high-speed train. He had a fixed smile on his face, but he wanted to stop this dance, put an end to this surreal interlude.

Senga said, 'Jackie loved to dance, he was so bloody light on his feet.' It was what Flora had also said about Jackie. He must have foxtrotted and waltzed into their hearts.

And then Senga was suddenly out of breath and had to quit, and she slumped into an armchair, head back, mouth open. Eddie looked at the long red hair and the gold blouse and the lipstick that had faded and the tears that continued to roll down towards the corners of her mouth. 'What I want to know is why some fucking bastard had to shoot him, for Christ's sake? Why, Eddie? Why? Why did they have to take his life?'

Caskie was quick to comfort her.

Joyce stood at Eddie's side. 'You're tired,' she whispered.

He shrugged and nodded towards Senga. 'I'm more worried about her.'

'I'll make sure she doesn't take any sleepers on top of what she's been drinking. I'll help her up to bed, then we'll leave.'

Joyce killed the music, and whispered in Senga's ear. Senga rose from the chair, leaning on Joyce's arm, and the two women walked together across the room.

At the door Senga looked at Caskie, then at Eddie.

'Joyce says I have to sleep, gentlemen. I have to drift away . . . Land of Nod for me.'

'Joyce is right,' Caskie said.

Senga said, 'Give me a kiss, Eddie.'

Eddie Mallon took a step forward and pressed his lips against Senga's cheek. She gazed into his eyes, not quite meeting them because drink had skewed her line of vision. 'We'll talk soon, you and I. We've got some catching up to do. Goodnight.' She blew a sad little kiss. 'The pair of you.'

The door closed.

'I think it's time for me to push off,' Caskie said.

Eddie said, 'He was shot in his car.'

'Yes.'

'And no witnesses.'

'Nobody's come forward,' Caskie said. 'But this isn't my case, Eddie. I'm not up to speed on it. If you want to know more about the investigation, Superintendent Tay's the man to ask.'

'I met him at the airport. He gives the impression he might not like questions.' Eddie gazed at Caskie's small white beard. It was tidy, well clipped. His eyebrows were perfect, no stray hairs. He had an easy smile. He was maybe fifty-four, -five, and in good shape.

'I'm sure he'll keep you posted if anything happens,' Caskie said. 'He's sympathetic. Don't let the veneer put you off.'

Eddie went on, his voice rising a little. He heard words echo in his head like gunshots in a tunnel. 'Tay told me Jackie hadn't been robbed. His wallet hadn't been taken and he had money in his possession. But who knows what else he might have had in the car? Something in the glove compartment, say. Or in the trunk. Something Tay didn't know about. So how can he rule out robbery? And then there's the secondary mystery of the missing driver, Bones.'

'He'll show up, I'm sure. Probably he's scared and imagines he's going to be implicated, so he's lying low, who knows?' Caskie rolled his glass of sherry between the palms of his hands, then set it down unfinished. He checked his wristwatch. 'I'm tired. It's been a long one.'

Eddie wanted to quit talking, but he couldn't. It was like jogging and not wanting to stop even if you were breathless, because the adrenalin rush was addictive. 'Either Jackie was shot during an act of robbery, or he was killed for other reasons we don't know about. If I was running this investigation and it turned out nothing *obvious* was stolen from him, then I'd dig deeper and ask myself what the hell he'd done that made somebody want to kill —'

'But you're not running the investigation, Eddie,' Caskie said.

Eddie stopped, subsided, leaned against the wall. The

hard truth of Caskie's statement silenced him. He'd been flying, buzzing in on questions that weren't his to ask. *What the hell am I doing exactly? I've come all this way to bury my dad; his murder isn't my business.* Whoever had fired a bullet into Jackie Mallon's face isn't my concern. Tay and his team were on the job. Justice would get done, but not by you. Take it easy, for Christ's sake. Slow down. But it was goddam hard to take the heat out of himself. *This ain't Manhattan, Eddie.* Remember that.

He said, 'I was getting carried away.'

Caskie said, 'It's understandable.'

Joyce came back into the room. 'She's out cold. I think we'll go, Eddie. If she needs me later, she can phone me. I don't think she'll wake for hours.'

All three left the sitting room and stood for a moment in the hallway at the foot of the stairs; the awkward etiquette of leave-taking. Who goes first? Who says what?

Caskie reached inside the breast pocket of his jacket and took out a business card. He handed it to Eddie. 'Here. If you need to get in touch while you're in Glasgow . . . It's been nice to see you again.'

'The same for me,' Eddie said. He tucked the card in a hip pocket of his jeans.

Caskie embraced Joyce. 'Call me if you need me.'

'I will, Chris.'

'Help with the funeral arrangements, anything at all . . .' Caskie raised a hand almost imperceptibly, and then he was gone, closing the front door with hardly a sound. Caskie had an undertaker's diplomacy, Eddie thought, listening to the quiet click of the latch. His body vibrated curiously to the aftermath of the spinning dance Senga had forced him through.

The dance of death.

He remembered he hadn't phoned Claire yet. He gazed up the stairway to the lamp lit on the landing. He touched the polished wood of the banister. He must have slid down that a thousand times when he thought Flora wasn't looking. He had a faded memory of Jackie coming down the stairs towards him, bright red braces and a white shirt with the collar open.

Jackie winked at him and said, *One day we'll hire a boat at Balloch and go fishing.*

That day had never come.

Joyce said, 'I don't suppose you want a quick tour of the old homestead, do you, Eddie?'

The prospect depressed him. 'But thanks for the offer,' he said.

'Another time.'

13

They drove the quarter of a mile from Onslow Drive to Joyce's place, a one-bedroom second-floor flat in a dark red sandstone tenement. Eddie took his bag from the car and followed his sister up the stone stairs.

'You can phone Claire from the living room,' Joyce said. 'I need a nightcap. You?'

'Maybe a soft drink,' Eddie said.

'Irn-Bru?'

'Irn-Bru, Jesus, I haven't had that in a lifetime,' Eddie said.

'You'll be happy to know it tastes the same as it always did. Dyed sugary water with loadsa bubbles.' She went into the kitchen.

Eddie looked at the bookshelves in the living room. They were stacked with paperbacks, many of them old orange-covered Penguins. Absently, he scanned the titles as he reached for the phone. Hugh MacDiarmid. Tom Leonard. A Scottish selection among European classics. *Kidnapped* beside *The Brothers Karamazov*. *Ivanhoe* leaning against *The Castle*. Joyce had always been buried in a book as kid. Granny Mallon, a sharp-eyed little woman with short silver hair and bulbous arthritic hands, used to say, *Get her out in the fresh air with a skipping rope before she goes blind.*

Eddie picked up the phone, then realized he didn't know the dialling code for the USA. He decided he'd call collect – but what was the number for the international operator? He looked for a phone book among the general clutter of the room, magazines, ashtrays, empty glasses. Joyce's private chaos. The prints on the walls were arranged in no specific pattern. Lithographs and sketches of famous writers, musicians, prints that publicized gallery openings or museum events, a few San Francisco Filmore examples, Bob Dylan, Hendrix. There was also an assortment of half a dozen busts in classical style, faces carved out of old stone, one missing a nose, another an ear: they looked like Greek philosophers pondering facial surgery.

Joyce came into the room carrying two glasses. 'I hope you appreciate I tidied this place up for you,' she said.

'I'm grateful,' Eddie said. He indicated the busts. 'Quite a gallery.'

'I found them in Dad's warehouse over the years.'

She handed him a long glass filled with a fizzy red liquid. He sipped it; exactly as he remembered. So sweet he imagined sugar armies scaling the enamel battlements of his teeth.

'How do I get the operator?' he asked. 'I want to make a collect call to Claire.'

She told him, he dialled, got through to Queens in a matter of moments. Claire sounded close at hand, a voice in the next room. They talked inconsequentially of the flight, then Claire wanted to know how Joyce was. Eddie glanced at his sister and thought she looked exhausted.

'Hard to say,' he remarked.

'You can't talk right now,' Claire said.

'You got it.'

'You met Senga yet?'

'I did.'

'And?'

'She's . . . I guess she's what I expected.'

'You sound tired. Call me tomorrow.'

'I will. Love you.'

Claire said the same thing, then Eddie hung up. Cutting the connection caused him a little jolt of sadness: *I still love my wife after all this time.* He guessed that seventy-five per cent of his colleagues, maybe more, were divorced, separated or serially unfaithful. He couldn't imagine another woman in his bed.

Joyce closed her book, picked up her wine. 'Claire's okay?' she asked.

'Fine.' Eddie nodded. 'I like this room.'

'I'm glad, because you'll be sleeping in it. The sofa you're sitting on opens into a bed. It's comfortable.'

Eddie took a swallow of Irn-Bru. 'Tell me about Chris Caskie. I didn't know about his existence until tonight.'

'I suppose his name just didn't crop up,' Joyce said. 'How many times have we met since you left anyway? I've been to the States, let's see – three times in thirty years, Eddie.'

'It's not enough, I know,' Eddie said, and sighed. 'It's my fault. I should have made the effort to come over –'

'I'm not blaming you, Eddie. You have a whole life over there. Responsibilities.' Joyce placed a cigarette between her lips, but didn't light it.

Eddie watched her and thought, I could have made the trip on any one of my vacations, but I didn't, I was afraid, not of seeing the city again – but of coming face to face with Jackie and entering the maze of my own emotions.

What would he really feel about his father? That first contact, whether handshake or hug, how would that have been? Stiff and tentative, warm and welcoming? Uncertainty had kept him from Glasgow. He'd become accustomed to the phantom he'd constructed in his mind – an unreliable man, touched by a wild streak, but honest: a man who meant well most of the time, although circumstance and his own flaws sometimes conspired against him.

Joyce blew cigarette smoke. 'Chris Caskie was the kindly uncle nobody else in our family knew how to be. He had contacts in universities, he could get the low-down on what universities had the best teachers – the kind of stuff that was light-years away from Jackie's world. It's a funny situation when you think about it, the avuncular cop wondering how he can arrest the father of his adopted niece.'

'Did he want to nail Jackie?'

'I think it became a kind of standing joke,' Joyce said. 'But a serious one. They enjoyed each other, only they just couldn't relinquish their roles. In the blue corner, Detective-Inspector Caskie, career cop. In the red, Jackie Mallon . . .'

'Mallon the what?' Eddie asked.

'How can I put it? The alleged criminal?'

'No more than alleged?'

'I really don't think he did much more than chisel the Inland Revenue any chance he got. Sometimes I had the feeling Dad said stuff deliberately to get up Chris's nose. He'd make a reference to a crime he'd heard about, and how he might know the names of a few guys responsible.

Chris always pretended he wasn't taking the bait, but you could tell he was storing it away to check later.'

I missed all this, Eddie thought. I missed Caskie's role in Joyce's life, the give-and-take between Jackie and the cop. He'd been robbed of something essential. Suddenly he wasn't the brother, he was a stranger staring through a window into a room he didn't know. His sister had made the transition from child to woman and whole areas of her life were blacked out to him. Her first lover, who was he? Her amphetamine infatuation, which she'd first mentioned five years ago, how had that come about? You could love her with all your heart, but you could never fill in the gaps.

He said, 'I want to know more about Jackie.'

'What exactly?'

'Anything.'

'Narrow it down, Eddie.'

'Start with his business. Tell me about that.'

'He mentioned retirement only a few weeks ago. He was saying how much he was looking forward to becoming one of the wrinkly leisure class. He was going to have a big sale of the inventory in the warehouse, then he planned to sell the building and the yard. I got the impression, right or wrong, that he may have had money worries.'

'If he sold his stock and his building, his cash concerns would have been over,' Eddie said. 'At least alleviated.'

Joyce said, 'Unless he had really big debts . . . but it doesn't matter any more, does it?'

'No, I guess not.'

'It's past, the business is history.' She stared into her wine. She ran a finger round the rim of her glass. 'You know, about a month ago he came here and his face was this boozy bright red colour, and he grabbed my hand and he said it had been a terrible mistake to hurt Flora, and it was something he'd regretted all his life. It was maudlin, but I believe he meant what he was saying. He hadn't been able to persuade Flora to stay with him, so he'd reacted with what he called "shameful cruelty". And then he just wept. I'd never seen him do that before. He buried his face in his hands and cried for a long time. It was the saddest thing.'

Eddie was quiet for a moment. 'Last time he phoned me, about six weeks ago, he said he wished he could go back and change the past. He'd been drinking then too.'

Joyce said, 'He couldn't express his feelings without a lubricant. It's all that macho Presbyterian stuff you get drummed into you when you're growing up in Glasgow. A real man never weeps, he just gets on with things.'

Eddie rose from the sofa and walked to the window and looked down into the street. The streetlamps were surrounded by so many small winged creatures the effect was of silvery liquid movement. His mind slipped back to the day of the departure from Glasgow, and he pictured Joyce as he'd stepped inside the taxi with his mother. He remembered Flora, weepy but trying to be all business, saying to the cabby, *Take us to the airport fast, we've got a plane to catch*, and the cabby, a man with a lazy eye that looked off into a wild blue yonder, coming back with something sarcastic like, *Are ye sure ye don't want a bloody police escort, missus?*

Eddie had turned his face as the cab pulled away and he'd seen Joyce watching from the shadow of the house in Onslow Drive, skipping rope held limp in one hand, her black hair curled and a big bright blue ribbon on the crown of her head. Her look had been one of puzzlement and pain.

The image made him ache.

Eddie said flatly, 'He cut the family in two.'

'Like a madman with an axe,' Joyce said.

She walked to the window and stood behind her brother, and put her arms around him, clasping her hands against his chest. He covered one of her hands with his own and said nothing, just watched the streetlights. A car slid past slowly below.

'I can't imagine Flora's state of mind,' Joyce said. 'Your husband tells you he'll fight for custody of both kids, he'll drag you through the whole legal system even if it takes years and he's got the cash to do exactly what he threatens. He issues an ultimatum – choose one kid, or risk losing both.'

This was the version Eddie had heard so many times from Flora. He looked at his sister. How frail she seemed in the soft light of the lamp; almost like a kid on the cusp of adolescence.

She said, 'Jackie always tried to do his best for me after Flora went. I couldn't bring myself to hate him for what he'd done. Oh, I tried. I really *wanted* to hate him. I used to get down on my knees and pray I could *learn* to hate him. God, teach me to hate . . . Daft. In the end, forgiveness takes less energy.' She smiled, sipped a little wine. 'Have you forgiven him?'

'I like to think so,' Eddie said. 'Or maybe I've just fudged what happened in the past. Discarded it. I'm not sure.'

'You know, I used to think Flora chose to take you to America because you were her favourite.'

'No. She thought I could cope with the upheaval better

94

because I was older. She was obsessed for years with saving money and hiring a hotshot lawyer in the States to fight for custody of you, but time passed, and she could never get the cash together . . .'

Fatigued, Eddie moved to the sofa, lay down. He crossed his hands on his chest and stared at the ceiling where the lamp created an oval of weak light. Giving up a child, he thought. It would hurt like hell. It would be a pain you could never alleviate. Day after day you'd haul a sense of loss around with you, and people might detect it in your mannerisms, the far-off look that would come into your face. But it wasn't only Flora who'd given up a child. Jackie Mallon had deprived himself of his son by his own brute act of spite. He'd punished himself as well as Flora.

That one big mistake, Dad. That heartbreaking cruelty. That's where the halo is corroded.

He was beginning to drift now. Couldn't fight it much longer. After a while he heard Joyce stub her cigarette. He felt her kiss his forehead softly and say, 'We'll get through all this.'

'Sure we will,' he said. She switched the lamp off. The darkness was comforting. He heard her cross the floor and enter her bedroom. She closed the door quietly.

He lay, fully clothed, on an unfamiliar sofa he didn't have the strength to open into a bed.

He slipped into sleep, dreamed he was dancing, he and Senga waltzing on board a cruise ship. The orchestra played 'Moonlight in Vermont'. The conductor had Flora's face. In the dream he looked at the tattoo on Senga's arm and he knew what it was. It surprised him. He thought: I'm mistaken. He woke briefly, considered the tattoo, then everything floated away from him and he fell into a sleep that was deep and this time dreamless.

14

At six thirty a.m., Billy McQueen, AKA Billy the Stump or Billy Wan-Fittit, read the morning newspapers in his Merchant City penthouse. The building in which he lived had been a derelict warehouse before razor-brained developers realized that the city centre of Glasgow was a very desirable place to live, if you were of the cellphone, fast-buck, nightclubbing slick-car generation; and so Merchant City had been created out of shabby Victorian warehouses and banks and offices, its new apartments purchased by lawyers and glitzy media types.

Billy McQueen didn't come into these categories. He was a middleman, a fixer who brought people together to make deals, and he took a generous percentage of profits for his troubles. He insisted on receiving a portion of his fee upfront as a token of goodwill. Officially he was an accountant, the profession specified on his income-tax returns, which were invariably works of superlative invention. He had no training in accountancy; he lived and operated in cracks and shadows.

He was insomniac because he drank gallons of rich coffee every day. His internal clock was in a state of confusion. His complexion was the colour of cigarette ash. He had a pendant lower lip that gave him the look of a man trapped in a lifelong grudge. He Brylcreemed his hair lavishly; wherever he slept he left grease-pits on pillows.

Dressed in sky-blue silk pyjamas and matching robe, he flicked the pages of the papers quickly; he was interested only in information about the murder of Jackie. What he read was bland and unsatisfying. *The investigation is ongoing . . . yackety-yak*. He felt the journalists were keeping facts back. Or maybe it was the police. You could go a step further and think they were in collusion, a clique of scribblers and cops.

He got out of bed, leaving a trail of newspapers. He limped into the kitchen. Twenty years ago, at the age of eighteen, he'd lost his left leg below the knee when he'd been drunk and taking a short cut across a railway line in Cowcaddens, and a train had whacked into him. Since then he'd worn a series of prosthetic limbs, some better than others. His present attachment chafed his stump a little, but he'd learned to live with discomfort, although he'd never grown accustomed to his demeaning nicknames. The Stump was an insult. So was Wan-Fittit – or, more properly, One-Footed.

That bloody short cut turned out to be a longer cut than you ever expected, didn't it? his father had said to him after the accident.

Ho ho. Comedian.

The kitchen was a big white room with granite surfaces. The skinny girl at the table was smoking hashish and reading the magazine section of an old *Sunday Mail* which was mostly fluff about rockers and film stars. McQueen hated tabloids. He liked the broadsheets. He liked to think he was scuba-diving in the Sea of Information, not just floating on the surface.

The skinny girl, who had an urchin's white face, said, 'I just made coffee.'

'I'll partake,' said McQueen. He filled a mug from the percolator. He sipped the coffee. His hands trembled. The girl's name was Leila, a regular supplied by a discreet escort agency he used. He liked to think of Leila as more than a call-girl. A friend. A lover.

Billy's life was separated into compartments. He lived with his manic depressive, ailing father in a four-bedroom flat in a respectable street in Hyndland. West End, red sandstone, classy. Larry McQueen didn't know about the penthouse in Merchant City. He thought his son travelled to distant cities on business trips.

Billy looked at the girl as he blew on the surface of his coffee. She wore a tight-fitting little sweater and black bikini underwear. He checked the time on his watch: 7:04. He knew his father would be awake. The old man slept only four hours a day, from midnight to four a.m. He was troubled by nightmares.

Billy picked up the phone, punched in a number and heard his father answer.

'How you doing?' McQueen said.

'Awright, awright.' Larry McQueen's voice was stressed. 'Where are you anyway?'

'Manchester,' McQueen said. 'Did you take your medi-cation?'

'What are you – my bloody nurse? 'Course I took my medication, for all the bloody good it does me.'

McQueen held the phone away from his ear and let his father rant. He pictured the old guy sitting up in bed, moaning and whining. Billy tried to be a dutiful son. He did his best. He really did. It wasn't easy. Some days the old fellow would lie on the living-room sofa and stare at the ceiling and say nothing, lost in secret melancholic depths, or else he'd take out his dilapidated guitar and strum a few truly depressing Jacobite folk tunes, like 'Will you no' come back again?'

He wanted to put Larry into a nursing home, but he didn't have the heart to evict the old fellow. He'd even hired a part-time nurse to look in on his father a couple of times a week, but Larry was abusive to this scrawny old biddy who was called Thelma Rogan. Whenever he could, Billy escaped to Merchant City, fifteen minutes away from the West End by taxi. In the penthouse he could have Leila and a sense of privacy in a place where his father couldn't find him.

'What year can I expect you?' Larry asked.

Sarcasm, always the dead-weight sarcasm. 'A few hours. I'm not sure.'

'You're never precise, are you? It's a wonder to me that you ever made it as an accountant when you can't even tell the bloody time. Eh? How did you manage it? Did you bribe the examiners? You're a numpty, Billy.'

Drone drone. Insult insult. Billy held the handset away from his ear. His father's voice sounded like a gnat trapped in a bottle. Jesus Christ, Billy had spent his whole life listening to Larry carping at him. You're a useless waste of space, Billy, you'll amount to nothing.

Bitter old git. Never a kind word.

Billy said, 'I'll be back before the TV gets delivered.'

'What TV?'

'I told you about it yesterday and the day before that.' What was the point? The old man rarely remembered anything from one day to the next except to insult his son. His brain was a decaying sponge in a bowl of stale fluid. 'A new TV is coming, Dad. Digital.'

'Digiwhat?'

'*Christ*. We went through all this.' Billy killed the line before he lost his patience entirely.

Larry would assume that the sudden disconnection was a flaw in the cellphone, even though Billy wasn't using one. Sometimes Billy found the unpredictability of cellphones a useful ploy. Just went dead, Dad. Must have gone out of range. He often escaped Larry's abuse by severing the connection. Larry didn't understand cellphones anyway. In fact, he'd been so unhappy since the country had converted to decimal currency that he'd never used a public telephone after they stopped accepting the old-style pennies and the big black coin boxes had been removed.

When can I expect you? When indeed. Billy didn't want to leave this penthouse. He wanted to sit here with the slatted blinds drawn and never go anywhere again.

The girl came back and poured some coffee. 'Want any more, Billy?'

'Fill me up,' he said.

The girl poured into his cup. Then she sat down and stoked up her little hash pipe. She inhaled deeply before offering him the pipe, which he declined. She looked very stoned. Her eyes were two damp rubies. Billy studied her face, which was pretty in an emaciated way.

Leila had some story about how she was working her way flat on her back through university, and Billy believed it. He liked to believe most things, because all he ever wanted was an easy passage through life; no bloody traffic cones.

He wanted simplicity.

But now he was on a slip-road he didn't like at all, and he wasn't sure what lay ahead or even the direction he was meant to be taking. In the beginning it had been straightforward. A little tricky, but most deals had an element of risk. You expected that. What you didn't expect was a participant getting himself killed along the way –

Shot in the face. Awful.

And way out of Billy McQueen's league. This is what comes of consorting with hard criminal types.

A stern voice in his head said, *Cut your losses and run, Billy.*

Run where precisely?

The smell of hash was strong. He got up, opened a window. Very thin sunlight was rising over the city. He didn't like that. He wanted the dark to last a long time because it was comforting. Now Leila, doped to the deepest recesses of her brain, had begun to chatter. She spoke ramblingly of her affection for wire-haired terriers, her fear of death by suffocation and Ronald Reagan's role in *The Killers* – there seemed to be some political point in what she had to say about this movie that escaped Billy McQueen.

Billy couldn't just sit here and listen to a stoned girl rambling on about nothing. He didn't have time for that. He grabbed the handset of the telephone and jabbed the number pad with a fingertip.

The voice that answered was quiet, almost a whisper. 'Gurk.'

McQueen said, 'Look, I know events have taken, uh, an unexpected turn. But who could have foreseen anything like this?'

The man called Gurk was silent for a while. Something about Gurk troubled McQueen. Even the name. *Gurk.* Sounded like the noise made by an air bubble popping in a waste-disposal unit clogged with custard.

'I was meditating, man,' Gurk said. He was black with a London accent, East End or close to it. 'I don't like being interrupted when I meditate.'

McQueen imagined Gurk sitting bare-chested in a hotel room. He wondered if Gurk was running on all four wheels along the cerebral highway, or if he had a mis-aligned axle. All this meditation, his strange utterances, his talk of transcendence and harmony and the music of the spheres and what have you – it made McQueen, a lapsed Presbyterian, deeply uneasy.

'You got any news for me, Billy?'

'Emm, no, not yet.'

Gurk said, 'Too bad. Here's the bottom line, Billyboy. You and your friend Mallon got something that belongs to me and my associates, and we'll expect it returned unless the deal is done and dusted.'

'Well, naturally,' McQueen said. 'But Mallon –'

'Yeh. Well. That's tragic. Fella gets shot. But it's not my problem, Billy. The world turns. We go through cycles.'

Cycles? Billy wondered. 'I'll arrange to return my commission. No problems there. And I'll cooperate with you any way you like.'

'I know, I know. You're a man of honour.'

'My reputation's excellent.'

'A man who tells you his reputation is excellent is using himself as a character reference,' Gurk said. 'I'd be very careful of a man like that. We need to meet.'

'Where?'

'Call me back in an hour,' Gurk said. 'And don't think about buggering off, old son. Confucius say one-legged man never gets very far.'

McQueen heard the connection click.

Leila was chattering about Lee Marvin in *Point Blank*

and whether the character he played, a guy called Walker, was actually dead or alive. In one sense, Leila remarked, the film might be construed as the tale of a vengeful ghost.

'It's a fucking *gangster* film,' Billy said.

'Ah, but only on one level, Billy. That movie has layers, man. Like strata.' She sucked her hash pipe and segued into a story she'd heard about a headless man alleged to be roaming the streets of Castlemilk, a housing scheme in the distant south of the city. Kids had reported sightings.

'Urban myth,' Billy said.

'Ah, but what gave birth to it? How did it get started?'

'I haven't a clue, Leila.'

'I have theories,' she said.

'Do you mind keeping them to yourself, hen?' Billy reached for her hand. 'See, I'm not clever like you, love. And who wants to be casting pearls before swine, eh?'

She gazed at him fondly. 'Am I too smart for you, Billy?'

'You're so far beyond me it's like I'm sunk in a trench and you're way up there in the bloody stratosphere.'

'I'm flying high,' she said.

'Bully for you. I'm up to my neck in shite and sinking.'

15

Eddie Mallon woke at first light. He was stiff from his spine-crunching sleep on the sofa. He rose slowly, rummaged inside his bag, finding toothbrush, toothpaste and comb. He left the room, guessed correctly that the frosted glass-panelled door across the hallway led to the toilet. He doused his face in warm water, brushed his teeth, ran the comb through hair that had always been too thick and springy to discipline.

He looked at himself in the mirror: sweet Christ, it was like seeing a younger Jackie Mallon just for a moment, a shade gazing back at him from the glass. It startled him, as if he'd stepped through the mirror into some other universe where the dead were resurrected.

Time zones and bad sleep, he thought.

He dried his face and went inside the kitchen. There was a note on the table with a Yale key placed on it. Joyce had scribbled: *Here's your key. If you wake before me, don't wake me. Appreciated. Love J.* He stuck the key in a pocket of his jeans, opened the refrigerator. He found a half-empty bottle of Chablis, a bunch of puckered black grapes, eggs, a can of Irn-Bru, a slab of cheese and a bruised orange. He plucked some grapes and opened the drink and sat at the table. Early light had begun to suffuse the backs of the sandstone tenements visible from the kitchen window. Brick changed from grey-black to red-brown as the sun rose. Pigeons flew among the tall chimney stacks.

He finished the drink and the last of the grapes. He left the flat and went down the stone staircase and out into the street where the colour of the sky awed him, because it wasn't a city sky thick with smoke and smog, it was limpid and sea-blue. Something unusual had happened to the weather here, a strange inversion, as if all the sun destined for the Mediterranean had gathered over Glasgow for a couple of days, creating this rarity.

He walked to the corner of Ingleby Drive and Whitehill Street then turned left and went south in the direction of Duke Street, a route that would take him past his old school. I must have come this way a thousand times, he thought. On either side of him the tenements were silent. Soon alarm clocks would rouse people and the day's outpouring of life begin, men and women rushing to their cars or hurrying to board crowded buses, children beginning another day of the long summer holidays.

Eddie could already sense heat building. He thought: All this was home once. These buildings, these streets and intersections, the school just ahead to his right.

He stopped suddenly. *Where was the damn school?*

That formidable 1890s dark red stone edifice, which had seemed so indestructible, had been demolished and now only the segregated entrance gates stood, one marked Boys, the other Girls; and where the school had been was a deep green forest of thistle and nettle and dock leaf and thorn. Shocked, Eddie stared into this density of foliage. You turn a corner, you expect a familiar landmark – but it's gone, the world has altered. This was the school he'd attended for almost two years before flight had been forced upon him. He remembered the narrow staircases, the classrooms, the toilets where everybody learned to smoke.

The disappearance of the school was one less thing to hook him to his boyhood. He wished he could blink his eyes and magic it back into existence if only for a minute, and see kids crossing the yard and the wind blowing scraps of paper into the bicycle shed. He wished he could see again the pretty brown-haired girl he'd fallen in love with at the age of thirteen: Dorothy, the name came back so easily. How miserable and how ecstatic that first love had been. This is how the heart works, young Eddie: welcome to the House of Paradox.

On a cold black winter afternoon in Alexandra Parade, she'd kissed him and he'd tasted sugar on her lips. He'd experienced his first real erection, and she must have felt it too, but it was a wonderful shared intimacy more than an embarrassment, and it added to the intensity of his love for her. Where was she now? in a middle-aged marriage? did she live in this city still? He had a sudden urge to see her, as if he might retrieve by looking at her the ferocious sensation of that kiss, that moment –

What the hell was he thinking? She was gone, a casualty of time. She'd drifted into the same slipstream that carried everything and everyone away. Eddie Mallon, 13, had been ferried off in the same spate as Dorothy McCallum. And drowned.

He continued to move, passed the corner of Roslea Drive. Nearby, in Hillfoot Street, there had been a snooker hall called Dan's that you reached by going along a dank narrow corridor, and he'd sneaked into it a few times to watch older kids stick coloured balls across green baize under lamps where cigarette smoke billowed. It was daring to enter this musty demi-monde. But the pool-hall would be gone by now, turned into something else. Bingo, he imagined. A video arcade. He didn't want to look to be certain.

He crossed Duke Street, the main thoroughfare that ran east–west in a long straggle of tenements and small shops. A few early buses blew foul smoke, a bakery van made a delivery of morning rolls to a store, newspapers lay stacked and twined outside a newsagent's door.

He stopped. He had a strange feeling, as if somebody had just touched his back lightly in a sensitive spot; it was shivery, and he couldn't attribute it to anyone because there was nobody within a hundred yards of him. Somebody walking on your grave, Eddie. More buses passed, a couple of lorries, passenger cars; he caught a tick-ticking sound, a metallic tapping, maybe a car with a flaw in its engine.

He walked a couple of blocks then turned right into Bluevale Street. There was something new in the sky-line, two tall concrete high-rise towers that resembled architecture he'd seen in photographs of old Communist countries, a suburb of Moscow or Minsk. The towers, drab and lifeless, had an oppressive quality.

He reached the warehouse at the foot of the street. The doors and windows were steel-shuttered and splattered with freaky Technicolor graffiti, and the enigmatic sign 'J MALLON, TRADER' needed a coat of paint. *Trader*: Jackie had chosen a description of his occupation that could mean almost anything. Eddie walked to the high wire fence that protected the open-air yard where the overflow from the warehouse was stored.

He saw a sign: BEWARE OF GUARD DOGS. He hooked

his fingers into the wire and gazed at the stock: weathered bricks taken from dismantled chimneys, old sinks and cisterns, bird baths, rolls of chicken wire, rusted wheelbarrows, broken tools that had served no apparent purpose. He also saw a large white delivery van, a Mercedes with the name J MALLON on the side panel and the address of the warehouse.

He found himself wondering if Jackie's killer had ever come down Bluevale Street, on foot or in a car; if the killer had ever gazed through the wire fence and watched Jackie in the yard; if Jackie's murderer had tracked his victim and created a timetable of the old man's movements and knew where to locate him for the purpose of assassination – but that implied premeditation. That meant Jackie had been marked for death. I want to believe it was utterly random, Eddie thought. Jackie was killed in the course of a robbery that went wrong, an innocent party.

He imagined this. The killer says, I want your wallet. And Jackie replies, Fuck off.

And then a struggle, hand to hand, a gunshot more accidental than intentional –

A dog barked from the yard, but there was no sign of the animal. I played here, Eddie thought. This was my kingdom. He gazed for a while, half-expecting Jackie to come out of the warehouse and cross the yard.

A man appeared and walked between the clutter towards the fence and stopped about twenty feet from Eddie. Sunlight made gold discs out of the man's glasses. He was in his early sixties and stooped and he wore a navy-blue warehouseman's coat with big breast pockets stuffed with pens.

I know this man, Eddie Mallon thought. What the hell was his name?

'You looking for something? You a reporter?'

'I'm Eddie Mallon.'

'Eddie Mallon? You? No way. You're kidding.' The man whipped off his glasses, came a few steps closer. '*Eddie Mallon*. In the name of Christ! So you are! Wee Eddie. Bloody hell. I wouldn't have recognized you in a hundred years. Look at the height of you! Jesus Christ almighty.'

The name came to Eddie. 'You're Joe Wilkie.'

'The very same Joe Wilkie that used to chase you out of here when we had a shipment coming in and we didn't want wee boys underfoot and getting squashed.'

Eddie lowered his hands from the fence. He realized he'd been gripping the wire tightly and it had left indentations on his fingers. He was tense without fully grasping why: this place so resonant with Jackie's life, so stuffed with reminders of his own boyhood, unsettled him.

Wilkie said, 'I'll unlock the doors and you can come inside and I'll make a cup of tea.'

He opened the gate in the fence and Eddie stepped through. Together, they entered the warehouse which smelled as it had always done, of rust and mildew and bird droppings. The ceiling was high and dark, pigeons infested the shadows, and shit covered whole areas like calcium deposits. In the poor light of the big metal building, Eddie saw Jackie's inventory in dim outline, the statues, stone columns, urns; it might have lain undisturbed for thirty years.

Suddenly a dog bounded out of the shadows, a massive Alsatian that circled Eddie and snarled, until Joe Wilkie said, 'Sit, Chet. Sit sit sit . . . Good boy,' and he thumped the dog's body with the flat of his hand a couple of times, and the pacified Alsatian slunk off to lie down a few yards away.

'He's all sound and fury,' Joe said. 'What are you, Chet? A right pussycat, eh? I always call my dogs after jazzers. Remember that? Chet Baker. The Alsatian before that was Lockjaw, after Eddie Lockjaw Davis. Then I had one I called Basie before Lockjaw. Oh, aye, and I had a Thelonious once too.'

'Wasn't there a Django?' Eddie asked.

'Django, aye, you're right. What a memory. He was a fierce bastard. I'd forgotten about him.'

Wilkie went inside the office, a small cubicle marked PRIVATE. Eddie followed, conscious of the dog's unbroken stare. Joe Wilkie plugged an electric kettle into the wall; the gas ring that had been used in the past was history. And so was the paraffin heater, replaced by an electric fire. The desk was the same – massive, strewn with invoices and phone messages on a long metal spike. The telephone was a clunky old black Bakelite job.

'No computer, I see,' Eddie said.

Joe Wilkie laughed. 'The idea of Jackie in the age of the Internet defies understanding, Eddie. I had to beg him to buy a bloody electronic calculator two years ago . . .' He opened a cupboard and took out a tin of tea bags and two china mugs.

Eddie found a chair and sat. 'It really hasn't changed much.'

'Not so many employees,' Wilkie said. 'There used to be four or five, now there's only me and my son Ray, and we run the place between us. Jacks of all trades. Nightwatchmen. Drivers. Stocktakers. We do it all.' Wilkie cleared phlegm from his throat and replaced his glasses. He sounded emotional. 'Your dad . . . You ask yourself: what's this bloody world coming to – but you don't get any answers. Scum's taken over everything.'

'It's no different anywhere else in the world,' Eddie said, a feeble response to Wilkie's remarks, yet all he could come up with.

Joe Wilkie made tea, handed Eddie a mug. Eddie tasted the tea, which was hot and unsweetened.

'Your dad was awful proud of you, Eddie,' Wilkie said. 'My son's a cop in New York City, he'd say. He'd show a photo of you in uniform every chance he got. He kept it in his wallet. He never tired of it.'

Eddie had no idea that Jackie carried a picture in his wallet, and showed it to people. The notion touched him.

'I heard Dad was selling.'

'So he said.'

'Did he have a buyer for the place?'

'He never mentioned one,' Wilkie said. 'A guy came a couple of times, and they shut themselves away in your dad's office. I could hear them arguing sometimes. I got the impression he might have been interested in buying the business, but maybe he didn't want to pay Jackie's asking price, whatever that was . . . I couldn't say for sure, I just know they had violent shouting matches and Jackie always looked furious afterwards.'

'You know the man's name?'

'I know his name all right. Roddy Haggs. A lot of people know him and his reputation.'

'And what's his reputation?' A son's curiosity about his murdered father's life: that was justification enough for asking a couple of questions. He wasn't trespassing on anyone's jurisdiction.

'Bent and bad,' Wilkie said. He shuffled papers and

looked tense. He didn't want the warehouse sold. This had been the only employment he'd ever known in his life. Without it, what was he supposed to do? His white face was a map of uncertainty and loss. 'I told the police Haggs was here,' he said. 'I told them about the arguments.'

'How did they react?'

'One of the cops – his name'll come back to me in a sec – wrote something in his notebook. That was that . . . Got it. Perlman. Detective-Sergeant Perlman.' Wilkie snapped thumb and middle finger together.

'When was Perlman here?'

'Yesterday afternoon. Nice enough fellow, a wee bit on the shabby side. But he has one of them faces that doesn't tell you what's going on in his brain.'

Eddie thought, The deadpan approach: give nothing away. He imagined Perlman, who looked as if he'd worked the streets for ever, would be adept at this.

'How's Senga?' Wilkie asked.

'It's a bad time for her. I don't know how she's handling it.'

'She loved Jackie. She used to come down here and help out now and again. I've often seen her roll up her sleeves and get stuck in. Never afraid of hard work. Some woman. Where are you staying?'

'At my sister's.'

Joe Wilkie said, 'How is Joyce?'

'Doing the best she can . . .'

'She's a good girl.'

Eddie, who realized he wanted to get out into the sunlight and away from the memories this place blitzed him with, finished his tea. 'Speaking of Joyce, I better get moving. She's probably wondering where I am.'

Wilkie walked with him into the yard and unlocked the gate in the fence. He held out his hand and Eddie shook it.

Eddie asked, 'You'll be at the funeral.'

'I'll be there,' Wilkie said. 'I knew your dad when we were growing up in the Gallowgate. That's a long time ago, Eddie. I wouldn't miss his send-off.'

Eddie clapped the old warehouseman's arm, then turned and walked slowly up Bluevale Street. And that was when it struck him again, the unsettling feeling he'd had before, the sense of something having brushed against him. The heat was sucked out of the day and he was cold for a moment as he gazed towards Duke Street where traffic was growing and bright red buses trawled along.

He stood still. He was conscious of the tenements looming over him, their dark secretive entranceways and the severe geometry of their windows, and suddenly he loved them as he'd loved them as a child because they were permanent, some part of himself would *always* belong here, but he had the feeling that these buildings, where people lived and bred and died, formed a protective shield around the mystery of his father's death, that if you could somehow penetrate to the hidden heart of the massive sandstone constructs you'd find the answer in the form of a man sitting at a table cleaning a gun, surrounded by oily rags and bottles of solvents, a cigarette crushed in an ashtray, pale lager going flat in a half-empty glass, and a cartridge clip lying alongside a lighter.

If you could find him. If you knew which stairs to climb, which door to knock.

16

'He's in Birmingham, is he?' Haggs asked.

'That's what he said on the phone. Birmingham. Or mibbe Liverpool.'

'Make up your mind.'

'He could be anywhere. How did he ever get to be an accountant? You need a brain for that, and Billy doesn't have one. His skull's empty. I mean, he lost a leg when a train ran into him. Hapless isn't the word. So, eh, where's the TV?'

'TV?' Haggs looked at the old fellow on the bed. He was thin and unshaven and had ketchup and egg stains down the front of his striped pyjamas. His face was thin as a hatchet-blade and his eyelids drooped. He looked as if he'd never smiled in his life. He had the expression of a man sitting on a thistle, but too self-willed to complain.

'Aye the didgie, whatever it's called. You're supposed to be delivering it, right?'

Didgie? Haggs wondered. He examined the army of little prescription bottles on the bedside table. The names of the drugs meant nothing to him. 'When's he coming back?'

The old fellow stared at Haggs in a vacant way. 'I

want to see the digital telly,' he said. He sounded like a spoiled kid.

Ah, digital. Haggs said, 'We'll get to that. Suppose you focus, McQueen, and tell me when Billy's coming back.'

'What's it to you? Just bring in the telly. Do you need his signature – is that it? Christ, man, I can sign for him.'

Haggs thought this was like talking to a brick edifice.

'Hey,' Larry McQueen said. 'How did you get in anyway?'

'You opened the door for me,' Haggs said. 'You don't remember?'

'My memory's . . .' With a look of irritation, Larry McQueen flapped his hand at the prescription bottles. 'I never remember when I'm supposed to take these bloody pills. They wreck my head and I get confused.'

Haggs walked around the room. He clenched and unclenched his hands, bones cracking. Note to self: be patient when there is no other strategy. The room smelled of pee and pot-pourri air-freshener. The area round the bed was littered with old newspapers, books about World War II, copies of *Watchtower*. 'What Christ's Resurrection Can Do In Today's World.' Not a fuck of a lot, Haggs thought.

A guitar with an ornate pick-guard was propped against the bedside table. A chamberpot of a blue floral design was visible just under the bed. It contained a little yellow pool of pish. The furniture in the room was good quality stuff.

'Larry,' he said. 'Would you happen to have a cellphone number for Billy?'

'He had a sky-blue marble when he was three,' Larry said. 'We lived in Kinning Park then.'

'Is that so?' Haggs said.

'Lost it, didn't he? Down a gutter. Plop and gone. Always losing stuff. A marble. A leg. Born a loser.'

Haggs walked to the bed. He grabbed the old fellow by the collar of his pyjama jacket and dragged his head up from the pillow. 'Where can I reach your son? Don't talk to me about digital TVs and marbles and such shite. Just give me a number for Billy.'

'Take your hands off me, Lew, I warned you.'

Lew? Who the hell was Lew? Some figure in McQueen's apparent dementia? Haggs said, 'I'm about to slap you in the mouth, Larry.'

'If I was a fifteen years younger, or even ten –'

'Aye aye aye. Let's not discuss the impossible.' Haggs raised a hand in the air. He wondered if a quick whack across the lips would do any good, if it would activate Larry McQueen's memory. Probably not.

Larry said, 'I don't remember any phone number, mister.'

'Think. *Think*.'

'Get your mitts off me,' and Larry McQueen made a funnel of his mouth and spat into Haggs's face, a wad of phlegm that struck Haggs in the eye.

'You disgusting old fucker,' Haggs said.

'Red card me for spitting then,' McQueen said.

Haggs punched McQueen half-heartedly in the nose, and the old man bled and cried out. Haggs had a mind to hit McQueen again but he knew it was point-less. Besides, there was no particular buzz to be had from bashing this defenceless old fart. The experience left him as flat as dead Alka-Seltzer. He'd crushed Matty Bones's hand, sure, but McQueen was a different matter.

116

Blood was flowing from the old fellow's nose. He appeared indifferent to it. As if the brief assault had never taken place, he glared at Haggs and said, 'Where's the telly then? In your van?'

Haggs stepped back from the bed. This encounter was like one of those weird nightmares where nobody ever answered your questions. You were inside a room and the walls sloped in a strange way, and people were staring at you as if the simple question 'Where am I?' was too difficult to answer.

He sighed and said, 'Okay. I'll bring up the telly. Where do you want it plugged in, Larry?'

'I don't want any sunlight shining on the picture,' McQueen said. Blood dripped from his lip to his pyjama jacket, where it brightened the dull red-brown of old ketchup crust.

Haggs wrote his name and phone number on a scrap of paper and placed it on the bedside table, wedged between the medication bottles.

'What's that?' Larry McQueen asked.

'When Billy gets round to calling, tell him I need to see him. It's in his own best interest. Can you remember that?'

'Think I've got a problem remembering, do you?'

'You? Never.' Haggs plucked a fistful of Kleenex from a pop-up box on the bedside table and shoved them into McQueen's hand.

'Wipe your face,' he said.

'Right, treat me like a baby,' McQueen said. 'It'll be a dummy tit next, and nappies, and talc for my arse.'

'I'll get the TV,' Haggs said.

He paused in the doorway and looked back. McQueen had let the tissues drop to the floor. He was staring at Haggs and blinking in the brassy early sun that gatecrashed the room.

'You got any smokes, Lew?' McQueen asked.

'I'll find you some.' Haggs closed the door and left.

17

When Eddie Mallon reached the corner of Onslow Drive and Whitehill Street he saw Senga standing barefoot outside her house in a dark green robe with short sleeves. Her hair was in some disarray. Eddie walked towards her, thinking how she looked pale and depleted. She turned her face when she heard him.

'You're up bright and early,' he said.

'I woke at dawn and I couldn't go back to sleep again, so I stepped outside and lo and behold here I am.'

'You're not wearing anything on your feet.'

'I like the ground against my skin,' she said. 'As a wee girl I loved to go barefoot every chance I got.' She looked at Eddie sadly. 'I have this cringe-making memory of forcing you to dance last night. I'm sorry about that. It was lunatic behaviour.'

'There's nothing to apologize for.'

She took a packet of B&H from the pocket of her robe, removed a cigarette and lit it with a gold lighter. She squinted her eyes against the smoke and looked at Eddie carefully for a moment. 'So . . . do I measure up to Flora?'

The question surprised him. 'I never thought of comparing you and her.'

'Apples and pears, eh?'

'You made Jackie happy.'

'It was hard work at times.'

'He wasn't happy with Flora,' Eddie said. He wondered if this remark constituted a tiny betrayal of his mother.

'Oh, I know all about that old soap opera,' Senga said. 'How to use your weans as pawns in a stupid game. Jackie realized it was stupid and destructive, but he could be inflexible beyond belief at times. Breaking a family up – for what?' Senga hesitated a second. 'He used to agonize over what he'd done. One day I told him, look, Jackie, if it's eating your heart out as much as you say, why don't you write to Eddie? Why don't you tell him how you feel?'

'You were behind that? I didn't know. I'm glad you did it.'

'*Somebody* had to kick his arse. I helped him write that first letter. And when you replied, he was over the moon. You'd opened the door for him a little way. A belated chance at redemption. You hadn't condemned him. You should have seen how happy he was after he made the first phone call and heard your voice.'

'I always wanted him to meet my wife and son,' Eddie said.

'It just wasn't on the cards.' Senga rubbed her eyelids. 'You want my honest opinion? Your mother was as much to blame as Jackie. She should've scratched and clawed to keep her kids together, but no, off she went to America with her tail between her legs. And don't tell me it was because Jackie frightened her, because if it had been me I would've moved bloody heaven and earth to keep my kids.' She puffed her cigarette quickly. Her words were expelled in little spurts of smoke. 'Flora chickened out, no argument. Jackie behaved like a major prick. And you and your sister were the ones that paid the price.'

Eddie thought of Flora immersed in her world of plants and big-band music. Her lifelong loneliness. Senga was right. Flora hadn't fought for her kids. She'd talked and talked about saving money for a lawyer, and how Joyce would be rescued and brought to America, but it was vapour, and it blew away. Maybe Joyce wouldn't have wanted to leave Scotland in any event. Had anyone ever asked her? Dysfunctional, Eddie thought. A family broken down and hissing steam like an old truck at the side of the road.

Senga folded her arms under her breasts. 'The neighbours probably think I'm completely daft standing out here like this. They think I'm eccentric as it is.' She looked down, wiggled her toes. 'Want some coffee?'

'Sure.' He found himself liking her, the way she shot from the hip, the apparent good sense she made when she talked about the Jackie–Flora saga. He glimpsed what Jackie must have seen in her, somebody straight, no hidden angles. *What you see is what you get.*

He followed her inside the house and walked behind her into the kitchen. This room had been redecorated since he'd last seen it – new stainless-steel appliances, recessed spotlights in the ceiling where a solitary bulb used to hang from a long flex.

'Pull up a chair, Eddie,' she said.

Senga was the kind of woman you found yourself obeying. She emitted, even in her grief, a sense of power and determination, as if heartbreak was something you could overcome if you worked hard at it. You got out of bed in the morning and kept on going, no matter what. She set cups and saucers on the table. He declined milk and sugar; he wanted his caffeine in an unadulterated rush.

He said, 'I walked down to the warehouse.'

'Was anyone there?'

'Joe Wilkie.'

'He's loyal,' she said. 'I like Joe. I like his boy Ray.'

'Joe hates the idea of the place being sold.'

'Jackie was always talking about selling,' she said. 'He blew hot and cold on the idea. But he couldn't have sold without my consent, because I own fifty per cent of the place.'

'I didn't know.'

'We'd been partners for more than ten years, Eddie. I invested a little cash of my own at one point when he was going through hard times, and in return I got half the company.' She stared at Eddie with a certain air of mock defiance. 'It's only a bloody scrapyard, Eddie, when you get right down to it. Okay, sometimes we get some decent stuff passing through, but not often. If I was a gold-digger, believe me, I wouldn't have taken up with your dad. In any case, I've got better business sense than Jackie ever had. I'm not just a pretty face.'

Eddie smiled. Partner in life, partner in business. What else didn't he know about the relationship between Jackie and Senga? For the first time since Jackie's murder, he considered the bureaucracy of death, a last will and testament, ledgers, files, bank accounts, unpaid taxes – all the stuff of life that the dead leave behind.

'Did Jackie make a will?' he asked.

'Damn right. I insisted on it. He left this house to me and his half of the business to your sister. I can't see Joyce wanting a half-share in the yard, so I'll cash her out if we can come to an agreement. We'll discuss it some time.'

Eddie was quiet a moment. 'Wilkie thought Jackie had found a potential buyer, a man called Haggs.'

'Skinnymalinky?'

'Who?'

'That's my name for Roddy Haggs. A long drip of a guy. His hands are always dead cold. He's like something dug up from the frost. It doesn't help that he looks a wee bit like Count Dracula on a bad day.'

'Tell me more about him.'

'He's one of those flash characters with his grubby fingers into everything going. A thug, but a rich one. Jackie pretended to like him, but he didn't trust him. I think maybe they did some business together a long time ago but they never got along. I met Haggs five or six times, usually if I was out having a drink with Jackie. He'd always shake my hand and hold it a wee bit longer than necessary. It was like he wanted to flirt with me right under Jackie's nose.'

'He wanted to think he could upset Jackie,' Eddie suggested.

'Worth a try.' Senga was overwhelmed a moment by an apparently sad thought, and she frowned, plucked a tissue from a box on the table and blew her nose. 'I'll tell you something that's bothering me. Where the hell is Bones? He was never far away from Jackie. Why hasn't he come round to offer his condolences? It's not his style. He was Jackie's shadow.' She smoked a cigarette and stared into the lit end. Her eyes watered.

'Have you any idea why he might have vanished?'

'Chris Caskie asked me that same question last night. I don't know, maybe something bad has happened to him.'

'Don't jump to gloomy conclusions,' Eddie said. He

123

thought of Caskie asking questions in his soft fashion. 'What else did Chris want to know?'

'You and him. You're a curious pair. Questions, questions.'

'Curious is a cross cops carry.'

She gazed at the kitchen window for a while. Eddie saw a certain earthy quality in her that must have appealed to Jackie. The large mouth, the powerful body, the long delicate fingers; she had a mature sexuality her air of grief didn't conceal. 'He asked why Jackie had left Glasgow last week, and where did he go.'

'And?'

Senga shook her head. 'And nothing. Jackie said he had some business to attend to. I didn't keep tabs on him. I trusted him, and he knew better than to disappoint me, believe me. I had the feeling he was going down the coast because he mentioned he was looking forward to getting some good sea air into his lungs . . . I drove him to Central Station, dropped him off, then picked him up the next day.'

Eddie saw a slight bafflement on her face now, the puzzlement that comes with the cold realization that everything's changed and your world will never be the same again. The structures have been blown away and you don't know what you're left with except the empty road that might be the rest of your life.

He finished his coffee. He found himself gazing at her tattoo, a tiny purple-blue figure etched into flesh; a man astride a horse. She caught the line of his eye and asked, 'Do you know who this is, Eddie? You remember your history?'

Old schoolbooks. Stories of violence and hatred. He said, 'It's William of Orange seated on a horse, and the date below it is July 1690. The Battle of the Boyne, if I remember correctly.'

'Right, when King Billy defeated James, and James ran away. A big day in the history of Protestantism.' She covered the tattoo with her hand.

Eddie asked, 'What did Jackie think of that?'

'He called it a disfigurement. He didn't have a sectarian bone in his body. I had this tattoo done when I was seventeen years old and I didn't know any better. I was brought up in a house of Loyalist maniacs who'd emigrated to Glasgow from Belfast and Derry, true blue do-or-die kill-the-Pope nutters. Catholics were beneath contempt. The Pope was the Antichrist. That was hammered into me. My dad, Willie Craig, was a high-up in the Orange Lodge and he believed the RCs were planning world domination. What chance did I have of an unbiased upbringing, eh? It's sick, all that stuff, and it takes a long time to break free of it.'

'But you're free now,' he said.

'I've been free a long time, Eddie.'

He got up from the table. 'I'll go see how Joyce is,' he said.

'Wake her up. She can be a terrible sleepy-head at times.'

Senga offered her cheek to be kissed and Eddie pressed his mouth against her skin and then let himself out of the house. He walked towards Ingleby Drive. His thoughts were like flashing detour signs directing him places he didn't want to go.

18

Charles McWhinnie spooned a touch of sugar into the foam of his cappuccino and surveyed the sunlit street from his table outside the café. Kelvinbridge, West End of town, McWhinnie's habitat of patisseries, food-of-the-moment bistros, upscale greengrocers where you could buy yams and Cape gooseberries; normally he would have been comfortable here, but this morning no, quite the opposite.

He sloshed some milky coffee down the side of his cup as he raised it to his mouth. A shadow fell across him and he raised his face and Chris Caskie was looking down at him through a pair of sunglasses.

Caskie sat, laid his folded copy of the *Scotsman* on the table and crossed his legs. He said, 'Glasgow's beautiful at times. The way stone changes colour in the sunlight. The varieties of sandstone. Pink. Red. Ginger. Blonde. Lovely place.'

'How is it all those marvellous colours look the same when it rains?' McWhinnie asked. 'How come they all look so damn *drab*?'

'Whoo. Tetchy, are we? Talk to me, Charles.'

'This whole thing isn't to my liking,' Charles McWhinnie said. 'I want that on record.'

'On record? Where? In a file? On a floppy disk? Hold your breath, Charles. You think this situation is a walk in the park for me?'

McWhinnie tried the coffee again. His hand trembled.

'The shakes, I see,' Caskie said.

'Sleepless nights.'

'I have a doctor who'll write you a prescription for Ro-Hypnol or something stronger, no questions asked.'

'Yesterday I had my Rover broken into in bloody Govan.'

'Dear old Govan,' Caskie said. 'Sometimes we go places we'd prefer to avoid.'

McWhinnie gazed at a double-decker bus roaring through a red light. His instinct was to note the number plate. 'I had honourable ambitions, Chris. Really. I saw my career in terms of nice little stages. I'd go from one case to another more important, then another more important still, a promotion every five or six years or so. Instead I'm sent to Govan with some sharp-faced little git with foul breath, and I get my damn car broken into and the sound system stolen. Now you've got me up at dawn and running around . . . I don't like these jobs. Even worse, I don't know why I'm doing them, and I don't know the reason behind them. What's this one all about?'

'You want advice, Charlie? You should have joined your dad's law firm. That way you might have kept your hands nice and clean. A little conveyancing. Drawing up a will every now and then. Being kind to nice old ladies in Bearsden.'

'I hated that prospect,' McWhinnie said. 'I would have been a partner within ten years. My father was *apoplectic* when I joined the force. Why are you so angry, I asked him. I'll still be on the side of the law . . . I remember exactly what he said to me in that stiff Victorian way of his. *I think you'll find the law has many branches, young man, and you're climbing out on the wrong one.'*

Caskie asked a passing waitress for mineral water then tilted his head back to receive the full blast of sun. He wasn't sympathetic to McWhinnie's situation. Nobody had forced Charlie into becoming a policeman. Nobody had twisted his arm.

'Don't go weak on me, Charles.'

'I'm not going weak,' McWhinnie said.

'I like fortitude and loyalty. Now tell me about your day.'

McWhinnie was quiet for a second. 'I think our man saw me. I can't be sure. He had a funny look on his face.'

'Funny?'

'You know the expression a piano tuner gets when he listens to a tuning fork vibrate? Similar to that. He appeared to be listening for something, but I got the impression he wasn't sure what.'

'Tell me his itinerary.'

'He left his sister's flat at five thirty,' McWhinnie said.

'An early bird,' Caskie said.

McWhinnie smiled. 'I must say Joyce Mallon is the one bright light in all this, Chris. I had the pleasure of her company after she identified her father. Easy on the eye. I drove her home.'

'She isn't your type, Charles. I can't imagine her sitting through a bloody rugby match. I'm prepared to bet she prefers a good book to camping in some sodden tent at the side of a freezing loch.'

'I could open new frontiers for her. She could recommend books for me to read –'

'The point, Charles. Where did our man go after he left his sister's?'

'To his father's warehouse. He talked to a fellow called . . .' McWhinnie referred to a little notebook. 'Joe Wilkie. He went inside, stayed perhaps twenty minutes, came out again. He walked back up Whitehill Street to Onslow Drive and encountered Senga Craig.'

'Encountered? Meaning what?'

'She was standing outside her house. Barefoot.'

'Poor dear,' Caskie said. He thought of Senga dancing last night. Sorrow and madness. He remembered how, after the death of his wife, he'd sat in the living room of his house in Broomhill and pictured the last holiday he'd ever taken with Meg, Bermuda, sun and sand, colourful rum cocktails, and how he'd been possessed by the need to mix some of these alcoholic concoctions for himself in the kitchen, as if he might recapture an element of what had been lost years before . . . And then a few days after the funeral he'd listened to the rain fall miserably on the glass roof of the conservatory and drip from the waxen leaves of the laburnums, and he'd snapped out of the mood and stepped out of the gloomy room of his mind – wherever he'd been.

He'd felt a deep relief then. He was free of Meg, free of her dreadful sickness, liberated from his oaths and his responsibilities to a love that had died long before Meg's physical departure.

'Our man went inside the house with Senga,' McWhinnie said. 'Fifteen minutes later he emerged, walked back to his sister's place. I waited for a time. Then at eight o'clock I left.'

The waitress brought mineral water. Caskie sipped it.

McWhinnie said, 'It looked perfectly natural to me, Chris. A little nostalgic walk around the old neighbourhood. I'd probably do the same thing.'

Caskie looked at his watch. 'He phoned me half an hour ago. He wants to see the scene of the crime.'

'Morbid,' McWhinnie said.

'Probably,' Caskie remarked. I hope that's all it is, he thought. He drank half his water and stood up. He was wearing a blue and white striped shirt, sleeves rolled to just below the elbows. He carried his jacket slung over a shoulder. 'Take a break. I think you need one. I'll call you when it's time to move again.'

'Joyce was married once, wasn't she?' McWhinnie asked.

Caskie said, 'Briefly.'

'What happened to the union?'

'It fell apart.'

'His fault or hers?'

'It takes two to screw up, they say.'

McWhinnie watched traffic in the street. Cars and buses glowed in the sun, mirrors flashed.

He said, 'About my car.'

'Send me a bill for the cassette deck. I'll see what I can do.'

Feeling despondent, like a low-rent private detective in the pay of dodgy lawyers working squalid divorce cases, McWhinnie watched Caskie turn a corner and disappear. He suddenly remembered what the little man in Govan had said: *You don't have the stuff for this work.* Maybe I don't. He wondered if he should call Lou Perlman. Perlman, an odd bird in the aviary that was Force HQ, had taken him under his wing when he'd first joined the Strathclyde Police. Dear old Perlman, smart and big-hearted, that hair cut in tough-guy spikes, always had time for him.

Perlman, he thought. My rabbi.

He took out his cellphone and punched in Perlman's number, then killed the power before a connection was made. Work it out for yourself, Charles, he thought, don't go running to somebody else when you need rancid water pumped out of your system. Lou Perlman doesn't need your problems.

McWhinnie ordered another coffee, took a small diary from his pocket and made a note. He thought, I should be writing something like *Dear Diary, I am melancholy*. He closed the little book and wondered if he should tell Chris Caskie his white beard looked damned stupid.

19

'What a dump,' the detective-sergeant said. His name was Anthony Bothwell. He was a tall man with red hair and a wide nose that might have been broken at one time. He had the soft accent of a Highlander. In his spare time, he was a bagpiper.

'Be a sweetheart and open a window, Vicky. Place pongs.'

The uniformed officer, Constable Vicky Kyle, thought, *I'll be your sweetheart any time* – and did as she was instructed. Brittle flakes of old paint fell from the window frame. The window probably hadn't been opened in years. She watched Bothwell, a happily married man for whom she had a doomed infatuation, stroll round the room. PC Kyle wasn't altogether downhearted; she liked the idea of a secret longing. You needed some passion in your life, even if it was only dreamy make-believe stuff.

'Look in there,' Bothwell said. He pointed to a small bedroom that adjoined the kitchen. 'I'll have a shufty here,' and he began rummaging through drawers and opening cupboards.

Vicky Kyle stepped into the bedroom. A blind had been drawn down on the window. She tugged it and it rose quickly on its roller, *swoosh*, releasing a cloud of dust. The window was dirty. Below, cars and buses slogged through the clogged thoroughfare that was Shettleston Road.

Discarded clothes covered the floor. Pyjamas, underwear, shirts, socks. The bed was unmade. A bedside table was littered with assorted cold medications and empty Nicorette boxes. Squeezed-out tubes and half-empty bottles and God knows what lay under a ceramic lamp which was crusted with dried gobs of gum.

Vicky Kyle opened the drawer of the table.

Old football pools coupons, three or four centrefolds, some of them obviously antique, a postcard from Skye signed by somebody called Tam. The message read: *Fishing's crap here and too many midges.* She looked inside a wardrobe; sports jackets hung crookedly, neckties dangled from hooks. There was a stink of camphor. A stack of old race programmes had been piled at the bottom of the wardrobe. She bent to examine them. A spider rambled across her knuckles.

She looked under the bed, saw dust compacted into balls and old newspapers and cast-off slippers and four empty scotch bottles, Haig's. She stood upright, straightened her skirt. The bedroom was airless and stale. She walked into the kitchen. Bothwell was checking under the sink.

'Nothing in the bedroom, Tony,' she said. 'This place is disgusting. I wonder when it was last cleaned. If ever.'

'The year dot,' said Bothwell, groping behind drainage pipes.

'BC or AD?'

Bothwell hummed 'Amazing Grace' and then 'The Black Bear'. Pipers' tunes. He loved getting kitted out in the full regalia, enjoyed the swinging weight of the kilt, the well-polished sporran, the *skean-dhu* tucked in the sock. He thrilled to parades and bagpipe competitions and Highland games.

He said, 'Ah hah. Now what have we here, I wonder.'

'You found something interesting?' Vicky Kyle asked.

Bothwell backed out from under the sink. The sleeves of his white shirt were covered in dark streaks. He held a plastic shopping bag in one hand.

He said, 'Let's see what secret the hidden bag holds, shall we?' He peered inside the bag. Then he looked at Vicky Kyle and winked. 'Well well,' he said. 'Well oh well.'

She thought his wink playful. She felt blood flush her cheeks. She wondered if it showed. If she was blushing. You're a big girl, Vicky, for the love of God, act your age.

'What have you got, Tony?'

'See for yourself.'

She looked inside the bag. 'Bloody hell,' she said.

20

The telephone rang at twenty minutes past ten. Alone in the flat, Joyce was still in bed; she answered on the third ring.

The caller was Flora.

'Ma?' Joyce said. Her voice was dry. Too much wine before bed.

'Surprised you, did I? Eddie have a good flight?'

'It was fine, Ma.'

'He has that daft phobia about flying.'

Joyce lit a cigarette – damned habit, why did she need it, especially when her throat was so dry? – and turned over on her back and looked up at the bedroom ceiling. She had a small unexpected flashback to her amphetamine days when the first thing she'd do on waking was drop a hit of speed and wait for it to fire her furnace just enough to get her out of bed and drive to school and babble at her pupils. *Wordsworth this and Keats that and here's what Coleridge wrote . . .* And the pupils, most of them dull-faced and sullen and listening for the bell that would free them, sometimes asked questions that turned out to be jokes so old they had beards . . . *Miss Mallon, what's a Grecian Urn? Five quid a week, ha ha ha.* By mid-afternoon she was always wilting; she'd go inside the staff bathroom and snap a tab in half and swallow it, saving the remainder for later. And so she got through her life, and her separation from Harry, riding the speed train through the hours of daylight and sometimes deep into the night too. She'd never loved Haskell, although she'd tried. She wept a lot back then, not because she missed Harry, but because she hadn't been able to get the marriage to work, she'd tried, oh Christ she'd tried, but she was never capable of sustaining the illusion of a healthy marriage. For his part, Harry couldn't come to terms with the fact that marriage wasn't always the beautiful dream he wanted it to be. You weren't always attractive and anxious to fuck. Your period was depressing, or you developed a cold sore at the corner of your lip, or you just drifted away into the private world of a book and you didn't want Harry to follow, dragging his hard-on.

All that. The mathematics of matrimony. The downs were troughs of low pressure. And suddenly there were just too many of them, and Harry had become a burden she couldn't carry and couldn't learn to love.

'Are you listening to me?' Flora asked.

'Of course I'm listening.'

'So how are you bearing up?' Flora asked.

'That's a tough one, Ma.'

'I know, dear. I know. I'd come to the funeral but . . .'

'It's okay. I understand.' Joyce thought, I dread the final goodbye. The ritual.

'I should have phoned before this . . .' Flora paused. 'Sometimes I just don't know what to say. Sometimes I feel so damn sorry for the way . . .'

'It's water under an old bridge, Ma.'

136

She tried to picture Flora in her tiny house on Long Island but all she could see were plants, a great forest of them. She remembered the afternoon five years ago when Flora had prepared a barbecue in her back yard and how the smell of burning meat had floated through the neighbourhood and dogs had begun barking everywhere. That was the day Joyce first realized her mother was shrinking with the passage of time. Becoming tiny, a little white-haired thing.

'I try to let it go,' Flora said. 'It's hard.'

Was she crying? Joyce wondered. Her voice sounded thin and quivery.

There was a long silence. 'It must be good to have Eddie with you,' Flora said eventually.

'It's great.'

'Is there any news?'

'No, Ma. Nothing.'

'Is Eddie there . . . can I talk to him?'

'You just missed him by about five minutes. He wanted to go into the city centre.' She was going to tell the truth, but held it back. 'He thought he'd buy some presents to take home with him. And I didn't want to keep him company. I hate shops, all the crowds –'

'You *love* shops. What are you *talking* about?'

'I've changed,' Joyce said.

'Last time you were over here, you couldn't wait for me to take you to Bloomingdale's. We did Macy's, and then all those funny little stores in the Village.'

'I remember,' Joyce said. 'I suppose that was my last shopping rush. Where do you go after Bloomingdale's anyway?' Why was Flora really calling? She telephoned maybe twice a year and it was always small talk, and now and again a family story that had assumed the status of folklore, a tale to be repeated and handed down.

'Joyce . . . he's not getting, well, involved, is he?'

'Involved, Ma? I'm not following you.'

'Interfering . . . in the investigation.'

'Is he acting the cop? Is that what you mean?'

'I guess so.'

'Ma, he's not a wee boy you have to worry over all the time. He talked to the police. But he's not out there trying to solve this crime, if that's what you're thinking.'

She thought: Of course Eddie's *involved*. He might not admit it to himself just yet, but he's *definitely* involved. The moment he stepped off the plane, he was *involved*. Somebody murdered his father: was he supposed to sit back and accept? And now he was at the crime scene with Chris because he'd asked to see it, he thought he might learn something, whatever. Because he couldn't help himself.

She imagined that hideous slice of wasteland, Chris and Eddie studying the place, Eddie thinking he might unearth something the local gendarmes had missed, a spent shell, a discarded comb the criminal had dropped. *Not in the real world.*

'If you want reassurance, Ma,' she said, 'I'll get him to phone you.'

'No, it's okay . . . Have you seen Chris Caskie?'

'Last night.'

'How is he?'

Good question, Joyce thought. 'Normally he's his charming friendly self. Sometimes he broods.'

'Meg's been dead only six months.'

Joyce didn't want to talk about Chris or Meg. Meg's

sickness. Sometimes she had the feeling that all human relationships ended in disaster.

Flora said, 'I love you, Joyce. You know that, don't you?'

'Yes,' Joyce said. 'And I love you too.'

'Keep in touch, sweetheart. And if you need me, I'm here.' Flora made a kissing sound and hung up.

Joyce rose, went inside the kitchen in her underwear, drank cold water. She found an old tartan dressing gown hanging on the back of the door, and she put it on, then she brewed coffee and drank it standing at the table, her robe open, her small breasts warmed by sunlight coming through the window. She felt a vague arousal she attributed to the heat; certainly there was nothing else nearby to cause it.

21

Billy McQueen sat in a black Ford Fiesta at the corner of Armadale Street and Ingleby Drive. Gurk, dreadlocked, was behind the wheel.

McQueen said, 'I'm not saying it's a waste of time, Tommy.'

'Spell it out. What the hell are you saying?'

'I'm saying mibbe it could be. *Mibbe*.'

Gurk looked at McQueen with eyes Billy thought just a little too intense to belong to a rational human being. There was a light in them that indicated either a form of madness or an extreme calm, Billy wasn't sure which. Gurk had an astonishing forehead, a brow that protruded prominently over his eyes like some abnormal outcropping of bone. His chin was almost a perfect square.

'I'm going up,' Gurk said. He prodded McQueen in the chest. 'And you, my old china, you sit right here until I get back.'

McQueen said, 'She may not be helpful.'

'It isn't experimental physics we're talking about, Billy. A, she knows something. B, she doesn't. No in-betweens. No fuzzy zones.' Gurk leaned close to Billy McQueen, eye to eye. 'You wear too much grease on your hair, mate. Grease is what you fry chips in. It's fucking unhealthy. Interferes with follicle development. Take my advice. Stop lathering your scalp in that shit.'

Gurk got out of the car and closed the door. Billy McQueen watched him in the rearview mirror as he walked along Ingleby Drive. Gurk moved with a confident kind of lope, lazy and loose. He obviously spent a lot of time in the gym, which showed in the rocklike musculature of shoulders under the red and yellow shirt he wore hanging outside his khaki slacks.

McQueen thought: This isn't a smart move. Coming here. I am unhappy. This has all gone wrong. He jumped when his cellphone rang, then calmed down enough to answer it.

Larry said, 'Where's that didgey TV?'

Billy wondered how Larry had found this cellphone number, then remembered he'd written it down months ago and the old man had stuffed it in the drawer of the bedside table. Okay, so he'd had one of his rare moments of clarity and remembered where he'd stashed the number and now the TV was worrying him.

'It isn't due to be delivered yet,' Billy said.

'Says you. The man was here. He said he was bringing it in from his van.'

'Are you sure?' Billy asked.

''Course I'm bloody sure.'

'He came into the flat?'

'No, he was shouting through a fucking loudspeaker from the pavement below,' Larry said.

Billy ignored the sarcasm. You had to. 'So, you let him in and he said he was bringing the TV –'

'Right. Then he went away and never came back. And

here's the nice thing. Here's the lovely part. The bastard punched me in the nose.'

'He *what*?'

'Do you no' understand English? Hit me, Billy. He hit me. He stuck one on me.'

A delivery man who doesn't deliver. A delivery man who punches a sick old guy in the face. Billy McQueen experienced an unexpected poke of dread. It was a brilliant sunny morning in dear old Glasgow, people were strolling in the city parks, it was picnic weather, ice creams were melting over cones and running sticky and white down people's fingers and crowds would be idling in their thousands through the Botanic Gardens: why was it so drab all of a fucking sudden?

Larry said, 'I mean, what the hell kind of delivery service is it when the man hits you right in the fizzog, eh? What kind of people are you *dealing* with, bawheid?'

I wish I knew, Billy thought. He slumped into depression. He wondered if it ran in families, this melancholy that increased as you got older. Would he eventually take to his bed like Larry and live in his own bleak little world?

'Here, I bet the telly was nicked,' Larry said. 'I bet it fell off the back of a lorry. Ask no questions and you'll hear no lies. Sometimes I think you and Lew are working together.'

Lew. Ah, good old Lew, the imaginary playmate who'd sprung fully grown from Larry's mind only last year. Larry and Lew had a relationship filled with contradictions, friends one moment, adversaries the next. A form of regression was going on in Larry's deteriorating brain: back to childhood and stamp-your-feet tantrums and people that didn't exist.

Billy glanced in the rearview mirror and saw Gurk vanish inside a tenement.

'By the way,' Larry said. 'This delivery man, he left a name and a phone number. Want me to read it to you?' Sounds of plastic bottles clicking, papers shuffling, the old man humming 'Charlie is my Darlin''.

Billy McQueen waited, tense as a rubber band in a cocked catapult.

'Haggs,' Larry McQueen said.

Billy switched his cellphone off at once and sat with his eyes shut. Haggs. Strike me down. Flatten me with a red-hot iron. Roddy Haggs. Jackie Mallon had once said that Haggs had been trying to find a way to muscle in. Gone to all kinds of trouble. Questions. People in parked cars watching Jackie come and go.

If there was a single soul you didn't want within a hundred miles of you or your property, one human being you wouldn't want to travel with on the last interstellar ship carrying to safety the few remaining survivors of the Final Nuclear Holocaust on Earth, it was Roderick Haggs.

22

Caskie gestured at the crime-scene tape hung round the small area of wasteland. 'The night Jackie was shot, his car was parked here. He'd been having a drink in Blackfriars just along the street. He returned to the car, got inside and he was shot point-blank by somebody in the driver's seat.'

Eddie Mallon stared at the empty plot of land. There was space for a dozen cars, maybe more, but none was parked here today. Eddie thought: Jackie settles in the back seat of the car and the driver turns and shoots him. Like that. If the shooter was Bones, Jackie wouldn't have sensed danger. If the man with the gun was somebody else – wouldn't Jackie have recognized from the back of the guy's head that he wasn't Bones? Or maybe he wasn't paying attention, and he was feeling mellow from drink, and the light wasn't good anyway . . .

Eddie stepped closer to the tape. He looked at the ground, which was stained by drips of oil and car lubricants. He wondered what forensics had discovered, if there had been anything useful in the car, prints, fibres, anything, no matter how minuscule, that might indicate the identity of the killer. He put his hands in the pockets of his jeans and swayed a second on his heels, rocking slightly. This close to the place where Jackie had been killed, he was unnerved, even though there was nothing to see, but what you created in your mind could be more savage than the reality. He imagined the gunshot. The end of his father's life. The dying. The roar of the gun rolled and rolled through him. He felt a hollow in his heart.

A man appeared, a familiar figure who flicked the tip of his index finger against the crime-scene tape several times as he studied the ground. Then he nodded at Caskie.

'Chris,' he said.

Caskie didn't smile. 'Can't stay away, Lou?'

'Drawn back like an iron-filing to a magnet. You look at a place once, it strikes you one way. Look again, you get another impression. A third time, it's different. And so on to an infinity of mirrors and insanity. I lost my brains years ago.'

Caskie said, 'Eddie, this odd-looking reprobate is Detective-Sergeant Lou Perlman. He's one of the many dedicated souls working your dad's case, although I couldn't tell you what he actually does. He's a mystery.'

'We already met,' Eddie said. 'At the airport.'

Perlman reached under his glasses and fingered his eyepatch. 'How are you bearing up?'

'So-so,' Eddie said. He could still feel that hole inside. He wondered what it would take to plug it.

Perlman said, 'It's a bloody rotten end to a life, anyone's life.'

'What's the reason for the pirate impersonation, Lou?' Caskie asked.

'Minor infection of the eyelid,' Perlman said. 'Some say the patch suits me. I may keep it. Makes me feel like a pirate. A life of derring-do and keelhauling people you don't bloody like. I could go for that.'

'I expect you have a list of candidates,' Caskie said.

'I do, Chris, I do.'

Eddie asked, 'Did you know my father?'

'No, we never met,' Perlman said. A sly smile appeared on his lips. The sun shone on the silver scruff of his unshaved jaw and glinted against his glasses. For a second his face was an oval of pure light. 'You got a minute, Eddie?'

'Sure,' Eddie said.

'What is this? A private convention for two?' Chris Caskie asked.

'A word in Eddie's ear,' Perlman said. 'Nothing sinister.'

Caskie shrugged, hesitated, then wandered slowly about ten yards away and tapped one foot in an impatient huff. He whistled quietly to himself, a man excluded from a confidence.

'This must be bloody frustrating for you,' Perlman said quietly. 'Looking on from the outside.'

'Yeah,' Eddie said.

'You're a cop. You want involvement. A sense of participation.'

'Yeah. You got it.'

Perlman drew Eddie a few more yards from where Caskie stood and lowered his voice. 'Yon Caskie has a lean and hungry look.'

'Meaning?'

'I don't trust him.'

'Is this internal politics? Or personal?'

Perlman said, 'I'm not a political animal, son.'

Eddie hadn't been called 'son' in years. 'You've got something you don't want him to hear.'

Perlman said, 'I never want Caskie to hear *anything* I say. He's a great eavesdropper, our Christopher. He's got an ear like a fucking satellite receiver.'

'What's on your mind?' Eddie asked.

'I've been thinking about you since we met. You shouldn't be left out in the cold.'

'Tay would disagree.'

'Tay's territorial. He's sprayed his musk across this turf. I'm thinking about something else.'

'I'm listening,' Eddie said.

'I'm a great believer in using every resource available in any situation. Why waste a good man just because he's got a funny accent and he's out of his own patch and doesn't know the score, eh?' Perlman laid a hand on Eddie's shoulder. 'I suggest we cooperate. You and me. A private arrangement. Nobody else knows.'

'Explain.'

'I'm your man inside the Force. Your ally. You learn what I learn. You get the unexpurgated truth from me, and not some sanitized version of the investigation that Tay chooses to tell you.'

'And in return you get?'

'You become my connection to the Mallons. Your gleanings become my gleanings.'

'I don't think there's a hell of a lot to glean inside my family,' Eddie said. He thought about Joyce, and then Senga: what could they know that might help Perlman?

'Ballocks, son. In my long and often colourful experience of this fair city, I've found there's always some black secret in any family. Some faded old whisper. It might

147

be repressed, or half-forgotten, but it's there. You just keep your eyes and ears open, and sometimes you notice the very thing you're looking for is staring you right in the face.'

Eddie smiled. 'You're saying some awful thing might be hidden in my family?'

'Don't go putting words into my mouth,' Perlman said. 'I'm not accusing anyone of wrongdoing. Maybe a friend of the family will be indiscreet. Or Senga will let some revelation slip without realizing what she's done. Maybe she knows somebody who had a murderous dislike of Jackie, only she's too upset to think about it. Or perhaps your sister knows something she doesn't even know she knows. The permutations are beautifully infinite. You'd be surprised how often families are sitting on a truth they don't even know about themselves. The trick for you is how well you pay attention.'

Eddie said, 'I think you're asking me to spy.'

'Boo hoo. Don't talk such shite. Spying, Christ. I'm asking you, Eddie, to lend a wee helping hand in the matter of catching your dad's killer. I mean, you don't expect me to believe you came all the way here to bury your dad without some part of you positively *gagging* to help find the killer, do you? I'm not buying that, son. Unless I've seriously misjudged you . . . in which case I walk away and this chat never happened.'

Eddie cleared his throat. His mouth was dry. The heat pounded him. His hands were damp. Okay. Why deny it? Why go on keeping it tamped down? Perlman saw through him. Perlman, tack-sharp and shrewd, penetrated areas of Eddie he didn't want to explore himself. Right to the heart of it, Eddie: you wanted more than just a sense of Jackie Mallon's life and times, more than the history of your estranged dad. This was no quick overseas trip to say goodbye to your father and console your sister in the process. He hadn't come three thousand miles to be a goddam mourner. It wasn't his style to stand by in passive mode, the grief-driven son surrounded by his bereaved sister and his father's black-veiled common-law wife. He knew it now: it was about justice, sure, but it was also about playing a role in getting it.

'What you're asking me to do could amount to nothing.'

'Aye, it might. I'll take that chance.'

'Why are you doing this anyway?'

'Because I'm just a kind-hearted old Jew. Because I don't care for Tay, who's like some fucking cardinal with a ring you're expected to kiss. Because I don't have intimate access to your family environment, and I want you to be my eyes and ears. Take your pick. I always have a diversity of explanations just in case.'

'Plus you don't like the rule-book,' Eddie said.

'I do this job my way.' Perlman looked up at the sun. 'You can trust me one hundred per cent. Game?'

Eddie said, 'Game.'

Perlman sniffed the air in an exaggerated way in the manner of a man seeking signs of a change in the weather. 'I wish to fuck it would rain. This isn't right, this kind of heat in Glasgow, it's a travesty of nature, it's driving me up the bloody wall . . . I'm in the phone book, Eddie. Perlman, L. The one and only. Don't call me at work.'

'One thing,' Eddie said. 'I understand you went to the warehouse and interviewed Wilkie –'

Perlman dismissed this with a gesture of his hands. 'Who told me Jackie and Haggs had words. Big deal. I'm not breaking sweat. Don't get me wrong, I'll talk to Haggs. He's on my list. But an argument Haggs had with your father doesn't excite me, because I understand they had more than a few over the years, and none of them ever led to Jackie's demise.'

'Who else is on your list?'

Sighing, Perlman said, 'An alkie who says he saw the killer's face in dramatic close-up. A deaf old guy who claims he heard a gunshot. A retired priest who saw a man running away from the area. One or two others. It's not a promising gallery, Eddie . . . We'll talk.'

Perlman turned and walked away. Eddie watched him go around a corner, the flap of his jacket bouncing, the cuffs of the slightly flared trousers revealing yellow socks. Eddie thought: an ally in yellow socks and flared brown pants. It was something, a chink, a peephole. He might not be directly at the official heart of things, but an association with Perlman was better than a dose of leprosy. He felt an unexpected quickening of his nerves. Perlman had opened a door for him. A corridor stretched ahead. All he had to do was keep an ear open for a hint, a nuance of speech; an eye ready for some off-centre piece of behaviour, something out of alignment. *Families are often sitting on a truth they don't even know about themselves.* Maybe so. Or maybe it would turn out to be nothing. Neither secrets nor gossip nor webby skeletons. It was just Perlman covering his bases.

Caskie approached, still whistling. 'What was that old sod after?'

'This, that. He's gung-ho to catch the killer. Wanted to reassure me.'

'He always looks so damn conspiratorial to me. He's been a cop since the year one. I've known him for about fifteen years and I couldn't tell you a thing about his personal life. If he has one.'

'Let's have a drink in this Blackfriars place,' Eddie said.

They walked along Bell Street. The sky was cloudless still, although the cross streets were in shadow. Building work was going on nearby, the transformation of a Victorian bank. Discarded chunks of concrete rumbled loudly as they clattered through a red plastic safety-tube into a skip.

'A new nightclub,' Caskie said. 'A restaurant maybe. The city grows and grows. You'll notice changes, Eddie.'

Eddie said, 'I keep expecting to see tramcars.'

'You'll only find them nowadays in the Transport Museum.'

The Transport Museum. Relics of old Glasgow displayed for public viewing. You could enter the lost city for the price of a ticket. His childhood was interred in demolished schools and motionless tramcars. That young Eddie had travelled a long way. *I grew up to spy on my own family. I'm staking out Senga and Joyce and whoever else comes into their orbit.* No matter how Perlman described it, it was still espionage, even of a small kind. But he couldn't hide from himself the fact he was uplifted by Perlman's proposal. A cop is a cop; and his dead father is his dead father. The one has to do something about the other, or else the world makes no sense, and everything's anarchy.

Blackfriars was just opening. A smell of food floated out of the big darkened room. Eddie stepped inside. *Jackie had come this way, crossed this threshold and he had maybe twenty minutes to live. Only he didn't know it.* What was in Jackie's head before he died? What thoughts and plans? Could Senga or Joyce know *anything,* even at the subliminal level Perlman had mentioned?

The dead left conundrums behind always. The living had the task of solving them. Or maybe it all vanished inside a mystery you can never penetrate.

Caskie asked, 'What can I get you?'

'Something ice cold. Lager.'

'Pint, half-pint?'

'A half's fine.'

Caskie attracted the barman's attention and ordered draught lager for Eddie, a shot of Macallan's for himself. He added a tiny measure of water from a jug to his glass.

'Your health, Eddie.'

'Cheers,' Eddie said. He tasted the lager, scanned the room. Maybe Jackie had stood exactly where he was standing now. Maybe this was the very place where the old man had had his last drink on the planet. The dead man's spot: Jackie drinks in complete calm, looks round, perhaps he nods to somebody he knows. And the executioner is outside in the heat of the night. *I can't see the killer's face*, Eddie thought. *I can't imagine the features. They're clouded.*

He swallowed half his lager and studied Caskie in profile. He had fine symmetrical features and he drank with a slow controlled movement of his hand. Friend of the family, good old Chris, a gentleman.

Caskie finished his drink. 'Another?'

'I'd prefer some air.'

'Fine,' Caskie said.

Eddie set his glass down on the counter and strolled towards the door. Caskie followed and they walked for a while and then George Square opened out quite unexpectedly, a large sudden sunny space in the aorta of the city; it was if the shaded side streets were no more than tunnels that had been leading you all along to this great expanse of red tarmac which was dominated by the elaborate architecture of the City Chambers, a building of

Italianate grandeur. Eddie approached the stone cenotaph located directly outside the Chambers and gazed up at the central tower, which rose with all the pomp and self-assurance of the mercantile class of the 19th century: *Glasgow was an important hub of the Empire, and that would never change.* Or so they believed.

The city's motto was 'Let Glasgow Flourish'.

He turned away from the building. Nearby, a bald guy with no eyebrows was selling copies of the *Big Issue*, and a deranged man, hollow-eyed and hair wild, sat on a bench and swatted the air with pale fluttering hands, as if to drive off imaginary flying insects. Lunchtime crowds sauntered in their hundreds, or sat eating sandwiches in the sunshine, ignoring the deprived and the demented.

The city flourished all right, Eddie thought, in the same way as cities did everywhere, vivid contrasts and screaming paradoxes, the gulch between rich and poor, sane and crazy. But today the sun shone and the sky was a sheet of pure cobalt and life was just fine and few people were thinking dark thoughts, except maybe himself.

He said, 'The place has changed a whole lot.'

'For the better,' Caskie said. 'It's cleaner. The air is breathable. It used to be a den of smoke and fog. There's more money around. You can see it in the amount of construction going on, and the way those wonderful old Victorian buildings have been cleaned up. Look about you, Eddie.'

Eddie stared back across the square. The busy buzzing pump of the city, Jackie's city. Where he'd lived and died.

And last week, for one night, Jackie had left Glasgow.

'Do you think there's a connection between Jackie's murder and his trip last week?'

153

Caskie frowned. 'Eddie, all I know is he caught a train at Glasgow Central.'

Eddie said, 'He got off somewhere.'

'He could have travelled to London and back. He might have gone anywhere in England or Scotland . . . I couldn't begin to guess.'

'And who did he meet?'

'You don't really expect me to know the answer to that.'

'It was rhetorical.' Eddie gazed at Caskie a moment, wondering why Perlman didn't trust him. Was it something Caskie had done? Something in his manner that Perlman didn't care for? They were opposites, sure, Caskie smooth and Perlman rough around the edges, but that wasn't grounds for mistrust. What then?

Eddie said, 'I heard some guy might be interested in buying Jackie's business. Haggs.'

Caskie said, 'Haggs?'

'You know him?'

Caskie blinked, scratched at his beard and looked across the square. 'No . . . I'd remember a name like that.'

Eddie said, 'So you don't –'

Before Eddie could finish, the cellphone in Caskie's pocket rang and he took it out, answered it, listened, then flipped the cellphone shut. 'That was Tay,' he said. 'He wants to see you.'

23

Joyce heard her doorbell ring. Since she hadn't buzzed anyone up, it meant that somebody in the building had forgotten to shut the outside security door properly – probably old Mimms in the flat above. Sweet old guy, but he was forever forgetting to close the security door. She knotted the belt of her dressing gown and walked into the hallway. Through the stained-glass window of her front door she saw the outline of a man.

She hesitated halfway towards the door and called out, 'Who is it?'

The man said, 'We've never met, Miss Mallon . . . I was a friend of your dad. I heard about this terrible tragedy. And. Well. I thought I'd pay my respects, sweetheart.'

She stared at his outline and how it was bevelled by irregularities in the coloured glass. His voice was unfamiliar to her. An English accent, somewhere in the south, maybe London.

'What's your name?'

'Your Daddy knew me as Tommy G.'

'And you were close to him, you say?'

'Peas in a pod, love. We did a load of business over the years.'

'I never heard him mention you.'

'Come on, he must've talked about me once or twice.'

'No . . . I don't think he did. How are you spelling your name? G E E?'

'Just the letter G. Plain and simple, pet.'

'Just G? That a nickname?'

'Yeh, a nickname, love. Listen, I feel like a prat standing out here. I'm not the bogeyman, you know. I understand your concern about a stranger turning up outside your door because God only knows we live in times of dread – but you don't need to be suspicious of me, pet. I'll pay my respects and go.'

She took two steps towards the door, then stopped. She felt apprehension. She looked at the panes, which were orange and red and green and blue. She'd thought many times of replacing them with a more secure door, thick wood with a spyhole, but she'd been reluctant to remove the glass, an original feature of the flat. She was attached to the past. She liked a continuity with the endeavours of the dead.

She gazed at the shadow beyond the panes. You live alone in a tenement flat and there's only stained glass between you and someone on the other side of the door. A rapist. Anyone.

She said, 'I don't mean to be rude, but this is a bad time for me. Can you phone me, and we can meet some other day?'

'I'm leaving Scotland tonight,' he said.

'Okay. Next time you're in Glasgow.'

He didn't move. Why didn't he just go away?

She said, 'My number's in the book. Under my married name. Haskell. Okay?'

He moved a few steps back from the door and his

shadow dimmed. She heard him say, 'Righty-o, sweetie. I'll give you a bell next time I'm here. Count on it. Ciao.'

She watched the shadow retreat from the stained glass. She went inside the living room. She'd sneak a peek from the window when he left the building, get an idea of what he looked like. Maybe she'd seen him before in Jackie's company and hadn't been introduced – people floated into Jackie's life and only a select few lingered for any length of time.

She stood to the side of the curtain and waited, clutching a wedge of dark brown velvet in her fist. He didn't appear. It took maybe thirty seconds, certainly less than a minute, to reach the street from the stairs, so if he hadn't emerged from the building, where was he?

She went back to the hallway. She opened the drawer of a small table and took out a can of mace and stuck it in the pocket of her robe. It was a Peppergard Pocket Model she'd bought on her last trip to America. She remembered it was advertised as having 'a finger-grip dispenser that fitted comfortably into a woman's hand'. It sprayed six to twelve feet. She had no idea if it worked, or if the chemical had lost its potency with the passage of years; she just knew she felt better with the cylinder in her robe.

She stared at the coloured glass for so long that the panes began to vibrate in her vision. This tension. He's gone. He was slow to leave the building, that was why you didn't see him from the window, perhaps he stopped on the stairs to tie a shoelace or roll himself a smoke, something, anything, you're getting worked up about nothing.

Perhaps he'd changed his mind and was coming back up the stairs to start all over again, wheedling, trying to get her to open the door. Why can't he just pay his respects through a closed door?

Tommy G. I've never heard of him.

She thought of picking up the phone and calling Chris Caskie and telling him about Tommy G and asking him if he could send a uniform round quick, but the Englishman hadn't done anything illegal, he'd just rung the doorbell and talked to her and that wasn't a crime. This is paranoia, she thought. This is what you used to feel on speed. The edge. People are watching you.

She saw a shadow fall outside the door and then coloured panes shattered and shards flew and the lead framework bent back as if dynamite had exploded, and Tommy G's hand came through the broken glass and grabbed the door handle and twisted it, and suddenly he was *inside her home, sweet Jesus,* and she was aware of his milk-chocolate skin and dreadlocks, and she found herself fumbling for the tiny canister of mace and she yanked it out and pointed it at him and pressed the button and the pressurized chemical mist struck him in the face but without any great force or density, and he covered his eyes with his hands and moaned, then he went down on his knees and made a choking sound. She wondered how long the effect of the chemical lasted. She stared at his colourful shirt and all the flecks of broken glass on the floor.

'I'm on fire,' he said. 'For the love of Christ, I can't see. Fucking hell.'

She thought, I'll spray the bastard again just to be sure.

He turned his face up towards her. His eyelids were shut. Tears ran over his cheeks. He was coughing harshly. She half-expected to see him spit out slivers of lung. She wanted to hit him, flatten him with something hard, an iron skillet. He crawled on all fours towards her then raised one hand blindly until his fingers touched the hem of her robe. He tugged at the garment.

'For fuck's sake, do something, get me some water,' he said, and he yanked harder on her robe and she felt herself being drawn down to the floor. He was strong and his hands were big. Even blind and gasping for air, he was capable of hurting her, and she knew it.

Use the spray again, she thought. Burn his eyes out.

She directed the canister at his face, pressed the button. Nothing happened. Panicked, she pressed it again, wondering if it was stuck through lack of use. The same result. Nothing. He reached up and his palm circled a naked leg. He tightened his grip at a place just behind her knee. He squeezed so hard she was forced to bend her leg. She lost her balance and the cylinder slid from her fingers and she fell against him and they rolled together on the floor. He smelled faintly of a long-ago scent. What was it? Some musk from hippie days. He kept coughing, like a man dying badly. Where the hell did his strength come from? Why wasn't he *screaming* with the pain of the mace? Why wasn't he on fire? Instead, he was on top of her, his eyes still shut. It seemed to her he had some weird way of seeing in the dark. He caught her hands and forcibly stretched her arms out on either side of her body and crushed her into the floorboards. Her robe fell open. The cylinder had rolled away, she wasn't sure where.

She could barely breathe under Tommy G's weight. She looked into his face. The red eyelids, the tears squeezed out between them, the white foam of spit at the corners of his open mouth. He coughed straight into her face. If

I could get the canister, she thought. If I could reach for it. If it worked. Where is it?

He opened one eye. The white was scarlet. She couldn't bring herself to look into it.

Why hadn't her neighbours heard glass smash? Why hadn't the pathologically nosy-parker Mrs Curdy in the flat across the landing called the police? Why hadn't she seen Tommy G intrude?

'Listen . . . to me,' he said. His voice croaked. She thought of sandpaper on rough wood. She pushed against his grip and tried to raise herself from the floor, but he had brute strength.

'Listen hard, darling. I had a . . . business deal with your father. A big deal . . .'

'I don't know anything about my father's business,' she said.

'He has something that belongs to me, my lovely,' Tommy G said. *Somefink. Loverly.*

'I don't know shit about that. Let me up. Get off me.'

'Why? You're soft. A woman ought to be soft. I'm in pain . . . my eyes are killing me . . . I need something nice, something soft, where I can lay my head.'

She thought: the chemical had lost its force since she'd bought it. Just the same, she had only herself to blame for the way she'd surrendered the initiative. She ought to have clattered him across the skull when he'd been crawling around blindly. She ought to have hurried inside the kitchen and picked up a knife and cut him.

'What did Jackie tell you?'

'Nothing,' she said.

'Come on, sweetheart . . . What did he tell you?'

She said, 'I swear. Nothing.'

Tommy G slapped her, hand open. The blow stung her

lip. She felt blood. It was the first time in her life she'd ever been struck by a man.

A morning of sunlight and broken glass. Her mouth ached.

He slipped a hand inside her robe and touched her breasts and she turned her face defiantly to the side. He whispered, *Nice tits, nice tits, oh yeh, warm.*

She pushed his hand away. He didn't resist. She felt strength go out of him, but she sensed he had the power to summon it whenever he liked. He rolled over on his back, coughed for a time.

Please just go, she thought. She listened to the hacking sound he made. She saw him draw the hem of his shirt up to his mouth. His brown body was muscular. He had long eyelashes. I could run, she thought. Get up and run. Out that door and gone.

He said, 'Pain is illusion. Pain's negative energy. Did you know that, love?'

'No,' she said.

She saw the canister. It was about a foot from Tommy G's right hand. She thought of reaching over him and getting it and maybe this time it would function.

'There's a portal through pain to the other side,' he said. His voice was a hoarse whisper. 'If you can reach it. If you know the way.'

Portal, she thought. Illusion. Had the spray affected his mind? He sat up. He turned his face towards her. His eyes were closed. His head was tilted to one side in the manner of a blind man listening. He had a menacing little smile on his face. He stood up with some effort, blinking madly as he peered through the slit of one eye. Broken glass crunched under his feet. He noticed the canister and kicked it and it rolled towards the door.

'You play rough, girl,' he said. 'Tell you what. Why don't you work on your memory, eh?' He tapped his skull with two fingers. 'I wouldn't like to come back . . . because the next time I'll really fucking hurt you.'

She watched him make his way to the door. He was unsteady. He stooped, picked up the canister, stuck it in his pocket. She heard him go down the stairs. Whistling. *Whistling.* She recognized the tune, couldn't name it, something cheerful out of Gilbert and Sullivan. 'My Object All Sublime' . . . was that it? She went inside the living room. She tried to light a cigarette but her hand was trembling. It took her four matches before she succeeded. She drew smoke deep as she could into her lungs. She sat down, still shaking, and she thought of Tommy G's eye, the colour of prime rib. *Christ, what is this legacy you've left us, Jackie?*

24

Detective-Superintendent Malcolm Tay's office was situated at Force HQ in Pitt Street, a few blocks south of Glasgow's most famous thoroughfare, Sauchiehall Street, which had had a certain bustling elegance at one time, but was now a yard or two downmarket, fast-food eateries and theme pubs and nightclubs, although a few department stores stood here and there. To the east of Pitt Street was Blythswood Square, formerly the red-light district, but genteel these days. South was the slab of the Hilton, close to the motorway that had been driven with civic disregard through the centre of the city.

Force HQ was a red-brick building attached to a glass office block that must have been constructed at an earlier time. The effect was of mismatched parts, botched architecture. The Strathclyde Police motto, Eddie Mallon had noticed in the brownish marble entranceway, was *Semper Vigilo*.

Tay's office was sparsely furnished. The walls were bare save for a cork bulletin board with a schedule pinned to it. Nothing personal here, no cosy family pictures, which didn't surprise Eddie. He imagined Tay's life as one of solitary self-containment. No encumbrances.

163

The superintendent, who sat behind a desk, was wearing the same charcoal suit he'd worn at the airport. Scullion was also present, standing with his back to the window. Chris Caskie leaned against the wall and looked up at the ceiling. Eddie Mallon felt he was a figure in a contemporary still life: *Hot Room with Policemen*.

Tay opened the middle drawer of his desk. 'I made you a promise last night, Mallon. I said I'd keep you posted.' He looked at Eddie, then reached into the drawer and produced a clear plastic bag with a cardboard tag. He laid the bag on the desk. 'And here we are.'

Eddie saw the gun under the kinks in the plastic.

'This is the weapon that killed your father,' Tay said. 'A Smith and Wesson 4006.'

Eddie felt blood hurry to his head and depth charges detonate in his heart. He was accustomed to guns every day of his working life, they were commonplace, but this one was different, this one was surrounded by static disturbances, as if an impression of the assassin's touch lingered upon the weapon. Eddie had an urge to pick up the bag, remove the gun and hold it in the palm of his hand and feel this instrument that had been used to slay Jackie. He looked at sunlight dulled in the folds of plastic.

'Whose gun is it?' he asked.

'Matty Bones's,' Tay replied.

'Bones?' Eddie asked.

'The only prints on the weapon are his. And there are any number of people who say they've seen Bones with this gun. It seems he liked flashing it when he was jarred. Something of the cowboy about our Matty.'

Scullion said, 'The weapon was discovered by DS Tony Bothwell and PC Vicky Kyle during a routine search of Bones's flat.'

'So you're saying – Matty Bones shot my father?' Eddie said.

Tay said, 'That's how it looks, Mallon.'

Eddie was incredulous. 'They'd known each other for more than thirty years. Long-time associate, intimate – then Bones suddenly decides to shoot his old friend. Why? A brainstorm? A seizure? You got any ideas?'

Tay picked up a pencil and tapped it on the desk. 'Who knows? In my experience, money's usually involved somewhere down the line. Maybe Bones owed your father cash –'

'Which he couldn't pay back, so he shot Jackie?' Eddie said. 'That's too goddam drastic.'

'Is it? People get killed for all kinds of reasons, some of them seemingly very petty, even ludicrous, to you or me . . .' Tay picked up the plastic bag and appeared to weigh the gun. 'Maybe there was an argument we know nothing about. Or a long-standing grudge. Or maybe Bones was indebted to somebody who wanted Mallon struck down. Bones had the weapon and the opportunity –'

'Now you're looking at a weird-ass scenario in which Bones is a hired gun.'

'I'm throwing darts, Mallon. See what might stick to the board.'

This metaphor struck Eddie as inappropriate in the circumstances of a murder investigation, reducing the search for Jackie Mallon's killer to a game. He stared angrily at Tay and said, 'Fuck darts. Jesus Christ. Let's talk about your whole line of inquiry. Let's look at the big picture. Why are you so cheerfully embracing the half-assed conclusion that Bones was the killer? Because it's easy? Because you're too goddam lazy to go out there and shake the bushes?'

'Eddie, for God's sake, calm down,' Caskie said.

He ignored Caskie. 'Have you interviewed the people he did business with, Tay? Have you been talking to auctioneers and estate agents who might have worked with him when an estate was coming under the hammer and who might be able to point you in the direction of any deals he was trying to make? Have you talked to any of his competitors in the salvage business? Have you got people looking into where he went when he left Glasgow last week? God knows, that might be important. You're pecking at the goddam surface. You're just scratching around. And now you've got the murder weapon and Bones's prints are all over it and that's it, case closed, no loose ends.'

He was thirsty, and glanced round the room; no sign of a water-cooler. He watched a muscle work furiously in Tay's jaw.

'You've crossed the line, Mallon,' Tay said.

Eddie paid no attention. 'This gun that belonged to Bones. You're saying he used it to kill Jackie, then he took it back to his flat and hid it? Why didn't he toss the fucking thing in the river? Why run the risk of it being discovered –'

'Criminals aren't neurosurgeons,' Tay said.

'Some of them know about survival,' Eddie said. 'They know about covering their tracks. I'm getting the feeling you just want to shut the book on this and save yourselves a load of legwork. Chalk one up on the old blackboard –'

Tay stood up. His face was tense and when he spoke his lips barely moved. 'Shut up and listen. I'm satisfied

166

we've got the murder weapon, and it's only a matter of time before we find Bones. And I'm damn sure he can be persuaded to tell us just why he shot Jackie Mallon.'

'Persuaded?' Eddie said. 'That has a nice sound.'

Tay beat a rhythm with the tip of his pencil, then he stepped out from behind his desk and unexpectedly clapped a hand on Eddie's shoulder. 'I'm not a sentimental man, Eddie. It's a well-known fact we Scots are only allowed that luxury on New Year's Eve. But I remember when my own father died I lost the plot for a while . . .' He appeared to run out of steam quickly, as if this moment of human contact was embarrassing to him. He sighed, raised then dropped his shoulders. 'I understand what you're going through. Grief. Pain. I understand all that. But trust me with this case, Eddie. I know what I'm doing. The Strathclyde Police knows what it's doing. Believe me. We'll find Bones . . .'

Eddie stood up. 'Thanks for the progress report.'

Tay said, 'You ought to get some medication to help you relax.'

I'll dope myself just for you, Tay. I'll be a zombie. I won't be a nuisance. Eddie went to the door, stepped out. Caskie followed him. In silence, they walked to the stairs.

Then Caskie said, 'That was bloody stupid.'

'Too upfront for you, Chris? Too open?'

'Bloody rude.'

'Oh, yeah, let's not forget rude. I'm the bad-mannered Yank. What do I know about fucking etiquette?'

Outside, in the shadow of the building, Eddie stuck his hands in his pockets and rattled some loose change. He watched uniformed cops enter and leave the hive that was Force HQ.

Caskie said, 'Even after you railed at him, Tay had the decency to open his heart to you. That doesn't happen often.'

'Was that his heart? I thought it was the hinge of a crypt creaking,' Eddie said.

'Give him some credit, Eddie. He was trying to be understanding.'

Eddie stepped out of shadow into sunlight. The blue sky was high and cloudless. The sun had no mercy. Why expect mercy anyhow? If Bones had killed Jackie, he'd shown no mercy to him.

If Bones had killed Jackie.

I'm not buying, Eddie thought. It doesn't make sense. Maybe to Tay it does. Cut. It's a wrap, guys. Go home.

A couple of black taxis were parked on the other side of the street. He wondered where Matty Bones, alleged murderer, was hiding.

'I think I'll grab a cab and head back to Joyce's place.' Eddie raised an arm, signalled, saw the taxi spin in a tight circle towards him.

Caskie's cellphone rang just as Eddie entered the taxi. Eddie watched him speak into the handset, saw his face change, that placid mask slip like flesh peeled from bone.

'Shit,' he said, and looked as if he'd just been struck by a club. He stuffed the phone clumsily in his pocket and climbed inside the taxi. His tone of voice was urgent. 'I'm coming with you, Eddie.'

25

Eddie's first impression was of broken glass everywhere, an explosion of bright colour, as if a rainbow of ice had fallen out of the sky and shattered. He saw Joyce standing at the end of the hallway holding a wet towel to her mouth. The cord of her robe was loose. He and Caskie hurried towards her. She fell into Eddie's arms, and he led her inside the living room and made her sit.

But it was Caskie who took her hand and stroked it with a slow gesture of concern. 'Eddie, there's some brandy in the kitchen. Would you mind fetching a glass for Joyce?'

Eddie thought, He's good with the women in Jackie's life. He's attendant physician, private nurse, counsellor, favourite uncle. Eddie wondered if he was envious of Caskie's role in Joyce's world. He looked at Caskie's neat little beard and the long fingers with the perfect nails, and he thought, yeah, I don't like the guy, and maybe it's connected to a mild jealousy or associated with Perlman's low opinion.

He went into the kitchen, found a bottle of cognac in a cupboard, returned with a half-filled glass.

Caskie was asking, 'Can you describe this character, Joyce?'

Joyce took the towel from her lip, which was only slightly swollen. Eddie handed her the brandy.

'Thanks.' She sipped, shuddered. 'He called himself Tommy G. G the letter, not G E E the name. He was black, wore his hair in dreadlocks. English accent. Sounded like London. Said he wanted to pay his respects to Jackie, but I wouldn't open the door. You see how expertly he overcame that trifling obstacle. I shot him with mace but it didn't work the way it was supposed to . . . He grabbed me, hit me. Right here.' She applied the damp towel to her lip again. She spoke through it, her words muffled. 'He was about five-eight. Muscular. Head sort of weird, square, I don't know what else . . . a line in oddball sayings.'

'Like what?' Eddie asked. He imagined somebody striking his sister. He saw a hand in the air, felt the contact of knuckle on lip. The picture angered him.

Joyce shrugged. 'Oh, some crap about how you can overcome pain. How there was a doorway into a pain-free life, I don't know exactly. Ouch. I wish he'd left me the key to this magic doorway.' She lowered the towel. The collar of her robe was wet. She pointed to her lip. 'How does it look?'

'It's nothing, Joyce,' Caskie said.

'It feels about three feet wide,' she said.

'Did he hit you more than once?' Caskie asked. He sat down beside Joyce, still stroking her hand.

Joyce said no. One blow.

'And he told you he wanted to pay his respects,' Caskie said.

Joyce said. 'Yeah, but what he really wanted was to know if I had any information about a business deal he said he had going with Jackie . . . I told him no, which is the truth. Then he belted me.'

Caskie asked, 'What kind of deal? Did he say?'

'He just said Jackie had something that belonged to him.'

'But he didn't spell out what?' Caskie said.

Joyce shook her head.

'Tommy G,' Eddie said. 'Does that name mean anything to you, Chris?'

Caskie said, 'No, nothing.'

Eddie looked at Caskie. 'Can you run the guy's name through your crime computer?'

'I was just about to do that.' Caskie took his hand away from Joyce and rose. She drank her brandy, glanced at Eddie, then lit a cigarette, which she smoked from the side of her mouth. Caskie stepped out of the room. Joyce patted the arm of the chair and Eddie sat, one arm hung loosely round his sister's shoulder. Caskie could be heard talking on the telephone in the kitchen.

'Did Tommy G say he was coming back?' Eddie asked.

'He said he wouldn't like it if he had to come back and hurt me.' She lowered her voice, as if she wanted to be sure Caskie couldn't hear. 'What in God's name was Jackie up to?'

'I don't know –'

'I mean, he mixed with some dodgy characters now and again, Eddie, but they were basically harmless. This is the first time I ever ran into anyone like Tommy G, and I didn't like it. This is one downright desperate bastard, and he scares me.'

Eddie looked into his sister's face. Jackie's deal, okay. But what kind of deal made a man smash through glass panes and attack Joyce? It was no ordinary transaction, no hundred-quid debt Jackie had left unpaid at his death. Jackie had something that belonged to the intruder and the guy wanted it back so badly it was worth physical violence to get it. One thing was sure: you didn't break and enter and cause havoc if you were walking the legal side of the street.

'I think Jackie was involved in something a tad more spooky than chiselling the Inland Revenue, Joyce,' he said. 'Unless they're sending out a whole new breed of tax collectors.'

'Definitely. So what was he doing, Eddie?'

Caskie came back into the room. 'We'll see what the computer spits out in due course.' He smiled at Joyce. 'I better make an official report.' He took a little notebook from his jacket. 'Let's run through it. He rang the doorbell and you went out into the hallway. Take it from there.'

Eddie only half-listened a second, drifted to the window, looked down into the street. He didn't need to hear this reconstruction. He thought about Jackie. He felt an ache that wasn't connected to Jackie's murder; it was the clouded insight into his father's world that disturbed him, that wherever Jackie lived was no place for the innocent. *Fuck it.* It was one thing to pull a few quiet strokes now and again, fiddle a ledger, massage the figures, buy merchandise that had quote unquote fallen off the back of a truck. That was part of the cash-and-carry business, and you winked at it and nobody got hurt. But when you were involved with a guy who behaved like Tommy G, it tethered you to something beyond crimes of funny accounting –

I was never a criminal, son. Remember that. That's the truth.

Yeah, Eddie thought: and I'm just loyal enough or dumb enough, or some weird filial combination of the two, to hold on to a sliver of hope that there's some

172

reason behind Tommy G's actions that will absolve Jackie Mallon. But what?

Think.

Could Senga know anything about the intruder's identity? Could she throw a little light on Tommy G? He walked across the hall to the kitchen, drank a glass of water at the sink. He felt depressed, confused, he missed Claire, he wondered what she was doing in New York right at that moment. Three thirty p.m. Glasgow, ten thirty a.m. Queens. What day was it? Was it one of her working days when she dressed in her Century 21 blazer and showed prospective home-buyers property available in Queens? He wasn't sure. I'm lonely, I miss my life. I miss standing with Claire in the shower stall, holding her hard under the water jet, and the way water runs into her eyes and flattens her hair against her skull and how she looks beautiful against the tiles. Go home, Eddie. Ignore Jackie's business dealings, whatever they were. Ignore his life and death, attend the funeral, fly away. Do what Tay would dearly love you to do, and leave it alone.

But Perlman, goddam, was correct: I'm not made that way. I'm the son. The only son.

He skimmed the pages of the phone book, found Perlman's number, dialled it. He'd report the attack to Perlman because it fell within the parameters of their arrangement, if that's what it was.

All he got was an answering machine. He didn't leave a message.

He stepped lightly around the stars and chips of stained glass, opened the door and went down the stone stairs. Outside, he turned right along Ingleby Drive. The surface of the street shimmered in heat. Tenements blurred like buildings immersed in rippling water. A dead cat lay in the middle of Whitehill Street. Black fur and blood on the tarmac, paws crushed, head back and mouth wide. Flies. Three kids stood in a circle round the cat. A small red-haired boy poked the animal with a stick. *Telt ye it was deid.*

Beyond all doubt, Eddie thought, and kept moving. He was sweating by the time he reached the house in Onslow Drive. He went up the steps, rang the doorbell, Senga appeared. She was wearing a black silk blouse and smart black slacks.

'Eddie,' she said. She was pleased to see him.

He thought: Don't alarm her with the story of the assault on Joyce. She doesn't need to know.

'Come in, come away in,' she said.

He went inside the house, which was dark and cool, and he followed Senga into the living room. 'I was just about to go out,' she said.

He said, 'I can come back when it's more convenient, Senga.'

She looked at her watch. 'I ordered a taxi, which should be here in a couple of minutes . . .' The horn of a car sounded outside. Senga got up. 'There it is. I have an appointment at the funeral home.'

'I'll go with you,' Eddie said.

'You don't have –'

'I do,' Eddie said.

'I'm supposed to choose a coffin. A casket.' She tried a smile, but her face wouldn't make it. 'I don't want to do it, Eddie. It's so damn final. I put Jackie in a box and the bloody box goes into the flames and that's it. That's the end.'

'Cremation?'

'That's what Jackie wanted.'

Flames. Eddie had assumed a burial. He hadn't anticipated fire. What difference did it make anyway? Fire, earth. He wanted to say something credible about an afterlife, immortality, paradise. He didn't hold these beliefs. He wished he did, if only to comfort Senga. He walked with her into the street. The cab was waiting, engine running. Eddie opened the back door, helped Senga in. Her perfume was strong.

She leaned towards the driver and said, 'McGlashan's Funeral Home. Do you know it?'

'Riddrie?' the driver asked. He was a young man with a shaven head that looked as if it had been dipped in wax. 'That's the one on Smithycroft Road, is it?'

'That's the one,' Senga said. She sat back and was quiet a moment as the cab pulled away, then she turned to Eddie. 'I don't know what kind of box to pick.'

'We'll look,' Eddie said. 'We'll choose something.'

'He wouldn't have wanted anything fancy. He'd have said it was a waste of money paying out huge sums for something you're just going to burn.' Senga checked her face in a small compact mirror then snapped the lid shut. 'He never talked much about dying. He was full of life. So full of it, Eddie.'

Eddie gazed from the window. The taxi was travelling along Alexandra Parade. The cigarette factories, in which hundreds of young women had once run the machines that rolled the cigarettes, were empty now. The air used to smell of cured tobacco, as if a cloud of the pulverized weed hung over Dennistoun. Eddie remembered the girls at the end of their day's work, how they wore headscarves and linked arms as they walked along brazenly, gum-chewing and wolf-whistling any young man who passed. They had attitude, he thought, before attitude was invented. Street cred. *Gallus.*

Senga opened the window of the cab and the sleeve of her blouse rolled up and Eddie looked at the tattoo and he had a memory of how Jackie had once answered a question Eddie had asked about the difference between Catholics and Protestants.

Here's the difference, son. You cut a Catholic's throat and he bleeds to death. You slash a Protestant's throat and guess what?

What, Da?

He bleeds to death as well.

And, Da?

That's it, Eddie. There's nothing else, no difference between them.

Eddie could even place this conversation in the context of a pale blue summer twilight when he and Jackie had been walking along this very street from a cinema where they'd seen a Randolph Scott Western, *Ride the High Country.* Jackie loved cowboy stuff. Eddie didn't care what the movie was, he just liked going to the flicks with his dad. He liked how he felt secure in Jackie's presence. Besides, there was always vanilla ice cream afterwards at a café called the Bungalow a few blocks from the tobacco factories and a waitress named Serafina who gave him extra raspberry sauce.

Wait . . .

Something in the memory struck a wrong chord. He shut his eyes and imagined Jackie burning and the hideous intensity of heat, the coffin rolling towards incineration and Jackie reduced to ash. What was wrong with how Jackie had answered his childish question about religions?

He felt the warm breeze against his face and Senga's perfume wafted towards him and he remembered his dad saying, *No difference between them*, and Senga saying only this morning, *Jackie didn't have a sectarian bone in his body*. And then Eddie was spinning back, and the years fell away from him like so many discarded betting slips, and he was standing on the stairs of the Onslow Drive house and the living room was filled with Jackie and his friends, and Eddie could hear the clink of dark-brown beer bottles and rough grown-up masculine laughter, and he could smell the heady reek of strong cigarettes. He paused the memory. Listened. The sound reverberated inside him. Jackie and his mates were singing 'The Sash My Father Wore', an Orange anthem, but that didn't make sense if what Jackie had said was true, and if Senga's claim was correct: why would Jackie be singing a Protestant song, an anti-Catholic song, why say one thing to your son and then act differently with your pals?

Eddie opened his eyes. Somebody had shouted: *Death to the Fenian cunts*. Then there was more laughter. A beer party, drunks, anything was possible. So Jackie and his mates sometimes sang Orange songs when they were inebriated, so fucking what? That didn't make Jackie a bigot. Eddie didn't doubt that when Jackie said there was no difference between Catholics and Prot-estants he was telling the truth. It was just that he felt obliged to act differently with his drinking pals and sing whatever they were singing, that was all. One of the gang. *O My Father Was An Orangeman, In the Good Old Days of Yore* . . . The words faded in Eddie's head. He'd never had any reason to memorize them. He hadn't been brought up in a sectarian environment. Flora never spoke of religion. But it jarred him now to be struck by this particular memory, which felt ugly and menacing –

'Something wrong, Eddie?'

He turned to Senga. 'I was miles away.'

'Let me guess. New York. You were thinking about your family.'

'You're clairvoyant,' Eddie said.

'You miss them.'

'Yeah.' Eddie experienced a flush of tenderness towards her and touched the back of her hand, feeling the big emerald ring on her wedding finger. The common-law wife's ring of respectability. He let his fingertips rest a moment against the stone. Senga's flesh was warm.

It wasn't a good time to ask her questions, but it was never going to be a good time. 'Tell me. Does the name Tommy G mean anything to you?'

'Who? Tommy G? No.'

'He's a black guy. English accent.' *He's vicious, Senga, he attacked Joyce:* but he didn't append this information. 'He was acquainted with Jackie.'

'People drifted in and out of Jackie's life,' Senga said. 'I couldn't keep track. Some he introduced me to. Some he didn't. Tommy G, no, I'd remember that name, I think. And I don't remember any black man.' She ignored the No-Smoking sign, lit a cigarette.

A dead end. A door clanging shut.

Eddie saw the massive structure of Barlinnie Prison loom up beyond the houses in the district of Riddrie, so dense and grey it swallowed the light of the afternoon sun. Row after row of narrow barred windows; men shut away in small cells. Jackie's *alma mater*, he thought. What was it Flora had said? *He was never quite the same after jail. He was harder under the surface.* The prison seemed

178

impregnable, impossible to escape. Maybe when a man left this place he took some of it with him. Perhaps Flora had been right and Jackie had walked out of Barlinnie a different person, one inducted in the ways of crime and cruelty. But Flora's view was coloured by loss and bitterness: how could it be accurate?

The taxi stopped. Senga got out, pressed money into the cabby's hand. McGlashan's Funeral Home was a red-brick building; the name of the firm had been painted, in sombre gilt script, on the curtained window.

Senga said, 'I hate this.'

Eddie led her with gentle pressure towards the door. 'We'll be in and out in a couple of minutes, Senga. If you don't feel like talking, leave it to me.'

She dropped her half-smoked cigarette on the ground, crushed it with her foot. The cab pulled away, leaving a scent of diesel on the air. Eddie opened the door of McGlashan's and a bell rang, and Senga hesitated a second before she stepped inside. The place, air-conditioned and cool, was shadowy. People who deal in the disposal of the dead don't need bright lights. They want shady corners, an easy sense of peace and eternity.

A man appeared in a doorway. He wore a three-piece black suit and a black tie with a large knot that had slipped slightly to one side. He had a drinker's red-tinted nose and he sniffed a lot.

'Robert Crichton?' Senga asked. 'We have an appointment.'

The man nodded. 'Mrs Craig?'

'Ms Craig actually.'

Crichton took her hand. He turned his face to Eddie. His breath smelled of gin.

'I'm the deceased's son,' Eddie said.

Crichton went directly into his spiel. 'This is always a sorry time. No matter what the circumstances are. You have my condolences. My most serious regrets. McGlashan's is totally at your service . . .' He led Eddie and Senga inside a room filled with coffins, dark glossy boxes in which muted overhead lights were reflected.

Crichton touched surfaces with a loving gesture, trailing his nail-bitten fingers across lacquered wood and brass handles and satin interiors. Senga stood very still, surveying the room with the look of a woman wishing herself elsewhere, because this, this damn *showroom*, was her idea of hell. All these bloody boxes and bolting Jackie down beneath a lid and turning the screws and into the fires with him. Bone-pale, she found a chair and sat down and gazed into her hands.

Crichton whispered to Eddie. 'She's not taking it well. It's hard. We'll do everything we possibly can. You're in good hands here . . . Shall we price some models?'

Eddie scanned the boxes. 'What difference does the price make?' he asked.

'It depends. The kind of send-off you want to give the departed. The matter of your budget, naturally.'

'You don't exactly budget for your father's murder,' Eddie said. 'It doesn't come into your general financial plans.' This room annoyed him. The boxes irritated him. Crichton's breath was offensive. They were supposed to be selling more than coffins here; factors like composure and calm came into the transaction. Eddie wasn't feeling calm. He hated the whole thing. Death was absurd, violent death more so. A gunshot in the night, a flash at twilight, snuffed out.

Crichton said, 'Well, murder, of course, you don't anticipate, you can't, I mean –'

'Damn right you don't anticipate,' Eddie said.

Crichton pinched his nose between thumb and forefinger as if he were about to plunge his face under water. Then he laid his hands on the edge of a shiny black casket whose interior was lined with off-white satin.

'This one is a bargain,' he said. 'And very handsome too.'

'And what do you call inexpensive?' Eddie asked.

Crichton mentioned a figure that Eddie tried to convert into dollars. He found himself gazing at Crichton's chewed nails and thinking it apt that a sordid little man with boozy breath and an off-centre necktie was the one to sell corpse containers, worm boxes.

Eddie touched the coffin. The wood was slick. Flames would peel the lacquer off in microseconds. 'It'll do,' he said. 'You take plastic?'

'Visa. Mastercard. We require, ah, a twenty per cent deposit.' Eddie gave him his Visa card and Crichton went off to swipe it through a machine.

Eddie walked to where Senga sat. 'Let's get out of here.'

'Did you choose that one, Eddie?' she asked. She pointed to the black casket.

'Yeah, that's the one.'

'It's nice. I'll repay you.'

'No.'

'I insist, Eddie.'

Crichton came back with the credit card and receipt. Eddie scrawled his name quickly on the slip, then escorted Senga in the direction of the front door. Outside, they stood together in Smithycroft Road, small shops behind them and square grey suburban houses facing them; the leaves of dense trees floated sunlight back into their eyes.

Eddie put a comforting arm round Senga's shoulders and she inclined her head towards him. Neither of them spoke for a long time: death laid a veneer of silence over them.

Then Eddie drew his arm away and said, 'Tell me a little more about Haggs. Is he well known in this city?'

'How do you mean, well known?'

'Would he be well known in . . . oh, let's say, law-enforcement circles?'

'You mean would the *police* know him? Of course they would. He was tried four or five years ago for – what's the expression – tampering with a jury? It made a big splash in the papers at the time. He walked away without a blemish.'

Senga slipped an arm through Eddie's and they walked together in the direction of Cumbernauld Road, where they finally stopped outside the public library, an octagonal building with a view of Barlinnie, and waited for a passing taxi.

'Where does he live?' Eddie asked.

'Rouken Glen. I've got the address somewhere.'

'I'd like it,' he said.

She spotted a taxi and raised a hand and the cab braked. She climbed inside ahead of Eddie and asked, 'Why?'

26

'He calls me, orders me to find Billy McQueen. I don't care what it takes, he says, find him. Break a few skulls if you have to.' John Twiddie slurped up a good measure of McEwan's heavy into the funnel of his mouth. 'Haggs gets on my tits something serious. Go here. Do this. Do that. I'm like a dog on a leash, doll.'

Rita was busy rearranging her rings. She liked to move them around. It's true what people said, she thought; variety is the spice of life. She liked the reflections the little gems made. She finished her Bailey's and stuck the glass on the counter and tilted her head to catch the afternoon sun that came in at an angle through the window of the upstairs bar at the Ubiquitous Chip in the West End of the city.

'And where do I find Billy McQueen? Eh? Where do I start looking? I don't know the guy.' Twiddie drained his pint. His nose throbbed where the stud was situated. 'He's not at his house, Haggs says. So give that a body swerve. He might be in England, Haggs says.'

'England? Big place, England.'

'Needle in a fucking haystack, hen.'

Rita was finally satisfied with the arrangement of her

rings. 'You have to respect Haggs. He's a self-made man. He's seen you all right with a few quid. You don't have to love him.'

Twiddie made a hawing sound, meaning mibbe, mibbe not. He was thinking of the way the van had caught fire last night. He was remembering flames filling the front, and black smoke drifting towards the wasteland, and the alkies waking up and pushing aside their sheets of newspaper and watching the van smoke and fizz for a time, then they crawled back under their papers or into their threadbare sleeping bags and wondered if they were having DTs.

Through the dull ache of hangover, Twiddie remembered the sound of the fire brigade in the distance, then him and Rita running away from the scene. Holding hands, laughing, collapsing near an old railway arch. And still laughing. They had fun together, and Twiddie liked that. He thought Rita was a knock-out in the looks division. She was sexy, firm tits, easy to arouse, keen to please.

Twiddie ordered two more drinks. Heavy for him, Bailey's for her. McQueen, one-legged man. How bloody hard could it be to track down Wan-Fittit?

He'd make some phone calls. He'd leave a few questions out there in the right places and mibbe get a few answers. He picked up his pint and winked at Rita. She leaned forward on her stool and adjusted the knot of his tie, which was an Armani knock-off, red with small pink dots. Twiddie thought it went well with his counterfeit Versace suit, a three-piece black number with very short lapels.

He set down his glass and spoke quietly. 'If that old fucker Mallon had talked, then we wouldn't have this shite to wade through –'

'*If* is a wee word with a big meaning,' Rita said. She adjusted the gold-plated paperclip that pierced her left earlobe then she poked Twiddie in the chest. 'Why don't you just make your phone calls, lover?'

'Will do.'

Twiddie looked round the bar. The clientele was mixed, some shabbies hanging about in the hope of a free pint from passing acquaintances, a few low-class criminal types, a well-known author and a gaggle of his girlie acolytes, an undercover detective Twiddie made immediately, a drunken Australian woman who kept wanting to sing 'Waltzing Matilda' only to be shushed every time she uttered a few notes. It was a drab sort of place, but fashionably situated in a narrow lane close to Byres Road, where an assortment of students and trendies shopped and ate. Twiddie, who'd been born in the clapped-out Cranhill housing estate in the east of the city, the Drug Casbah, thought he'd come up in the world when he drank in The Ubi.

He found a quiet corner where he could use his cellphone. Reception wasn't terrific but at least he had a good view of Rita sitting up on her stool, long legs and red leather miniskirt and some spangled stuff in her hair that sparkled when the sun caught it. She looked a picture. A wanker's dream. He loved when they went to clubs and she danced her arse off for hours.

Twiddie punched in numbers. He talked to people in different parts of the city. Mad Cross-Eyed Logan, who ran betting shops in Shawlands and Govan, said he hadn't seen McQueen in months. Bobby McPherson, operator of a profitable ticket-forging enterprise and nicknamed Bobby Christ because of his intense religious beliefs, said he hadn't heard a dicky bird about Wan-Fittit in weeks. Patrick 'The Cowboy' O'Hare, who'd once borrowed heavily from McQueen to establish a chain of dry-cleaning establishments throughout the city, said he no longer did business with Billy, and his loans were all paid off. Teejay Guptah, owner of the Patna Palace Curry House in Bath Street, said he thought he'd seen McQueen the day before yesterday near George Square, but he wouldn't swear to it.

He made one last call, this time to Gio the Gasman, so-called on account of his occasional habit of wearing a World War II gas mask because he was allergic to petrol fumes and pollen. Most of the time the Gasman hung out on the corner of Sauchiehall Street and Dalhousie Street, chain-smoking cigarettes hand-rolled in dark brown paper. He spent hours watching the street, grooving to the sounds of his Walkman.

He answered Twiddie's call with his usual greeting. 'Hazzo.'

Twiddie asked, 'You know Wan-Fittit McQueen? You know his house?'

'Nope,' said Gio.

Twiddie mentioned the address in Novar Drive, Hyndland. 'I want you to go there. Keep an eye open for him.'

'How much is it worth?'

'I'll give you twenty.'

'Twenty-five and I'm scooting, Twiddie. Vrooom. Vrooom.'

'Right. But leave the mask at home, eh? Keep a low profile.'

Twiddie stuffed his phone into a pocket. He walked back to the bar, where Rita was finishing her Bailey's and was just about to set the glass down on the counter when a man approached her, and Twiddie thought, *Aw Christ, no*. The man, who wore a flesh-coloured eyepatch over his left eye, was Lou Perlman.

'Well I declare,' Perlman said. 'The Bobsy Twins, Rita and John. This is my lucky day.'

'Lemme guess,' said Twiddie. 'You played a horse and it won.'

'Only mugs gamble,' Perlman said. He moved close to Rita and Twiddie and extended his arms in such a way that he managed to draw them both into his embrace. 'My babies. My wee babies. And what have youse two been up to lately?'

Lou Perlman, in brown suit and a gold kipper tie that might just have been fashionable when Carnaby Street was new, had been born and brought up in old Gorbals, before city planners had demolished the place. Twiddie feared him: he was as hard as a bag of shaved steel.

'Up to nothing, Lou,' Rita said. 'Do you never shave?'

'Every third day.' Lou Perlman tightened his embrace. 'Your beauty takes my breath away, Rita. I gasp. I feel like Willie Wordsworth strolling through a field of daffodils when I look at you.'

'Pull the other one,' Rita said, and shook a leg at him. 'It plays "The Bluebells of Scotland".'

'So. Bring Lou up to date. Lou likes to be au courant with affairs.'

'Oh coo-rawn?' Twiddie asked.

'French, Tweedledum. Comprenez? I see your wee moustache is flourishing. Frankly I've seen more hair on a parrot's arse. You still running errands for Long Roddy, eh?'

'Who?'

Perlman laughed, a smoker's bark. Twiddie didn't like

this proximity to the cop. Perlman smelled of police stations. Tobacco and sweaty shirts and something dusty and metallic, maybe rusty, like old radiator pipes, and a hint of cheap soap. These scents reminded Twiddie of hours he'd spent in custody.

Perlman released the pair. He looked at Twiddie, who couldn't hold the policeman's hard stare, then he turned to Rita, who was altogether more defiant.

'I wish you'd piss off and leave us alone,' she said. 'We've got a right to privacy, don't we? We've got a right to sit here in the Chip and have a quiet wee drink, don't we?'

'Rights,' Perlman said. 'People are always moaning and whining about rights. You know what rights do, Rita? They get in the way of *law and fucking order*.' He caught Rita by the wrist. Her assorted jewels jingled. She rang like a cash register. 'Where were you last night?'

'At home watching a video.'

'Boy Wonder here was with you, right?'

'Yeh, he's always with me,' she said. 'Aren't you, lover boy?'

'Aye,' said Twiddie. 'Never leave her side.'

'And what were you two scumbags watching? *The Towering Inferno*? *The Day the Earth Caught Fire*? Or something new from the Arsonist's Video Rental Emporium?'

Rita said, 'Just because I once set fire to an abandoned building you've got me down as a pyro.'

'You play with matches, dearie. Fire intrigues you. You're like the moth, Rita. Can't stay away from the candle.'

'That was years ago,' she said. 'You never let a person live anything down.'

'I'll try again,' Perlman said. 'Where were you pair last night?'

Twiddie asked, 'You deaf?'

Perlman caught Twiddie's nose firmly at the place where the stud had caused the bulb of inflammation, and he tugged Twiddie's head downward. 'What did you say, John?' Perlman asked.

'You're hurting me,' Twiddie said.

'Speak up!'

'I said you're fucking hurting me.'

'SPEAK UP, I'M LOSING MY HEARING.'

The suppuration on Twiddie's nostril erupted under the pressure of Perlman's fingers. Pus spurted into the policeman's hand. He gasped in disgust and grabbed tissues from the dispenser on the bar and wiped his fingers. 'Oh for fuck's sake, Twiddie. This is *scunnering*.'

'I got some on my suit,' Twiddie complained.

'It was *your* nose that exploded,' Perlman said. 'It was *your* conk that burst.'

Twiddie cleaned the lapels of his suit with tissues. 'This is pure Versace, Perlman. One hundred per cent. I'll sue. I'll take you to court.'

'Why don't you just shut your fucking face? If anybody's going to court, it's you.' Perlman crumpled the napkins and tossed them over the bar into a wastebasket. He had absolutely no desire to have Twiddie's body fluids on his skin; it was an intimacy he didn't need. He had better things to do than question the Weird Couple about their whereabouts. He had a murder on his mind. But he was the resident expert on Twid and the Fire Goddess.

He glared at Twiddie. 'You see? This is what happens when you don't deal with things, laddie. They fester.

Sooner or later, oy, you've got a right bloody mess. One more time. Where were you last night?'

'Watching a fucking *video*,' Rita said wearily.

Perlman yawned. 'Name?'

'*Scream*,' Rita said.

'Engrossing.' Perlman turned to Twiddie. 'So you were nowhere near the vicinity of Orr Street last night?'

'I don't even know where Orr Street is,' Twiddie said.

Lou Perlman slid a finger under his eyepatch. 'Insect bit my eyelid, which is infected,' he said. 'This heat brings out some very strange flying things. As well as other oddities, such as a burning van near Orr Street in darkest Bridgeton, and a report – made by an alcoholic who was once an eye surgeon, if you like irony, if you know what irony *means* – that two people were seen running from the smouldering vehicle. This surgeon, a poor soul fallen on very hard times indeed, peered out of the cardboard box he calls home, and he saw a young man and woman flee the scene, positively *hooting* with merriment. It was the good doctor's impression that the couple was drunk and celebrating . . . And you two were watching a video called *Scream*?'

Rita raised a hand in solemn mode. 'Honest to God.'

Perlman sighed. 'You stand by this, Twiddie?'

'I do,' Twiddie said.

Rita said, 'Every time there's a fucking fire, I *swear*,' and she glared at Perlman, letting her sentence die.

Perlman looked round the bar. Then he said, 'The fire brigade did a damn good job, got the flames out quickly. It wasn't much of a fire, I'm told. An amateur job. Those fire-brigade guys, masters of their craft. I like to fish through debris. Get my fingers filthy.'

'Zatafact?' Twiddie said.

Rita shrugged and looked at her fingertips.

Perlman stared at the pair for a long time before he said, 'Hope and pray you don't see me again too soon. *Vaya con dios*, my wee pals.'

Twiddie and Rita watched him leave. Twiddie was sweating, and ran a finger between collar and neck. His nostril ached where the abscess had burst.

'You think he knows anything?' Rita asked.

'No. He's full of shite.'

'Will you mention this to Haggs?'

Twiddie said no, no, definitely no. The word *amateur* bothered him.

Rita asked, 'What does *vaya* – what did that old bampot mean?'

'Something to do with God,' John Twiddie said.

'Was that Spanish or Jewish he was talking?'

'They call it Yiddish,' Twiddie answered and frowned at the door through which Perlman had passed.

27

When he dropped Senga off, Eddie remained in the taxi and rode south. *What did he think he could prove by talking to Haggs?* she'd asked, but she'd dredged the address out of an old address book anyway. He opened the window and sat back and watched the city flicker past in the afternoon sun, shadow and light, fragmentary eclipses created by tenements and an occasional high-rise. *Trying to prove . . .* If Haggs had been the defendant in a prominent criminal trial five years ago, it was *impossible* that Chris Caskie didn't know his name unless he'd been vacationing outside the solar system at the time. Caskie, Caskie, confidante of the Mallon clan, friend to Senga, Joyce and Flora – for Christ's sake, *why* deny knowing Haggs's name?

Eddie had the feeling everything was connected in a way that was nebulous to him yet, a string of knots he couldn't unravel, Caskie's prevarication, the relationship between Haggs and Jackie, and the whereabouts of Bones, whose motive for the slaying of his old pal remained utterly obscure – unless you were Tay, who seemingly wanted quick closure.

Eddie felt the warm breeze in his hair as the cab headed

down Bellgrove Street. This trip to Rouken Glen, think about it: did he expect Haggs, even if the guy happened to have information about Jackie's life and times, and Caskie's dishonesty, to volunteer his knowledge freely?

Eddie Mallon, imbued with bright-eyed Yankee innocence, seeker after truth, pilgrim: Why did I never develop the deep cynicism of the long-serving cop? His partner, Tom Collins, once said, *You want to believe the best in everybody, Eddie, doncha?* The question concealed a criticism: Why doncha grow the fuck up, Eddie? The world is populated with sleaze. People will deny their wrongdoing until hell becomes a fucking health spa.

It's me, Tom. It's the way I am. Everybody deserves a chance to tell their side of a story, don't they? You don't rush to judgement.

Tom Collins said, *In fucking Walt Disney's head, sport.*

The taxi passed the expanse of open land that was Glasgow Green, and the former Templeton's Carpet Factory, built in the late 19th century to resemble the Doge's Palace in Venice. An extravaganza, exotic, *bold*, it should have been a wild incongruity, but somehow it managed to look as if it belonged here on the north bank of the Clyde.

The cab headed along Pollokshaws Road towards Shawlands, after which the tenements gave way to less cramped housing, some stout red sandstone villas whose tidy appearance suggested the inhabitants were prosperous and lace-curtain prim. God was in his heaven, and all was well in this corner of Glasgow.

The cab driver turned his face and glanced at Eddie. 'You said Langtree Avenue, jim?'

'Right,' Eddie said.

'Where money grows on trees. So they say.' The driver laughed.

Beyond Giffnock now, Fenwick Road, a big round-about, a right turn followed by a left into Davieland Road which adjoined Rouken Glen Park, where Eddie saw sunbathers stretched on grass and dogs scampering and teenagers sitting in a huddle that emitted a blue fuzz of smoke that might have been tobacco or something illicit. The cab swung left away from the park and entered Langtree Avenue. Eddie, a little tense and uncertain, leaned forward in his seat as the driver looked for the house, which turned out to be a big detached white-painted structure surrounded by a tall hedge.

Eddie paid the driver, then walked towards the gate, carved walnut with a white enamel plate screwed into the wood. The word Drumpellier was painted on the enamel in blue floral letters. A house with a name. He pushed the gate and entered the drive and his feet crunched on gravel the colour of a flamingo. The windows struck by sun were like long mirrors. A burgundy Jaguar was parked in a shaded space at the side of the house. The lawn was trim and a single monkey puzzle tree stood in the dead centre. The thick interlocking branches of the tree resembled a pine with advanced arthritis.

He walked to the front door, noticing a security camera about four feet above him to his right. He pressed the doorbell. He heard the camera whirr quietly as it shifted a couple of inches. He understood. You didn't get inside by ringing a bell. You gained entrance only if the person staring at a monitor inside granted you permission.

Eddie looked up into the eye of the camera.

A man's voice came out of a hidden speaker. 'Who are you?'

Eddie was startled, but tried not to show it. 'Eddie Mallon. I'm looking for Roddy Haggs.'

The voice said, 'Come in.' The door opened without human assistance.

Eddie went in, found himself in a big square entranceway with a marbled floor and a number of marble columns. The original rooms of the house had been demolished to make way for this one enormous space. From a hidden source came a muzak version of the soundtrack of *South Pacific*.

He crossed the floor a few yards, then paused at the edge of what people used to call conversation pits. Five steps down to a sunken square area furnished with casual chairs and huge pillows. 'Happy Talk' finished. Now it was 'Some Enchanted Evening'.

The man who approached Eddie was tall and cadaverous, and his head was too small for the body that supported it. But there was more to the man's unusual appearance than the size of head in relation to frame. It was his skinniness, the quality of near-transparency, that made it seem as if his height was artificial, as if he'd been stretched on a rack.

Eddie didn't need to be told that this was Roddy Haggs; he fitted Senga's description. And when Eddie accepted Haggs's handshake he wasn't surprised to discover that the man's skin was chilly. He sleeps in a box of his native soil, Eddie thought.

'Let's go down into the pit,' Haggs said.

The pit. How appropriate. Eddie descended, Haggs followed. 'Sit. Make yourself comfortable. Drink?'

Eddie refused the drink, then said, 'Quite a place.'

Haggs fixed himself a small tumbler of scotch from a decanter. 'Should be, considering the cash that went into it.'

A certain kind of person always wanted to tell you

what they'd spent on their houses. They were usually self-made types. Eddie looked up; where the columns met the high ceiling assorted angels had been painted skilfully on plaster. He half-expected God to appear, staring down at him stern-eyed, a white beard in the clouds. Behave cautiously, Eddie.

Haggs said, 'You've come home for the funeral, I assume.'

Eddie nodded. 'Yeah.'

'Fucking *tragedy*.' Haggs sipped his drink. 'Me and Jackie had our differences. But I like to think we respected each other. I feel bad for Senga.'

If Haggs was an act, he was a pretty good one, Eddie thought. The sorrowful intonation in the voice, the expression of concern.

'You knew each other a long time,' Eddie said.

'Years and bloody years.'

Eddie hesitated before his next question. Haggs had a way of looking down the length of his nose at you, as if you were a specimen on a slide, something very small and hard to categorize. 'You ever do any business together?'

'I once gave him an opportunity to invest in a car-hire company, but he was a wee bit slow opening his cheque-book, and the chance passed.'

'And that's all,' Eddie said.

'Aye. Did you expect more?'

Eddie shook his head. 'I'm not sure. I thought maybe you had some joint ventures in the past.'

Haggs shook his head. 'The big difference between Jackie and me is that he was interested in what he could pluck out of history, whereas I'm more intrigued by what I can make of the future. Show Jackie an old country mansion and he'd wonder what he could salvage. Show me that same house and I'd be thinking of pulling it down and putting up a block of flats. So, what brings you out into the wilds of Rouken Glen to see me?'

'I'm the executor of Jackie's will.' Sometimes the capacity to fabricate was so slick it frightened Eddie.

'And what does Jackie's will have to do with me? Unless he's left me something, a keepsake maybe.' Haggs laughed. It was a high-pitched sound, a hinge squeaking. 'Old bugger wouldn't leave me a cracked chanty.'

A *chanty*, Eddie thought. A chamberpot. 'About the warehouse.'

'That dump in Bluevale Street?'

Eddie nodded and went into his storyline. 'It's going on the market soon to satisfy some tax demands Jackie hadn't paid.'

'Jackie had a useless accountant, some fucking quill-pusher from the Victorian age. I told him a hundred times. Get up to date. Throw out every last abacus and plug into the new age . . . Did he listen? Did he fuck. And now the whole kit and caboodle is going up for sale, you say?'

'Probably at auction,' Eddie said.

'I still don't see any connection to me, Eddie.'

'No? I heard you were interested in the property.'

With an expression of amazement, Haggs laughed loudly. His long body shook and he fine-sprayed the air with saliva. 'Me? *Me?* Do I look like a junk dealer? Do I look like a man who'd be interested in buying and selling rubbish?'

Eddie said, 'I heard you'd visited the warehouse and you and Jackie had arguments about the valuation of the business.'

'Jackie and me – we were oil and vinegar. We liked

197

to argue. Christ, we thrived on it. Who remembers the reasons? When conflict's finished, I let it go.'

Eddie didn't buy that. He had the feeling Haggs was the kind of man who'd never forget a grudge or a slight or the name of anyone who'd walked on the wrong side of him. Okay. Realistically, what the hell *did* a rich man want with a rundown warehouse? Demolish the place and build a supermarket or a bingo palace or a leisure complex? Wrong part of town, Eddie thought. Fine. Say it wasn't the warehouse or the space Haggs wanted, and Joe Wilkie guessed wrong. Say it was something else.

What did Jackie have that Haggs needed? What exactly?

He thought of Tommy G. Jackie *definitely* had something Tommy was looking for.

Had Jackie left troublesome loose ends all over Glasgow?

'I hear you're a cop in New York,' Haggs said.

'In Glasgow I'm just somebody's son trying to make sense of his father's affairs, and if I got the wrong end of the stick about you and the warehouse, let's drop it.'

'Gladly,' Haggs said.

The muzak played on. 'There is Nothing Like a Dame'. Suddenly Haggs slapped his thigh and laughed again, and said, 'I'm trying to imagine myself sitting in Jackie's grubby wee office arguing about the price of such-and-such a sundial or an old HMV gramophone. Sorry, Eddie, I don't mean to mock what Jackie did for a living –'

'No big deal.' But it was, and Eddie felt a surge of irritation at the way Haggs belittled Jackie.

Haggs asked, 'You talked to the police about the murder?'

'Yeah, we've talked.'

'Is Glasgow's finest close to finding the killer?'

'They believe Bones did it,' Eddie answered.

'*Bones?*'

'Bones's gun was the murder weapon.'

Haggs asked, 'That wee man went around *armed*? Have they brought him in for questioning?'

'They can't find him.'

'Then he fucked off. Probably scared shitless. I can't believe he killed Jackie.'

'So who did?'

Haggs shrugged. 'I'm baffled.'

'Then we're all baffled – apart from the cops,' Eddie said.

'The cops won't change their minds. They're inflexible. And it wouldn't be the first time they've jumped to the wrong conclusion.'

'Am I hearing contempt for the Strathclyde Police?'

'You don't need to be a mind-reader. They're a right evil bunch of wankers.'

'I heard something about a trial you were involved in . . .'

'That was a bloody attempt to railroad me.'

'Why?'

'How many reasons do you want? They're jealous of my lifestyle. They don't like some of my business partners. They don't like to see somebody from my background get ahead. You read the sign on the gate when you came in? You see the word *Drumpellier* there?'

Eddie said, 'I saw it.'

'I was born in Drumpellier Street, in a district of this fair city called Blackhill. You're born and brought up in Blackhill, Eddie, you're not supposed to get out. It was crime and drugs and gangs, some of the hardest fuckers in Glasgow. The police didn't like to visit Blackhill, and they didn't like people spilling out of Blackhill into other places, especially people like me drifting into respectable areas like this . . . Are you getting the picture?'

'You've risen above your station.'

'And I stepped on a few toes climbing. And some people don't forget that. And some of these people have friends in the police . . .'

'So you have *Drumpellier* out there to remind you where you came from,' Eddie said.

'More than that. It's me giving them the finger, Eddie. It's me saying, fuck the lot of you, I walk where I bloody well please.' Haggs tossed his scotch back and drew a hand across his mouth. 'So the trumped-up trial, Eddie, was a scheme planned by morons who wanted to show me that even if I'd come up in the world, I could go down again as fast as *that*,' and he snapped his fingers. 'The police case against me was a load of ballocks. I walked out of that courtroom free as a bird.'

Eddie stood under the angels and the blue sky and the cloud clusters. Haggs carried deep black grudges against the social order. Did he have grudges against Jackie too?

'Who told you about that trial anyway?' Haggs asked.

Eddie plucked an easy lie out of nowhere and tossed it like a paper dart. 'Guy called Caskie. A cop.'

Haggs said, 'Caskie . . . Is he the one friendly with your family?'

'The same,' Eddie said.

'And how did my name happen to come up in conversation?'

'Because I told him you intended to buy the warehouse.' Eddie smiled.

'Now you can tell him you were wrong.'

'Consider it done,' Eddie said. 'Thanks for your time.'

Haggs walked with Eddie towards the door. On the right was a small wood-panelled room filled with glass display cases.

Eddie glanced at them. 'Quite a collection,' he said.

Haggs asked, 'You interested in guns? I've been collecting them for years.' He strode towards the display cases. There were almost fifty blackpowder pistols here, most of them genuine antiques, each gleaming and imbedded in dark brown wood. Haggs took a keychain from his pocket and unlocked one of the cases and removed a long handgun with a walnut stock and held it out for Eddie's examination.

'Kentucky Flintlock,' he said. He handed the gun to Eddie, who was surprised by its weight, and then he carefully removed another weapon from the case. This one had a fancy curved handle and a barrel more than a foot long. 'This beauty is a Le Page Percussion Duelling Pistol. Lovely feel to it. I've also got a very fine original Colt 1860 Revolver and a mint-con Remington Percussion dating from 1858.' He gestured towards the display proudly. 'Been a hobby a long time. I always take my hobbies very seriously, Eddie.'

'This Kentucky is a very fine gun,' Eddie said, admiring the craftsmanship.

Haggs held out his hand and Eddie gave him back the flintlock and he returned it to the case, which he locked.

'Beautiful things make me forget my origins,' Haggs remarked. 'I'll walk you out.'

Outside, both men gazed at the monkey puzzle tree. To Eddie it seemed as if the tree had been tortured by sea storms, a thing you might find growing in godforsaken sand dunes.

He asked, 'You know Caskie, I assume?'

'You think I'd want a cop for an acquaintance?' Haggs laid a hand on Eddie's shoulder and massaged it a little too firmly. 'I'd rather use shite for toothpaste.'

Eddie smiled thinly. Sun reflected from the branches of the tree in a zigzagging pattern of light and a drab bird – probably a sparrow – popped out of the foliage and flew directly overhead.

28

The calamitous drumming in Caskie's head just wouldn't quit. Hot and flushed, he kept going over the same thing – his denial of ever having heard of Haggs. Reason, give me one good reason, he thought: I panicked. I slipped. I gave in to a kind of idiot seizure of guilt. Moron. It was downright stupid, a magician dropping his cards during a sleight of hand, and Mallon – certainly no dummy – had picked up on it. Caskie was convinced of that.

What would it have cost me to say I knew Haggs by name? Nothing. He'd answered without thinking. *Haggs? Never heard of him. Nothing to do with me. Not part of my world.* He'd rushed into the denial too quickly.

The burden you've been carrying. You're on overload.

He watched Joyce, who stood at the window and looked down into the street. She smoked a cigarette. 'Where the hell did Eddie go? He just disappeared. He didn't say he was leaving. It's been more than an hour, hasn't it?'

'I don't know.' Caskie had lost track of time.

From the hallway came the sound of a man drilling screws into sheets of plywood. Caskie had telephoned him and he'd come at once to put the plywood in the place where the glass had been, a temporary solution, security for Joyce. She'd wondered how Caskie could find somebody so quickly. One phone call and *voilà*. The carpenter appeared within ten minutes. Probably an old favour. Caskie had hundreds of strings he could pull in this city. He'd already arranged for a patrol car to remain in the vicinity in the event that Tommy G returned. She had the feeling a single car wouldn't worry a man like Thomas G.

'It's the middle of the afternoon and I'm not dressed yet,' she said.

'School holidays,' Caskie said.

She looked at Caskie. He had a strange lifeless tone in his voice. 'I'd better put some clothes on,' she said.

She stepped into her bedroom, closed the door. She pulled on a T-shirt with the logo *McCools*, the name of a bar she sometimes visited when she was in a jazz mood. Then blue jeans tight at her hips. She stood in front of the long mirror of the wardrobe, thinking she looked undernourished. She remembered how the intruder had dragged her to the floor, the way his hand had parted her robe. She'd have bad dreams about him. He'd crash her head uninvited.

She sat in a green velvet chair, an item salvaged from Jackie's yard. She saw her image again, this time in the oval mirror of the Victorian dressing table that had once belonged to Granny Mallon, funny how bits and pieces of furniture and small items of jewellery are handed down through generations like genetic material passed from one person to another, and she thought of how often Granny Mallon must have gazed at herself in this very mirror, a young wife, barely more than a girl, brushing her hair stroke after stroke.

She touched her lip where Tommy G had struck her. It didn't hurt now. She'd pressed ice cubes to it for a while, and they'd helped. She heard a knock on the door. Caskie appeared. She looked at his reflection in the mirror.

'You all right?' he asked.

'I'll be fine. Just give me a minute to myself, Chris.'

'Checking,' he said. 'You want aspirin or anything else?'

'No. But thanks for asking.' She smiled at him in the mirror. He closed the door, retreated. She couldn't read his expression. Concern, certainly. Always. She wasn't sure what else. Something troubled him. Probably Tommy G. She heard the buzz of the carpenter's drill and a big delivery truck pass in the street and how it made the glass vibrate in the window frames. Flora popped into her mind and she thought, I want my mother, I want to lay my head in her lap, all the things lost to us in the crap of the years, all mother–daughter moments ripped away from us. Thank you for that, Jackie. Thank you. I loved you anyway.

Caskie fingered the spines of books. *A Scots Quair*. *Growing Up in the Gorbals*. *The USA Trilogy*. Motes of dust drifted in sunlight. He walked the room restlessly. He brought his face close to one of the busts Joyce kept on shelves. This one, smooth-eyed, blind, a Roman copy, seemed to be peering into a world outside the range of everyday senses.

'Counsel me, Senator,' he whispered to the bust. 'Look at the bloody awful state of things. Where do I go from here?'

'Are you talking to a statue?' Joyce asked.

Caskie turned quickly. He hadn't heard her enter, and he was a little embarrassed. 'I was conferring,' he said.

'Talk to statues often?'

'All the time,' Caskie said. 'They don't judge, you see.'

'You're afraid of judgement?' Joyce asked.

'Now and then.'

There was a noise in the hallway, and Eddie Mallon came into the room.

He looked weary, Joyce thought. His eyes were lightless. 'Where the hell have you been?' she asked.

'Choosing a coffin,' he said.

'Oh shit, *damn damn*, I was supposed to help Senga do that and it went out of my mind. I feel awful.'

'Under the circumstances,' Caskie said, 'you're allowed a little amnesia.'

Eddie flopped on the sofa and stretched his legs.

Joyce said, 'You've been gone a long time.'

'When you're buying a coffin you don't simply leap into the first one you see,' he said.

'Comical,' Joyce said.

'I need some light relief,' Eddie said.

'Don't we just? I think I'll walk round to Senga's. See how she's doing.'

Caskie looked at his watch. 'It's time I was going too.'

Eddie glanced at Chris Caskie, whose face was lightly tanned. It made his small beard seem whiter.

'Did you process Tommy G through your computer, Chris?'

'It's in,' Caskie said. 'Nothing's come back to me yet. We'll get something, I'm sure.'

'I'm sure,' Eddie agreed.

Joyce ruffled his hair. 'Back soon.'

Caskie said, 'See you later, Eddie.'

I know how to empty a room, Eddie thought. He heard the front door close. He thought of phoning Claire, but before he could lift the phone the motion of the day caught up with him – the taxi-rides that had zoomed him from one end of the city to the other – and he shut his eyes and dozed in a shallow way for twenty minutes, dreaming of Glasgow, a black-and-white Glasgow he'd never lived in, steamships on the Clyde, crinolined ladies stepping out of horse-drawn carriages, shoeless kids begging on street corners. The air stank of raw sewage and the dank river. Women in shawls sold fish from wheelbarrows, and men hauled on their shoulders sides of butchered animals.

He woke dry-throated, walked into the kitchen, drank some water at the sink. He felt a deep frustration. He didn't see how he could stay in Glasgow long enough to penetrate the reasons behind Jackie's murder, or identify the killer, as if the slaying and the people involved belonged in a Glasgow so secret it was out of his reach – like the monochromatic city he'd seen in his dream. He was due to leave the day after the funeral. What could he achieve in so short a space of time? He couldn't drag out his visit, he had work at home, the case of the dead junkie girl in the abandoned brownstone, her identity and cause of death, and God knows what else might have happened in the meantime, what files dropped on his desk, what mysteries he was paid to solve –

Caskie and Haggs. Haggs the gun collector and Caskie the cop. What did they have going between them that required such facile fabrications? It was a fair assumption, he thought, that Haggs knew Caskie. He certainly knew *of* him. Say their paths had crossed. It was possible they'd met in orbit around Jackie. Assumptions, and Eddie wasn't enamoured of them, but sometimes they were the little building blocks that led to truth. He dipped his head under the cold water tap and let the stream run for a minute. Then he turned off the tap and stepped back from the sink and enjoyed water running over his scalp and down his face and thought: Caskie, lying sonofabitch.

You and Haggs are involved in something –

It was always *something*, this mystic *something*, this object that couldn't be defined. He dried his face and walked back to the living room and opened the phone directory.

29

The motorway roared half a block away. Petrol fumes hung brown in the still air like old muslin. Haggs, hands deep in pockets, gazed at the street through a high wire fence. This site, protected by the fence and an expensive electronic alarm system, was the location of a car-hire company called EasyGo, which Haggs owned. The lot was filled with Puntos and Ford Mondeos and VW Golfs. The Clyde was about five hundred yards to the south.

Haggs stared into the street, which had a derelict look. Across the way was an abandoned warehouse with broken windows. A gang of teenagers smoked crack and eyeballed the EasyGo lot as if they were thinking wads of drug money might be stashed inside.

Wasted fuckwits, Haggs thought. 'He comes to see me,' he said. 'On my fucking doorstep, bold as brass.'

Caskie, arms folded, leaned against the chassis of a Golf. 'I can't keep him chained, Haggs. He's not an easy customer.'

'Tells me he's the executor of the will and do I want to buy Jackie's warehouse.'

'He's not the executor of the will,' Caskie said. 'I happen to know Jackie's lawyer is the executor.'

'Okay, so he's lying. Then he asks me who do I think murdered his father and do I know a policeman called Caskie who, it seems, told him about that trial of mine years ago. I don't like this Yank cop turning up on my fucking doorstep.'

'I didn't tell him anything about you or your trial, Haggs.'

'So he's got a private agenda.' Haggs glared at the crackheads passing a pipe around.

'Private? His agenda's as bright as a lighthouse,' Caskie said. 'He's looking for the killer.'

'And that brings him to my doorstep.' Haggs cracked his knuckles a couple of times. 'He doesn't believe Bones did it.'

Caskie had the urge to ask *Where is Bones?*, except he didn't want the answer. Bones was to take the fall, and then he'd be smuggled out of Glasgow to safety. That was the understanding, the deal. But Caskie was having a hard time picturing Bones strolling down Regent Street to Piccadilly Circus or drinking ice-cold beer at a sidewalk café on the Boul St Mich, and clocking the passing crumpet. He felt cold inside.

Haggs said, 'I don't like the way Mallon stares at you when you're talking to him, because I get the feeling he's seeing right through your fucking head.'

'He sticks,' Caskie said.

'I wish he'd fuck off back to America. Is there a chance he knows anything about Jackie's business?'

'You think Jackie telephoned his son in Queens to tell him he had some furtive deal going on? Straws, Haggs. You're clutching.'

'I wonder.' Haggs made a V-sign at the scruffs across the street but they were too buzzed to be bothered by him. They had their crack and that was the limits of their universe and some tall skinny fucker gesticulating was an alien drop-in from another galactic system. 'Why's he so desperate to connect you and me?'

'Because he doesn't trust his local sheriff,' Caskie said. 'He doesn't believe anything you tell him unless he can verify it for himself.'

'I'd hate it if he became too much of a nuisance, Caskie. I'd hate to . . .' Haggs shrugged and looked serious.

Caskie saw a plane far to the south, rising out of Glasgow Airport. He wondered about its destination. Far away. Far far away.

Haggs said, 'The business we were discussing yesterday. Where are we with that?'

Caskie watched the plane vanish, a silver dot of light. 'Senga first,' he said. 'She knows nothing about Jackie's plans.'

'You're absolutely sure about that?'

'One hundred per cent. And the same with Joyce.'

'So what you're saying is Jackie confided his plans in nobody.'

'Nobody in the family anyway.'

'You're not just being gallant, are you, Caskie? The bold knight figure. The big man.'

'No, I'm not.' Caskie realized, not for the first time, how deep his hatred of Haggs had become; the emotion was hard and black like a stone dropped down a bottomless well. *I'll get you, Haggs.*

Haggs said, 'I've relied on you to suss out what these two women know, but if I find out you're lying and you're protecting either of them, you can forget all about your police pension and any perks you might be expecting. What you'll get instead, pal, is public humiliation so

211

fucking shattering you'll need to slip out of Glasgow in the back of a turnip lorry –'

Caskie interrupted. 'I'm not lying, and I'm not protecting Senga or Joyce.' He looked up at the sun, blinked. 'It might interest you to know Joyce was attacked today.'

'Attacked?'

Caskie told him about the assault, and Tommy G. He was pleased to see that the story had a distressing effect on Haggs, who clamped his hands together and cracked his fingers quite rhythmically. 'Let me get this straight. This Tommy G said he had a *deal* going with Jackie?'

Caskie nodded. 'A *big* deal. His very words. Maybe it's even the same deal as the one you're so interested in, Haggs. Wouldn't that be a kick in the teeth? Competition for you.'

Annoyed, Haggs asked, 'Who the hell is Tommy G?'

'He's up from London.'

'That's really helpful. And what else?'

'Tommy G alias Tommy Gurk alias Thomas Gilfillan alias Tommy Zen. Any of these ringing your chimes, Haggs?'

'No.'

Caskie said, 'Jamaican Londoner. Did a short stint in the Scrubs for possession of hashish with intent to sell. A year, time off for good behaviour. Then he entered a monastery.'

'A monastery?'

'He became a Buddhist, Haggs. In Tibet.'

'So you're telling me that our dear wee Joyce was attacked by a pacifist vegetarian? What did he hit her with – a fucking bean-curd egg-roll? Note to self: always make sure you're armed with a sharpened parsnip when you're in conversation with a Buddhist.'

212

'Buddhist or not, he's connected,' Caskie said. 'He takes trips. Rotterdam sometimes. Also Zurich. He has associates in both places.'

'What kind of associates?'

'Business types.'

'Straight business or funny?'

'Funny, I'd say.'

'How funny?'

Caskie didn't answer. He loved to keep Haggs dangling. He looked at the dopeheads beyond the wire fence. The druggy underclass. Thin stoned faces blissed to the hilt. A wine bottle, label peeling off, was doing the rounds. One of the kids, a girl dressed in baggy jeans with a plaid shirt knotted round her waist, blew him a kiss and called out, *'Hey Santy Clause! Can I suck yer beard, eh?'* She tugged her khaki blouse open and flashed a small sad breast at him and then sat down with her back to the wall and rolled a cigarette.

'Nice wee tit,' Haggs said.

Caskie ignored the remark. 'As far as I can gather from the skimpy data I was able to access,' he said, 'Gurk is associated with a dubious character in Zurich called Josef or Joe Kaminsky. According to police surveillance reports, Gurk stays at Kaminsky's country house when he visits Switzerland.'

'And what's so special about Tommy Gurk that he merits surveillance? What business is he doing with this Kaminsky?'

'Anything that pays is my guess.'

Haggs said, 'Give me specific.'

'Kaminsky is wanted by the Israelis on charges of – I quote – currency irregularities. The Swiss have resisted extradition efforts.'

'Currency irregularities? Fuck does that mean?'

'It sounds like a catch-all phrase. Maybe he's evaded taxes, or traded illegally in securities . . . I don't know. There's also the chance it's a smokescreen to cover activities which have absolutely nothing to do with fiscal matters.'

'That's it?'

Caskie nodded. What he'd told Haggs wasn't the whole truth. But enough to rattle Haggs's cage. Haggs didn't need to know everything in the database. 'The Police National Computer has its limitations, Haggs.'

Haggs thought, *Jesus Christ*. Rotterdam. Zurich. Israel. A monastery in Tibet. It was getting out of hand, going international, spreading to places where he had no control and no affiliates, where he didn't know the bloody languages. He didn't like it when his ventures had connections beyond Glasgow or, at a pinch, the Scottish border, because it increased the chance of complexity, elaborate rip-offs, encounters with men whose ways of doing things might be alien to him. He couldn't make the link between Jackie Mallon and the Jamaican Buddhist called Tommy Gurk or G or Zen, between a terraced house in the east end of Glasgow and a country house in fucking Switzerland. He couldn't connect a junkyard near Duke Street with 'currency irregularities' in Israel. Weird planets were colliding. He felt as if the road he'd been travelling towards the hidden world of Jackie Mallon – badly signposted as it was – had suddenly reached a fork where the directions were posted in languages he couldn't translate.

'Get me more, Caskie. I need more.'

'Easier said than done. I could go through Interpol, but there are protocols.'

'Fuck protocols,' Haggs said.

A rock thrown from the old warehouse smacked the wire fence and made it vibrate. Haggs wished he had a rocket-launcher and he'd just blow those crack-smoking guttersnipes all to hell.

A young man with wild hair called out, '*How much is it to rent one of them fucken cars, eh?*'

Haggs turned his back on the crack crew and looked at Caskie. 'I suggest you dig a wee bit deeper, pal. If you know what's good for you.'

I'll dig your grave, Caskie thought. That's how far I'd like to dig.

A shadow moved at the back of his mind. Then it took definite form, brightening. He thought: Maybe. Why the hell not? He recalled what he'd experienced when he'd first run Tommy G through the computer – a dim awareness of possibilities, a disjointed sense of enlightenment – but it was expanding now, it was growing from seed to shoot.

Another rock struck the fence, then another, a third, eventually a fusillade. The restive crackheads drifted across the street. Ragged, white-faced, skinny, these kids looked like extras from a cocaine version of *Night of the Living Dead*. More rocks thudded the fence. Then faces were pressed to the wire and grubby fingers hooked the metal strands. The fence was kicked and rattled and shaken vigorously. A rock flew into the lot and struck the roof of a Ford Mondeo.

Haggs roared, 'Fuck off out of here, the whole bloody lot of you! You shower of shite! You bunch of arse-wipes! *Fuck off!* You hear me?'

Some of the kids laughed and hooted. A gaunt girl in yellow-tinted glasses and a mini-kilt and purple Doc

Martens climbed a few feet up the fence before she fell back. A few of her friends cheered and helped her up and she began to climb again.

Haggs looked at Caskie. 'You're a cop. Do something about this scum, for God's sake.'

'They won't get over the barbed wire at the top,' Caskie said.

'I'm not counting on it,' Haggs said. 'Have I got to dial the police myself?'

'You know the number, Haggs?'

'Fuck you,' Haggs said. He took his cellphone from his jacket. The girl climbing reached the top of the fence and tried to seize the coiled strands of barbed wire. She cut her hand and fell, clattering against the pavement.

'You can never find a policeman when you need one,' Caskie said, enjoying his moment of supremacy – that and the fact the shadow was taking on ever more solid form, and he saw it clearly now. He felt a jolt, a thrill, of inspiration. *How to get Haggs out of my life* . . . How often had he asked himself that? And now he had a possible answer. But did he have the guts?

'Bloody joker,' Haggs said, punching buttons.

Caskie was miles away, thinking. Yes. One long-distance phone call.

30

Lou Perlman said, 'This pub's a kind of shrine for addicts like me.' He indicated old football photographs and posters that filled every available space on the wall. Glass display cases contained various editions of the green-and-white hooped jerseys of Glasgow Celtic Football Club. Medallions hung here and there, and scarves had been stapled to the ceiling beams.

Perlman went on, 'Traditionally, Celtic has had a predominantly Roman Catholic support – on account of the club's Irish origins – but not exclusively so. You remember your social history, Eddie?'

Eddie Mallon remembered. Jackie was usually disappointed when Celtic defeated their Southside rivals, Rangers. Eddie took the half-pint of lager Lou Perlman pushed along the bar towards him, and sipped. Perlman had a shandy, which he rapped cheerfully against Eddie's glass, and said, 'I'm a nut about Celtic, a passionate headcase – so what can I do? Some of these players on the walls are old heroes of mine. Charlie Tully, a right comedian on the wing, Willie Fernie, played like he had the ball attached to his boot with an invisible thread, Billy McNeill, tower of strength in defence . . .

I'm boring you, right? I always bore people when I go on about Celtic.'

Eddie said, 'I liked the game when I was a kid.'

'Ah, the game's only a small *part* of it,' Perlman said. 'It's the culture. It's Glasgow. It runs in the blood of the city. Of course, you'll find people who'll try to tell you they've got no interest in the two teams. View such individuals as suspect, son. They may be aliens from beyond the city limits. You'll find other people who take the game to extremes, and see it as a holy war. On one side is Ulster and the Union Flag and our beloved monarchy, on the other is the IRA. View these nutters with suspicion as well. They may be dangerous. And then some people will tell you we've moved on from all that shite, we're liberated from old hatred . . . take that with a pinch of salt, Eddie. We're impaled on the past like a pig on a spit.'

Perlman stared at the various posters in silence for a time. He smiled. He had a good smile. It changed his face the way sudden sunlight transforms a dark room. His lower teeth were slightly misaligned and discoloured by tobacco. 'So what's an old Jew like me doing supporting Glasgow Celtic, you wonder? They've been the immigrant underdogs, and Rangers the establishment. So who's a Jew with a liberal streak to support, eh?'

'Not the Presbyterian establishment,' Eddie said.

'Got it,' Perlman remarked.

They carried their drinks across the bar to a table hidden in a corner behind the jukebox. A few drinkers, wearing team colours, stood at the bar and argued about an arcane footballing matter. Perlman removed his glasses and wiped them on the sleeve of his jacket. The knot in his wide gold tie was undone and his collar unbuttoned. 'I'd rather talk football than crime any day of the week. Except crime pays my wages and football only fuels my passion . . . So crime it is. On the phone you said somebody attacked your sister.'

Eddie described the break-in, the assault.

'Your sister's never seen this character before?'

Eddie said, 'No. And Senga had never heard of him either. Slim gleanings for you, huh?'

Perlman held his glasses up to the light, then replaced them. The lenses were still smudged. 'The next question is – what's this situation between Tommy G and your late father? I assume you've asked yourself a few questions and come up with nothing.'

'Less than nothing.'

'No conclusions, no inspired guesses.'

'None. I thought Roddy Haggs might be able to throw a little light –'

'You talked to Haggs?'

'Was that a faux pas?'

'Didn't I tell you he was on my list?'

'I didn't think it could do any harm to see him. I hoped he might know what Jackie was up to, and maybe I could somehow hook that information to Tommy G –'

Perlman said, 'Let me tell you this. I'm the Force's numero uno Haggs Watcher. When it comes to Roddy, I'm like a fucking encyclopedia. The main thing to remember about Haggs is he's driven by a completely disgusting greed. He sees something he wants – slurp, out comes the tongue like a demented anteater, and the object of desire is digested. Roddy belches, and moves on to the next acquisition. If he believes your dad had something tasty, he'd want to suck that down too. Haggs is dangerous, Eddie. He's got some unpleasant cronies.'

'Are you saying I could be in trouble?'

'I'd be lying if I denied it.'

'I'll look out for myself,' Eddie said.

'See that you do. Seriously.' Perlman tore the filter off a cigarette. He lit the vandalized cigarette and regarded the filter with scorn. 'I hate these sorry attachments. So you say Caskie phoned Tommy G's name into Force HQ for a crime computer check?'

'Right,' Eddie said.

'I'll double-check, see what result came through.' He coughed and swallowed some shandy.

'Why? You think Caskie might just be going through the motions?'

'There's a whisper about good old Chris. I've been hearing it on the streets for donkey's. It's always been constant but quiet as a lullaby, and what it says is that Caskie's very friendly with Haggs. This isn't to accuse Caskie of anything illegal, don't get me wrong. Cops and criminals, they're in the same industry basically, so why shouldn't they know one other? But with Caskie the talk has always suggested something more, like he's maybe a wee bit *too* close to Haggs. People in Pitt Street have heard this gossip, but nobody's ever done anything about it. Most cops would put it down to criminal malice. Some wanker out there wants to spread a bad word about a cop, undermine him. But this particular whisper has been unusually long-lived.'

'Nobody ever looked into it?'

'Eddie, the world is bursting at the seams with criminals and assorted louts. Who's got time to probe a groundless rumour, eh?'

Caskie and Haggs, Eddie thought. Friends. What kind of friendship was it? What sort of benefits could they derive from such an alliance? He imagined Caskie and Haggs meeting in dark places, heads close together, whispers. An exchange of information, favours flowing back and forth between them. *Find out what Jackie Mallon is up to*, Haggs says. *You've got the inside track.*

Caskie, maggot in the apple, agrees.

A kid approached the jukebox, spread his hands against it, studied the playlist. He dropped in a coin and pressed a couple of buttons and then swaggered back to the bar. The music was an Irish tune played by a folk band.

'"Fields of Athenry",' Perlman said, and laid a hand on his heart. 'My anthem.' He listened to the music a moment before he leaned across the table and said, 'Tay showed you the gun, I'm told.'

'I saw it.'

'Did he tell you where the gun was found?'

'Bones's flat.'

'Did he say where exactly?'

'Just the flat. That's all I was told.'

Perlman beckoned Eddie closer with his finger crooked. 'It was wrapped inside a Tesco grocery bag and stuffed under the kitchen sink. The *fucking* sink.'

'No way,' Eddie said.

Perlman said, 'Does the word transparent come to mind?'

Eddie said, 'See-through. A man has a gun that was used in a murder and he wraps it in a grocery bag and sticks it under his sink, which must be the most blatantly obvious place in the history of crime for stashing *anything*.'

Perlman said, 'Too fucking easy to find.' He blew smoke. 'You can bet your mortgage Bones didn't stash it there.'

'Then who did?'

'There's no other candidate *but* Bones, Eddie. That fact has come down from a very high place indeed. It's the gospel. Tay wants it signed and sealed.'

'What is it? Is Tay lazy? Is he too busy to dig any deeper?'

Perlman crushed out his smoke. The cigarette paper burst and flakes of tobacco stuck to his fingers. He blew them away. 'Laziness isn't a factor, Eddie. Tay is at his desk dawn till dusk some days. His assistant Sandy Scullion also works all the hours sent by God, although he's altogether a more pleasant human being than Cardinal Tay. But you know the shitty way it works. If the murder victim had been the Lord Mayor of Glasgow, you can bet your arse Tay would have been crawling all over the crime, witnesses and potential witnesses would have been hauled in on crowded charter buses.'

'And Jackie was a nobody,' Eddie said.

'Not quite,' Perlman said. 'Jackie Mallon wasn't the Marquis of Govan, right, but he had a criminal record, albeit small. Also he was suspected of various wrongdoings down the years. Theft of artworks. Masterminding a scheme to persuade some decrepit aristo in his dotage to part with precious pre-Revolutionary Russian coins. Stuff like that. None of it ever stuck to your dad, but it occupied police man-hours, it produced paperwork and more paperwork, and so Jackie Mallon was something of a fucking nuisance if you worked in Pitt Street.'

'Now he's not a nuisance.'

'Score,' Perlman said.

'It sucks. It's –'

'Unacceptable? Unfair? Sure it is. It's like the fucking National Health Service, Eddie. If you're rich, and can go

222

private, you'll get good service. If you're *Untermenschen*, you can wait a year or two for a hernia operation. Same with the law. If you're a star, you'll get star treatment. If you're a small-time fucking pain-in-the-arse like Jackie Mallon, and somebody shoots you – oy – you're off the books. It's the system, Eddie.'

'And that's what Jackie was, a small-time pain-in-the-arse?'

Perlman said, 'That's what they tell me.'

'Never big-time.'

'Unless he changed horses lately.' Perlman opened his cigarette packet and saw it was empty. He began to tear it in strips. 'You want him to have been sweetness and light, eh?'

'He'd never been that.'

'Okay. Let's say . . . worthy of love.'

Eddie finished his drink. 'That,' he said.

'Boys and their fathers,' Perlman said. 'Dear God, the complexity of it all. I'll walk out with you.'

They left the pub. Eddie looked at the darkening sky, then at Perlman who was smoking thoughtfully. 'You married?'

'Not any more.'

Eddie detected nothing in the response, no regret, no sadness: it was a dry fact dryly uttered. 'Any kids?'

'Never had the time. I'm going home. What about you?'

'I'll stroll for a while,' Eddie said.

'I'll be in touch. Mind how you go.'

'I will.'

Perlman turned and moved away.

Eddie walked to the end of the block, looking for a taxi, seeing none. *A small-time pain-in-the-arse*, he thought.

It wasn't a bad judgement. He could live with that one.

But small-time didn't get you killed.

He paused on a street corner. The city was all noise, unfiltered and vibrant. He listened to the drone of the city. He picked one or two distinct sounds out of the auditory pile, a muted trumpet being played in a tenement, a vandalized version of 'I'll Be Seeing You' – bum note, stop, try again – a man tapping the sidewalk, the *pavement*, with a cane, and the sound of a dog-chain rattling quietly.

Another sound reached him, a constant ticking, and it occurred to him that there was a weird familiarity about this, he'd heard it before only he couldn't remember where, it had sunk into a deep pool of his awareness and lain there unexamined under the silt. For a second he was touched by mild apprehension, something that settled on him with the fleeting touch of a furry summer moth.

He gazed across the street. The car was dark green. The motor was idling. Something inside the engine was out of whack, a minor malfunction. *Tap tick.* The driver, face half-shadowed, was staring straight ahead, not looking at Eddie at all, not interested.

Go for it, Eddie thought.

He crossed the street quickly and caught the handle of the door on the driver's side and hauled it open and, reaching in, grabbed the man by the lapel of his dark blue blazer and dragged him out of his seat.

'Jesus Christ.' The driver slid to the ground, banging an elbow and rubbing it vigorously.

Eddie looked down at him. 'Funny bone?'

'Yes, but not remotely amusing, alas,' the driver said.

31

Larry McQueen woke, got out of bed and went in search of the TV deliveryman and wondered, as he padded in pyjamas and slippers from room to room, if he'd dreamed the fellow up, and all this TV delivery stuff was just a nonsense. But his nose ached and there was dry blood on his hands and he remembered the fellow punching him. He wondered how long he'd slept.

'Hallo? You there? Coooeeee.'

No answer. He looked in the kitchen. Checked out the bathroom in case the fellow was answering the call of nature. In the living room, where a bowl of wax fruit sat on a long coffee table, Larry looked from the window down into the street, which was clogged with parked cars.

He walked into the hall and stepped into his son's bedroom and gazed at the prints on the walls. Modern art. All lines and paint spillage, any moron could do that, what the hell did Billy pay for these bits of crap? Billy had more money than sense. And precious little sense anyway.

Back into the hall.

'Hello? TV man, where are you?'

The flat was silent.

Larry opened the front door and went out to the landing and stood looking down the flight of stairs that led to the street. Maybe the telly man was having trouble getting the box out of his van. Could be. Needs a hand. Larry descended a little shakily. He clutched the banister rail. At the bottom of the stairs he stopped and peered at the front door, a rectangle of dimming light. He stood motionless for a time.

Who was he fooling? He couldn't help the fellah lift the TV box if it was heavy. He wasn't young any more. He didn't have –

Then blank. He couldn't remember why he'd left the flat.

Bloody hell.

You get old. The brain. You don't. Things slip. Tilt. You used to play bingo every Wednesday night. You remember when the lamps in the street were lit by gas flame and coal was delivered in a horse-drawn cart and you needed a ration book for sugar and that time the Queen visited Glasgow after her Coronation and the population lined the streets and waved their little flags, that was when people had respect for royalty –

He was outside now and the royal-blue sky was very very high and he felt a wee bit dizzy between the tall red tenements and sun glancing off windows and he thought, if I sit down on a wall I'll be fine, and his heart was awful fast and when he reached for a wall he found it wasn't solid, it was shrubbery, and it parted under the weight of his hand and he fell through it and landed arse over elbow in somebody's garden where there was crusty dogshite and some old fast-food boxes containing onion rings from a prehistoric age and a burger covered with blue fuzz oh Christ and I can't get up.

'Billy,' he said quietly. 'Come and help me. Help your dad.'

His mouth was dry as cinders. He felt weak.

I am lying here because because . . .

He rolled on to his back and looked up. The sky had an inky quality. His left foot had become twisted in a tangle of shrubbery and the slipper was gone.

O Billy, help me.

Or that nurse Thelma, where was she, where was she?

Then somebody was speaking to him. 'Let me give you a hand up, mister.'

Larry had big spots in front of his eyes, like raindrops. The face that loomed down was young and friendly. Sideburns and short hair a funny orange colour and an unlit cigarette end between the lips.

'Come on, let me get you up. I'll just grab you under the shoulders and you hang on to me, right?'

'Aye, right,' Larry said.

'I saw you come out of the close,' the young man said. 'I'll take you back inside.'

'Aye,' Larry said. 'I need my bed.'

'Where did you think you were going dressed only in your pyjamas, for God's sake?'

'I was . . .' Larry's head emptied like a cistern flushed.

'Never mind. Just hang on.'

Larry leaned against the young man. They went inside the tenement, then up the stairs. Ascending, Larry had a sense of having discarded his body.

Inside the flat the young man said, 'You live here on your own?'

'My son sometimes,' Larry said.

'Where is your son?'

Larry sat on the sofa and shook his head.

'You don't know where he is, eh?'

Larry said, 'He moves here and there. I need my nurse. That's who I need.'

'I'll give her a bell. What's her number?'

'In the kitchen by the phone, Thelma's her name.'

'Leave it to me,' the young man said.

Larry said, 'What's your name, sonny?'

'Giovanni. Gio.'

'That's a foreign name.'

'I was born right here in Glasgow. Nitshill to be exact.'

'I'm McQueen,' Larry said.

'Aye, I know, I saw the nameplate on the door.'

Larry listened to the young man go inside the kitchen, then the low rumble of his voice. Giovanni returned. 'Stale in here,' he said, and blew his nose into a big handkerchief. 'Your nurse is on her way.'

'You're a right Samaritan, lad,' Larry said.

'She also said she'd contact your son.' The young man looked round the room. 'I'll be off then.'

'Can you not stay?'

The living room was already empty. Open-mouthed, Larry wondered about dreams and that fuzzy borderline where what was real and what was not just melted into one incomprehensible experience. He wiped drool from the corner of his mouth.

32

The driver sat on the kerb and rubbed his elbow and made a moaning sound.

'How long have you been tracking me?' Eddie asked.

'Tracking you? What do I look like? A bloodhound? This is an outrage –'

Eddie said, 'First thing this morning I had the feeling somebody was scoping me out. I'm betting it was you. You were driving along Duke Street early this morning. I heard your car. That same goddam sound.'

'My blazer's filthy,' the man said. His car was still idling, still ticking.

'Nice jacket, too bad,' Eddie said. 'Who's paying you?'

The man rubbed dust streaks from his sleeve. '*Paying* me? Ah, yes, to keep you under observation, of course. I'm being reimbursed for that, I suppose.'

Why didn't the guy get up and launch a few punches? He was at least ten years younger than Eddie, and he looked fit and strong enough to retaliate instead of just sitting limply near his car and fingering his funny bone or dusting his blazer. Was he a coward? Gutless? It's not that, Eddie thought. The guy looked stressed; his indignation was only a front.

Eddie said, 'Unless I'm way off target, you've spent most of the goddam day hound-dogging me, and nobody works for nothing. So who's your paymaster? Simple question.'

'There's no such beast as the simple question.'

'It's been a long day. Talk straight.'

The guy stretched his arm out slowly, as if checking the integrity of his elbow joint. He held the arm level for twenty seconds, then lowered it. Eddie gazed at him impatiently. *Fuck this.* His mood had darkened. Reaching down, he gripped the lapels of the blazer and dragged the man to his feet and pushed him back against iron railings that surrounded a scrag of garden at the front of a tenement.

'Talk to me,' he said.

'I'm not tracking you. You're out of your skull –'

'Who's paying you?'

'I'm tired and my temper's frayed, friend –'

'My temper's not altogether unruffled either, *friend.*'

The man pulled himself free of Eddie's hold and took a step towards his car. 'If your fit of madness has passed, do you mind if I get in my car and bugger off?'

Eddie saw the man move purposefully to his vehicle, and he went after him at once, caught him by the shoulder, spun him round. Face to face. He smelled something sweet on the guy's breath.

'Show me some identification,' Eddie said. 'I want to know who the fuck you are –'

'I'm a motorist assailed by a deranged pedestrian,' the guy said.

Eddie shoved him against the body of the car. 'Your name, fucker. Your name, your *name.*' And he thrust his hand inside the guy's blazer and hauled out a slimline wallet of soft kidskin. The guy panicked and made a frantic effort to grab it back, but Eddie turned to one side and flipped the wallet open just as the man threw a punch that was partly blocked by Eddie's shoulder, but forceful just the same, sending a stab of serious pain like a corkscrew into the side of his neck. Bullseye. Starry nights and bright sunsets. Tenement buildings collapsing. The scream of motorways. Disoriented, he had an image of gridlocked traffic in the Holland Tunnel.

He went down on one knee, still holding the wallet, and he thought: I'm fucked. The guy made another swift lunge and Eddie held the wallet against his chest, covering it as if this were a game of football and he was shielding the ball. The guy launched a kick that hurt Eddie just under the ribs, but he didn't fumble the wallet in spite of the pain. Dear Christ, there had to have been a smarter way to control this from the first exchange, Eddie thought. I'm hurt and I'm really goddam *losing* it, down on one knee in a darkening Glasgow street, clutching the wallet of a man you've never seen before, one you think has been following you all day – is this squalid escapade why you came three thousand lousy miles through space and time in a *motherfucking aircraft*? Where's the dignity in this?

He made it on all fours to the railings, grasped one, hauled himself up. The guy grunted and stuck his knee sharply into the base of Eddie's spine and all air was expelled, and Eddie had the sense that his lungs were about as useful in the oxygen-processing function as two sun-dried apricots. He gasped and coughed and felt his stomach rise into his throat. But he still had the wallet, oh yeah, *the wallet is mine*. He collected his strength and, in the manner of an out-of-condition prizefighter, swung his arm round in a direct line, hard and fast, fist a ball of lead, and he made contact with the guy's face, and the guy went down like an empty set of clothes in a conjuror's illusion.

Eddie turned, leaning against the railings, and looked down at the man motionless on the pavement. He heard the rattle of his own hurried breathing. You used to be in great shape. American life has wasted all the muscle in you, endless bad coffee in waxy cardboard cups, donuts in sickly sugar-pink all-night joints, burgers dying in grease and hot dogs simmering in water that might have come unfiltered out of the Hudson, white bread and ketchup, the Beginner's Basic Cardiac Arrest Kit. Claire kept telling him, *Wholemeal bread only, Eddie. Nothing fried. Fresh fruit. Chew on a raw carrot if you have the munchies.*

Carrots were terrific if you were Bugs Bunny, he told her.

He opened the wallet with a hand that shook from exertion. He saw the ID. *Detective-Sergeant McWhinnie, Charles. Strathclyde Police.*

He stared at it.

A cop.

He raised McWhinnie to a sitting position and propped him against the side of the car, which was still pumping out exhaust fumes, and ticking. Eddie reached into the car and switched off the engine and then went down on his knees beside the glazed McWhinnie. You never forget a name. The guy who'd driven Joyce home from the identification of Jackie's corpse had been called Charles McWhinnie. This had to be the same one. He was young and good-looking enough to cause Joyce a flutter.

'I think my jaw's broken,' McWhinnie said in the thickened voice of a novocained man.

'Let me get you inside the car.'

'Why? I'm comfortable here,' McWhinnie said.

Eddie said, 'We've attracted some attention. Just get in the car.'

A few faces in ground-floor windows. Lovers of street violence. Not so gory as telly, but more authentic. A pot-bellied man in a white undershirt stood at the mouth of a close. 'Feeble,' he said, and he slow handclapped. 'If you have to resort to fisticuffs, you might at least put on a proper show.'

Eddie said, 'Quit whining. It was free.'

'Free or not isn't the bloody point. That encounter was pure crap. You both need some time in the gym.'

'Fuck off, fatso.' Eddie raised McWhinnie and manoeuvred him into the passenger seat.

The man in the white T-shirt shouted, 'Pair of diddies. Big girl's blouses.' He turned and vanished inside the close.

Eddie got behind the wheel and slammed the door and drove away. His ribcage throbbed. His neck was filled with forks of pain.

'We drive on the left in this country,' McWhinnie said. He rubbed the side of his face where Eddie had connected. 'By morning I'll look like the bloody Hindenburg. After the crash.'

'I'm not going to be bruise-free myself,' Eddie said. He aimed the car directly ahead, then somehow found himself on a motorway where the traffic that whizzed past him was disconcerting. He took an exit and steered carefully into the car park of the Hilton. He killed the engine and sighed and tried to ignore his aches and pains.

'It's a crime to assault a police officer,' McWhinnie said.

'So you'll report me.'

McWhinnie shrugged. He held one hand, palm flattened, to the side of his face. 'I don't know how much I feel like a police officer.' The tone in McWhinnie's voice was that of a man to whom promises made had been violated. Oaths had been empty words. He squeezed out a kind of smile. His face was already beginning to swell.

Eddie said, 'Talk to me some more.'

McWhinnie looked in the direction of the hotel. Taxis came and went. Porters hauled baggage. Beyond the glare of the hotel darkness was total. The sun was done with the day.

'I don't have to tell you a damn thing. I have no obligations to you. In fact, I should be cuffing you and asking you to accompany me to the station.'

'What's stopping you?' Eddie asked.

'Ha bloody ha, I don't have the strength for it,' he said. 'Damn, this fucking *jaw*! Christ, did you have a lead pipe hidden in your fist?'

'Pure bone,' Eddie said. 'You were saying?'

'Do you want to hear about the cop movie I saw at a Saturday afternoon matinée and it made me think I'd like to be a detective when I grew up?'

'You don't have to go that far back, Charlie,' Eddie said.

'You Americans always want to cut to the chase.'

You Americans, Eddie thought. He wanted to correct McWhinnie, *this is the city of my birth, my country*, but why bother? 'Hurry's our style. Rush rush. Go go.'

'You were right about one thing. I've been following you.' He touched his jaw again. Blood leaked from between his lips. 'You've dislodged one of my back teeth. Do I look like a balloon yet?'

'You're heading that way. Who gave the command?'

'Ah, the command. Follow the American.'

A tall man in a dinner jacket stepped out of a limo and, with an angelic gowned woman on his arm, entered the hotel. There was a sound of dance music as the doors opened, brassy stuff from the big-band era. 'Just One of Those Things.' Eddie was reminded of Flora. Flora in her greenhouse, thinking of Jackie, remembering the honeymoon in Largs, her long-lost love and his cruelty.

McWhinnie said, 'I don't want to go all philosophical on you, Mallon, but do you believe that in order to maintain the law we sometimes have to break it?'

'I think we walk very close to the edge at times,' Eddie said.

'But not over it?'

'It's debatable, Charlie. It's all grey areas and no maps. Why? Have you broken a law?'

'I'm an upstanding policeman,' McWhinnie said. 'I do what I'm told. If I have questions, I keep them to myself. If I have doubts, I choke them down.'

'And you're choking now,' Eddie said.

'I have . . . let's say, gristle lodged in my gullet.'

'I'm listening.'

'A small thing perhaps – but why the hell was I following you?'

'Yeah. Why?'

'The truth is, nobody told me and I didn't ask. I drove around. I watched. I made notes. But I'm not some bloody espionage agent, Mallon. I joined the Force because I had this notion of upholding the law, achieving something positive I could be proud of, if that doesn't sound Pollyanna and risible – not to waste my time and training running after a cop from New York who, as far as I could tell, wasn't armed and represented no threat to public order. Work like that . . . don't have a clue what its *purpose* is. And obviously I'm not even very good at it.'

Eddie thought, Charles McWhinnie in a nutshell: no sense of self-worth, needs to be valued, praised now and then. 'Somebody thought the job was important, Charlie. Who?'

McWhinnie swivelled his jaw from side to side. It made a clicking sound. 'I'm no Judas, Mallon.'

'I haven't heard the clink of thirty pieces of silver, Charlie.'

McWhinnie said, 'It's not only following you that depresses me, Mallon. It's not just that . . .'

Eddie waited. He understood he couldn't force McWhinnie to talk. He couldn't threaten him. He'd spent his violence. Anyway, what good would it do? McWhinnie would say what he had to in his own time.

More couples entered the hotel dressed for a formal dance. Women with crisp hairdos and long dresses, men in evening wear. It's too hot to dance, Eddie thought. Jackie and Flora in Largs, had it been too hot for them to dance, or had they held each other close and sashayed across the floor of their hotel? A fast foxtrot, a whirl, Jackie's delicate feet barely touching the floor and Flora desperately in love.

Why did he keep coming back to that honeymoon, like a man returning to the origin of a myth he'd never understood? An effect of pain, confused signals rushing this way and that through his head, messages coming in from unusual sources tapped out in a neural Morse he'd never heard before. He *hurt*. It was as if a ghostly figure, with no training in the healing arts of the Orient, was sticking acupuncture needles into his ribs in all the wrong places.

Oh boy. He needed painkillers, strong ones. Darvon. Percodan. Soon you can lie down and stretch out on the sofa in Joyce's flat. She's wondering where I am. The brother who goes missing. Sometimes for years in a faraway continent.

McWhinnie said, 'I'd like to step out of this car with the feeling that I haven't betrayed anyone, Mallon. I'd like to unload some of the dung I'm choking on, but at the same time I don't want to feel that I've regurgitated it in such a way that I'll have long sleepless nights bedevilled by questions of loyalty. Is that clear?'

'There's stuff you can't tell me, I understand that.'

'No. Stuff I *won't* tell you. I have a conscience like a sack of coal, Mallon. I'll set it down for a moment . . . Here's a shock to your system: Bones, alleged killer, was under police protection.'

Bones: the name fished out of the air. 'Protection? I don't follow that.'

'He was ensconced in a flat in Govan for his own safety after the killing.'

'Safety from what?'

'Don't interrupt me. This is hard enough. The flat, I assume, is used from time to time as a kind of secure house. It's a dump, a place people pass through. Witnesses, say. Informants. I bought groceries for Bones. I delivered them to the flat. I told him to stay there and I left. He was a reprehensible little shite with bad teeth. I didn't ask myself why we were being hospitable to him. Probably I just assumed it had something to do with the murder of your father, and maybe Bones needed protection in case the killer was looking for him too. I just did the job.'

'And?'

McWhinnie said, 'This job also involved paying off certain debts Bones had incurred with questionable bookmakers throughout the city. It was over two thousand pounds, it doesn't matter the exact sum. I gave the markers to Bones. I wasn't sure why we were buying him in such a *blatant* way – except perhaps to keep him cheerful while we interviewed him in connection with your father's murder. That's what went through my mind, I suppose. We were oiling a potential witness. We were bribing him, after a fashion . . .' McWhinnie tried another smile but the side of his face had swollen up, as if he had a crab-apple stuffed in his cheek. The smile looked like a gash. 'Some time that day, Bones disappeared. I went in the evening to the flat to check on him, and he'd gone. Where and why? I don't know. Did he leave under his own steam or did somebody come for him? Again, I don't know. But that's only a part of the conundrum, Mallon . . . Answer this. Why was he stuck inside a safe house when he should have been taken to Force HQ for questioning immediately after the murder? Why were we being so cooperative to a man who's suddenly become the major suspect in the killing?'

'He wasn't a suspect immediately,' Eddie said.

McWhinnie said, 'He *should* have been, Mallon. That's my real point. Why wasn't he in your father's car when Jackie left Blackfriars pub? Where was he when somebody was shooting your dad? And then what – did he walk around for a while before he returned to the car and saw cops everywhere? You see, he should have been taken in and questioned hard as soon as he reappeared. Instead, he gets the soft-shoe treatment. Safe house. Gambling debts paid. Groceries. Scotch. He was given preferential treatment – why?'

'Where was he apprehended?' Eddie asked.

McWhinnie said, 'I don't know. I've talked enough. I draw a line here.'

'Did he go back to the car and somebody took him into custody? Did he walk into a local station and say here I am? Did he meet somebody by prearrangement? Who took him to the safe house in the first place? Whose idea was that? There must have been some short preliminary interview at the very least before he was given sanctuary. There has to be a written record somewhere.'

McWhinnie smiled. 'Oh really? A written record, you say? I used to be a big believer in written records. Now? Who knows? I've nothing else to say. I'm in pain and it's getting harder all the time to speak.' He opened the passenger door, and stepped out. 'Keep the car. Use it. I feel like drinking. Medicinal reasons. Sorry about the punch-up, it's not really my style, far too uncivilized, if you knew me better you'd realize that, and you'd know how sick to my soul I've become,' and he turned and walked stiffly towards the hotel.

Eddie got out of the car and called to him. 'You haven't told me who issued the order to have me followed.'

'Right, I haven't,' McWhinnie answered, without turning to look.

'A name,' Eddie said.

McWhinnie kept moving. 'Not from these lips.'

'McWhinnie, wait,' Eddie shouted. 'Who gave you the cash to pay off the gambling debts?'

McWhinnie stopped and looked back. 'This is all I'll say. You know him.'

It had to be somebody inside the Force. Somebody who could pull strings, play power games. 'I know him . . . Is it Caskie?'

McWhinnie turned away, kept moving. He pushed the door and stepped inside the Hilton and Eddie saw the glass swing back in place in a quick little disturbance of distended light. He thought of going after McWhinnie, but he knew McWhinnie had nothing more he was prepared to say. Eddie didn't get back in the car. No way was he driving to his sister's place. Wrong side of the street, one-way systems, few recognizable landmarks. He was dragging ass now, and the night was closing down on him.

Outside the hotel he found a taxi to take him to Dennistoun. He sat in the back and he thought of what McWhinnie had said, and how he'd make sense of it.

33

On the phone, Billy McQueen told the nurse he couldn't come to see his father. It was inconvenient, he had business meetings, he plucked excuses out of the air. The call-girl, Leila, was dead asleep on the floor. She'd passed out here a dozen times.

Thelma said, 'Look here. He's your father. Your dad. He was wandering around in his pyjamas in the street. In the street, mind you. That's serious. God knows what the neighbours are thinking. I've given him something to help him relax, but he's going on about a TV delivery and somebody called Giovanni and I can't follow him. I strongly suggest you make an appearance, because if you don't, well, I can't be responsible if he decides to go walkabout again. I do have other patients, Mr McQueen.'

Billy McQueen thought: I have had better days.

The deal is fucked.

Gurk gets maced.

And now Larry is wandering the streets in his pyjamas. Plus this Giovanni – who the hell was he?

He said, 'It's difficult for me, Thelma. I'm up to my neck.'

'Neck? You'll be in over your head if you don't get here, because I'll phone Social Services and tell them your father needs to be hospitalized for his own safety –'

'Thelma, I pay you to deal with all this –'

'I have other patients, Mr McQueen. I'm already late for a Parkinson's in Bearsden.'

'Right, right, I'll be there as soon as I can.'

'It better be quick,' she said.

Billy put down the handset. *Fuck you, Thelma*, he thought. He limped to the window and looked out. Darkness and orange lamps. I don't want to go out there. I don't fancy the streets tonight. Climbing in a taxi, take me to Hyndland, no way José. Bloody Larry in his pyjamas.

Leila turned over in her drugged sleep and muttered, '*On an ocean liner sure.*' Night trips, Billy thought. Seagoing escapes under cover of darkness. He wished he was inside Leila's dream and the big propellers of a ship were churning. Destination Tahiti, oh aye.

He picked up the cordless, punched in the number of Gurk's hotel room.

'Yeah?' Gurk said.

'I was wondering . . . are you all right?'

'Rinsed my eyes out a few times with Evian,' Gurk said. 'Sight has been restored. Lamps working, happy to say.'

'Glad to hear that . . . Look, I was curious to know if you wanted to step out, have a bite to eat, a drink, something? I know a nice place in the West End.'

'Kind of you. Have to decline, sorry.'

It's not your company I want, Billy thought. It's the safety of your presence. Be my bodyguard, please. 'It won't take long, Tommy. Half an hour mibbe. I'll send a car down for you.'

'No can do, me old son. I been talking with some of my people. Options are being discussed. People are openly worried. Money is out there, to say nothing of vanished articles. Makes me wonder about other dimensions, Billy. Can things disappear into alternative realities? Are there diversions along the everyday continuum? Anyway, I'm stuck here waiting for the sodding dog to ring again.'

Billy said, 'But –'

'Tell you what. Gimme a bell later.' Gurk hung up.

Billy phoned the number in Hyndland. Thelma answered on the first ring. 'I hope to hear you say you're on your way, Mr McQueen.'

'Even as we speak,' Billy said.

'Your dad's ranting.'

'Fifteen minutes,' Billy said.

I should have stuck him in a home. He's dead weight, he's lumber I have to carry on my back, he's my cross. All I wanted was his affection. You've worked at that, and you're still not getting it, Billy. He put on an expensive black silk shirt, then black trousers and shoes. Camouflage. Creature of the night. He covered Leila with a cotton sheet then phoned his usual cab company for a taxi.

While he waited, he thought about Gurk's dark-red eyes. Beyond bloodshot. Like Halloween contact lenses, the colour of terror. He remembered how Gurk had come stumbling out of the tenement in Ingleby Drive after his visit to Joyce Mallon.

Why hadn't he tried harder to persuade Gurk to keep him company? The Dreadlocked One was obstinate. He made up his mind and that was that. Phone calls, associates, outstanding debts, a transaction gone all to hell: the pressures were stacking up. Gurk managed to escape into meditation and fanciful questions about diversions along some continuum.

Billy's questions were less esoteric but just as mysterious, such as: who shot Jackie Mallon and why did this sweet deal go all wrong? Sometimes the stars were light-years out of joint.

He sweated. His stump chafed against his prosthesis. He needed a splash of industrial-strength moisturizer. Go to Hyndland, appease Larry, stuff him with more medication. Why can't I just wash my hands of you, Larry, you bitter old sod?

His buzzer sounded. He pressed the button on the wall.

'Taxi, Mr McQueen.'

'Is that you, Alec?'

'Aye.'

'I'll be down in a flash.' Alec McGroaty. One of his regular drivers. He didn't want strangers. He turned the lights off, left his penthouse, descended in the lift where the mirrored interior reflected a multitude of Billy McQueens dwindling to infinity. I feel that tiny, he thought. A dot in a frozen eternity of silvered glass.

He entered the foyer, nodded at the night security man, Cutcheon, who'd once been a professional wrestler. He looked hard and bulky in his black suit. Alec McGroaty was standing at Cutcheon's desk. A small man in a fawn cardigan and baggy tartan trousers such as a golfer might wear, McGroaty had a deferential manner.

'Hot outside, Mr McQueen,' Cutcheon said.

'Aye, it's like the Costa del Sol,' McGroaty remarked.

McQueen didn't feel like small talk. He followed McGroaty outside to the taxi. He climbed into the back.

'Novar Drive,' he said.

McGroaty said, 'On our way.'

McQueen observed the streets. He had the feeling he was travelling through the veins of the city. At Charing Cross he saw the lights of the Mansions Café & Bar. Fun. Life as average people live it. He had the urge to instruct McGroaty to drop him off at the café where he could lose himself in the throng, have a couple of drinks, loosen up. Then he thought of Larry in his pyjamas.

Out west now, over the River Kelvin and buzzing along Dumbarton Road and then up into the dark red sandstone maze of Hyndland where Billy eyed the well-maintained tenements, the ornate cornices and rosettes and high ceilings you could see in rooms where curtains hadn't been drawn. Comfortable lives. He longed to scratch his stump which had begun to itch seriously. He felt fevered.

Somebody will be watching the house. It's a dead certainty.

He leaned forward to the driver. 'Alec, go round the block.'

'Awright,' McGroaty said.

The cab completed a circle of the building. Billy McQueen glanced up at the windows of his flat. The light was on in his father's room. The other windows were dark.

'Go round again,' Billy McQueen said.

McGroaty drove round the block a second time. Then he parked outside the entrance to the tenement McQueen would have to enter sooner or later. Billy peered from the cab at the security door. No sign of anyone loitering. But how could you tell if it was safe beyond the security door? How could you know there wasn't an intruder waiting for you? And even if the close was empty, there were about a million cars parked along the street and a dark figure could be sitting in any of them, just biding his time until you got out of the cab.

Billy, Billy, this is no kind of life. He said, 'Alec. Do me a favour.'

'If I can, Mr McQueen.'

'See if it's all clear.'

McGroaty turned and looked back at his passenger. 'Eh, how do you mean all clear?'

'Go inside the building, see if there's anybody loitering.'

McGroaty said. 'Is there the possibility of danger here, Mr McQueen?'

'There's somebody I don't want to see.'

'Aye, but is there *danger*? Do I have a guarantee of my *personal* safety?'

'I'll make your tip excessive,' McQueen said.

'You're scared, right? And you want me to test the waters for you?'

'Scared? Not at all. Just a precaution, Alec.'

McGroaty appeared to consider this. 'How much of a tip are you talking?'

'Fifty.'

'Could you make it an even hundred? I've got a kid –'

'– at Eton, and the fees are high?'

McGroaty laughed. 'Aye, they're extortionate.'

McQueen said, 'A hundred then.'

'I'm to make sure nobody's loitering in the building, zat all?'

'Exactly. Here's the key to the outside door.' McQueen handed McGroaty a key-ring. 'The big brass one opens the security door. Just go inside, see if anybody's hanging around, then come back and tell me. Got it?'

McGroaty said, 'Got it.'

McGroaty left the engine running. McQueen watched him walk up the path to the security door. McGroaty unlocked it, entered the building. The door swung shut behind him. Billy thought, I'm having a bad moment. I'm cut off from my lines of communication.

A man materialized in the driver's seat. A black shape.

Billy banged a fist on the glass partition that separated him from the driver. 'Hey, you, what the fuck? This is McGroaty's taxi.'

The man said, 'Just a wee detour, Billyboy.'

The cab moved slowly forward.

His heart scampering like a hot greyhound sprung from a trap, Billy reached for the door handle. I'll step out, I'll get away, I can do it, gammy leg or not. The door to his right opened and a girl jumped in beside him. She was big and wore black gloves with spiked attachments on the knuckles, and under the muted glow of a streetlamp Billy saw that her face was battle-hard and unforgiving and that her mouth was set in an expression of vicious determination.

'What the hell's this?' Billy shouted.

'Shut your fucking gob.' The girl slammed him in the mouth with one of her spiked gloves.

Billy felt brutalized, his face lanced with buckshot.

'Not another word out of you,' the girl said. 'Unless I say so.'

'Right,' Billy mumbled.

'That was a word, diddy,' and she backhanded him hard, and he felt the taxi turn upside down like a carnival ride that was making him ill.

34

Eddie let himself into Joyce's darkened flat. He switched on lights, calling his sister's name. No answer. He remembered she said she was going to see Senga. She was probably still there. Inside the bathroom he rummaged through the medicine cabinet and found Solpadeine capsules. He read the ingredients on the side of the box. Codeine, *far out*. He swallowed a couple of caps then walked into the living room, sat down on the sofa and massaged his face. He was motionless for a long time, weary. He had to stay alert to call Claire.

He thought about time differences, then his mind wandered to sequences of time lost – such as the period between Bones's disappearance from Jackie's parked car and his sanctuary in the safe house. Okay, Lieutenant, what have we got?

One: by prior arrangement Bones had abandoned the car, leaving the way clear for Jackie's killer. So Bones was an accessory to the murder. At some point after leaving Jackie at Blackfriars, Bones was conveyed to a police safe house.

Two: the killing of Jackie Mallon had been sanctioned by at least one cop, who'd ordered McWhinnie to pay off Bones's gambling debts and then smuggled him to safety. But Bones, for reasons unknown, had vanished from the safe house. Why leave a secure place? Why take that chance?

Was he forced? Coerced?

Eddie felt the Solpadeine begin to kick in, the glaze of codeine, the way pain receded behind a barrier, and he lost track of his thoughts for a time. You could grow to love codeine, he thought. He suddenly wished he had Tom Collins with him and they could toss ideas back and forward, bounce notions off one another the way they usually did. Tom bites into his maple-glazed donut and takes a drag on his cigarette, smoke and sugared dough all mixed up in his mouth, and he mumbles, *This whole scenario involves a bad cop at the heart of it, Eddie. I don't like these things, when the good guys go off the track.*

They don't thrill me either.

And Caskie's your candidate. What's in it for him? Money? Power?

Eddie shut his eyes. What does friendly Chris stand to gain from any of his machinations?

Tom Collins said, *The next step is the real toughie, Eddie –*

I know, I know where you're going –

Unavoidable, man. If Uncle Chris smuggled Bones to safety, then he colluded in the murder of Jackie Mallon –

Yeah –

Even if he didn't pull the trigger himself, Eddie, even if he's a shoo-in for fucking sainthood in Senga and Joyce's eyes, he told Bones to take a hike because he was setting Jackie up. He promises Bones a safe haven where he can wait for things to die down.

Eddie felt a certain druggy slippage, a mind-slope he was slithering down. Scree.

Tom Collins says, *Hey, if Caskie's really and truly tight with Haggs, then you gotta consider Haggs is also involved. Maybe he's the shooter. Maybe he just provided the shooter.*

Caskie and Haggs. Laurel and Hardy. A team. Did they have secrets from each other, or were they joined at the hip? In a codeine haze, it was tough to concentrate. He shook his head, massaged his eyelids. He reached for the handset on the coffee table, remembered the number of the international operator and asked to make a collect call to Claire.

'Hey, how are you?'

'I'm okay,' Eddie said. 'You and Mark?'

'We're great. You sound kind of . . . flat?'

'I'm just tired.'

'No, it's more than that,' she said.

How could she tell from a distance of three thousand miles? It was a gift she had. She knew from the first syllable of 'hello' if he was in a good mood or bad, if he'd had one beer too many, all kinds of things.

'I miss you,' he said. 'You're hearing a blue note.'

'By the way, Flora phoned,' she said. 'Wanted to know if I was doing okay. Like I'd founder in your absence. I love you with all my heart, Eddie, but I can still manage things here.'

'You told her so,' Eddie said.

'Gently.'

'Is Mark home?'

'He's at Chuckie Roth's house.'

'Tell him I called, would you? Give him my love. Tell him to look out for you.'

'I think you got that last sentence the wrong way round,' she said. 'Is Joyce hanging in?'

What was the point of mentioning the assault? He

said, 'I think so. You know Joyce. She has different levels.'

'And you don't go there.'

'Nobody goes there, sweetie. Not even Joyce, I suspect . . .'

'Any news? Any developments?'

'Nothing special to report.'

'Are you being straight with me, Eddie?'

Fuck. She missed nothing. He pictured her in the kitchen, phone tucked between jaw and shoulder. He heard water running in the background. She might be cleaning salad leaves at the sink, or filling a kettle for tea.

'It's complex,' he said.

She said, 'Murder usually is.'

He covered a yawn. 'I'm beat, love. I'll say goodnight.'

'Stay out of trouble,' she said.

'I always do. I love you.'

'Likewise, Eddie.'

When he put the handset down he sat for a minute and let the codeine flow easy through his system. The pains diminished. He had a flash of the encounter with McWhinnie; he smelled the rust on the railings he'd stumbled against. He got up, walked the room, tried in vain to summons Tom Collins again.

Blanked, he walked to the kitchen, drew a glass of water, felt a slight swoon. He bent down under the tap and soaked his head, and tried to ignore the tweak in his spine, that ripple of nerve. Dripping, he went back inside the sitting room and then he stopped on the threshold of Joyce's bedroom.

He went in, flicked on the overhead light.

Double bed unmade, a big quilt of American Indian design, a pile of books on the floor by the bed, an ashtray

251

filled to the max on the antique dressing table, books of matches from various bars and restaurants, *Groucho St Jude's*, *Trattoria Trevi*, *The Polo Club*, little mounds of clothing scattered here and there. It was a comfortable messy lived-in room. Eddie moved towards the fireplace which was made from carved walnut, little clusters of dark brown grapes and cherubs. The wood imparted warmth, like dark flesh under a hot sun.

There were photographs on the mantelpiece, some framed, others thumbtacked to the wall in a haphazard way. He saw Joyce on her graduation day, mortarboard and black gown and a smile on her face that suggested relief: I'm through with school. World, here I come. Jackie was alongside her, his hair not yet completely silver, sideburns a little unruly. He wore what looked like his best suit, the kind men always wear with an air of deferential discomfort, holding themselves as if the waistband's too tight and the pants starched. There was a wolfish quality to his smile. The light in the eye was sharp, but it was a middle-aged rake's light on the cusp of dimming. In this photograph Jackie had been – forty-nine? Fifty? He looked proud of what his daughter had achieved.

Next, photographed on the same day, Joyce and Caskie standing side by side. Joyce has the mortarboard held in front of her and her hair, long then, falls across her shoulders. Her smile in this shot dazzles. Caskie, beardless and strong-chinned, middle to late thirties, is as proud of Joyce as her own father. He's gazing into the camera with the straightforward honest look of a dad who's given wholehearted support to a daughter worth every drop of his sweat.

Fuck you, Chris, I want to scissor your goddam face out of the photo.

At the end of the mantelpiece there was a black-and-white picture Eddie had never seen before, and the sight of it disturbed him, although he couldn't say why precisely, except that the subject of this particular shot had been going through his mind like a hallucination only an hour or so earlier. Jackie holding Flora off the ground, cradling her as if she were as light as a baby, and Flora's black hair falls away from her face and she's smiling, she's happy, he's never seen that hot smile before, and Jackie – good-looking in a blazer and flannels, a genuine dude – has his head thrown back just a little, face frozen in mid-laugh. And just behind the stone steps where they're standing, just beyond wooden tubs of flowers, is the edge of a sign – 'IEW HOTE'. Eddie picked up the photograph and turned it over. Somebody had written, *Largs, June 1954, Seaview Hotel*. The honeymoon, Eddie thought. Young lovers. That blood fever, the crazed magnetism that binds husbands and wives together in a way that will never be quite the same again. It may stay strong, it may grow even stronger, but it will never be the same kind of bond as the first flourish, when even those simple words 'husband and wife' have an erotic charge.

Eddie fingered the picture as if he were trying to divine something that wasn't immediately apparent. He was suddenly depressed: the happy faces in the photograph couldn't know what thunderclouds were gathering ahead. You always saw old pictures with the privilege of hindsight. You knew the partings and the losses, the sorrows and the pains, that lay before the subjects. People were innocents when the shutter clicked. Frozen in a particular second, they had no futures.

He stepped away from the fireplace.

'Hello.'

He turned, saw Joyce. 'Caught me. I was snooping.'

'Feel free.'

'I'm sorry, Joyce.'

'No, seriously, I mean it, look around, take your time, I have nothing to hide from my own brother.'

'There are a couple of pictures here I hadn't seen before. Your graduation –'

'Lost youth,' she said. 'I look like I'm off to discover a new continent in those pictures. The intrepid explorer. Instead I teach secondary school in Shawlands.' She stepped closer to him. 'Have you been in a war? You're all wet and funny-looking and you've got a bruise like a map of Italy on the side of your neck. How did you get that?'

'I had an accident,' he said. 'I slipped.'

'Right, I noticed it's icy outside.'

He wondered if his ribs were purple too. The Solpadeine made these concerns remote.

'Tell the truth,' she said. She put a hand on her hip. He imagined her doing this in a class while she waited for one of her students to explain why he hadn't completed his homework.

'I was in a fight,' he said.

'A fight? You mean with fists? Who were you fighting?'

'I had a brief encounter with your acquaintance McWhinnie.'

'McWhinnie? You've taken to fighting with Glasgow policemen? Jesus Christ, Eddie.'

'We ended with a kinda truce,' he said.

'Dare I ask the reason behind the conflict?'

'He's been following me.'

'You're paranoid.'

'Bullshit.'

'Truth, paranoia, whatever. Are there any good reasons to get into a punch-up with a cop?'

'You sound like Flora when she was angry with me,' he said, and he looked at her small hand and how tightly it was clenched against her hip, which was thrust aggressively forward. Blue jeans, T-shirt, sneakers, even her clothes seemed combative. She wore no make-up, so no lipstick or face powder detracted from her eyes, which were burning on all cylinders.

'Well, fuck it, you deserve to be scolded,' she said. 'It's perfectly understandable that the Strathclyde Police don't like a cop from outside wandering round on their territory. You'd take kindly to some Glasgow policeman in Manhattan, I suppose –'

'Depends on what he was doing.'

'Tell me what it is *you're* doing exactly?'

'I have some questions about Jackie's death.'

'You and me both,' she said. 'We want the same thing, like what the hell he was up to at the end of his life, and what got him slaughtered in the back of his car, but fighting with the cops isn't going to help get answers.'

'You know what they're saying about Bones?'

'Chris told me.'

'Oh, right, Chris, good old Chris, he's practically family, after all,' Eddie said. The codeine forcefield short-circuited for a moment and he was a nest of pains, and suddenly furious. Restrain yourself. Chris was sacrosanct. He was a temple you couldn't enter unless you kicked off your shoes, then genuflected.

'I'm not a fan of easy sarcasm, Eddie. What have you got against Chris anyway?'

Eddie chewed the words in his mouth as if they were made from a substance he couldn't swallow. Pig's liver raw. *He's a goddam liar and crooked as a carnie game. You want the skinny on dear Chris, sister? He's bad to the bone. Let's ask Chris about Jackie's murder . . .* But he didn't get these words out. Instead, he took the merciful option. 'Look, the way I feel has probably got nothing to do with Chris. My perceptions are skewed, it's the shock of Jackie –'

'Shock, I'm beyond shock,' she said. 'Right now all I want is to get through this funeral.'

'Right now, what I'd like best is to drive a goddam nine-inch spike into the skull of whoever triggered the old man.' The vehemence in his voice surprised him; it was his first direct encounter with a raw need for retribution, an ugly jagged emotion.

'Hard words,' she said. 'Maybe later I'll feel the same way as you. Maybe I'll develop a deep longing for revenge.' She stepped closer to him. Her smile was sad. 'We shouldn't argue, we need each other.'

He held her. She felt limp.

He saw them reflected in the oval mirror, brother and sister clinging together. He looked big and ponderous compared to the wispy appearance of Joyce. 'I guess I've missed too much of your life. I'm out of the loop.'

'Then get back in,' she said. 'The door's open.'

'I'm working on it.' He looked over her shoulder, drawn back to the photograph of Jackie and Flora, honeymooners in 1954 in the Seaview Hotel, Largs. But it was Christopher Caskie he was thinking about, and his eye drifted to Caskie and Joyce, graduation day at the University of Glasgow, a man and a young woman who might, to an untrained eye, have been father and daughter.

Eddie squeezed his sister, then let her go.

'I just want away from death,' she said, 'and back into the light, if you know what I mean.'

'I know what you mean.'

He looked at Joyce and saw her once again as that little girl staring at him as he vanished in the back of a black taxi, bright ribbon in her hair and skipping rope dangling from one hand, but now another form took shape to complete the mural of that day, a memory he'd misplaced or buried, a recollection of Jackie standing just behind Joyce, his hands resting possessively on her shoulders, his face shadowed a little by shrubbery, his expression that of a proudly stubborn man who thought it a sign of courage to conceal his feelings, a man above showing the pain of departures, one who wouldn't beg for another chance because begging was a weakness. He'd sooner let his family disintegrate than ask for a fresh start. He understood only the terrible logic of endings. And yet – there was something else, a look within a look, masked, and Eddie realized it was the first inkling of a sorrow that would take Jackie Mallon many years to discover and explore.

A sadness filled Eddie, and he turned his face away from his sister and gazed through the window at the moon climbing the warm night sky, and he wondered what the weather had been like on the day of his enforced leave-taking, but that was one memory lost in the dross of things.

35

'I think you've had enough, sir.'

Charlie McWhinnie, clutching a napkin filled with ice-cubes to the side of his face, looked at the fat-necked man behind the bar of the Hilton and asked, 'Have I been aggressive? Have I been insulting to your other customers? Can you honestly say –'

'No, sir,' said the barman, who had a bright red face and long sideburns. 'You've been generally well behaved. It's just that you keep falling off your stool –'

'Gravity is the drunk man's enemy,' McWhinnie said. He scooped a palmful of peanuts from a little silver dish and tossed them towards his mouth. Mostly they went shooting past his face. 'A question. Are you happy in your work?'

'Aye. It has its moments.'

McWhinnie belched. His perceptions were unreliable. The room was turning in a slow circle. He felt he was a passenger on a precarious carousel. He narrowed his eyes and looked at his little notebook, which lay open on the bar. The pages were wet with booze and his fountain pen lay in a puddle of spilled drink. *Dear Diary, life is shit. When I was six years of age I fancied playing rugby for Scotland, heroics in the Murrayfield mud.*

'I'm working on a story,' he said.

'You a writer then?'

'More a keeper of records,' said McWhinnie. 'This barkeeping lark, you think I'd be good at it?'

'Requires social skills,' the barman said.

'Those I have in abundance.'

A hand fell heavily over McWhinnie's shoulder. 'What are you doing to yourself, my young pal?'

McWhinnie turned, saw Lou Perlman. 'Lou? What brings you here?'

'You did. You phoned.'

'Fuck me. Did I?'

'And the Good Samaritan came running. You're pissed as a newt, son. What happened to your face?'

'My face is irrelevant, Lou. Listen. Listen to me. A question. Am I or am I not cut out to be a cop? Honest opinion, Lou. No fluff. Straight answer now.'

'You don't want any kind of answer in your present state of mind, Charlie. Why don't you let me just drive you home, eh? What do you say? Come on.'

McWhinnie felt his stool listing to one side. 'I don't wanna go home, Lou.'

Perlman said, 'You look like hell. You need to lie down. What are you drinking for anyway? You feeling sorry for yourself?'

'I'm questioning my purpose, Lou.'

'Usually better to ask the really deep questions when you're clear-headed, Charlie. Just lean against me and we'll get you out of here. Okay?'

McWhinnie stuffed notebook and pen into his pocket and stepped down from his stool. He lurched towards Lou Perlman, missed and fell over. Perlman and the barman hauled him to his feet, then Perlman moved him a few steps in the direction of the exit, but it was a struggle.

'I do not want to be a fucking solicitor, Lou. Uh-huh. Not on your life.'

'What's biting your arse, Charlie?'

'My hands are dirty.'

'Is that a metaphor?'

McWhinnie planted a slobber of a kiss on Perlman's cheek. 'You're my best pal, Lou. The very best. You're a great man.'

'Right, I'm a fucking hero,' Perlman said, and guided McWhinnie down a short flight of steps. 'So your hands are dirty, and you're feeling worthless and your life has no direction?'

'Spot on,' McWhinnie said.

'And you want to quit the Force, eh?'

'You see into my soul.'

'No, I'm only remembering what you told me on the phone. Let me tell you what I see, Charlie. One weary cop plastered to the gills. You need sleep.'

'And dreams.'

'Aye, good ones.'

'Fucking *Caskie*,' McWhinnie said. *Cashkey*. 'That fucking Caskie gives me shite jobs to do. He thinks he's God.' He stumbled into a wall. Cubes of ice spilled from the napkin and cascaded over his blazer.

'He *is* God, Charlie. He invented *your* world, didn't he?'

'Bastard,' McWhinnie said.

'Steady there, son.' Perlman steered McWhinnie towards the exit doors. 'Caskie's got no supernatural powers. He's just an ambitious turd with a black heart.'

'I want to be inside a murder investigation, Lou. I want to be right at the heart of a hurricane.'

'Don't let Caskie get you down. The time'll come when you won't be spinning in orbit around him. You'll have moved on. Patience, laddie. There's no fast-track to happiness, in love or work.' Lou Perlman nudged McWhinnie out of the hotel. The sky over Glasgow was clear, a great star-show. 'Me, I'm a lucky sod, I love my work. It's the only thing in my life, Charlie. Do you think it'll ever be that way for you?'

'Suffering Jesus,' McWhinnie said, and tripped. He sat on the ground and smiled and looked up at Perlman. 'Not if I can bloody help it.'

Lou Perlman helped McWhinnie to his feet. 'By tomorrow you'll think you dreamed all this, Charlie.'

36

A building site where, except for a couple of pale bulbs strung around the perimeter wire, there wasn't much illumination, and Billy McQueen stumbled, pushed from behind by the girl. Sometimes the guy with the little moustache and the nose ring elbowed him sharply in the ribs.

'There's some confusion here,' Billy said. 'I don't know either of you. You've got me mixed up –'

'Shut your face,' the man said.

'I have money, I mean, I think we can come to some kind of understanding,' Billy said.

'One more word out of you,' the girl said. 'Warning you.'

Billy glanced back at her. She was fearful, a frightener with the spikes on her knuckles and the black leather gear that creaked as she walked, and a face like Desperate Dan's sister – if Desperate Dan had a sister, Billy was in no frame of mind to remember the comics of childhood. Desperate Dan ate enormous cow-pies, he remembered that. The horns of the beast protruded from the fucking pastry.

Why were they forcing him across this building site?

What part of Glasgow was this anyway? And what did they want with him? He had a flickering suspicion they were connected to Gurk, but he dismissed this because they were locals and he couldn't imagine Gurk using Glasgow heavies. He'd bring up muscle from London if he needed it.

The skeleton of a building loomed up in the dark, a structure in process, metal girders and framework and floors half-laid. It rose, solitary and sinister, to a height of about twelve storeys. Billy was aware of cement mixers and wheelbarrows and piles of brick around him, but these were marginal impressions because it was the incomplete building that seized his attention. What was it? A future block of flats? Offices? Another hotel? He thought: I was a moron to walk into this, to be lured from my beloved penthouse, to care enough for that bitter old sod Larry that I'd venture out into a night filled with danger – and for what?

This. A trap. I'll run. I'll run like the wind.

The Wan-Fittit Wind. You'll get nowhere, Billyboy.

He stared at the dim outline of the tower, saw here and there sheets of protective plastic.

'Here,' the man said.

'Here where?' Billy asked.

'You blind or something? Get on that.'

'On what?'

The girl shoved him forward. 'Move your arse.'

Billy McQueen shook his head. 'I'm not stepping on that,' he said.

The girl whacked his mouth with the spiked fist. Billy's head spun. Glasgow was going round and round.

'Just move,' she said.

She shoved him aboard the contraption, which was a

wooden platform of the kind used by window cleaners. It was attached to the outside of the building by a couple of ropes – a pulley, a bloody pulley, and that meant only one thing: I'm going up, Billy thought. I'm going way way up. I don't have a head for heights.

The man and the girl stepped on to the platform beside him. Billy shivered. His lips were numb. The night, although warm and wonderful if you were out on the town, felt arctic and spooky to him. He'd never been this cold. Well, maybe once, when the train in Cowcaddens went over his leg and he thought he felt the sub-zero chill of death settle on him as the ambulance-men raised him on to a stretcher.

'Up up and away,' the man said. He tugged on a rope and the platform began to rise.

'*On my beautiful balloon*,' the girl sang.

'Oh Jesus,' Billy said.

The platform swayed as it rose. It shoogled from side to side like an old Glasgow tramcar. Billy grabbed one of the ropes. There was nothing else to hang on to. No protective barrier, no handrail, just this sodding bloody rectangle of wood rising in the dark by means of ropes.

'Anything you want,' he said. 'Listen to me. I can give you each a hundred K cash. Just set me down on the ground and let me go.'

'*Would you like to fly, on my beautiful balloon*,' the young man croaked.

I am going to throw up, Billy thought. 'Two hundred each. Two hundred grand. Best I can do.'

The girl punched him in the stomach. The pain snatched his breath away. The platform continued to rise. Up and up, brushing close to metal girders, passing sheets of plastic, tendrils of unconnected electric wires that dangled and sometimes brushed the side of Billy's face. The air smelled of paint and fresh concrete and dry metal and epoxy.

The girl sang, *'On the roof where everything is free.'*

The young guy lit a cigarette. 'Great fucking view,' he said.

Billy looked, saw lights everywhere. The city was a triumph of the electric arts, yellow lamps, lights that shone on radio masts, traffic on motorways. Great view, completely terrifying.

Up and up, swaying, the creak of the pulley. He shut his eyes, but that was worse. How high was this tower? Height was an abstraction, the distillation of his fear. You couldn't measure it in feet or metres. You couldn't weigh it either. His body felt weird and buoyant.

'Must be great up here when there's a big wind blowing,' the young guy said.

I can only imagine, Billy thought. 'I can get you more money mibbe, if you give me a day or two.'

'Think you can buy anything you like, eh?' the young man asked. 'Sometimes that's not possible, McQueen.'

Suddenly the platform plunged six feet downward – and Billy thought, oh Jesus, this was the moment, this was when death came and took you. The grinning skull: *You're mine, sucker.* He was trapped in an airless space. The girl laughed, the platform swung away from the building, then the contraption levelled itself and the ascent continued as if nothing had happened, but Billy's heart was like that of a man wired to an electric chair and the clock is only seconds from the throw of the final switch. Oh sweet mother of Jesus, he thought. I'll do anything to get off this thing – and still it was rising, up and up for ever into a cosmic darkness.

Then the contraption stopped. The night was still and eerie.

'Step off,' the young guy said.

'Step off? Are you fucking mad? Step where?'

'Get off,' the girl said. 'End of the line.'

Billy saw only darkness stretch in front of him. The door of eternity. 'I'll fall, for Christ's sake.'

Suddenly a light went on inside the unfinished tower, a high-powered lamp at the end of a thick black cable. Billy blinked.

The figure who held the light said, 'Nice of you to come all this way, Billy.'

'Haggs,' Billy said. Oh Jesus.

'The very same, Billy. Now step off the platform and move towards me.'

'You're out of your mind, Haggs.'

The girl thumped him casually on the back of his skull. 'Do as you're told.' She said to Haggs, 'I think he wet his nappy on the ride up.'

'He's challenged in the lower limb department,' Haggs said. 'You need patience and understanding sometimes. Generosity towards your fellow man.'

'Aye, right enough,' the girl said, and snorted.

'Come on, Billy,' Haggs said. 'There's a good strong wooden bridge between you and me. No funny spaces. No loose planks. The support girders are magnificent. The building isn't going to fall down. Come on now, get your arse over here to me. It's only ten feet and there's bags of room. Nothing to be afraid of. We'll have a nice little chat.'

'Oh, this is standard practice for you, is it, Haggs? Hauling people a thousand feet up in the air for a meeting?'

266

'Just move, Billy,' Haggs said.

Billy McQueen stepped on to the wooden bridge. He felt wood under his feet, but it didn't fill him with a sense of security. The planks shifted a quarter-inch or so under his weight, and creaked, and he sensed the long drop, the horror. He thought he felt the tower sway. He looked down at the wooden crosswalk, judged it to be six feet wide, so if he stayed in the dead centre away from the edges he'd be fine, just fine, yes indeed. He stared into Haggs's lamp. It blinded him.

'Well done, Billy,' Haggs said.

Billy stopped about two feet away from Haggs, aware of movement on the bridge behind him. The girl and the young man stood on the walkway.

The girl said, 'Wheeee, it's magic up here,' and she balanced on one leg.

Haggs put an arm round Billy's shoulder. 'You can see all the way across the city. The lights over there? That's Castlemilk. You can see Rutherglen and Pollokshaws and Cathcart and if you look just to your left you'll notice the lamps round the City Chambers –'

My turf, Billy thought. My penthouse. Where I belong. Not out here on thin wood suspended between metal girders God only knows how high above the earth.

'There's Central Station and Buchanan Street – and look at all the bridges across the river and the way light reflects in the water. Can you see the Moat House Hotel, Billy?' Haggs had a certain proprietorial enthusiasm in his voice.

'I see it. Why am I here, Haggs?'

'Straight to business, eh? Don't like the spectacular panoramic view of our fair city?'

'I'm not fond of high buildings,' Billy said.

'Are you shivering, Billy? On a warm night like this?'

'I'm scared to fucking death,' Billy admitted.

Haggs clapped him on the shoulder. 'You've been hard to find. Why's that, I wonder? Troubles, Billy? Problems?'

'Oh, the usual business stuff. You know.'

'I think it's a wee bit different this time. Right? It's not your normal situation, is it? Speak to me about Gurk.'

McQueen shook his head. *There.* He was sure he felt the tower sway. It was one of those jerry-built affairs with cheapskate reinforced concrete, a corner-cutting operation, a fly-by-night cowboy piece of work. He wished he had something firm to hang on to. He wished he had a Velcro safety suit and could attach himself to a receptive surface.

'Gurk, Billy,' Haggs said. 'Talk. I am all ears.'

'Gurk. Right. Here's what I did. Mallon had some capital he wanted to invest. Sometimes I put people in touch with one another. One man has commodities, another man money. I get a commission.'

'Fuck's sake. Spare me your job description, Billy. So Mallon had money and Gurk had a commodity.'

'Right,' Billy said. He was morbidly drawn to peer over the edge of the walkway. He saw girders crisscrossing in the reach of Haggs's lamp; they were the colour of a battleship. Then you couldn't see the steel ribs, only dark, a big mouth waiting to be fed.

'What was Gurk's . . . commodity?'

'Don't ask me, Haggs. I only bring people together. I don't want to know what's passing from place to place. I only want my commission based on the total amount of the transaction, usually ten, sometimes fifteen, per cent –'

'I don't have the slightest interest in your fees, Billy. I'm asking you a simple question for the second time. What the fuck was the commodity Mallon wanted from Gurk?'

'I don't know. I didn't ask. The less I know the better. That's how I operate, Haggs. It also makes the principal parties feel better about doing business. Secrecy, confidentiality. They value that.'

'Twiddie.' Haggs nodded.

The planks of wood creaked. Billy was aware of movement from behind. His throat was seized in a fierce lock by the man Haggs had called Twiddie. Billy didn't have the strength to resist. Twiddie forced him to his knees then released him. Billy remained in this position, a supplicant before Roddy Haggs.

Haggs said, 'What you're telling me is you put Mallon in touch with Gurk, but you don't have a clue what was transacted between them?'

'Only in the fiscal sense.'

'Fuck fiscal! *Twiddie*.'

Twiddie's boot went into Billy McQueen's back. Billy felt a serious jolt of pain rush ruinously from spine to skull, and he fell forward on his face.

'I'll ask again, Billy. The commodity. The package. Whatever the fuck it was.'

'I told you, I don't ask questions like that.'

'Maybe you should. Maybe you should be more interested, Billy. *Twiddie*.'

Billy McQueen braced himself for more pain, but it didn't happen. Instead, Twiddie caught him by the shoulders and swung him round until his head dangled off the walkway and he was looking down into the void. How many storeys below, how far to fall? Billy shut his eyes, fought back a scream.

Haggs said, 'The leg, Rita.'

'The leg?' Billy asked.

'Remove the leg,' Haggs said.

'Will do,' said Rita.

'Hold on, wait a bloody minute,' McQueen said.

He heard a switchblade knife open and he tensed himself, expecting to be cut. But the girl didn't slash his flesh, only the material of his trousers, making a quick sharp slit to a point above the knee.

'Undo the thing,' Haggs said.

'Undo my fucking *leg*?' McQueen said. 'Wait, Haggs. Please.'

'Why? Have you got something to *tell* me?'

McQueen looked down into the black heart of the tower. He felt the girl's hand on his skin above the stump. 'It's the way I always do business, Haggs. I swear to God. I couple parties who may have mutual interests, and that's all I do.'

'Like a financial dating service, eh?' Haggs was quiet a moment. 'The leg, Rita. Yank the fucker off.'

'Please, Haggs,' McQueen said. 'If I knew anything more, do you not think I'd bloody well tell you?'

'The leg, Rita,' Haggs said.

The girl pulled on the exoskeletal prosthesis and said, 'It's hard. I never touched one of these before. What's it made of? Plastic? Wood?'

'It's a fucking peg leg and McQueen's Long John Silver,' Haggs said. 'Just tug the bloody thing, Rita.'

Rigid urethane foam, Billy McQueen thought. An inner foam core, outer lamination flesh-coloured, a solid ankle cushion heel foot – a SACH – attached with a bolt. *I am a trans-tibial amputee*, he thought. Clutching the edge of the wooden walkway and gazing down into the hollow spine of the building, he felt the girl remove the attachment roughly from his stump, and there was a jab of pain, and he shut his eyes.

'Toss it,' Haggs said.

'Toss it where?' Billy asked.

Rita let the prosthesis drop from her hand. It struck the walkway and bounced off the edge and fell into the dark and Billy listened to it bounce against girders as it plunged and then there was a long silence and he knew what Haggs had planned for him and he didn't believe it.

Talk your way out of this, Billy. He had tears in his eyes. He turned his head, looked up at Haggs.

'Don't, Roddy. Don't. Oh God, don't even think about it.'

Haggs put his foot on Billy's spine. A little pressure. 'Here's the story, Billy. You only have to tell me what the transaction was about. That shouldn't be hard.'

'Haggs, listen to me, please, a guy called Kaminsky phoned me from Zurich, and asked me did I know somebody with cash to invest, and about the same time Mallon had been asking me if I knew how he could make a good quick profit, something for his retirement, and all I *fucking did*, Roddy, was plug the parties into one another. Kaminsky's man Tommy Gurk and Jackie Mallon. That's gospel . . . Maybe it was drugs.' Think hard think fast, Billy, think like you never thought before.

'Drugs? Jackie Mallon? Nope. He wouldn't touch narcotics. He considered them evil. Work of Satan.'

'Okay, how about stolen property, antiques and stuff?'

'He's got nothing but junk in that warehouse,' Haggs said. 'Floor to ceiling shite. I've seen better antiques at a dump.'

'He planked them somewhere else, a safe place.'

'You know where?'

Think harder Billy harder. 'Mibbe he rented an empty house and stored these antiques inside –'

'And you have the address, Billy?'

'No –'

'You're guessing, chuck. And I'm wasting my time.'

'Wait, Roddy –'

'Ah, fuck this,' Haggs said. 'Twiddie.'

Twiddie stepped towards Billy. Haggs said, 'Send him in search of his leg.'

You're sending me nowhere, you bastarts. Billy McQueen gripped the edge of the walkway as hard as he could. His fingers locked. His knuckles were like rivets. His body was bolted to the wood. Nobody is moving me. Not so much as an inch. Then Twiddie stepped hard on his hand. Billy heard bone crack and pain fuse through him and he hauled his hand out from under Twiddie's boot. And before Billy could think of a response that might save him Twiddie smashed the boot down on the other hand, and Billy yelped and felt himself being pushed towards the edge, shoe-horned into the brink of a long dark descent. Rita and Twiddie dangled him from the walkway. Rita held the stump, Twiddie the ankle, and Billy hung lopsided in the air.

'*Roddy oh no, for God's sake, have a heart.*'

'It's not such a distance to fall, Billy,' Haggs remarked. 'Be brave. Be a soldier. Meet your maker with a brisk salute.'

'*Noooo, Roddy, dear Jesus, no –*'

Billy McQueen was released as casually as the wrapping of a toffee-bar and he plummeted, screaming for barely a few seconds, down the cylinder of the building.

On the descent he had an illusory sense of flight, of angels feathering the air about him with their wings. *We'll save you, William McQueen.* He was dead before he hit the ground, his skull shattered against a girder.

Rita said, 'I bloody hate it when they scream.'

Haggs stared out across the city. He thought of his taxicab fleet going back and forth, ferrying passengers through the night. He thought of people driving hired cars from his company. Cash registers rang in his head. But he wasn't satisfied.

What he sought was out there somewhere, secreted in one of the many thousands of black pockets where no light fell. He thought: I'm missing something. And whatever it is I'm obsessed with it.

37

Was it Thursday, or had he mislaid a day somewhere?

Eddie woke at nine a.m., got up from the sofa. He pulled open the curtains: the sun was ruthless. He glanced into the street, saw a patrol-car parked diagonally across the street: Caskie's watchdog keeping Joyce safe. He showered quickly and dressed in a white SUNY T-shirt and black jeans. In the kitchen he found a carton of fresh orange juice. He poured some, drank quickly. He was dehydrated and his neck ached and his ribcage creaked like the hull of an old boat. There was a niggling friction in the small of his back and he pictured tiny vertebrae knocked a fraction out of alignment. He cut a chunk of cheddar from the block in the fridge, then filled his glass again.

Joyce stepped into the kitchen. She was smartly dressed in a green linen jacket and brown slacks. 'I overslept. I don't even have time for coffee.'

'What's the rush?'

'I have a meeting at school, some bloody boring committee business about the curriculum for next year.'

'You can't get out of it?'

'I could, but I feel I should keep busy, even if it's only

half-hearted.' She drank orange juice from the carton, then stuck it back in the refrigerator and looked thoughtfully at Eddie. 'Did you ever hear of a man called Billy McQueen?'

Eddie shook his head. 'Who's he?'

'I just caught an item on the news,' Joyce said. 'I wasn't concentrating on the details. A guy by the name of Billy McQueen was found dead last night . . . there are probably a dozen Billy McQueens in Glasgow, but one of Dad's old cronies was called by that name. I was just wondering if it was the same guy. Senga might know.'

'Dead in what circumstances?' he asked.

'Sorry. I wasn't paying close attention . . . the name just popped out at me.'

'I'll ask her,' he said. 'I was going to drop in on her anyway.'

She kissed Eddie's cheek, then she was gone in a flutter, before he could ask any more questions. He heard the front door close. Billy McQueen: the name meant nothing to him. How could it? He swallowed a Solpadeine. He rose from the table slowly; a mass of aches, bundled pains. He wondered how McWhinnie felt this morning. He walked back into the sitting room where the old busts regarded him balefully. He felt a kinship with their battered broken faces.

He left the flat. The morning was hot. The shadows between the tenements were warm and lifeless. He longed for a breeze, even one so weak it barely stirred shrubbery. He crossed Whitehill Street. He was sweating by the time he reached Onslow Drive.

Senga let him into the house, hugging him exuberantly in the doorway. How could she know the sensitive condition of his ribs? In pain, he bit his lower lip. He smelled gin on her breath; she kissed his cheek with her lipsticked mouth. She led him into the living room.

Two men sat side by side on the sofa.

'Joe Wilkie, Eddie,' she said. 'You already met at the yard.'

Wilkie wasn't wearing his glasses, and his pallid round face had the look of a full moon. 'Eddie,' he said. 'Nice to see you again.'

'Same here,' Eddie said.

Senga said, 'The good-looking one is Ray, Joe's son.'

Ray got up. Eddie shook hands with the young man. Ray Wilkie's grasp was slack and quick, as if he disliked the connection of flesh. Shy, Eddie thought. Or evasive. It depended on your point of view, on what you wanted to see. Ray Wilkie held himself in a slightly stooped manner – which he may have copied from the stance of Joe – and he had a tendency to avoid eye contact, looking down at the carpet much of the time. He wore a sharp black suit, lightweight, short lapels.

'Pleasure,' Ray said. His voice had the same pitch as his father's.

'You been in the wars, Eddie?' Senga asked.

Eddie smiled. 'I slipped, dumb of me,' and he wondered how many times he'd have to explain his bruises.

'We were just having a drink. Can I get you anything?' Senga asked.

'Water's fine,' he said. She went out of the room, patting Eddie's shoulder as she passed. He watched her go in big strides, her arms pale in her long-sleeved black blouse. A silvery thread ran through the material and glimmered.

Not ten a.m. yet. She'd started early, Eddie thought. He noticed a half-empty glass of beer in Joe Wilkie's hand, and Ray nursed a small shot of scotch. They'd all started early.

Joe Wilkie said, 'You must be thinking we're hard-core boozers, Eddie. Eh? When Senga forces a drink on you, you don't refuse it.'

'I can believe that,' Eddie said. He looked at Ray, who gazed into his drink. He had fair eyelashes.

Senga came back carrying a glass of water stuffed with ice cubes. Eddie took it. 'Cheers,' he said.

The Wilkies raised their glasses. Eddie held his iced water in the air. The atmosphere in the room struck him as a little awkward, as if he'd intruded on something of a private nature.

Senga said, 'We were talking about a man called McQueen.'

'McQueen? Is this the same man who was mentioned on the radio?' Eddie asked. He felt a weird little flutter in his chest, a shudder of pulse: it was as if he'd had a premonition and it was coming true.

'Aye,' Senga said. 'You never knew him, did you? He was a friend of Jackie. They did some business together.'

'What happened to him exactly?'

'They found him on a building site in Maryhill,' Wilkie said. 'He fell off a high-rise tower some time last night. Workmen found him this morning early. Nobody knows what the hell he was doing up there to begin with. The place isn't even completed. A man with one leg . . . what's he climbing up there for? It's all scaffolds and ladders, for Christ's sake.'

Wilkie said, 'He lost the lower half of a leg in a subway accident years ago.'

'I heard it was a train,' Ray Wilkie said.

'Train, subway, what damn difference does it make?' Joe said to his son.

Ray shrugged and looked into his scotch, his expression one of deflation. It was obvious he never won arguments with his father.

Eddie said, 'You're telling me this guy McQueen climbed a building in the dark – an unfinished building – and *fell* to his death.'

'Aye, right,' Wilkie said. 'Fell . . . they say. On the other hand, mibbe he was shoved.'

'Shoved?'

'Well, I'm betting he didn't climb that fucking building just for the hell of it,' Wilkie remarked. 'I'm betting he had company *egging* him on.'

Senga shook her head, sighed in the manner of somebody retreating from the horror of the real world. Eddie glanced at her and wondered where she'd gone in her mind, what sanctuary behind those closed eyes, and then he thought of a man plunging from a high building through darkness. He remembered the jumper in downtown Manhattan the morning of the day he caught a flight to Glasgow. Now a one-legged man, an occasional business associate of Jackie's, climbs a high-rise block in a place called Maryhill, then falls to his death. He was either a suicide or somebody had forced him to climb in the first place. You could menace the hell out of somebody if you were twenty storeys up and the building had no floors. You could get them to promise you anything, tell you anything.

An associate of Jackie's.

Coincidence? Was it a fluke that Jackie and McQueen had died within days of each other? Sometimes if you chipped away at coincidence you unearthed a message,

278

if you knew how to decode it. At other times all you got was gobbledygook.

'What kind of business did he do with Jackie?' Eddie asked.

'He was sort of a financial adviser,' Senga remarked.

'Something like that,' and Joe Wilkie made a wobbly gesture with his hand, to suggest that 'financial adviser' was a term to be interpreted loosely in McQueen's case.

Senga said, 'Jackie liked him. Now he's dead. A couple of days after Jackie . . .' She reached for his empty glass. 'Refill?'

'Please.' He got up and followed her into the kitchen. He watched her fill his glass at the sink. He felt a heavy sadness: it was as if Jackie had fallen from that building and not McQueen, a complete stranger. They're connected, he thought. *They have to be.*

She handed him his glass. Eddie sipped. 'Tell me more about McQueen.'

'I didn't know him all that well. I saw him maybe half a dozen times in all. We exchanged a hello, how are you, but that was it. I seem to remember he lived with his father, who's an invalid.'

'Had he done business with Jackie recently? Did Jackie mention his name lately?'

'I'm racking my brain, Eddie. McQueen . . .' She drifted into silence, gazing at the kitchen window, the garden beyond, the entanglement of shrub and stalk that was dry in the sunlight. She looked at Eddie and snapped her thumb and middle finger. 'It seems to me Jackie said he saw Billy McQueen about two weeks ago. Maybe less than that. Jackie came in, sat at the kitchen table, opened his newspaper and then he said, quite casually, he'd seen Billy. It was an aside. Small talk.'

'Did he say why they met?'

Senga shrugged. 'He didn't say whether it was by arrangement, or if they'd run into one another on the street or in a pub. No details. I got the impression he *might* have talked to McQueen, but I didn't get the feeling it was for business reasons. Maybe they had a drink together, and passed the time of day and talked football. I don't know, Eddie.'

Senga reached out and held both his hands in a gesture he found strangely comforting. She emanated warmth. 'There's an expression on your face that puts me in mind of the look I used to see on my own mother when she was trying to stitch together a patchwork quilt. It's concentration with a dash of frustration. Is that what you're doing, Eddie? Trying to make your own patchwork quilt?'

'I didn't think of it that way,' he said.

'She pricked her finger with the needle sometimes,' Senga said. 'I remember that. When she bled, she always stuck her fingertip inside her mouth. Funny what we remember and what we forget.'

Eddie imagined the tip of a needle puncturing his skin: the moral of Senga's fable didn't elude him. He sipped water, played with a cube of ice on his tongue. McQueen meets Jackie. They talk. Both of them are dead within days of each other. What did it mean?

He looked into the back garden. Years ago, a wooden swing had hung from an old elm. The elm was no longer there. The swing was a phantom.

'You took Jackie to Central Station last week,' Eddie said. 'What time?'

'You're just like the tide, Eddie. You keep rolling in. Ten thirty-five a.m.'

'You sure about that?'

Senga said, 'That's a precise answer. Jackie was adamant about it. We had to get to the station no later than ten thirty-five. We got stuck in a traffic jam for about ten minutes and I thought he was going to blow a fuse.'

'But you made it,' Eddie said.

'We made it.'

Eddie touched the side of her face. He liked this woman. He imagined her looking after Jackie. Cooking his food, ironing his shirts, all the domestic support. Jackie was of a generation that didn't know how to do these things. He imagined Senga and Jackie Mallon fretting in gridlocked traffic, Jackie hunched forward and tense in his seat, Senga reassuring him. We'll get there. Don't worry. You'll make your appointment, whatever it is.

'He said he wanted sea air,' Eddie said.

Senga nodded. 'Aye.'

'Where could he go from Glasgow Central for sea air?'

Senga was quiet a moment. 'Ardrossan,' she said. 'Troon.'

'Largs?' Eddie asked.

'Largs, certainly.'

38

Tommy Gurk focused on his dish of passion-fruit ice cream so hard that the small pink confection appeared to glow. Staring at things to the exclusion of objects or happenings on the periphery of his vision – the other customers in the café, the clack of cutlery, the flutter of waitresses – produced an intensity of such purity he felt he melded in some way with the object of his attention. This ice cream was more than a concoction of fruit pulp and cream and sugar: it became an inherent part of Gurk's being. *The Oneness of Things.* Beyond appearance there was essence. Essence was eternal. Life was without end. You came back time and again. A human, a goat, a toad, whatever.

I want to be an eagle next time out, Tommy Gurk thought. His karma worried him, though. He had too much going in the debit column. He'd be a worm or woodlouse or tick, his bleeding luck.

His cellphone rang.

It was Joe Kaminsky, whose heavy accent Gurk sometimes couldn't penetrate. Polish, Russian, who could tell? Kaminsky, who'd feed you vodka until you were hallucinating, and force piles of wild boar and truffles and Beluga into you, who'd take the shoes off his feet and gift them to you if you happened to mention how handsome they looked, was an absolute skinflint when it came to his past. Like he was drawing a blackout curtain across his history. End of. Past is dead, man.

Gurk wondered, but never asked. Asking would be unhealthy. Perhaps fatal. He wasn't finished with this incarnation anyway. Things to do. Discoveries to make.

'I picked your message up,' Kaminsky said. 'McQueen has perished. This is bad.'

'Yeh,' Tommy Gurk said, remembering McQueen's invitation to dinner last night. If he'd accepted, then Billy might be alive today. You just never knew these things.

Kaminsky said, 'Murdered, of course.'

'He fell from a high place.'

'I know many people who have fallen from high places, friend. So now. What to do? What is next step?'

'I was hoping you'd have some wisdom to impart,' Gurk said.

'McQueen was the lemon. He might have been squeezed a little harder. Now we have no McQueen, and that means no lemon juice, correct?'

'As you say.' Gurk looked at his passion-fruit ice cream, which was melting. Buddha is in everything, he thought. In melting ice cream, McQueen's death, a canister of mace. All life was an encounter with the True Path.

Kaminsky said, 'I have always said this deal was stinking. Like a dead cod. It has never felt to me right. Find the ones who killed McQueen. Start there.'

'I can't just pluck names out of thin air, Joe.'

Kaminsky sucked on something. A slice of orange. Coffee. Maybe that tea with honey he liked. 'I will help you, of course. Information has been telephoned to me only in the last hour. It has come to me from a source in Glas-cow. Unexpectedly, but why look inside a gift horse's mouth, huh? I will give you this name. You memory it.'

'My ears are pricked.' Gurk pictured Kaminsky's small black shades and the set of whiskers he sported. They made him look like an Eastern potentate.

'And no writing this on paper,' Kaminsky said.

'Gotcha.'

Kaminsky spelled out the name with exaggerated care, and then an address. He went on to add, 'To your hotel will be delivered a package. In a few hours from this time now. You will need what it contains. In Glas-cow, a car will be available to you. You will find details of the location in the package. Do this job. Do it fast and do it well.'

'Gotcha. Nod's as good as.'

'What is this, this nod?'

'Slang, Joe.'

'I never understand this English slang, never.'

'You need to be born into the environment, Joe.'

'Pah,' Kaminsky said, and cut the connection.

Gurk went out of the café and stood for a time watching seagulls in the morning sky and sun on bright water. He drew the smell of brine into his lungs: satisfying.

39

Eddie walked from the house in Onslow Drive towards Alexandra Parade, where he'd find a taxi for the city centre. On the corner of Craigpark and Golfhill Drive a wine-coloured Jag drew into the kerb directly in front him, braked hard and Roddy Haggs stuck his head from the window. Surprise surprise, Eddie thought. Haggs had been tracking him. How else to explain his sudden appearance in this part of the city?

Haggs said, 'Just the man I'm looking for. Get in the car.'

Eddie hesitated.

'A minute's all I need. Come on.' Haggs opened the passenger door without getting out. Eddie climbed in. The interior smelled of leather and cigar smoke. Haggs, dressed in an expensive pin-striped suit, smiled and cracked his knuckles. The car stereo was playing 'Rhapsody in Blue'.

'I like this,' Haggs said. 'Gershwin. Always like a bit of George and Ira. Funny name for a fella, Ira.'

'Yeah. What's on your mind?'

'You,' Haggs said.

'Any specific context?'

Haggs laughed: *chukka chukka chukka*. 'Always looking for the angles, eh? You've got a cop's brain.'

Eddie didn't like Haggs's laugh. He tapped his fingertips on his knees.

Haggs said, 'I won't delay you, wherever you're going. I have something for you. A wee present.' He reached behind, retrieved a white paper bag from the back seat and opened it. He removed a varnished pine box about eighteen inches long and six wide, with brass hinges. It was highly polished and Eddie saw his reflection in it. Haggs set the paper bag, which bore the name Emporio Armani, on his lap, and then laid the box on top of it.

'Here's the thing,' Haggs said. 'A man dies, and you realize maybe you should've been closer to him when he was alive, and a wee bit kinder. You following me?'

'You're talking about Jackie,' Eddie said.

'Right. I could've tried harder. We might've done business together if we'd been less stubborn. Allies. Know what I'm saying?'

Eddie looked at the box. 'Now you regret missed chances.'

'Aye. I was up late last night thinking about them and . . .' Haggs's voice faded away. 'Take this last deal he was into. We could've done something together . . .'

'What deal is that?'

'He never mentioned the specifics, Eddie. And I've been less than honest with you, I admit.'

'Really,' Eddie said.

'You heard we argued. I told you I'd forgotten the reason.'

'And that was a lie?'

Haggs looked contrite. I'm expected to buy the expression, Eddie thought.

Haggs said, 'This is the way it was. Jackie needed some extra cash to finance his deal. He asked me to participate. He didn't say what the biz was. I was supposed to trust him. I said, you're asking a hell of a lot, Jackie. He said, Haggs, you're too fucking cautious. And if I ever decided to put my faith in him I could come back with the green. Then I thought, what the fuck, I'll take a chance, a bit of a flyer, I'm not short of a few quid after all – but it was just too bloody late, and Jackie was . . .' Haggs shut his eyes a moment and looked sadly pious.

'He invited you into a deal,' Eddie said. 'Only you didn't know what it was.'

Haggs, eyes still shut, spoke softly. 'Aye.'

'You didn't tell me this yesterday.'

'I felt fucking awkward about it, Eddie. I didn't want you thinking I'd turned your dad away like that. Let him down.'

No way, Eddie thought, although he enjoyed Haggs's act, the flicker of shut eyelids, the dry solemn tone of contrition in the voice, the *mea culpa* of it all. He watched Haggs's eyes open and how they swivelled towards him without the man's face having to turn.

Haggs said, 'Maybe the deal still has legs. Maybe it's alive and kicking and just waiting to be financed. I'm thinking of Senga, Eddie. She might be hurting for money.'

'Ask her,' Eddie said. 'Maybe she'll be able to tell you something.'

'I have a sneaky feeling Senga doesn't like me,' Haggs said. 'Some past misunderstanding. I have every regard for her, Eddie. Believe me. But I think my best approach . . . well, it's through you.'

'You want me to ask Senga? You want me to tell her

that Roddy Haggs would like to partner her in a business deal? Maybe even become her benefactor?'

Haggs smiled. 'You've picked me up wrong, Eddie. I'm not thinking along that road. I'm wondering if . . .' He hesitated, eyeballed the street as if he suspected that the scraggle of shrubbery might conceal an enemy.

'Wondering if *I* know anything?' Eddie asked.

'Right.'

'If Jackie confided in me?'

'Now you're talking.'

Eddie smiled, tilted his head back. From the corner of his eye he was aware of the glossy box in Haggs's lap. His gift. 'I hate to disappoint you, Roddy. Jackie phoned me a few times when I was in New York, but he never talked business.'

'Not once, eh?'

'Not once,' Eddie said.

'Ah well.' Haggs sighed and opened the box and took out the Kentucky Flintlock pistol and weighed it in the palm of his hand. 'I brought you this, Eddie. You seemed to admire it yesterday. I want you to have it.'

'I can't accept that,' Eddie said.

'Take it, for Christ's sake. I'll be annoyed if you refuse.'

'I can't take it, Roddy. It's too expensive.'

'Money, money's pish, there's always loadsa money,' Haggs said. He lifted the pistol and levelled it and, closing one eye, stared along the barrel at Eddie.

He held this position and the light in his eye was pure concentration, as if Eddie were a target. 'You could blow somebody's head clean off from this range,' he said.

'No problem,' Eddie remarked.

'You really could.'

'I'm convinced.' Eddie gazed into Haggs's face and the

fierce brightness in his eyes and for one bad moment he wondered if the man had gone insane and planned to kill him. *American Cop Slain in Glasgow Suburb.* A random murder, inexplicable and irrational. He imagined Jackie looking down the barrel of a gun. Jackie's terror. Jackie's life came to this in the end, a hole, a bleak aperture.

'One shot,' Haggs said.

'That's all it would take for sure,' Eddie said.

He felt sweat form on his body and his T-shirt stick to his skin. Haggs wasn't going to shoot, this was some form of threat, a demonstration of what he could do if he took it into his mind. This was Haggs flexing muscle, pumping his own kind of iron. The gun was a Nautilus machine, an exercise bicycle. *I can shoot you the fuck into oblivion if I want, Eddie baby.*

Haggs said, 'Now if I had a beef against somebody. Boom.'

'Yeah,' Eddie said.

'Do I have a beef against you, Eddie?'

'I hope not.'

'I wouldn't like to have a beef against Jackie's son.'

'I wouldn't like to give you a reason,' Eddie said.

'Sometimes I wish duelling was still legal. Pistols at dawn. Name your seconds. One man facing another. Equality of chance. You'd tell me if you remembered Jackie mentioning anything.'

'Yeah, for sure.'

'I'm fucking serious, Eddie. I'd like to give Senga a helping hand. After all, she's a widow, give or take a legal document. So don't just put the matter out of your mind. Understand me?'

Haggs moved the gun an inch closer to Eddie. It was one of those moments when your life is a gyroscope turning on a wire. Eddie felt a drop of sweat slide down his nose and trickle to his upper lip.

'You have my word,' Eddie said.

'Your word, terrific. Wonderful.' And Haggs laughed, lowered the weapon. 'Note to self: Eddie Mallon doesn't like looking down the wrong end of a gun. Even when it's unloaded,' and he laughed again, delighted with Eddie's visible unease. 'Oh, Christ, I enjoy a wee bit of mischief. The secret lies in looking serious.'

'You looked pretty serious all right,' Eddie said. He felt strangely out of balance, as if sunstruck. He was thirsty.

Haggs boxed the weapon, shut the box and stuck it back in the Armani bag, then passed it to Eddie. 'She's all yours, Eddie. Look after her. Grease her from time to time.'

Eddie took the bag. 'I don't know what to say.'

'Just don't forget where you got the gun,' Haggs said.

'Count on it.'

Eddie pushed the passenger door open.

'Need a lift anywhere?' Haggs asked.

'No, really, I'm fine.' Eddie got out of the car.

Haggs laughed again and said, 'Hi-ho Silver,' and the big Jaguar screamed away, tyres burning, engine roaring. Motionless under the high hot cinder sun, Eddie clasped the Armani bag to his chest and thought, Yeah, Haggs looked pretty serious all right, goddam serious, like a man with more than a passing acquaintance with deadly violence.

40

Sometimes when Detective-Sergeant Lou Perlman listened to experts, forensic know-alls with their university ties and big brains, his attention wandered. After all, what did he *really* need to know about the temperature at which paper burned, or the amount of oxygen required to conduct flame through a narrow enclosed space? Cubic this and cubic that. It was all just so much slosh, like milky tea spilled into a saucer.

'Is there a point you're getting to, Sid?' he asked, sounding raspy and sullen. 'No hurry anyway. I've got all bloody day to waste.'

Sidney Linklater, a graduate of Edinburgh University, thirty-three years of age and a Force Support Officer – a *civilian* – blinked at Lou Perlman in surprise. It always astonished him that others could fail to be fascinated by his world of fibres and threads, of flames and melting points, of decomposition and putrefaction. He likened the non-scientific mind to an asteroid turning pointlessly in space.

'All right, I'll hurry along, Lou, if you're finding this a bit of a bore,' he said.

'Don't get your knickers in a twist, Sid. Some of us

are cut out to be scientific. Others of us are just men with big feet and big bunions and wee brains. Like me. The dogged sort. We pound pavements. We're happy just chugging along. Clip clop. Fucking Clydesdales in human clothes.'

'I find false modesty indigestible,' Linklater said.

'So is all your fucking data, Sid. No offence intended.'

Linklater said, 'Sometimes I feel like a missionary preaching to savages.'

'I *am* a savage, Sid. Keep that in mind when you talk to me. Simple words. Short sentences. See Dick pish. See Spot shit. Remember, I was brought up in the Gorbals. Correction. I was *dragged* up. We'd only just got electricity installed the day before the demolition people moved in. I'm a child of the gaslight generation. We didn't have PCs and websites. Ours wasn't the Information Age. We knew fuck all.'

'And I was delivered by a stork.'

'Oy vey,' Perlman said. 'Those hankie deliveries can be tricky.'

Linklater shrugged and looked round his workroom. Assorted objects, seemingly unconnected to one another, sat on shelves. Two pairs of Wellington boots. A charred shotgun. A couple of hunting knives with shiny blades. Bottles of various chemicals. A bicycle bent out of shape. Spades, trowels, a big fishing net. A microscope, also a load of computer gear that Perlman, who was quite proud of being misaligned with the electronic age, couldn't identify – maybe they were scanners, or photograph enhancers, or some kind of UV equipment, who cared?

Not Lou Perlman.

Linklater, whose hobby was making charcoal rubbings from ancient tombstones, pushed his glasses up his long nose and gazed down at his work-table. He wore see-through plastic gloves. In his right hand he held a pair of tweezers. 'Let's go the number one route just for you, Lou. No frills. No fancy cocktails.'

'My boy,' Perlman said.

There was debris on the table, and Linklater poked at it. One plastic ashtray, a couple of misshapen cigarette filters. A small pile of wet ash and scraps of scorched paper. A square wallet of black leather lay to one side in a small dark puddle. There was a smell of petrol.

'These would-be arsonists splash a little petrol inside the van,' Linklater said. 'Strike a match, drop it in, buzz off. They leave the window on the passenger side open – a slit, no more than that. They overlook a basic principle of the firemaker's skill. Flame needs oxygen. This fire goes, but it isn't the spectacle it's supposed to be. Some of the spilled petrol burns, sure, but this isn't a movie, Lou. The tank isn't going to blow up. We get some flame, enough to destroy the fabric on the seats. More dramatic black smoke than flame. The fire suffers oxygen deprivation, so it's too slow for the light display the arsonists must've wanted. Anyway, there's bugger all in the back of the van to burn, no rags, no papers, nothing, just this wallet . . . then along comes the fire brigade, hoses blasting. The wallet was just beginning to ignite. There was blood on the floor of the van which the firemen, despite their zeal, didn't manage to hose entirely away. It's AB neg. No fingerprints on the steering wheel. Some in the interior. There's mud on the tires. Fresh.'

Linklater touched the wallet with a latexed fingertip. 'I emptied it carefully,' he said. 'I set the contents over here,' and he tweezered to the side a sheet of opaque plastic, under which lay banknotes that had been browned along the edges, scarred first by fire then doused with water. Linklater gently shoved the wilting money aside and concentrated on a sheet of lined paper.

'This appears to be a page out of a cheap notebook, Lou. The writing's felt-tip and the water's made it run. It seems to be some arrangement of numbers. An accounting, maybe. Somebody adding and subtracting.'

'Ah-hah. What else have you got?'

'It wasn't exactly *stuffed* with goodies,' Linklater said. 'But there's this.' He edged a piece of folded pink and green paper towards Perlman, who bent forward and looked at it through his one good eye. The other eye, lid still swollen from the insect bite, smarted beneath the patch.

'A driving licence,' Perlman said.

He bent until his face was only six inches from the table. There was no photograph in the licence, but the name of the owner was legible. Perlman heard birdsong in his head. He straightened up and smiled, and in a very bad voice cranked out an 80s song lyric. *'The tide is high, I'm moving on.'*

'What in God's name is that appalling noise?' Linklater asked, feigning great terror.

41

Eddie Mallon met Christopher Caskie in a café a couple of blocks from Force HQ. It was a fashionably relaxed place with ferns and high arches and pretty waitresses, unlike the mutton-pie and strong-tea brigade of grim aproned matrons Eddie remembered from Glasgow restaurants years ago. The girls who served you were good-looking, moussed hair, modishly pale complexions. Eddie ordered a bottle of mineral water, espresso and a chocolate croissant. Caskie, with a prim little nod of his head, asked for tea.

'Nice room,' Eddie said.

'I come here now and again,' Caskie remarked. 'Is that a bruise on the side of your neck?'

'I had an upset,' Eddie said. 'I lost my footing.'

'Sorry to hear that. I hope it's not too serious.'

'It's fine.' Did he know? Had McWhinnie told him? Eddie seriously doubted McWhinnie would make a report of their encounter.

'Been shopping?' Caskie nodded at the bag.

Eddie set it on the floor and said, 'Just something for Claire.'

'Nice thought,' Caskie said. 'You phoned, so am I

forced to assume you have more tricky questions for me? See if I can guess. It's about Tommy G.'

The waitress, a lovely trim girl in short black skirt, had a good-natured face. She set coffee, croissant, Strathmore water and tea on the table. 'If you need anything else, let me know,' and she was gone discreetly. Eddie swallowed the mineral water instantly, then tasted his coffee and bit into his croissant.

Caskie said, 'I ran the name, Eddie. The computer has no record of Tommy G.'

'I'm surprised,' Eddie said.

'I am too.'

'You'd expect –'

'I always try to avoid expectations,' Caskie said. He tasted his tea and made a face. 'I don't remember asking for herbal . . .'

Tommy G: a blind alley. Eddie swallowed the last of his croissant. 'Did you run it as Tommy G or Tommy G E E?'

'Both.'

'Are there other sources you can try?'

'They take time.'

I don't have time, Eddie thought. A funeral, then home. The end. Back to Queens. Back to a dead junkie in an abandoned house. 'You heard about Billy McQueen?'

Caskie said, 'On the radio.'

'You knew the guy?' Eddie asked.

'Barely.'

'Friend of Jackie, they tell me.'

'I believe there was a vague fiscal relationship over the years,' Caskie said.

'Why would anyone murder him?'

'Has it been confirmed that he was murdered?'

'Come on. You think he had some freaky thing about scaling unfinished buildings in the dead of night? Like a dangerous hobby that just got out of hand and he slipped? Maybe he dressed in some Spiderman get-up and went out across the scaffolding to look for handy dangling places.'

'A touch theatrical,' Caskie said. 'I can't begin to guess, Eddie. If I knew the man better, maybe I could proffer an opinion.'

Caskie had a small half-smile on his face: Detective-Inspector Enigma. *This man might have been involved in the death of my father*, Eddie thought. He gripped the edge of the table and felt his hands tighten, and he saw the inside of his head change colour – as if emotions were tints – and the pattern of his thoughts went this way and that, and he suddenly wanted to reach out and grab Caskie by his striped necktie and drag his head down to the table and pound it and pound it. Then he let the feeling go, and he tried to relax, and he pushed his chair back from the table a few inches. *Complicity in a brutal murder*. What if you're wrong, Eddie? What if you've miscalculated? But your heart, sometimes reliable in the past, and occasionally impetuous too, says you're right. Believe in it now.

He leaned towards Caskie and said, 'Tell me about safe houses.'

'What houses?'

'Safe. Places where cops put witnesses for security reasons.'

'I've never had any use for such places personally, Eddie. I assume they exist. I may be wrong.'

'But you don't know for sure.'

'Why are you so interested in the subject?'

'It popped into my head, Chris.'

'Without reason?'

'All kinds of things pop into my head without reason.'

'You ought to control that tendency.'

'I try, Chris, I try. Here's another one. For example: Do you think it's possible for a cop – a senior officer, say – to run a kind of private fiefdom inside a force? Like his own little kingdom, I mean, where he could do what he liked, he could make his own personal use of manpower, use police property – like safe houses – any way he wanted, he could decide what was right and what was wrong without involving his fellow officers. This guy would be unaccountable. Up to a point.'

'The man who would be king, eh?' Caskie smiled. 'It's hard to imagine an officer abusing his power to such an extent.'

'Sure. But it could happen, right?'

'Is there some reason behind this little fantasy, Eddie? Or does it simply amuse you?'

'Is it a fantasy, Chris?'

'I imagine so.'

'Come on, Chris. Give me a better answer than that.'

Caskie pushed his cup aside and sighed, a long sound. 'When did you first decide you disliked me, Eddie?'

'You changed the subject, Chris. Didn't enjoy the last one?'

'I had a feeling it wasn't going anywhere. Now it's my turn to be curious.'

'Fine,' Eddie said. 'Dislike you? Funny, I can't decide if it's simple dislike or a more complicated contempt.'

'Contempt is strong. Where does it come from, Eddie? Do you despise me for being closer to your family than you? Is that the root of it? I knew your own father better than you ever did. Is that it, Eddie? I'm this stranger, this outsider who got to know your dad and your sister and you can't cope with that.'

'You wanted to sling Jackie's ass in jail, Caskie.'

'If I'd had the chance. Jackie knew that. He understood the rules. It didn't stop us being close.'

'The best of pals,' Eddie said. 'I doubt that. You didn't even trust each other.'

'We had a working arrangement. We were friends despite the obstacles. Which is more than you ever achieved.'

'And that was my fault? I was taken away, for fuck's sake. What chance did I have?' Eddie gazed past Caskie to the far side of the room where one of the waitresses was watching him in the glazed manner of the daydreamer. His eye travelled beyond her and into a shadowy place. He could have shown Jackie his home in Queens. Toured him around Manhattan. Empire State Building. Staten Island Ferry. The whole works. He could have taken him to a soccer game. Jackie might have liked that, hotdogs, cold beer in waxy cups, the passion of the Hispanic fans. Lost ambitions. Such simple ones.

Eddie pushed his chair back from the table. Dislike. Contempt. He wished he had the kind of dignity that didn't allow him to yield so easily to these feelings. Claire would have said something like how we're only human after all and that means weakness as well as strength, vanity as well as humility, but right now Eddie could only think of the fact that his mind was smoking and the smoke smelled of sulphur. Claire had a world of her own, where charity and understanding reigned.

He got up from the table and looked down at Caskie. 'Tell me, Chris, how long have you known Haggs?'

'I believe I answered that question before,' he said.

'Why the fuck are you lying?'

Caskie asked. 'I don't remember lying to you, Eddie. You asked if I knew the man, I told you I didn't.'

Eddie smiled. 'You're cool, Chris. You're a fucking cucumber on ice.'

'I've been called worse. Don't forget your bag.'

Eddie picked up the paper bag. Outside he blinked in the unrelenting sun of this pink and blue city. Tarmac shimmered. Starlings flocked above rooftops, a glossy black swarm. He looked this way and that, thinking how clumsily he'd cut the ribbon of polite pretence between himself and Caskie, then decided his destination.

42

Although he was superior in rank to Perlman, Sandy Scullion felt like a trumped-up impostor in the older man's company. Lou Perlman, a legend in the Force, was a throwback to the old days, when DNA might have been the acronym for a savings bank, and electronic gizmos were primitive hand-held Asteroid games that came direct from Taiwan to the Barras market and lasted about forty-five seconds before going on the blink.

The car in which the two men travelled moved along Moss Road on the south side of the city. Scullion drove because Perlman hated cars. They always broke down on him. On the right was the dark-brown Victorian façade of the Southern General Hospital. A couple of young nurses walked across the lawn in front of the hospital; in sunlight their white uniforms had a fluorescent look.

Perlman watched the girls. He had a feeling he'd forgotten something he'd promised to do. It dogged him. 'Some days I feel my age,' he said.

'Don't we all?' Scullion eyed the rearview mirror. 'Where do I turn?'

'Left. Langlands Road.'

Perlman coughed into his hand. His lungs hurt. He

wished he could kick the nicotine habit. 'Some mornings I get up and my throat's scratchy and I need to pee like my bladder's bursting and my bones ache and I think this is it, this is the day I'm writing the resignation note, and ballocks to it all.'

'Retirement,' Scullion said.

'Aye. Downhill Drive,' Perlman said. 'I could sit in the park and give crumbs to birds. I could buy a wee dog, take it walks, wait patiently while it poops.'

'You've got a couple of years in you,' Scullion said.

'Could you put a wee bit more enthusiasm into your voice when you say that, Sandy? I want to be convinced. What am I without my work? A hollow man. The walking dead. Take a left here.'

Scullion turned the car into Kennedar Drive, a street of shabby tenements. Kids played on the pavement. A van with a punctured tyre listed at the kerb.

'Number twelve,' Perlman said.

Scullion parked, pulled on the handbrake. 'You lead,' he said.

'I know these buggers,' Perlman said. 'They try my patience something fierce.'

'I'll be a silent presence, just along for the ride.'

They went inside the tenement. The close was dim and the air cool. They climbed to the second floor. Perlman held the banister rail, which was sticky – probably from some kid's ice cream or sweetie. At least he hoped it was something as innocent as that. The city rubbed off on you, he thought, in bad ways and good. Live in it all your life, you know its corners and its angles, you can rattle off bus numbers and routes, all fifteen names of the underground stations in any order, you remember the streets where the trams used to run, those clattery old bone-rattlers that travelled in seeming defiance of Newtonian physics, you recall buildings long ago demolished, even the names of people who lived in them. He remembered the old Jewish families. The Sakols. The Finemans. The Jesners. Others. Take a couple of Jews and you've got a potential diaspora. Where had they gone? Where had all that piety gone? The respectable suburbs. Giffnock. Newton Mearns. Beyond.

You and the city, he thought, you're an old married couple conscious of each other's faults, and forgiving of them at least some of the time, but irritable the rest. He coughed again. The city was in his lungs, the spoor of the place. He wondered if a city could kill you. *Cause of death: Glasgow.*

He wiped his sticky hand on the side of his trousers. The brass plate on the door ahead of him read ELVIS PRESLEY & ANNIE LENNOX.

'Pair of wits,' Scullion said.

'You're half right.' Perlman rang the bell. It played the first few bars of 'Are You Lonesome Tonight?'

A man's voice came from the other side of the door. 'Who is it?'

'Perlman. Your friendly cop.'

'Aw, what the fuck is it now?'

The sound of a chain sliding, a key turning, the door opening half an inch. Twiddie's unsmiling face appeared in the slit.

'We're coming in,' Perlman said. 'Get the kettle on.'

Twiddie, in black T-shirt and yellow briefs, moved back from the door and Perlman stepped in, followed by Scullion. A Harley-Davidson motorcycle, big and malignant, was propped against a wall, dripping oil on newspapers. Perlman had long ago ceased to be surprised by anything he came across in the homes of people. A Pekinese in a microwave, a chopped hand in a food processor, and on one memorable occasion an entire car, a Vauxhall Astra built from stolen parts, inside a third-floor flat. How to get the vehicle downstairs hadn't been part of the scheme. *Er, what do we do with the car now? Ooops.*

'I see we've caught you with your trousers off, Twiddie.'

'I was sleeping,' Twiddie said. He touched his swollen red nostril in a self-conscious way.

Rita appeared in a doorway at the end of the hall. Her hair was in blue plastic curlers. Without make-up, her face resembled a blanched potato. She was dressed the reverse of Twiddie. She wore black panties and a yellow T-shirt.

Perlman said, 'Look at this, Sandy, a match of clothes and a match of love. It's so adorable it just makes me want to take up embroidery. Little hearts on tiny cushions. Rita, you never looked more alluring.'

'Piss off,' Rita said.

Twiddie said, 'She's not at her best before she's had a cup of char.' He glared at Scullion. 'Friend of yours, Perlman?'

'This is Detective-Inspector Scullion, Twiddie. He's my boss. The way Haggs is your boss.'

'Haggs, Haggs, I wish you'd drop that. I haven't seen Haggs in a long time.'

Perlman said, 'I might look like a simpleton, Twiddie, but don't be deceived. You're never far away from Hot Rod. He snaps his fingers and you run. You're the messenger boy. Phone calls, quick meetings in out-of-the-way places, I know how it works.'

Twiddie waved a hand dismissively. 'That's shite.'

Rita retreated into the bedroom and slammed the door. Twiddie wandered into the kitchen and grabbed a pair of jeans from the back of a chair and pulled them on.

'How come you're still working anyway, Perlman? How come you've not retired?'

Perlman said, 'The Force needs me to keep an eye on the likes of you and the Bride of Frankenstein,' and he gestured with a thumb towards the bedroom door.

Twiddie muttered something that might have been *auld bastart*, then stuck the plug of an electric kettle into a wall socket. The kitchen was a mess. Sinkload of dishes. Pizza boxes and red sauce stains and dead cigarettes filling an old milk carton, and rolling papers spread around. No sign of dope.

Rita came into the kitchen now, wrapped in a red Chinese-style robe adorned with dragons. They breathed fire, Perlman noticed. Very appropriate. She was Arsonia, Goddess of Arson. She sat at the table and folded her arms and stared at him fiercely. 'Can you not leave us in peace?'

'That's not in my job description, love,' Perlman said.

Rita glanced at Scullion. 'Who's this prat?'

Twiddie said, 'He's Perlman's boss.'

Rita lit a cigarette, blew smoke at Perlman. 'So what is it this time, Perlman?'

'You know, Rita, I look at you and I wish I was thirty years younger,' Perlman said. 'Ah-har, shiver me timbers, Jim lad. My heart's tripping the light fantastic. Feel it. Give me your hand –'

'I don't want to touch any part of you, Perlman. Just get to the point.'

'That van,' Perlman said.

'Oh for fuck's sake, not *again*,' Rita said. 'The van this, the van that.'

'Something nags me about that van,' Perlman said. 'You want to hear it?'

'Not especially,' Rita said. 'But I'm going to anyway, I suppose.'

'Right, so you might as well pin your lugs back, my dear, and listen close, while the Swami, the Great Perlman, speaks. The van, the mysterious van. What is it that bothers the Swami?'

'Is there a point to this?' Twiddie said.

'You better fucking believe there's a point,' Perlman said. He moved quickly and stepped towards Twiddie and slammed him against the wall. Twiddie looked surprised, neck stiff and face held back by Perlman's forearm.

'Police brutality,' Rita said.

'No, police brutality would be if I was to give Twiddie a right brutal kicking,' Perlman said. 'If I was to whack him bloody hard in the ballocks, say, and when he dropped to the floor I'd kick the shite out of him. Now *that* would be police brutality. Right, Inspector?'

'Absolutely,' Scullion said, and smiled uneasily. He heard pages of a regulations book fly free from their binding.

Perlman continued, 'This is just to get your fucking attention, the pair of you. Just tell me who else was with you in the Transit the other night. That's all I want to know.' He stared at Twiddie through his one good eye. His unshaven face was set in belligerence; he had a street-fighter's jaw. Twiddie struggled to free himself from the strength of Perlman's forearm, but couldn't.

'Not bad, eh, Twiddie? Not bad for an old fart that should have been superannuated ten years ago. Who was with you in that fucking van?'

Twiddie's eyes popped. 'We told you, we were watching –'

Surreptitiously, Perlman kicked Twiddie hard on the shin. 'A video, I know, I heard that one. Tell me another.'

Twiddie groaned. Rita got up from the table. She appeared quite ready to launch herself at Perlman, but he had a way of glaring – even one-eyed – that made people hesitant about physical confrontation. It was the demonic look of a man who could promise you nightmares, and deliver them if you pushed him too hard.

'Understand this, my wee pals, I'm not pussy-footing,' he said. 'Who else was in the fucking van?'

'We don't *know* about any bloody van,' Rita said.

Perlman released Twiddie now. Twiddie rubbed his neck. Perlman paced the floor, hands in the pockets of his brown trousers. He had a grease stain on his wide gold tie; some of the older officers at Force HQ claimed to remember that same mark from the mid-80s.

'We've got brilliant new sciences these days,' Perlman said. 'We've got electron microscopes. We can test a single strand of hair and tell you the name, address and phone number of whose noodle it was attached to. Now this is *way* beyond my understanding, just as I'm sure it's way beyond yours. No matter, it's enough just to know that all this bright shiny new stuff actually works, which makes it harder for people to do things without leaving traces of themselves. A fleck of dandruff. Belly-button lint. These trifles are the gateways to whole new worlds . . . keeping all that in mind, if you can, I'll ask again. Who else was with you in the van?'

'I want my lawyer,' Twiddie said. 'I want Binks.'

'You think that babyfaced piss-artist can help you, John? You think Mr Henry Binks, solicitor and bullshitter and drunk, can help you out? He wouldn't know his arse from a hole in the ground, our Mr Binks. He's probably having a champagne cocktail in the Rogano even as we speak.'

'This is just bluff,' Rita said.

'Are you sure of that?' Perlman asked.

'Slurry I can smell a mile off. John, don't you listen to anything he says. And don't run to phone your bloody lawyer either. This old bastard,' and she pointed a finger sharply at Perlman, 'is blethering.'

Perlman pulled her towards him, clutching a fistful of her Chinese robe. She stared at him. The eye-lock, the contest. She wasn't yielding, nor was he. He saw in her eyes a lack of generosity and charity. Life was a sore struggle and she'd survived a loveless upbringing inside a decrepit rat-infested building in a world of cracked cups and broken porcelain sinks and outside toilets and all the hard crap a city conspired to throw in your path, and somewhere along the way she'd attached herself to Twiddie, minor thug, villain. It wasn't for love she'd barnacled her world to Twiddie. It was their mutual interest in the arcana of violence that bonded them.

Perlman felt a dip in his emotion, a leaking of energy, as if this brief insight into Rita's world forced him to confront an unfamiliar sensation: pity, or something like it. Getting softer as the years roll, Lou. My sand isn't packed quite so hard any more. It drifts through my fingers. I'll be a bleeding heart next. God forbid, a man with a social conscience.

He shook this mood off and zoomed back in on the ugly face that was so determined not to flinch from his look. But he'd lost eye contact. By the rules of this contest, he'd lost.

He recovered quickly. 'I forgot to mention. We've got blood samples from the back of the van.'

'And this is supposed to worry us?' Rita asked. She yawned, covered it loosely with a hand.

'To death,' he said.

Twiddie said, 'Perlman, for God's sake, we don't know anything about this Transit. I swear it.'

'Apart from the blood,' Perlman said, and paused, and held the silence a beat. 'We've got a wallet.'

'Wallet? What wallet?' Rita asked.

'You tell me,' Perlman said.

'I can't tell you a fucking thing,' Rita said. 'That's my last word on the subject.' She looked at Scullion. 'Unless you have some kind of warrant, Inspector, could you and your senile sidekick please see yourself off the premises?'

'Bones,' Perlman said. 'Matthew Bones. Name familiar to you?'

Rita shrugged. Twiddie turned away, picked up the kettle, made tea. 'Only from the newspaper,' Twiddie said.

Hand on chest, Perlman feigned cardiac arrest. 'A newspaper? You actually read, Twiddie? Quick somebody. Pass me the digitalis.'

'Excuse me if I don't laugh,' Twiddie said. 'This guy Bones is missing, right? Something to do with that shooting.'

Perlman said, 'Missing is correct. The jackpot of pennies rattles down Twiddie's chute.'

'So he's missing, who gives a fuck?' Rita asked.

'Why was he in the van you and Twiddie torched? I stand corrected: *tried* to torch.'

Rita spoke to Scullion again. 'Do you usually employ cops hard of hearing?'

Perlman said, 'Did I not mention it was Bones's blood we found in the back of the van? Did I not tell you that even as we speak men are going through the van looking for fingerprints – which they'll find. Yours and Twiddie's. And those of Matty Bones. So suppose you spare us all the time and trouble involved, and tell us exactly what happened that night, and where Matty Bones might be found? Eh? What do you say?'

'Go fuck yourself.' Rita picked up a magazine and thumbed the pages. Skinny girls in lingerie flickered past. Gaunt ghosts with druggy expressions.

Perlman thought: You don't break down a wall like Rita's with bluff and bluster. You don't make a dent with threats. Magic microscopes and forensics and blood samples and all the rest of it – it was a bag of cold chips as far as she was concerned. She had an in-built alarm-system manufactured on the streets and so far it hadn't issued a beep, and thus she felt secure. Somebody's wallet in an old Transit, so what? Blood? Gimme a break. And fingerprints . . . well, Rita and Twiddie would've been wearing gloves. They might possess stunted IQs, but they weren't suicidal. They weren't going to be linked to that van. Perlman had known that coming here. He'd known he couldn't con them into an incriminating statement, or menace them into giving up information loosely. No, this was something else, this was sifting the dross to see how it was constituted.

Rita buried herself in her magazine. Twiddie, clanking cups on a tray, said, 'Tea's up.'

'I'll skip the tea,' Perlman said.

Scullion looked at his watch. 'Me too.'

'Suit yourselves.' Twiddie set the tray on the table, edging aside an HP Sauce bottle to make space. It was,

Perlman thought, a bleak little montage of a certain kind of tenement life: the brown sauce bottle with goo on the cap, the milky tea, the mismatched cups, one of which had no handle, cigarette burns on the surface of the table.

'When you two decide you have something to tell me, something to get off your chests, you know where to reach me,' Perlman said. 'I'll be expecting to hear from you. I'll be your Father Confessor . . . But don't try my patience. I'm waiting.'

He looked at Scullion, raised an eyebrow. They left the room. Twiddie, slurping tea, escorted them into the hall. 'Cheerio.' He closed the door.

Perlman and Scully went downstairs, out of the building and into the street. Scullion unlocked the car, got inside. Perlman slipped into the passenger seat, gazed through the windscreen. At the top of Kennedar Drive was a primary school and a row of terraced houses.

Scullion asked, 'You think they had Bones in the van?'

'Yes.'

'And you see Haggs's shadow fall across this.'

Perlman nodded. 'Twiddie and the Bride of Frankenstein are not what you'd call initiative-driven. The kind of ideas that occur to them wouldn't power a ten-watt bulb. Haggs tugs a string in Rouken Glen and Twiddie jumps in Govan.'

Scullion drove to the end of the street, turned right. He adjusted the sunshade. 'Let's say Haggs told them to take Bones for a drive. Why?'

'Maybe they were instructed to mess him up. A wee reminder of something. But it all got out of hand. Bones was Mallon's man, and we know there was no love lost between Jackie and Long Rodney. It gets tangled, Sandy.

Maybe it's one of those fucking gangster sagas where somebody gets shot and it all boils down to nothing more than a matter of territory, or an insult blown out of proportion . . .' Perlman realized he didn't sound very convincing. It was more than territory, more than some inflated outrage.

'Tell me, Lou. How good is this witness of yours?'

'The alcoholic eye doctor? Bloody useless. For an eye-doc he's blind as a bat. Plus his head's scrambled permanently.'

'Oh,' Scullion said.

'But I believe he saw what he says he saw. Because I'm a fucking cockeyed optimist, Sandy.'

'And the blood?'

'Matty was AB negative, according to a report from the Victoria Infirmary where the wee jockey was taken in 1984 when he fell from a horse at Ayr races, and his face split like a pomegranate dropped from the Scott Monument. But AB neg is common as dirt. So common, Sandy, it's my blood type as well.'

'You're just an old-fashioned bullshit artist,' Scullion said, and smiled.

'Probably.' Perlman watched a big black mongrel strut in front of the car, pursued by a snot-nosed infant, in turn chased by his teenaged mother who wore her hair in curlers under a scarf. *Come back, ye wee bugger.* Perlman sighed, and his eyelid throbbed, and he remembered what it was he'd intended to do, and that was to see if Caskie had run Tommy G through the computer. Growing old, things slipping, fuck it.

*　　*　　*

Rita said, 'What do you think, doll?'

'I don't know what I think.'

Rita asked, 'Call Haggs?'

'No fucking way.'

'Haggs'll go mental, John, if it turns out Perlman's got something up his sleeve.'

'Haggs is already mental.'

Rita pouted and said, 'We can always shag this situation out of our minds.'

'I'm up for that,' Twiddie said.

'I notice.'

43

Eddie Mallon entered Central Station and walked under the high glass roof that allowed bright light to illuminate the huge interior. He stashed the Armani bag containing the pistol in a left-luggage locker. A smell of strong coffee floated in the air, and a vendor sold fruit and an assortment of nuts in the forecourt. Eddie bought a bag of cashews. He chewed on them while he walked to the location of the timetables, which were arranged on boards.

He found the schedule he was looking for.

A train left Central, destination Largs, at forty-five minutes past each hour. Jackie had been anxious to be dropped off at the station by 10.35 a.m. Why? Because he needed enough time to buy a ticket, he wanted to make sure he had a cushion of about ten minutes to spare him a crazy rush to catch the train.

Eddie looked at the station clock: 11:37. He went inside the ticket office and bought a day-return, then he walked quickly to the platform and took a seat on the train. The carriage was filled with women and little kids. A trip to the beach, a release from the dry streets of the city. He stared out, and wondered if McWhinnie had followed

314

him to the station, if he was somewhere on the train. Or if McWhinnie had even bothered to go to work today.

The train moved. Eddie gazed at warehouses and factories, the unplanned outskirts of the city. Kids, some of them in swimsuits, scampered up and down the aisle. The Kiddy Express – except it wasn't an express, it stopped at a number of stations on the way. The first was a few miles from Glasgow: Paisley, Gilmour Street. More kids and mothers boarded here. Fugitives from Paisley. Eddie had an impression of bright sun-hats and pacifiers and baby-bottles containing orange juice. The women, pink-skinned for the most part, were dressed in lightweight shorts and summery blouses. They had the cheerfully relieved smiles of people jettisoning the drudgery of the city for a few hours at the beach.

He observed the landscape yield to deep green pasture. Out of the city's reach he felt a certain freedom. The sky had no limits here. The small towns and settlements the train zipped through were blinks of an eye. He imagined his father travelling this way a week before. He wondered if Jackie looked from the window, or if he read a newspaper, or if he sat with his eyes shut and dozed. Did he think of the honeymoon in Largs, the old days, first love? Had he chosen Largs as a meeting place because it had associations for him? Had somebody asked, *Where will we meet, Jackie?*

And had Jackie replied: *Largs, I know a hotel where we can talk in peace*?

Largs, Christ. All this could be a crazy construct of your own brain, Eddie, he thought. The conviction that Jackie had travelled this way for a meeting could be something you've cobbled together from the assorted odds and ends of your own imagination. The big hunch that turns out

315

a total disaster. A misguided step in the dark. You just don't know.

Suddenly, startling as a great mirror of quicksilver, there was the sea, and in the distance through the haze of heat the awesome grey spine of an island – Arran, which looked like a man at rest. The train stopped at Saltcoats Station. The kids yelled and laughed and pressed their faces to the windows as if they might smell the sea through glass.

Fifty minutes after it had left Glasgow Central, the train arrived at its destination. Eddie made his way on to the platform and walked to the main street. He smelled the sea air that stirred in a breeze so soft and slow you could barely feel it. He strolled past shops – the Baker's Oven, the Craft Shop, the Bagel Basket – until he arrived at the seafront, where a ferry of the Caledonian MacBrayne line was taking on passenger cars for the short trip to Cumbrae, a humpbacked island less than a mile off the coast.

The ferry was mobbed by screaming gulls. On the pebbled beach, gaggles of kids paddled in the shallows under the vigilant eyes of mothers. The kids consumed copious amounts of ice cream. Bold seabirds approached, scavenging for broken cones or any kind of appetizing spillage. The air smelled of salt and burned toffee.

Eddie turned right, away from the pier. Small, with well-kept gardens and neat bungalows in side streets, Largs lacked that tawdry quality he associated with resort towns. No high-roller casinos, no cheap eateries. Ahead, facing the sea, stood a couple of large structures that might have been hotels. The first one he reached was indeed a hotel, but it wasn't the Seaview. He continued to walk. *Am I getting warm, Jackie? Am I close?* He thought of

Jackie and Flora, arm in arm, strolling this promenade. Young lovers who couldn't wait to be shut inside their room away from the world.

The board with the name 'THE SEAVIEW HOTEL' had been freshly painted in blue and gold. 'Bed & Breakfast. 70 Rooms En-Suite. Function Room. Bar & Restaurant.' The building was grey stone, flowerboxes on sills, a cheerful midsize hotel with an unimpeded view of Cumbrae.

Stay away, son, Jackie said.

Hey, you just don't go in here blind, unprepped, Tom Collins said.

Eddie climbed the steps, entered. The air was cool inside, venetian blinds half-shut. For a second he couldn't see anything except the ghosts of things left in his eyes by the sunlight. Then he could make out the reception desk, a smiling girl in a floral dress, a wall-map of North Ayrshire, a sign with an arrow: BAR & RESTAURANT. He went inside the bar, a narrow room beyond which was a large fern-clogged dining room half-empty. He asked for a club soda with ice, then he sat down in a darkened corner of the bar and drank quickly. He ached. His head. His body. He wanted Solpadeine. He had none.

'Hot one,' said the barman.

'Pleasant,' Eddie said.

'I like it cooler.' The barman wiped the counter. 'There's a change coming. So I hear.'

Eddie finished his drink, set the glass down. Now. I get up, I go back to the reception desk, I ask them if Jackie Mallon was a guest here one day last week, did he have company, I show my NYPD identification and hope it pulls strings and opens door for me. *Jackie Mallon, you say? Did he stay here? I'm sorry, we can't give*

out information about guests, sir. And you're well out of your
jurisdiction, I believe.

Eddie paused in the doorway between the bar and
the reception area. The girl at the desk, pretty, Nordic,
smiled at him. She had wonderful straight teeth and a
kindly look. Eddie took a step towards her, reaching in
his hip-pocket for his ID, then he stopped, because a
man in a bright floral shirt appeared at the desk and
said something that made the receptionist laugh, and the
man laughed too, then ran a hand over his dreadlocks and
turned his face, scanning Eddie quickly before returning
his attention to the girl.

Eddie couldn't move, affected by a sudden paralysis.
He imagined this man breaking the stained glass of
Joyce's door, charging inside her flat, attacking her.

The man made another joke and the girl smiled and
said, 'I always forget jokes. Every time I hear one, in one
ear and out the other.'

'Takes a special kinda brain, pet. An empty one.' The
man laughed and then turned his face a second time to
Eddie. Eddie felt he was being filed, stored for future
reference. The eyes were sharp and calculating, no sign
of mirth. The man moved from the reception desk and
passed close to Eddie on his way to the bar.

Eddie stood still a moment. What now? What move to
make now? You've come this far. You take the next step.
He went back inside the bar and stood next to the guy,
who was making banter with the barman.

'Biggest mistake the English ever made in Scotland was
building a road that led south,' he said.

The barman said, 'Now that we've got our own Parliament, we'll throw all you English out.'

'Your own Parliament? That lot in Edinburgh are all

gums, no teeth. They can't even fart unless they get the green light from Westminster.'

'At least we beat you at rugby last time,' the barman said.

'Once in a blue moon, mate.' The man turned to Eddie and said, 'What do you think, chief?'

'Think about what?' Eddie asked. This man *struck* Joyce, Eddie thought. Gurk's strength was evident from his muscularity. The powerful crag of brow suggested brute force. Joyce would have no chance with a man like this.

'Hallo? Is that American I hear?'

'Right,' Eddie said.

'Don't tell me. Lemme guess. Noo Yawk. The Great White Way. Times Square.'

'Cool,' Eddie said.

'There isn't an accent I can't get,' the man said. He held out a hand. 'Tommy Gurk.'

'Eddie.' The grip was very strong, combative, almost a challenge.

'Nice to meetcher, Eddie. You on holiday here?'

'Right. You?'

'Business. I sell novelty items to shops. You want suggestive picture postcards or a yo-yo that whistles – I'm your man. Don't knock it, mate. It's a living.'

'I wouldn't think of knocking it. Been here long?'

'I'm in and out. Off and on. What's your game?'

'Retired,' Eddie said.

'At your age? Lucky sod. What was you before?'

'A cop.'

'Some of my best friends,' Tommy Gurk said. 'Drink?'

'Club soda. Thanks.'

Gurk ordered two club sodas. He clinked his glass

against Eddie's. For a time Gurk was silent. He stabbed at an ice cube with a long brown finger.

'I didn't catch your last name, mate,' Gurk said.

'I don't think I mentioned it.'

'Travelling incog, are we?' Gurk nudged Eddie. 'I understand that. Bloke has his reasons for going around free as he likes using any name he likes. On the run from a wife, or more likely a wife's lawyers, hey, a geezer has the right to change his own sodding name . . . People looking for you, Eddie?'

Eddie shrugged, left the question unanswered. Let Gurk think what he liked.

'You play your cards close to your chest,' Gurk said.

'Force of habit, nothing personal,' Eddie said.

'No offence taken. None whatsoever.'

Gurk set his glass down. 'I'll be running along. Maybe we'll meet again.'

'Yeah,' Eddie said.

Gurk dropped a pound coin on the bar and inverted his glass over it. 'Your tip, Jack.'

The barman said thanks.

Gurk stepped out of the bar. Eddie heard him exchange some words with the receptionist. More laughter. This Gurk was a joker. He spread good cheer wherever he went.

'He's a character,' said the barman. 'Laugh a minute. He's been here more than a week and had us all in stitches.'

More than a week, Eddie thought.

The time-frame was right.

He felt the ghost of Jackie in the bar and imagined that if he turned his head he'd see the old man sitting at a corner table, inclined over a drink. The feeling of being

320

haunted spooked him. He took a five-pound note from his pocket and slid it towards the barman.

'I've got a question,' he said.

The barman looked at the money, but said nothing.

'Has he had visitors?' Eddie asked.

The barman rubbed the side of his face. 'That wouldn't be for me to say, sir.'

Eddie dropped another note on the bar, a tenner. 'Now can you say?'

The barman leaned forward. He had a skinny face and his eyes were dark slits. 'Mr Gurk, our resident comedian, had two visitors last week. Dinner companions.'

'Describe them,' Eddie said.

'One was a guy in his late sixties about. Thin black hair. Looked dyed. The other was maybe fortyish. Walked with a pronounced limp. They had a few drinks, they stayed the night. That's all I know.'

Eddie looked at the ice melt in his glass. He smelled roasted meat waft from the direction of the kitchen, and strong vegetable matter boil, brussels sprouts, cabbage maybe. Gurk and Jackie and McQueen – all three of them had come to the Seaview to discuss business, but the deal had gone sour. Jackie and Billy McQueen had been murdered, and Gurk was left holding the bag, and probably under pressure from somewhere.

He was out in the cold.

And he wanted to come back in.

Tommy Gurk took the stairs up to his room. It had dark blue wallpaper. He sat on the centre of the bed, lotus position. He had the slats of the blinds angled in such a way that the sun coming into the room was sliced. Light, dark, light, dark. He shut his eyes. He searched for the inner place, the garden, but it kept eluding him. He'd glimpse the path to the tranquil centre a moment, then he'd hear the niggling whisper of voices, the natter of all the monkeys in his brain, and his mood fell apart.

He walked the room. *I don't need any static*, he thought. He spaced the slats of a blind with his fingers and looked out at the water. A ferry was ploughing towards the island.

He thought about Kaminsky's missing property.

Then the American in the bar. That was bothering him. Ex-cop, or so he said. Listen, he's just a guy skipped out on his responsibilities, how do you know he's anything else? He's running away. He's got that fugitive look. Heavy alimony, can't hack it, takes a hike. That was one plausible scenario.

The American looked familiar, didn't he?

How could that be? You see a guy for the first time and he looks familiar, how so? He reminds you of somebody else, say?

He let the question go. He didn't have an answer for it.

He sat on the bed again. He took off his wristwatch and set it on the night-stand. He let his arms dangle loosely at his sides. Think of the garden. The garden. The garden. Think all the scents of the garden. Now let it go, let these pictures fall away, and step into the white zone beyond the garden, seek the peace where birds don't sing and nothing stirs because nothing exists in this zone except the thump of your heart and the thud of your pulses and soon you won't even hear these drumming reminders of life. You enter a place beyond nothing. You call it the Zone.

Here you are capable of anything because you are nothing, the embodiment of a paradox –

A wayward fly buzzed his face.

He opened his eyes, *damn*, pawed at it, missed. It flew to a corner of the room and settled. A common housefly. The disturbances small things can create. He got up from the bed. He was out of the Zone because of a fly, but he still felt a measure of peacefulness, so much so that when he opened the padded envelope that lay on his pillow and let the stainless-steel pistol, a Ruger P90, slip into his palm he felt a glorious detachment from the violent capabilities of the weapon.

He studied the piece of paper stuck in the envelope. He memorized the information, looked at his watch. He had twenty minutes before the train.

He returned the gun to the envelope and he thought, The secret of doing violence well is self-knowledge.

Eddie waited in the Atlantis amusement arcade, surrounded by zap-technology, the roar of interstellar weaponry, lizard-monsters kids chased at high speed through mazes in space, the beeps and kapows and blasts of a form of entertainment whose attraction eluded him. Kids stuffed coins into slots and entered these strange worlds without having first of all to make any kind of mental adjustment, or so it seemed to Eddie; they passed effortlessly from the non-electronic dimension to its opposite.

He moved as far away from the machines as he could but the noise tracked and assaulted him. He watched the street. Across the way, tiny kids went round and round in miniature cars. Eddie thought, I can handle that. It's nice.

Teensy cars that went in an undeviating circle lacked the evil complexity of electronic games where Space Wizards could take you to infinite dimensions –

Tommy Gurk appeared. He was carrying a black leather briefcase. He'd changed clothes. He wore a loose black linen jacket and blue jeans. Eddie drew back into shadow. Gurk strolled straight past. His expression was one of intense focus: *I'm going where I'm going, and nothing will stop me.* Eddie gave him thirty seconds, then left the arcade and walked about fifty yards behind him.

Gurk was heading for the railway station.

44

Christopher Caskie answered his telephone on the third ring. He gazed through french doors into the back garden of his house in Broomhill and remembered how Meg, when her health had begun to decline, used to sit in the conservatory with a book in her lap. Catherine Cookson sometimes. A P.D. James mystery now and then. Invariably she fell asleep and Caskie had to go out and fetch her and carry her inside. This bloody house was like a prison, too big for one person, he'd sell it, anyone with any sense would put it on the market.

'Mr Caskie?'

'Speaking.' Caskie was conscious of his hand shaking slightly. He fought to still it.

'Christopher Caskie?'

'Yes –'

'I have had you checked.'

Caskie said, 'Of course. I expected that.'

'A phone call from somebody in your position was unusual. But you pass muster – is that the phrase?'

'That's the one.'

'I am wary. I check. Always. Check this. Check that. Check check. No mistakes.'

'Naturally.' Caskie shut his eyes. The room was too bright. It was like standing inside a tube of neon. Was it too late to take things back, to say no, *I've changed my mind, this isn't the way I want my personal affairs conducted?* I was a good cop once, an exemplary cop. I have awards, medals, citations. Now this. This rot I can't stop.

But I have to stop it.

He heard a sound at the other end of the line, a liquid falling, perhaps tea or coffee being poured. Say no to your conscience. Just say no to that interior sniper who shoots down all your bad thoughts. You never asked for him in the first place. It came with the way you were brought up. Here, swallow your daily spoonful of John Knox Juice. You'll feel bad if you don't take it. You'll feel a whole lot worse if you do.

'Now we will take the next step,' the caller said. 'My man will be prepared.'

'And the two women will not be involved.'

'My word. My hand is on my heart.'

The line was cut. Caskie put the handset down. He looked at his watch. Four p.m. exactly. He called McWhinnie's cellphone.

'Christopher, I'm sick,' McWhinnie said.

'How sick, Charles?'

'Flu type of feeling. Draggy.' McWhinnie's voice was thick, like a man speaking from inside a ski mask. 'Headache, upset stomach, the runs.'

'I know the symptoms. You've been in bed all day?'

'I went out for a time,' McWhinnie said. 'Our man visited Senga in Onslow Drive . . . then I felt sick in the car, so I came home and lay down. I don't know where he is.'

'You'll be right as rain tomorrow,' Caskie said. He

thought of his conversation with Eddie Mallon, that stuff about a safe house. Out of the blue. It could only have come from McWhinnie. Ergo: they'd met, and McWhinnie, whipped by that conscience of his – so akin to Caskie's own – had talked. And Eddie Mallon had dropped the subject into the conversation as if to say: *I'm ready to play any game you like, Chris.*

Caskie said, 'Stay warm, Charlie. Drink fluids, take aspirin. We'll talk in the morning.'

'Fine.'

Caskie hung up. Poor McWhinnie, saying he was sick. He lied badly. But it didn't matter. There was no hard evidence to link Christopher Caskie to any crime. McWhinnie might have broken the code of confidentiality in the presence of Eddie Mallon, and talked of safe houses – but it stopped there. How could McWhinnie verify his tale of carrying groceries to a safe house in Govan? Who at Force HQ would listen and believe? *Poor Charlie, nervous breakdown, terrible thing.* As for Mallon, well, he had no evidence either, and little credibility in Tay's eyes.

Caskie walked out to the patio and stood in shade. As if affected by heat, bees were cumbersome as they moved from flower to flower. This confounded weather. It couldn't last. Not in Glasgow. Global warming. This was more like global meltdown.

He walked back inside the house and poured himself a gin, which he packed with ice. He held the glass in the air and said 'Cheers' to himself, then he drank. He thought of the man saying, *My word. My hand is on my heart*, and he wondered if the same dry heat that held Glasgow in its grip also prevailed in Zurich.

His doorbell rang. He went down the hallway to answer it. He couldn't remember when he'd last felt this liberated, nor this awful. He had a war going on in his head and the heavy machine-guns were bombarding those trenches where the soldiers on the side of the angels flew white flags of surrender.

He opened the door. The sunlit street was harsh, the light like a lake of petrol burning.

45

Eddie Mallon stepped off the train at Central Station, walking about a hundred yards behind Tommy Gurk. It was a long time since he'd stalked anyone. He remembered the vigilance required, the almost unnatural sense of anticipation, the ability to detect any sudden alteration in the quarry's movements – such as that pause when the target turned and, as if struck by an inexplicable uneasiness, glanced back and thought: *Somebody is walking on my grave.*

Gurk moved along the crowded platform at a regular pace. He was in no hurry. Neither was he lagging. He held the briefcase close to his side. At one point he paused, scratched his head. But he didn't look back. If he turns, Eddie thought, if he sees me and raises a hand in greeting, it's no big deal, I'll say hey, we meet again, small world, whaddya know.

Gurk went through the ticket barrier. Eddie kept his distance. Gurk passed a couple of coffee shops and then, changing his mind, wheeled round abruptly and entered one of the cafés. He didn't look in Eddie's direction. Head down, Eddie kept moving, then turned after twenty yards and walked back. He glanced inside the café and saw

Gurk pointing to a pastry in a glass case. A young girl slid the pastry on to a plate, handed it to Gurk, who said something to make her laugh – what a gift, the guy was a walking joker – and she put a hand up to her mouth as if laughter was against management policy. Tommy Gurk made another crack, the girl turned her face to one side and her shoulders shook. She poured him a coffee and he took it – coffee in left hand, pastry in right, briefcase clutched under his armpit – and he wobbled from side to side like a man who'd lost his balance, all part of the funny-man routine. He moved to a table, sat down, took a healthy bite from the pastry. He set the briefcase on the floor between his feet.

Eddie walked to a newsagent's that faced the café, bought a paper. Textbook. You bought a newspaper and pretended to read it and all the while you felt completely ridiculous, like somebody wearing a wide-brimmed hat in a hoaky black-and-white spy movie set in a foggy Balkan town before the outbreak of the Second World War.

Eddie opened the *Evening Times*. The front page depicted the skeleton of a half-finished high-rise surrounded by scaffolding. A photographic insert showed the plump face of a man with shiny black hair. The headline was lurid: *Mystery Death of Local Accountant*. The face was Billy McQueen's. Eddie read: *Police are baffled by the discovery of the corpse of William McQueen on a Maryhill building site early this morning. McQueen, who ran an accountancy business in Glasgow –*

Eddie moved, narrowing the angle of his view. Gurk was finishing his pastry, licking crumbs from his fingers. Where do you go from here, Tommy? Who do you hurt next? Senga? Is she on your list? Or do you have another shot at Joyce in your search for whatever it is that Jackie left behind? That fucking grail, that unholy treasure chest, whatever.

'Fancy meeting you here, Mallon.'

Startled, Eddie turned. Charles McWhinnie had materialized next to him.

'You almost stopped my goddam heart,' Eddie said.

'I can affect people that way.' One side of McWhinnie's face was discoloured, but there was little swelling.

'How the hell did you find me?'

'I saw you get on the train, which I managed to miss by the width of a pubic hair. So I waited. I knew you'd come back.'

'Terrific patience,' Eddie said.

'Now and again,' McWhinnie said.

'You don't look too bad,' Eddie said.

'Considering I sat up half the night rummaging through the nooks and crannies of my soul, while I sipped Macallan's with an ice pack pressed to my face. I concluded that I'm not a happy fellow. This job is a waste of my time. I have one life to live, why spend it on angst? So I called in sick, and I'll stay that way until I've decided what to do with the rest of my time on planet earth. I've decommissioned myself . . .'

Eddie scanned McWhinnie's face a moment. Changes were going on inside Charlie McWhinnie. You could see a darkness in his eyes that might have been tunnels going places Charlie had never been before.

Eddie said, 'Listen, that rough-house stuff last night, I apologize. That's not me, McWhinnie. Maybe twenty years ago, when I had a more aggressive streak, but last night I lost control. Put it down to frustration. Annoyance.

A bunch of stuff, people giving me a hard time, being obstructive –'

'Let's forget it.'

Eddie laid a hand on McWhinnie's arm and positioned himself in such a way that if Gurk looked in this direction he'd see only Charles McWhinnie's back.

McWhinnie said, 'Why do I get the impression you're using me as a shield?'

'There's a guy in that café,' Eddie said.

'I'm not supposed to look, right? And he's not supposed to see you either. Is there a reason for this surveillance?'

'Here's the story, Charlie. The guy's called Tommy Gurk. He's looking for whatever the hell it was my father was doing before he got killed.'

'*Gurk*, you say? Caskie ran a PNC search on a fellow by that name yesterday.'

'He told me it came back negative.'

'Dear me, he lied,' McWhinnie said.

'No kidding.'

'Gurk, who has a bunch of aliases, is some kind of demented Buddhist who took a wrong turning down Satori Street and has been trapped in a cul-de-sac ever since. He's linked up with some characters on the Continent, in particular a guy called – let me think – Josef Kaminsky, who is reputed to be *seriously* dangerous, and involved in black-market activity.'

'What kind of black market?'

'Name it. He can get you anything.'

'Anything isn't very specific, Charlie.'

'Because, my friend, the computer says he dabbles in everything. You want American cigarettes from Norfolk, Virginia, delivered direct to anywhere in the world at one-fifth US retail price? Unused outboard motors in their original cartons or shock absorbers from Detroit as unsullied as the day they came off the assembly lines? No problem. Something less mundane perhaps? How about works of art pilfered from galleries? Perfectly valid credit cards stolen from the manufacturing companies? Easy for Kaminsky to acquire, if you have the scratch . . . Oh, yes, and if you step out of line, you might well disappear for ever. People who cross Kaminsky have a tendency to vanish. Nice, eh?'

'This is in his file –'

'I'm not making it up, Eddie. And the only reason he isn't behind bars is because he can walk on fucking water. I imagine he sits in Zurich and issues orders on his cellphones and his minions go out and do his bidding while the man himself sips Campari and nobody can point a finger at him. And Gurk is, quote, an *associate*. Which almost certainly means that Tommy is quite capable of anything.'

Eddie assimilated this, wondering what the deal was with Jackie. Stolen artworks? Cigarettes? It was going to be a big score for you Jackie, right? Eddie looked at Gurk and his head clouded and he thought, The deeper I dig into Jackie's world, the less I like.

Where was the good father every kid wanted?

The good father I wanted.

And now there are two of them, Gurk thought. He didn't need this. He didn't need interference. He didn't want any fucking *aggro*. He couldn't afford wankers looking inside his fucking briefcase.

He'd wait, pick his moment, get up, walk out. They

think, *He hasn't noticed us. He's just supping his brew and digesting his Danish.* He reached down and picked up his briefcase and laid it on his lap.

Then he got up. Immediately sat down again. Keep them on their fucking toes. Keep them dancing.

Any minute now, you go.

Eddie saw Gurk get up from the table, briefcase in hand. A train was disgorging its passengers and suddenly the area around Eddie was more crowded than it had been, a throng of red-faced people disembarking after hours at the beach.

McWhinnie said, 'He's on the move, Mallon.' Then he was swept aside by the tide of the crowd, but managed to push his way back to Eddie. Gurk stepped out of the café. It was confusing, this buzzing surge of people and the smell of their suntan lotion and sea-salt, men in baggy shorts, kids scurrying around, getting entangled in the legs of adults and playing games and making weird sounds like *zoop zoop zoop*, women carrying souvenirs of the outing, beachballs and baskets of seashells, and one little kid had a water pistol he fired into McWhinnie's face and said, *How's zat feel, eh?*

Gurk was moving quickly now, losing himself in the multitude that pressed towards the main entrance just as office workers and insurance agents and salespersons hurried inside to catch their regular commuter trains. McWhinnie rubbed water from his eyes and followed Eddie, who was shoving his way through the crowd and wondering if Gurk knew he was being dogged. So many goddam people pushing in opposing directions. Eddie felt like a man swimming against a mutinous current.

McWhinnie was close, a few yards to the left. Gurk was maybe twenty or thirty yards ahead, barging forward to the main exit.

Then suddenly Gurk found some space for himself and jack-knifed right, hurrying towards the stall where a few hours before Eddie had bought cashews. Eddie kept after him, conscious of McWhinnie making a turn to stay in touch with Gurk's abrupt change of direction. A voice boomed on the tannoy system. *The train now standing at Platform Three is the 1800 hours for Ayr, stopping at Paisley Gilmour Street, Johnstone, Dalry . . .*

Gurk was moving in the direction of a side exit. We could lose him, Eddie thought, and ran into the swarm of commuters hurrying towards the Ayr train, elbowing his way through, ignoring the grunts of disapproval, the snide little remarks about his rudeness. *What happened to manners?* Eddie could see McWhinnie to his left still. He was making better progress than Eddie, he was closer to Gurk, fifteen yards behind the quarry.

Eddie was sweating. The air trapped inside the station was hot. Gurk knows, he thought. He has to know. Nobody moves like that unless he's being hunted. He's seen me. He's seen McWhinnie. He can't get bogged down in a goddam railroad station. He's got business ahead.

A beggar tried to thrust a tin cup into Eddie's face. *Please help.* Sorry. Another time. McWhinnie, somehow, had managed to shorten the distance between himself and Gurk to about ten yards. Maybe he had a better knack for sliding through crowds than Eddie. Gurk was already vanishing into the corridor of the side exit. Eddie found himself surrounded by a group of Germans with backpacks. Six or seven of them, poring over a big map.

I think Culzean Castle will be nice, yes? Eddie swept the map aside and the Germans murmured in irritation, and one, a standard-issue Aryan, reached out for Eddie as if to drag him back and demand either an instant apology or rapiers at dawn, but Eddie was already beyond him.

Now he'd lost sight of both McWhinnie and Gurk.

He reached the exit passage. There were stairs he hadn't expected, and a metal barrier bisected the stairway. People obeyed no rules here, left side for those ascending, right for those in descent, some process of order. Instead, they went up and down as they pleased. There were collisions, dodges, confrontations narrowly avoided, the whole commuter lunacy, the urgent madness of the citizenry rushing to various destinations. So many people in flight. The city was burning. The doors of the asylums had been thrown open. Everyone was free to create chaos. Eddie was pressed to the rail in his descent. His back hurt. His arm was crushed to his side.

He saw McWhinnie at the bottom of the stairs, but no sign of Gurk. Maybe Gurk had been devoured by the city, disappeared, one of those posted missing in the mystery that was contemporary life. McWhinnie looked up, caught Eddie's eye, motioned towards the street with his hand. Did McWhinnie's gesture mean he still had Gurk in his sight? Eddie kept descending through the scrum until he reached the bottom of the stairs. He felt he'd been forced through a sieve. I'll have a portion of mashed Eddie, please.

A rectangle of sunlight ahead, a street, traffic, flocks of people entering the station or escaping it. Was there no end to the number of bodies? McWhinnie was outside now, and so was Gurk. From where Eddie stood it appeared McWhinnie had caught up with Gurk and grabbed his arm, and Gurk was arguing, trying to free himself. This altercation was observed by Eddie in an intermittent way, as if he were inside a cinema where the patrons in front of him kept getting to their feet and obscuring the view. Now you see McWhinnie, next second he's vanished. And Gurk was going in and out of the frame too –

Then there was one of those moments when your heart feels like glass that has suddenly developed a flaw, and you know something has gone badly wrong, something beyond normal commuting-hour activity has happened, something so extraordinary and unexpected that nobody knows how to react. There's a clearing in the crowd, a pocket of quite unnatural space, and people are hurrying back from the epicentre of the event, ground zero, and somebody shouts, somebody else screams, and Eddie finds himself rushing forward, stomach tumbling, knowing that whatever has taken place here isn't a happy occurrence, and before he realizes it he's reached the clearing and he sees McWhinnie lying on his side, his white shirt stained with blood, and more blood on the grey pavement, a bright pool reflecting the sun, so much blood you can't tell where it's coming from, and then Eddie is on his knees beside McWhinnie, who's dead, dead beyond dispute, dead as a body that might have fallen from a high ledge or a passing plane. Dead as McQueen, dead as the jumper in Manhattan.

McWhinnie's eyes are open. His mouth.

Eddie stands up, just as a woman with a pale shocked look points a finger without speaking, but Eddie knows she's indicating the direction the gunman took, and he turns and moves quickly and although his legs feel disconnected from his body he runs as if the woman's finger was a starter's pistol whose explosion he alone in all the world has heard. Renfield Street, through traffic, then crossing St Vincent Street against the lights, aware of buses and taxicabs and the sheen of sunstruck cars, but then he doesn't know where to go next – up St Vincent or down?

He stops moving, leans against the wall of a building, gasping, head down, a thin thread of saliva hanging from his open mouth, all his pulses raging. *I have one life to live,* McWhinnie had said.

Short life, Eddie thinks. Oh, you sad bastard, Charlie.

His back to the wall, he hunkered down, arms dangling uselessly over his knees. He didn't move from this position for a long time. He didn't know where he was. He didn't know how far he'd come from Central Station. A passer-by in a business suit said, 'Clean yourself up and find a job, for heaven's sake, have some pride in yourself, man,' and dropped a pound coin between Eddie's feet. Eddie said thanks but the man had already vanished round a corner.

Gone.

And Gurk had gone too. Into the ever more narrow arteries of the city, side streets, alleys, lanes, passageways too tight for any car to travel, places to which Eddie had no access.

46

Haggs had never liked the Jew, who brought to life a nascent anti-Semitism in him. Haggs rarely ran into Jews and generally had no feelings about them one way or another – but Perlman, this guy in need of a shave and a haircut and a complete sartorial overhaul, stirred up some deep resentments Haggs had acquired by chance on his way through life. Haggs believed, on the basis of no experience, that Jews were pushy, acquisitive, clannish, secretive, and loved to control great flows of cash.

This fucker Perlman clearly wasn't into the cash aspect, but he fell right into the pushy category. The way he blew cigarette smoke straight into Haggs's face, for instance, and the aggressive lock of his jaw, and how he flaunted his disgusting soiled tie, which anyone with any taste would have hidden *inside* the jacket – these things weren't designed to endear Perlman to you. What also troubled Haggs was the fact that Perlman had strutted into the members-only room in the clubhouse without a member's approval, and that was downright bad manners, like pishing on the floor.

Perlman said, 'Posh place. What does membership run you?'

'If you have to ask, you're not membership potential,' Haggs said.

'Relax, Haggs. I wouldn't join any club that accepted you,' Perlman said. 'So don't worry your arse about me filling in an application. Golf gets on my tits. There's something depressing about grown men hitting a wee ball for miles and chasing after it in clown-coloured clothes. I don't know about you, Haggs, but I sense retarded development and a Freudian thing.'

Haggs smiled and secretly longed to land a fist in the centre of Perlman's grizzled chops. 'You've got some gall to talk about clothes, Perlman.'

'I've got a lot of gall, Roddy, old son. Keeps me young and spry. As for my clothing, I don't give a shite. I'm a cop. I'm not on some bloody catwalk. In fact, I'm proud – in a contrary way – of my total lack of nous in the world of couture. I hope my appearance here is embarrassing the crap out of you.'

Haggs was uneasy. Of course he didn't want to be seen with Lou Perlman. He looked round the dark-panelled room, glanced at the roll of honour on which were gold-painted the achievements of past members, the windows that overlooked the first tee, a stand of pine, a stretch of glassy water in the distance. At polished circular tables members with prosperously ruddy faces and rings of chub under their polo shirts drank expensive single malts and smoked fat Cuban jobs and laughed at crude jokes they couldn't have shared with their wives.

'It's a man's world in here, right enough,' Perlman said. 'Dead butch. You can just smell the pong of rich leather polish and the Old Spice aftershave and a tiny wee hint of sweaty groin that's been talcumed. Very nice. You've come up in the world, eh? You're a star, Haggs.'

'I played my cards right,' Haggs said.

'Aye, but it was always your deck,' Perlman remarked.

'Control is power, Perlman.' Haggs lit a cigar which he poked at Perlman, who fingered his eyepatch. 'I come here for a quiet time and then you turn up looking like a lost dog, darkening my doorstep. What do you want anyway?'

'I like the way you carry all this off,' Perlman said. 'This swanky place. The clothes you're wearing. What do you call those trousers – plus fours?'

'Right.'

'And those fine red and blue diamond socks. Magic.'

'Get to the point, Perlman. What do you want?'

'Information.'

Haggs said, 'Information?'

Perlman scanned the room. 'I wonder what the good people in here would think of your association with John Twiddie and Rita whatserface, both lowly denizens of Govan, both incurably violent sociopaths. What would they say if they knew you consorted with scumbags like that? Would you be blackballed, Roddy? Would they sling your arse out on to the street, eh? *Off you go, you fucking impostor, and no refunds.* Oh the shame, oh the scandal. Haggs expelled for fraternizing with nasty bastards.'

'Twiddie and Rita,' Haggs said and shrugged. 'I can't say I'm intimate with them, Perlman. They passed in and out of my world once or twice. It's not as if I'd have them at my house. I wouldn't sit down to dinner with them.'

'They wouldn't know what fork to use, would they,' Perlman said. 'They'd think the fish knife was for the butter. Rita would stub out her fags in the left-over

341

mashed potato. Oh, it's a scary picture. When did you last see this awesome pair?'

'Who remembers?' Haggs said.

'Try, Roddy. Try for me.'

'I'm drawing blanks,' Haggs said.

Perlman said, 'What if I was to knock this table over and this nice Rennie Mackintosh lamp with it? What if I was to spill your drink in your lap? What if I pretended to vomit on these lovely waxy floorboards, I mean, give it the full boke choke right out of my gullet, you know what I mean? Wouldn't that be a humiliation for you, Roddy?'

'You can dance on the fucking table for all I care.'

'You wouldn't blink?'

Haggs shook his head. 'Neither eyelid would move.'

'And you wouldn't be embarrassed?'

'You can't pressure me, Perlman. You ought to know better.'

'You want to test me, Roddy? I'll go down on my knees and make puking sounds. Members will show grave alarm. Disgust will be evident. You're judged by the company you keep in the rarefied atmosphere of an expensive boys' club. It's no bloody skin off my back to be seen rolling on the floor. I don't give a fig, old son. Ready?' Perlman clutched his stomach and made a sound of discomfort. It was barely audible, but the threat was there. 'After I've rolled on the floor and made rude gurgling noises and farted, I'll throw this ashtray through the mirror behind the bar where all the single malts are lined up like smart wee soldiers. Glasgow Policeman Loses Control At Exclusive Golf Club. Sound good to you, Roddy?'

'Fuck you, Perlman.'

'I hear that refrain a lot.'

'Twiddie and Rita, when did I last see them – that's all you want to know?'

Perlman lit another cigarette. 'Tell me.'

'A week ago.'

'In what circumstances?'

'Passing on West Nile Street. We exchanged quick chat about the weather. I went my way. They went theirs. I wish I had more, Perlman. I wish I could bring sunshine into your life. But that's it.'

Perlman sucked smoke. Haggs was a good liar. He didn't have a giveaway of any kind. He lied barefaced. Probably because he believed what he was saying. He invented alternative realities and lived inside them. 'I was hoping for more, Roddy. Truly. Here's the thing. They set fire to a van, a Transit, but they're such rank fucking dildoes they didn't exactly light up the sky with their effort. I have a witness, a fellow that saw Twiddie and Rita run from the scene of their incendiary flop.'

'Stop right there,' Haggs said. 'You think this interests me? A pair of morons try to burn a van – come on, Perlman. Tell me a better story.'

'This one picks up,' Perlman said. 'In the back of the van is a wallet.'

Haggs had the sense of travelling in a small boat towards rough waters. 'A wallet?'

'Aye.'

'And?'

'The property of Matty Bones.'

Wallet, Haggs thought. *Bones*. The two words echoed in his brain like coconut shells struck together.

Oversight. Big time. The ship was drifting towards rocks and the lighthouse wasn't working. Haggs said, 'So what?'

'So how did Bones's wallet get in the back of this van, together with bloodstains that are precisely Matty Bones's type?'

I could kill, Haggs thought. 'I'm not exactly Twiddie's keeper, Perlman. How the hell would I know what he and that deranged crumpet of his get up to? I move in another world altogether.'

Perlman looked round the room and remarked, 'And very nice it is too.'

'I wish you luck, Perlman, I really do. But as for a burning van and Bones's wallet, listen, you've come to the wrong place if you're looking for alms.'

'I had my hand held out and I was expecting you to cross it with the silver of information,' Perlman said. 'Daft of me. I live in great expectation, Roddy. I always believe that behind every closed door lies the dark truth. And in every burning Transit van is the clue you don't expect. Funny old world.'

'Funny's right,' Haggs said. Note to self, he thought: stay calm in adversity. Don't let it show.

'The van was stolen in Renfrew three nights ago, matter of interest. Were you in Renfrew by any chance?'

'Give me a break, Perlman. Do I look like I'd steal a Transit van?'

'Maybe you do,' Perlman said, and gazed in the direction of the trees, the lake, light from the sun spreading across still water. A golf ball was flying through space, insignificant against the vast blue of the world. It came down like a shotgunned bird in the dead centre of the lake. Plop.

'People pay to play golf.' Perlman shook his head. 'Downright amazing.'

'Are you done with me?'

'Aye,' Perlman said. 'For the time being.'

'Call me first next time,' Haggs said. 'If there's a next time.'

'But you're such a hard man to reach, old son.'

'If at first you don't succeed.'

'How does the rest of that go, Roddy?'

Haggs clapped a hand against Perlman's shoulder. 'You're a smart arse, Lou. But I like you anyway.'

'The admiration is mutual, Roddy.'

'I never doubted it,' Haggs said.

'Remember, Roddy. I've got my eye on you. The good one. I'm this close to nailing you for *something*.'

Perlman walked towards the exit. As he pushed open the glass door and stepped outside, his cellphone rang in his pocket and he felt the closing door slap lightly against his back.

He spoke into the handset. The caller was Sandy Scullion, who said, 'Central Station, Lou. Now. It's bad.'

47

In his room at the dosshouse in Duke Street, Tommy Gurk stood at the sink and plugged an electric razor into the wall-socket and, concentrating on his reflection in the mirror, ran the razor across his skull. His dreadlocks dropped like newborn minks into the sink. He thought of the young geezer at the railway station. *I want to have a word, you don't mind.* I was out of the Zone, Gurk thought. I wasn't in a place of peace. I wasn't in the garden. Where was calm? More locks fell into the sink.

Take your hand off me, chief.

A word, won't take a minute. You have some ID?

Never carry any. Don't need it. Free country, ennit? You a copper?

Could I take a wee peek inside the briefcase?

What's in this briefcase is private, mate. For mine eyes only.

I'd like to just check that, sir.

You're not listening to me, are you, copper?

Zzzzzz. Tommy Gurk switched off the razor and leaned forward over the sink until his face touched the mirror. He put his hands into the pile of dreadlocks that lay nestled in old brown porcelain. Strip the identity down.

Change. You can't go around this city looking the way you did. You can't do what you've come to do unless you alter your appearance. He pulled his lower eyelids down. Underneath, the pink tissue was pale and looked unhealthy.

He stepped back from the mirror. There. Bald now. Shaved to the skin. He gathered the thick lanks of cut hair and put them in a wastebasket, then ran water into the sink until all trace of stray hair was gone. The room smelled of old cigarettes and piss and disinfectant and the stale flesh of all those men and women who'd come and gone. A dosshouse. In the lobby downstairs he'd paid his money at the desk and the clerk in the cage hadn't even looked at him and the people who sat in beaten-up leather chairs paid him scant attention, they just shuffled newspapers or played draughts or snoozed and twitched in their wino dreams. He'd felt invisible. That was what he wanted.

He remembered, saw it clearly, how the gun came out of the briefcase.

Wait a minute, think, put away that weapon, sir.

All the faces in the crowd at the railway station had receded like people suddenly diminishing in size, the sky pressing down, the planet wobbling on its course through space, all topsy-turvy.

Just give it to me.

You want it, you got it, china.

The explosion jarred his hand but he didn't have time to feel the kick because he'd stuffed the gun back in the briefcase and then he'd run, he'd fled down side streets, this way and that, lost, not caring, needing to be beyond reach and recognition, then he'd found an underground station in Buchanan Street and gone down the escalator to the platform and boarded a train that carried him into the sweet anonymity of a black tunnel, and he'd come up into brassy sunlight in another part of the city and bought the razor in a second-hand shop and boarded a double-decker bus and after he disembarked he walked a few blocks until he found this dump, this great drab Victorian building where rooms were cheap and the clientele cheaper.

Catch your breath. Find the place. Enter the Zone.

He ran a hand over his hairless head. He felt bumps in his skull, and tiny crevices his dreadlocks had hidden. He couldn't find the calm. He was a long way off and his compass fucked. He was tuned to static. He thought, I'll phone Kaminsky, I'll tell him what happened, unforeseen circumstances – but Kaminsky never wanted to know about failure. The word wasn't in his vocabulary.

Down in the street an ambulance raced and screamed, an auditory explosion, how could you reach out for tranquillity in such a place? He had a flash of Tibet, the placid shadows of the monastery, monks in saffron robes, the gong that echoed in the arched passageway, wind-chimes, unflavoured cooked rice in his mouth. He'd go back to that if he could. Like a fucking shot.

He emptied the briefcase on the bed. The gun. The toothbrush and tube of tea-tree toothpaste he always carried in the event he couldn't get back to wherever home base might be. Healthy gums, very important. A disposable razor. A small phial of Total Shaving Solution. A bar of hemp soap in its original box. That was all.

The ambulance faded but now there were police cars and sirens and all hell. The city was a cauldron of jarring noises. He had to get the whole job done successfully and go back to Largs and collect his gear from the hotel – if that was possible, if the place was safe – and then head south, maybe by bus, he'd decide later. He walked to the window and pulled the net curtain back a little way and his fingers penetrated the dry moth-eaten material. He looked into the street and thought how a simple business deal – *let's shake hands on it, Mr Mallon, or can I call you Jackie?* – could go so easily to ruin.

He tossed his few belongings back into the briefcase and left the room. Punter's name on the paper, what was it, why was he panicked into forgetting simple things?

Too much chaos, too much swirl. Rise above it.

Begins with an 'H'. Higgs?

No, Haggs. Spot on. Got it.

48

Eddie Mallon sat in the back of a taxi with his head tilted back and the window down and warm air blowing at his face. Even with his eyes open he kept seeing McWhinnie, poor dead Charlie blown away – and for what? Some questions hung in the air like toxic gases. You couldn't analyse them any more than you could disperse them. *What did McWhinnie die for?*

The driver said, 'They say it was a policeman.'

'Huh?'

'A policeman,' the driver said and glanced back to look at Eddie. 'The fella that was shot. You hear about it?'

'I heard,' Eddie said.

The driver's plump neck spilled over his shirt collar. His jaw was nicked from shaving cuts. 'The way this city's going,' he said, and he shook his head because he had no vocabulary for the horrors he saw.

'The whole world,' Eddie said.

'Aye, the whole world, right enough. I don't remember the last time a policeman was shot in Glasgow. It's bloody terrible, so it is. I blame Hollywood pictures and the general decline in Christian values. We used to look up to policemen when I was a wee boy. They told you what was right and what was wrong and gave you a good kick up the arse if you needed it. Nowadays that sort of thing would land them in court.'

Eddie wasn't listening. He was conscious of the number of police cars on the city streets. An officer was dead. Consequently, visible police presence everywhere. A communal sense of shock, grief, a dismal black mood dominant inside Force HQ. Subdued officers whispering together, sharing a single visceral truth: *one of our own has been murdered.*

Charlie McWhinnie should never have been involved, Eddie thought. If Caskie hadn't used him as his personal hound-dog and private gofer, McWhinnie would never have become entangled in the life and movements of Eddie Mallon, and maybe the disillusion spreading like bindweed through Charlie would have withered. But Caskie had forced Charlie into tasks he felt either demeaning or futile, and so he'd fallen asunder, baffled by the point of his life and the direction of his career.

Eddie stared at the passing buildings. To his right the turrets and spires of the Art Gallery, an extravaganza in red stone. The building seemed to float on air. He felt numb, then angry. His mood swung this way, that way. He shut his eyes tight, experienced the sway and vibration of the cab.

'Broomhill Drive you wanted?' the driver asked.

'Right,' Eddie said. He looked at Caskie's business card crumpled in his hand. 'Sixty-five.'

'Sixty-five. Here we are.'

Eddie stepped out, paid. He stared at the grey house, the stained-glass panes in the upstairs windows, the carved stonework above the front door. Grapevines and wheat sheaves, a rustic effect. What good does it do to come here? What can I possibly get out of this? A blind man and his fawn labrador guide dog went past and Eddie thought, That's what I need, something to lead me, show me the way. The man's white stick tapped on the pavement.

Eddie moved towards the front steps of the house. He'd tried twice to phone from the city centre to announce he was on his way, but the line had been busy both times, so he quit. He wasn't in the mood for politeness anyway, he was beyond niceties. He climbed the steps, rang the doorbell, waited. He gazed at the nameplate. I'll turn, walk away, leave. This is wrong. Confrontation isn't the approach. But the anger kept coming back in waves and he was powerless to stall the feeling. His skin was hot. His hands sweated. His scalp too. He rang the bell again and this time heard a sound from within, a click, a shuffle.

The door opened.

Caskie said, 'I'm surprised.'

'Invite me in,' Eddie said. He didn't wait to be asked, he stepped past Caskie into a hallway where a ceiling fan turned and there was awful wax fruit in a bowl and some cheesy watercolours of seascapes adorned the walls.

'Consider yourself invited,' Caskie said, closing the door.

Eddie entered a room to his right. A sitting room, some good solid furniture, glossy wood surfaces, shrubbery at the window, a leafy big garden beyond.

'You seem agitated,' Caskie said.

'Have I disturbed your siesta?' Eddie asked.

'I wasn't napping.'

'You go around in a robe usually?'

'When I'm unwinding, why not?'

Eddie looked at the navy blue robe and the pyjama

352

trousers that matched and the marbled white feet tucked inside pale blue slippers. Hadn't Caskie heard? Hadn't this bastard heard about his boy McWhinnie?

Then Eddie noticed that the telephone handset was off the hook and dangled close to the floor. 'I tried to phone you,' he said.

'I was resting, Eddie. It's my day off. I hate being disturbed.'

'So you haven't heard?'

'Heard what? Clarify, Eddie.'

Eddie told him about Charlie McWhinnie.

Caskie stood slightly stooped, head forward, like a man listening to a radio station he hasn't been able to tune. His expression didn't change. Sometimes he touched his beard. Eddie, throat dry, was light-headed. Memory bytes: *He was back at the station, looking at McWhinnie on the ground. He didn't want to see the dead man's blood again.* When he finished talking he watched Caskie step towards a chair and perch himself on the arm. Caskie drew his eyelids together, middle finger and thumb, and sighed, and shook his head. The material of his robe shimmered.

Eddie said, 'Probably your colleagues have been trying to contact you, Caskie. They want to tell you what's happened to Charlie.'

Caskie made no move to replace the handset. He stared at Eddie. 'You saw this murder happen?'

'I saw,' Eddie said.

'How did you know Charlie?'

'Oh, for Christ's sake, why don't we just strip the whole charade down? Why don't we pack up the fucking tents and admit the circus and all its illusions have left town? You had McWhinnie follow me from day one. He wasn't terrific at the job. So we met. We met, we talked, he was an okay guy.'

'Cosy,' Caskie said.

'He had problems,' Eddie said. 'You got him to work surveillance, Caskie, but you didn't say why. It's dog's work and long fucking hours, and he had these terrific cops-and-robbers dreams, but you didn't even stroke him a little, or lie and tell him what he was doing was of great importance to the Force. He desperately wanted to be good at his job. He was keen, Caskie. *Eager*. You remember what that was like, Caskie? When you were enthusiastic. You wanted to set the world on fire. But you – I know what it is, you're out of touch with people. You're arrogant. You don't know how ordinary people tick. You don't know what weighed on Charlie's conscience.'

'No? Let me clear it up for you,' Caskie said. 'It's standard operating procedure in our part of the world, Mallon, that subordinates do what their superiors tell them. We don't expect misgivings and self-doubt and neurotic little twitches. And if any man has a problem with his conscience, we don't expect him to wallow in it. We expect only obedience. I'm deeply sorry about what happened to Charlie. Profoundly sorry. Shocked. You don't know how much I mean that. But he knew law enforcement work was not without its dangers.'

'What about *your* conscience, Caskie?'

'I don't have a problem with it,' Caskie said. 'I sleep at night. Deeply.'

Eddie heard a sound from the room overhead. A slight creak, then silence. An old house. Mice under floorboards. Whatever. He'd had mice in his house in Queens. He'd baited traps with cheese, and listened to them snapping murderously in the dark. Ah, Queens. I want to go home. I want Claire in my bed and the knowledge my kid is asleep in his room down the hallway and there's strong coffee in the morning and Danish fresh from Fiedler's Bakery on the corner. I want what I've left behind.

He gazed at Caskie. 'No problem, huh? Okay. Tell me how you square your conscience when it comes to my father. Did you arrange to meet Bones the night my father was shot? Did you ask him to leave the car at a certain time and meet you someplace nearby? Then what – did you drive him to a safe house in Govan while certain parties murdered my father?'

'I know you've been through a rough experience this afternoon, Eddie, you need something to relax you –'

'Don't even try to take me down that road, Caskie.'

'Too late. I think you're well and truly on that road already. Let me get you a drink. Scotch?'

'Fuck the drink. I don't want your booze. I want the truth, Caskie. You set my father up. You had to get Bones out of the way. You made promises to him. Just leave the car for a while. We'll look after you. Gambling debts? No problem, Bones. We'll take care of them too. So Charlie goes round squaring debts with bookies. And somebody shoots my father with Matty Bones's gun and then you stash the weapon in the old guy's flat under the sink – hidden in plain fucking sight – so a couple of hapless cops on a search can't possibly overlook it.'

'Surmise,' Caskie said. 'All of it.'

'Not according to McWhinnie.'

'Who isn't around to verify any of it, alas.'

'Sadly,' Eddie said.

'You're fucked,' Caskie said.

'I'll go to Tay. I'll tell him all this.'

'He'll listen? Ballocks.'

'I'll make the bastard listen.'

'How? Handcuff him to a radiator? You can't make Tay do anything he doesn't want to do. And he doesn't want to listen to you, Eddie. Believe me.'

Eddie slipped into silence. Exhaustion, weary to the marrow. A long brutal day. Shadows formed in corners.

'Just tell me. Is Haggs in this with you? Are you helping him in some way? I know he wanted a slice of whatever my father was getting into, and I guess Jackie wasn't sharing. So you decided to give Haggs a hand, you're well placed, you've got all kinds of connections –'

'That's a stretch, Eddie. You're overreaching. You're always trying too hard –'

Eddie held a hand up to silence Caskie. 'What can Haggs give you in return? Cash? Information? What can Haggs possibly do for you?'

'You're playing head games, Eddie.'

'Or it's something else,' Eddie said. 'Maybe he has a hold over you. Is that it? Behind the nice home and the respectable position in law enforcement, there's something festering in a closet, there's a grub inside the lovely red pippin, and Haggs knows about it, and it could ruin you – how about that? Am I getting warm?'

Caskie said, 'Ice floes. Polar bears.'

Eddie felt defeated. He moved this way, Caskie blocked him. He moved that way, Caskie blocked him again. He was weak suddenly, and hungry, but he knew he wouldn't keep food down. His stomach was like that of a man sailing on a rough tide. He thought he'd drift off into sleep if he didn't get up and leave this house. He'd go back to his sister's and rest for a half-hour and he'd think of another approach, and maybe he'd go straight down to Force HQ and find a sympathetic ear for his story. Perlman's ear. But he had to get it clear first. He had to be sure of his direction. And suddenly he was woozy. The margins of his vision were fogged.

He moved into the hallway. Caskie stepped behind him.

'You also lied about Tommy Gurk,' Eddie said. One more deceit: what did it matter?

'I was protecting confidential police records,' Caskie said. 'Don't tell me you haven't done that once or twice in your life, Eddie.'

I can't remember, Eddie thought. Head blank. Whiteout. 'It's pointless to talk with you,' he said. 'I just don't have the energy for it, Caskie.'

He looked at the wax fruit and then raised his face to observe the slow-turning fan and the shadow it cast on the ceiling, and his eye was drawn beyond that to the stairway leading to the upper part of the house and he saw a figure in the dimming light at the top of the stairs, small and thin and wrapped in a robe six sizes too big for her, her short hair a mess, and he felt as if a hammer had been bludgeoned into the side of his head with such force that his brain emptied and his eyes failed.

She said, 'Eddie,' and her voice came out of the blackness.

49

The streets around Central Station had been cordoned off: a no-go zone. So many cops, more than a hundred certainly; Perlman couldn't remember when he'd last seen his colleagues out in such numbers except when they worked security at big football games.

He had to push his way through the crowd of spectators constrained by a phalanx of uniforms and a barricade of patrol cars and police vans. Mounted horses were present, big steady beasts seemingly unperturbed by the mass of people. There were cops making announcements through a loudspeaker system, telling the crowds to disperse, everything was under control – the usual pabulum for the public. But crowd control was no simple choreography in this situation; apart from the sightseers and sensationalists, there was the added complication of huge numbers of people trying to make their way out of the station, and others desperate to enter because they had trains to catch.

Madness, Perlman thought. Murder during rush hour. Commuter chaos. He was buffeted and elbowed as he pressed through to the Union Street exit where Scullion had told him to come. He wanted to say, Let's make it fun, let's turn it all into a bloody big outdoor fair, a massive fête, hotdog stands and barbecues and brass bands, games the kiddies can play, helter-skelter and merry-go-rounds and three-legged races. Why not? Do away with all this morbid vigilance and bring on the dancing girls. If the crowd wanted entertainment, give it to them.

Bitterness, Perlman, he thought. Watch out for that. *En garde*. A young man dies – but not everyone in the crowd is a ghoul, there are those who want to get home to their families, and can you blame them for that? You solitary old fart. Been alone too long. You don't remember what a family was like.

He saw Sandy Scullion when he finally flashed his ID in front of a uniformed cop who ushered him through the throng. Scullion, in white shirt and red tie, raised a hand wearily. Perlman walked towards him. He was aware of Tay loitering in the background and a couple of other heavyweights from Force HQ – DCI Ralph Hannon, known as Ralph Cheeks because of his resemblance to a squirrel whose mouth was stuffed with crab apples, DCI Mary Gibson, a cheerful woman in her mid-forties who dressed like a woman in a Laura Ashley catalogue, and DCI Benjamin Bennet, sharp, a bachelor with a trim moustache and a ladykiller's rep. They were out in numbers, showing the flag.

The Force is with you, Perlman thought. Not always. Not for McWhinnie.

Scullion said, 'They tried to resuscitate him in the ambulance. But he wasn't coming back, Lou.'

'Who shot him?'

'We've got some witnesses,' Scullion said. 'The killer's a light-skinned black, five-eight or nine, muscular, wore a hat that was either brown or black, hair in dreadlocks.'

'Dreadlocks?'

'A hairstyle, Lou. Rastafarians, reggae bands. Don't tell me you don't know.'

'I know, dammit, it just slipped my mind a minute. You think I don't keep up with things?'

'You're snapping, Lou. Don't snap at me. I didn't ask for this situation.'

'You're right, Sandy. I apologize. Read my face.' Perlman felt his breath catch at the back of his throat. He didn't want to show emotion. Maybe later, when he was on his own. But not here, not now. You reserved a private table for your feelings and you said, Charlie, too bad it didn't work out for you. I'm sorry and I'm sad. You had a few things to fix in your life, but you didn't get your allotted span, son. You didn't get your biblical quota of years.

'What else have we got?' he asked.

Scullion said, 'The killer ran in the direction of St Vincent Street.'

'And then what.'

Scullion shrugged. 'I don't know. Jesus Christ, how damn difficult can it be to find a man with dreadlocks in Glasgow?'

'He won't have the fucking dreadlocks now,' Perlman said. He made scissors of his index and middle fingers. 'Snip snip.'

Tay came towards them. He appeared uncomfortable, like a man whose shoes are too tight, or whose cummerbund is pinching him after a heavy formal dinner. 'This has been a private nightmare for years. I keep arguing the police shouldn't carry guns, and then this happens and I wonder if I'm wrong, if my support of that policy's addle-headed, and we ought to be toting those bloody Magnums like they do in America.'

Irrelevant, Perlman thought. Whether you armed the Strathclyde police or you didn't, it was academic as far as Charlie's life was concerned. He ignored Tay and looked at Scullion. 'What else have we got, Sandy?'

'The killer had a briefcase – black or brown or tan, take your pick – and seemingly McWhinnie apprehended the man and demanded to see what was in the case.'

'Why?' Perlman asked.

'I don't know.'

Tay said, 'McWhinnie worked under Chris Caskie. Why isn't he here? He could tell us what McWhinnie's workload involved.'

'Caskie's not answering his phone,' Scullion said.

'Then I'll send some bloody uniforms to find him,' Tay said. He wandered off, clapping his hands for attention, roaring orders, stirring up the gendarmerie. The crowds all around seemed to simmer, like a human broth.

Perlman saw dry blood on the pavement. He looked again at Scullion. 'So Charlie hassles this black guy into opening his briefcase. And then what? The man whips out a gun and shoots Charlie dead?'

'That's the essence of it, Lou.' Scullion looked sad and placed a hand on Perlman's arm. 'I know you tried to guide him through the Pitt Street minefield, show him the ropes, I know you were a friend to him, Lou –'

'For Christ's sake, that doesn't have any bearing,' Perlman said. 'A fellow officer is dead and whether I liked him or despised him isn't even a consideration, Sandy. I know you want to be helpful and I appreciate it, but this is work. This is what we do for a living. Anything personal, drop it. Save it.'

'I was only . . .' Scullion didn't finish whatever he'd set out to say.

Perlman looked in the direction of St Vincent Street. So many people in the evening sun. Cops. Civilians. The buildings created warm pools of shade. 'What else do our witnesses tell us?'

Scullion said, 'I have three female witnesses who think there was another man in McWhinnie's company. This third party apparently went down on his knees beside McWhinnie, then he got up and took off in pursuit of the killer. According to one of our witnesses, he looked as if he'd seen a ghost.'

'And we don't know who this concerned citizen might have been?'

Scullion shook his head. 'We've got a description. Six feet or thereabouts. Thirteen stone rising to fourteen. Black jeans. Trainers, variously white or beige. White T-shirt with a logo. The guy had thick hair, curly, black going grey. One woman described it as "a mass" of curls. Another said he was handsome, kind of.'

'Anybody read the logo?'

Scullion looked skyward. 'The shirt said something like Sunny on it.'

'Sunny?'

'I'm only telling you what I've gleaned from hysterical people. Sunny, one woman said. But spelled with only one "N".'

'Suny. What's that? A Japanese fish treat?'

'Take it or leave it, Lou. Two of the witnesses were also certain that the T-shirt had the word Brook on it.'

'So we've got Suny and we've got Brook. We've got a funny T-shirt and a mass of curls and handsome kind of.' This was ringing a tiny bell in some remote steeple at the back of Perlman's brain. His memory often yielded details he had no idea he'd committed to it.

Suny Brook. Mass of curls. Wait for it to come. Don't force it.

Always treat memory with courtesy and patience, Lou.

Scullion said, 'The man who went in pursuit never came back.'

'So he vanished into the mystifying air of dear old Glasgow,' Perlman said, and his eyes were drawn back to the blood on the pavement. One of the police horses whinnied. The crowds were beginning to thin in the manner of people who, having expected a spectacular of sorts, were shuffling off because the event had been cancelled and their tickets made null and void. The uniforms were allowing commuters to leave the station, pressing them into orderly lines. Those who awaited permission to enter, even if they knew they'd missed their regular trains, were being directed inside the station through the Hope Street entrance.

Perlman tried to imagine the man in the white T-shirt run towards St Vincent Street. But he couldn't see facial detail; his memory had stalled. Getting old, Lou. What is it they say? Memory is the second thing to go. But what's the first? Can't remember. That joke had blue mould growing on it.

He stuck his hands in his pockets and wondered why he'd been so careful of Charlie McWhinnie's welfare, his state of mind. *The son you never had*. Bullshit, Lou. It's something else inside you. It's that jellybaby heart of yours. You see unhappiness and you want to go to its rescue because you're the bloody schmuck who climbs trees to save stranded kittens or young kids clinging to limbs. You grit your teeth and you haul yourself up branch by branch.

Charlie McWhinnie had something of the quality of a

kid dangling from a limb. And you wanted to help him down to safety.

Aye. You're a hard bastard, Perlman. A man to be feared, right enough.

Why was Charlie so unhappy with Caskie?

Fucksake. That wasn't a question. Everyone who'd ever worked for Caskie had been miserable. He treated his subordinates with all the affection of a 19th-century plantation owner for his indentured slaves. He cracked the whip. You worked for Caskie, you became a non-person. He lorded it over you. Smug strutting bearded *pupik*.

This is not going to bring back McWhinnie.

'Somebody'll have to tell his parents,' Perlman said. 'His dad's a lawyer somewhere. Bearsden, I think.'

Scullion said, 'Tay's already assumed that role.'

'Somebody's also going to have to ask Caskie if he knows anything about the identity of the alleged killer and why Charlie confronted him.'

'You'll do that, I suppose.'

'Oh, aye,' Perlman said.

50

Haggs spoke into his cellphone: 'We need to meet, Twiddie.'

Twiddie asked, 'Something up?'

'I want a chat.' Haggs was aware of a happy bunch of golfers walking past, toting their bags. *A birdie at the twelfth*, somebody said. *When did you last see a birdie at the twelfth? One of the players laughed and said, It's not nice to toot your own horn, Archie.*

Haggs waited until the party had gone inside the clubhouse before he spoke again. 'Bring Rita.'

'Name a place,' Twiddie said.

'The usual,' Haggs said.

Twiddie powered off his cellphone and looked at his sausage sandwich. Brown sauce oozed out between the two pieces of bread and dripped on to the table. Rita, dressed only in a pair of pink panties that matched the glitter she'd applied to her nipples, smoked a cigarette and leafed the pages of one of the glossy magazines she so enjoyed. Other lives. Glamorous ones. Big houses with gardens, bright flowers and kids. Places where it never rained. You never saw rain in any of these glossy journals. People fried in eternal sunshine. I want to go there, she thought. Out of here. Away from these streets.

'He wants to see us,' Twiddie said. He sucked brown sauce from the back of his hand.

'What for?'

'He sounded sharpish. Mibbe it's about that . . . van.'

Rita tossed the magazine to the floor. She dropped her cigarette inside a beer bottle and it sizzled briefly. 'The van, the van, I wish this bloody van would just go *away*.'

'You'd better get dressed. Haggs wants us. We've been ordered. Our Lord and Master has spoken.'

Rita stood up, stretched her muscular arms. 'And we obey.'

'I think I'm turning into one of them – what do you call them – an atheist.'

'An atheist?' Rita made a mocking *ooooeee* sound. 'Mother Philomena always told us atheists go to hell.'

'There's no such place.'

'If you're a dried-out old Mother Superior there is.'

'My nose still hurts,' Twiddie said, and touched his reddened nostril gently.

51

Shocked, angered, bewildered, Eddie walked into the sunlight in Broomhill Drive. *I didn't see it coming*, he thought. I didn't even get a sniff of it. He'd been preoccupied in a number of ways, sure, but just the same he felt he should have sensed *something*. He'd had a breakdown of his peripheral vision, of instinct. No, it was more, it underlined the distance between his world and his sister's, how far apart they'd been forced to grow. He stopped walking and thought of her as she stood on the staircase wrapped in what must have been one of Caskie's bathrobes, and the quiet way she'd uttered his name. A whisper. He didn't remember turning and marching out of the house, nor if she'd called after him. He had to get out, that was all he recollected, leaving her on the stairs, the big fan turning and Caskie's expressionless face in the hallway.

His throat was dry, and he had pain at the back of his eyes. He stopped at a traffic signal. He heard Joyce call his name and he turned, saw her half-walk, half-run, towards him. She wore a tan lightweight silk shirt that hadn't been tucked very well inside the waist of her dark brown slacks, and the strap of one shoe was undone, causing her foot to slip in and out, and the heel of the shoe to cluck against the pavement with each step she took. She looked as if she'd been glued together hastily and the parts were already coming undone.

She caught his arm and said, 'Eddie, I'm sorry.'

'It's your life, Joyce. I figured you might have better taste, that's all.'

'Fuck you,' she said, and her small face was pinched and pale and sharp. 'I'm trying to apologize for not telling you about this before, but if this is your attitude I'm wasting my time.'

'He's a shit,' Eddie said. 'Big-time.'

'You don't know him, Eddie.'

'I know enough. He lies. He manipulates. Where he should have a heart he's got a fucking icebox.' He fell silent, because the next sentence that came into his mind was one he wanted to withhold, to spare her, to leave her with something. Choke on it, Eddie. Tamp it down.

'You need to see it from his angle,' she said. 'He's been through a lot. His wife was ill for a long time.'

'And you were his solace, huh? You were his comfort.'

'Christ, you have a way of making things seem down-right cheap.'

'Talk to your boyfriend. He knows about cheap.'

He turned away but she tightened her hold on his arm and swung him round to face her. 'I know how it might look to you. But he needed me. She was dying, and he hadn't loved her in years. Even so, he stayed with her until the end, Eddie. He went through her pain with her. He nursed her. He dispensed her medication. He bathed and fed her. He sat up with her for hours at a time, watching her pain. He's caring and he's good-hearted and maybe that eludes you, Eddie, because you don't know him –'

'Okay, the guy's a saint, a real sweetheart,' Eddie said. 'But he had you on the side to ease his burden, so that must have helped.'

She swung a fist suddenly. Eddie didn't see it coming. It stung his ear and he heard a whining sound in his head. He caught her hand and held it against his chest.

'Don't make me hate you,' she said.

'Did Jackie know about you and your Romeo?'

'You can be so fucking childish, Eddie.'

'Did he *know*?'

'No.'

'Couldn't tell him? Ashamed to confess?'

'What was the point in telling him?'

'You were sparing his feelings?'

'Yeh, that's it. He and Chris were on different sides of the fence, Eddie.'

'Bullshit. When you come right down to it, they were on the same side of the fence. They were both crooked.'

'I don't believe that, Eddie.'

He touched the side of her face as softly as he could. He had to tell her now. He didn't have an escape route. 'Listen to me. Caskie knew Jackie was going to be murdered before it happened. Caskie, whose bed you've just come from, was involved in the mechanics of the killing – in conjunction with a man called Roddy Haggs.'

She put her hands on her hips and stepped back a pace. 'What kind of fucking person are you? How can you *possibly* say something like that, Eddie? How can you stoop so damned low? You really know how to get down into the gutter and come up with some pretty vile stuff, don't you? Why in God's name would Chris want my father killed? You want to hurt me because I lied to you, I omitted the truth, fine, I apologize, I am sorry to

369

the bottom of my heart, but there's no bloody need for you to make up all this shite and throw it in my face, is there? We don't need this between us, Eddie. It's a wedge, and I don't want it.'

She doesn't want to believe, he thought. Who could blame her?

'I tried to kill off the relationship, I really did,' she said. 'When I married Haskell I thought, this is a way out of a bad situation. But I couldn't get Chris out of my mind. The whole Haskell thing was doomed. I didn't want him. I wanted Chris. I'm not getting any younger, Eddie, and love is a substance that is bloody hard to find. What do you know? You've got Claire and a kid.'

Love, Eddie thought. Love was a thing you wanted so desperately you didn't always see things clearly. It was more than a life raft that kept you afloat in solitary waters, or the sound of another human voice in an apartment or the ruffle of somebody turning the pages of a newspaper while you read the magazine section on a Sunday afternoon. Love was a commitment of the heart, not a salve against solitary confinement. *I'm not getting any younger, Eddie.* 'How long has it been . . .' He left the question hanging.

'How long has it been going on?' she said.

He looked away. Butterflies flapped out of a hedge and flew close to his face, startling him. *Forget I ever asked, Joyce.*

'Buckle your seatbelt, Eddie,' she said. 'The first time was a few months before my thirteenth birthday.' She delivered this statement in a flat way, as if it were something she was reading from a prepared health bulletin. *The patient is comfortable and is off the critical list. We don't expect any further complications.*

370

Dear Christ. He didn't know what to say. Stunned. He'd assumed the affair was of more recent vintage – maybe the last six or seven years, on and off again. Now she was telling him something else, and he couldn't take it in. He couldn't find room for it. Couldn't get his mind round it.

'He'd always been so kind to me, Eddie, it just seemed that what we did was natural,' she said.

'Twelve,' he said.

'Almost thirteen.'

'What's the difference?' He thought, Twelve is only a word. Let it go. But no, he couldn't, twelve was a child, a kid, an innocent. Caskie had committed a crime.

'You consented to it,' he said.

'Yes.'

'Even if you gave your consent, it's still –'

'I know what you're going to say, and I know what you're thinking,' she said. 'How could he do it with a girl that young? He must be some kind of perve, a monster. Look at me, Eddie. Don't turn away. I *wanted* him to do it. It was all I had to give him in return because he'd been good to me. Here, my body, it's all yours, take it, I want you to have it –'

'I don't need to hear this,' Eddie said.

'But I damn well need to tell you. He was twenty-nine and married, and I was almost thirteen, and after that first time it became a regular occurrence. We'd meet, he'd find some place to take me, a hotel out of the city, he'd book us into different rooms just in case . . . So it went on.'

'And on, and on.'

'We tried to break it off a few times over the years.'

But true love conquers all, Eddie thought. It can vanquish any enemy. He couldn't picture Joyce, *twelve years of age*, spreading her legs for Caskie in a hotel room, Caskie entering her, man into child: did he speak of love, did he talk of a future? She'd fall for it. She was a kid, and optimistic. Yeah, she'd go for it. Eyes closed, a supplicant before her own future, she'd dream her romantic dreams even as Caskie thrust himself inside her and grunted, and the years rolled away and still he remained married, and her hopes diminished to the extent that she met and married Haskell just to escape – what? Her own disappointment? Some sense of shame? Twelve years of age, he thought. Jesus Christ. He felt unsettled, queasy. It wasn't his thing, schoolgirls and their little skirts and their blazers and their gymslips, their smoothly innocent faces and tiny breasts. For some guys, sure, it was a big twisted kick, they sat in the half-light of their computer screens and scoured the Internet for images to incite them, the Web pimped for them – but he'd never understood that kind of lust. He'd perceived it as sickness. He'd seen too many runaway schoolgirls raped by middle-aged men, sodomized and forced to participate in orgies and drugged and God knows what else. He'd seen them dumped inside derelict buildings or on abandoned railroad lines, alive, half-alive.

Joyce said, 'We couldn't stay away from each other, Eddie. It was a kind of insanity. It's always been like that.'

'It's an insanity, granted,' he said.

'Oh, you don't have to sound so damn smug. Who are you to judge?'

'I wasn't judging.'

'You prick. You can't help yourself.'

'Okay. I'm judging. I have a moral view. It's instinctive.

I can't help it. Who else knows about you and your boyfriend?'

'Nobody.'

He placed his hands on his sister's shoulders and, lowering his head, looked directly into her eyes. What did he see in there? A tiny hint of sorrow because she'd kept her secret and the effort made her lonesome, or a touch of relief that she'd finally told somebody? He wasn't sure.

Twelve, he thought. 12. Two times six. Three times four. Work the figures any way you like, it still came out twelve.

He said, 'I think somebody knew.'

'I'm positive they didn't, Eddie.'

'Here's an educated guess. Roddy Haggs.'

She shook her head. 'No, not –'

'He found out. He had the knowledge. So he had the power. Do whatever I ask you to do, Chris old pal, or I'll blow the whistle and it's going to be heard all over the land. High-level cop fucks underage girl. Field day in the tabloids. They have a name for this crime, Chris. So cooperate with me, Inspector, or you're going to hell on a fast bus . . . It makes sense, Joyce.'

'We were careful, Eddie. Very careful.'

'You thought you were.'

'I *know* we were.'

'Secrets are the hardest things to keep. You're seen on the street by chance, or you're noticed stepping into a taxi or catching a train, or maybe in the parking lot of some rustic hotel you think is remote and nobody knows you, but it's a small world . . .' He dropped his hands from her shoulders. 'Do you really love him?'

'I don't know. I'm not sure what love is. When I was

twelve I would have died for him. I thought he was damn adorable. He could've asked me to jump off a bridge and I would've done it without hesitation. When I was twenty I wanted to live with him, the whole domestic bit. Cook, clean, have kids by him. By the time I was thirty I realized I'd become accustomed to sex with him. There was still this spark, this passion. Now . . . now I think it's a pleasant habit, Eddie, one I can't imagine living without. Is that what love is in the end? A habit? I have an addictive personality anyway, for God's sake . . .'

'I hope to Christ you don't love him, Joyce. I think he's got all kinds of problems coming down on him sooner or later. I don't want to see you hurt. I don't want you drawn into something that can only end unpleasantly.'

'I don't believe he had any involvement in Dad's death,' she said. 'I'll never believe that. Not in a hundred years. No way.'

'In a hundred years we'll all be history,' Eddie said. 'And none of this will matter a damn.'

'You can't live your life from that perspective, Eddie.'

'When stuff gets unbearable, you can try.'

She suddenly wept then, pressing her fingertips against her eyebrows, inclining her face. He watched tears roll down her cheeks and he reached out and held her and he thought of the little girl with the ribbon in her hair who played *Chopsticks* on the piano with flamboyant movements of her hands, like a melodramatic concert pianist, and Jackie would say, 'Good Christ, girl, is there nothing *else* you can learn to play?'

Jackie's voice echoed in his head.

He was filled with a deep yearning to go home, and leave Joyce to the misadventures of her heart, and forget Jackie Mallon. What do you owe him anyway? Whatever illicit activity he was involved in was a link in a chain of lies and violence. You didn't do business with a killer like Gurk without making a statement about yourself: okay, so you didn't pull a trigger and kill somebody, Jackie, but you were prepared to associate with a man who was a shooter, so what did that make you? If you knew what Gurk was capable of, you were an accessory. And if you *didn't* know, then greed had made you blind. And if you were trying to recover any decency with your phone calls to Queens, and your regrets about how you'd driven a stake through the soul of the family, and how love had to be restored, goddammit, you let it all slip through your fingers, didn't you, Dad?

And yet he couldn't resist the thought: *Jackie wasn't responsible for his associates, was he?* You went into business with someone, and he turned out bad, it happened all the time to people . . . Screw it, Eddie, even now you're looking for an avenue leading towards forgiveness. Even after all that has happened, you still come back to the hope that you can find a cleft of light in your heart and a way to rescue Jackie from damnation. Why can't you just despise him, and let it go like that? You're a kid again, and he's telling you how he'll take you to Balloch and hire a boat and go fishing, except that day never came, *but you're still fucking waiting for it*, aren't you, Eddie, even when it's impossible . . .

The sun began its very slow summery descent. He listened to his sister crying, and he had the impression that the city all around him was built on foundations of deception and greed.

52

When she left Eddie, Joyce walked back to the house. Caskie was standing at the table in the conservatory and she pressed herself against his back and circled her arms round him and locked her hands upon his chest. She knew without looking that his eyes were closed. She knew him so well. She knew him better than anyone ever had.

'You told him,' Caskie said.

'I felt so bloody fraudulent, Chris. I don't want that feeling. Skulking, lying. I don't want that.'

'You went back to the beginning?'

She said yes, she'd gone back.

'How did he take it?' Caskie said. 'I don't have to ask, do I?'

'He looked unpleasantly surprised. Distressed. What do you expect?'

'And angry. He'd feel angry.'

She laid her cheek against his spine and smelled the cologne he wore and she wondered what it always reminded her of, she could never quite reach the heart of the scent. 'He said Haggs knew about us.'

'Did *you* tell him that?'

'He guessed Haggs had you in a bind. A stranglehold.'

'He's smart,' Caskie said. 'It's not always a good thing to be.'

Say it, she thought. Say the next bit. Spit it out. 'He thinks . . . He thinks you might have had something to do with Jackie's death. You and Haggs colluded. You conspired in some way.'

'That's what comes of being just a little *too* smart.' Caskie turned, caught her chin between his fingers. 'Look at me. Do you really think I had *anything* to do with your father's killing?'

'No, of course I don't.'

'You feel absolutely certain when you say that?'

'Yes,' she said.

He caressed her cheek. 'Haggs has had me in chains for years, you know that. I've done him some favours, things I shouldn't have done. Maybe I could have been strong enough to tell him no, turn him down, but that's water under the bridge. Killing, though, good Christ, no no, there's just no way – that's something else, Joyce.'

'I know that.'

'It's beyond consideration. I'd never agree to anything that brought you misery, never.'

She thought of their relationship, this little world they'd created, and how private it was. You could withdraw inside it and lock the doors and shutter the windows and light candles, and then it was only you and Chris and everything else could go to hell.

'It's going to change,' he said.

'What is?'

'This situation with Haggs. I'm going to change it.'

'How?'

'Just trust me. I have to get dressed and go into the office.'

'No, not yet.'

'I have to,' he said.

'No, don't hurry away.'

He hesitated, then lowered his face to hers, and she felt his warm breath upon the side of her neck and she enjoyed the soft touch of his beard, and she slid a hand down to the belt of his robe and she thought how easily he led her, how easily she wanted to *be* led, and how he'd had this same effect on her for years, even during the period of her miserable marriage to Haskell when she'd deliberately cut Caskie out of her life, but oh God she'd *longed* for him, Mrs Harry Haskell dreaming of her lover and how tender he was, and considerate, and remembering all the times they'd met in hotels, even when Meg was dying, yes, even then. He'd have a nurse come in to look after Meg and he'd slip away.

Sometimes she detected Meg's ghost in this house, like a quick shadow in a stairwell, or a brush of clothing against a wall. *I hadn't loved Meg in years*, he'd once told her. *Not in the man–woman sense. I don't feel guilt, Joyce, I never have about you.*

He slid her blouse off, and inclined his head to her shoulder and she felt his open mouth on her flesh and the touch of his teeth. She had her hand inside his robe, his cock in her palm, and she went down on her knees and pressed her face into him. She listened to the soft moan of pleasure he always made and it struck her that at the core of this sound there was something else, another tone, a kind of subdued lament. As if, like her, he regretted the years of subterfuge, and the voluminous lies. As if in some secret corner of himself he was sad, and this diminished his pleasure. She cupped his testicles in her palm and when she needed it least she heard an echo of Eddie's voice, *he helped arrange the mechanics of the killing*, and she dismissed the whisper, exploded it, sent the splinters flying out of her mind. One day, maybe, Eddie would know that the real Christopher Caskie was a sweet man, genuine, gentle and warm. One day.

'My girl,' Caskie said. 'Oh my dear girl. My love.'

53

Tommy Gurk took a taxi to Gorbals Street, south of the Clyde. The car was a bottle-green Fiat, parked close to the Citizens' Theatre. The keys were inside a magnetized steel box attached to the underside of the bumper. Gurk opened the box, got the keys. The heat inside the car made his hairless skull sweat. His head felt raw, like a rash was developing. He'd worn dreadlocks a long time now. It was bizarre having a scalp as naked as a baby's bum.

He glanced at the directions somebody had left on the passenger seat. Written on a sheet of blue-lined paper, they were easy and explicit. Gurk shook his head, amazed. See, this is where you had to hand it to Kaminsky, the way he had of doing things, he had minions all over the shop, geezers who did stuff without even knowing who they were working for, locating weapons, delivering envelopes, providing cars, no questions asked – there was a big intricate network of connections in different countries. People always owed Joe Kaminsky favours. And they always obliged. The consequences of failure, well, they didn't bear consideration.

Off we go, Tommy Gurk thought.

He drove along Pollokshaws Road, heading south.

There were cop cars all over the place, and once or twice he felt he was being scrutinized, once or twice he had a little electric-prod of paranoia, but the trick was to look cool, and that meant you had to feel you had your shit together inside. You had the juice. Cool within, cool without. All the way, baby. You were just a guy driving along Kilmarnock Road, and the fact you had brown skin, tally-ho, that was no impediment. Just follow the directions, get into the rhythm of the road, put some miles behind you, drive into the sweet Zone. Then the directions got a little more complicated, but not much, he could handle it, he was beginning to feel more like himself.

Into the roundabout, zippedy-doo, no sweat. A few more blocks and here we are. And a jolly nice street it is too. Prosperous. Very much so. Go slow. This is white bread land and you stand out like Malcolm X at a Klan convention. He sang to lull himself. He did his Paul Robeson voice. *Old man ribber*. He was close to the house now, he checked the numbers, noticed how some of the homes had names because jokers who lived here thought that was posh. He sang Belafonte's 'Banana Boat Song' and stared at the name of the house and waited, slouched in the driver's seat, motor running.

54

Caskie usually made Lou Perlman feel that he was an inferior being, a dunderhead allowed five minutes of human conversation. Caskie's bearing was one of low-grade tolerance. They sat in Caskie's office in Force HQ and Caskie sipped coffee out of a plastic cup.

'It's tragic about Charlie,' Perlman said.

'It's a heartbreak.'

'He was a nice young guy. I'm sorry for his parents.' Perlman noticed how tidy Caskie's desk was. Pencils in containers. Pens lined up on the leather cover of a notebook. Caskie's fingernails were immaculate. He must have them manicured, Lou Perlman thought. Maybe at the hairdresser's he has the whole *schmear*, beard trim, manicure, hot towel shave.

'Tay's asked me to clarify a few things,' Perlman said. 'For the record.'

'Of course.'

'What was Charlie doing at Central Station, Chris?'

Caskie shrugged. 'I gave Charlie a broad remit, Lou. We'd have to look through his records, the logs he kept.'

'So you gave him his head, you let him run, is that what you're saying?'

'Exactly.'

And pigs have wings in that world, Perlman thought. You never gave Charlie an inch of breathing space. You kept Charlie in a black room of your own design. 'You're telling me you have no idea what he was working on that would've taken him to Central Station?'

'Come to think of it, he was quite excited about information he was gathering in a case involving the theft of a valuable coin collection from a house in Langside a month ago. We can examine his notes, Lou.' Caskie glanced at his watch.

A young man's dead and you're checking the time, Caskie. What does that tell me? You have another appointment, better things to do. 'So you have no idea about the identity of the killer?'

'I wish to God I did. Again, I can only say that we should look at McWhinnie's papers and maybe we'll find some kind of hint.'

I'm hearing a looped tape, Perlman thought. Check Charlie's notes. His log. Aye. Sure. Maybe Charlie had written, *I suspect a black called Winston Smith, 24 Garturk Street, Govanhill, of stealing a valuable coin collection and I intend to arrest him at Central Station during rush hour.* And that also belonged in the same world as jet-propelled pigs.

'He never mentioned a black guy to you?' Perlman asked.

'No, never.'

'All right. We'll look through his stuff. See what there is.'

Caskie was quiet a moment. 'I intend to take retirement, Lou.'

'Is that a fact?'

'I've written a letter I'll give to Superintendent Tay in the morning. You're the first to know.'

'Is this not a wee bit sudden?' Perlman was surprised that Caskie had confided in him. But it wasn't exactly an act of intimacy. There was no sense of sharing involved, no exposure of self. Perlman felt Caskie simply needed an audience to make his announcement, and it didn't matter who was in the room with him. A tea-lady, a janitor, anybody.

'It's been coming a long time,' Caskie said. 'Maybe the death of McWhinnie's the last straw. I don't know.' He got up from his desk and walked to the window and stood with his hands tucked in the pockets of his double-breasted jacket. He stared down into Pitt Street where the falling sun had begun to create shadows and he wondered if he was being premature in announcing his retirement. What if things went wrong? What if the scheme he'd devised with Kaminsky became derailed? No, don't think that way. It'll work. Even as you stand here, it's in motion.

He thought of Eddie Mallon striding out of the house in Broomhill Drive, leaving the front door open behind him. And of Joyce, how tiny she looked inside the bathrobe, how quickly she dressed to catch up with Eddie Mallon. She wanted her brother to know she felt bad concealing the truth from him – all very fine and honourable, but Caskie wasn't so sure Eddie could take that truth calmly. He'd disapprove furiously. Adult men and pubescent girls – Eddie Mallon would see it as an immoral equation. He wouldn't understand that kind of love; it was socially unacceptable as well as criminal, and had to be carried out in hotel rooms and cars parked in lonely places. Caskie had never found delight in the illicit aspect of it.

384

He'd feared the condemnation of men, and the disgrace of imprisonment.

And then there was Haggs.

Once, many years ago in a gloomy little motel outside Edinburgh, he and Joyce had been checking out at the reception desk when Joyce, in an ill-judged moment of impetuosity, a spark of affectionate mischief, had linked an arm through his, and laid her head against his shoulder, and run the tip of her shoe against the inside of his leg –

– and there in the lobby was bloody Haggs, registering this intimacy with a leer. Two days later Haggs had phoned. *I've been studying this situation, Chris. And you know what? I've got you by the family jewels. You're all mine, pal.*

And down the years Caskie did Haggs a favour here, a favour there. Overlook this, ignore that, help me out with this allegation of stolen property. Assist me with this, gimme a hand with that. You are my private cop, Caskie.

And then one day: I need help with the Mallons, Chris.

I need some assistance with Jackie.

When exactly had the final escalation begun? Caskie couldn't remember the date, there was a passage of time when everything accelerated, and he could recall only fragments. Haggs had become frantic because Jackie was up to something, and he couldn't find out what, and so he dreamed up a plan, and he needed Caskie to get Bones out of the way for a while, a few hours, take him someplace safe overnight, you can arrange that, Chris, dead easy for you, eh?

Caskie thought: Haggs didn't really need *me*. He could

385

have used *anyone* to pressure Bones into taking a walk at the appropriate time. All he wanted was to drag me deeper into the mire of his life. Show me he had control. Remind me of all the years he had a hold on my world.

And make me a partner in murder.

Caskie tried to shut down his memory as a man might close a very old door, but the hinges were stiff with rust.

You want Jackie alone, Haggs?

Aye, for a wee while.

I'll see what I can do.

Try to deny it, but you knew in your heart that there was murder in the air. You could smell it as certainly as the stench of a long-dead carcass. You knew Jackie Mallon was being set up. Joyce's father. You wanted to stop it. Let Haggs blast his revelations all over the tabloid sheets. Live with the disgrace. You can go down in people's memories as that cop who molested a wee girl. Caskie, pervert.

But you couldn't. You turned your face, looked away.

You even took the murder weapon in a plastic grocery bag.

He felt deeply depressed. He thought, Soon I'll be free. 'It's time to draw the blinds and lock the door and hang a Gone Away sign.'

'You'll miss it,' Perlman said.

'Miss what? The hours? The flood of crime?'

The power, Perlman thought. That's what you'll miss. 'I take the point,' he said.

Caskie seemed suddenly expansive, but in his own detached way. It was as if he'd come down a rung or two on the ladder where he lived his life, and found it a risky descent. 'It's a liberation, Lou. I feel I've been carrying a backpack of bricks around for years. I've wanted to let go before now. But the time wasn't quite right . . .'

'And now it is.'

'Yes. I'm ready. It's time.'

You don't have the look of a man anticipating serenity, Perlman thought. There's no air of celebration about you. Where's the champagne spirit, Christopher? Where is that I-don't-give-a-shit good cheer?

Maybe McWhinnie's death has done you in after all.

Caskie released a smile, as if it were a lick-penny's offering dropped into a collection-box. He looked at his watch again. 'I have a few things to do, Lou.'

Perlman got up. 'Fine.'

'Feel free to ask me anything you like about McWhinnie. I'll be available.'

'Thanks,' and Perlman turned towards the door and that was when his brain kicked him. *Sunny. Brook. A mass of curls.*

55

Haggs drove his Jaguar along Nitshill Road for a mile before taking a right turn, which led him through narrow suburban streets. He marvelled at the tidiness of some lives. Blackhill, where he'd been born, was a squalid pit of tribal divisions and deprivation, of runny-nosed wee kids screaming in shite-soaked nappies that hadn't been changed in days, of men standing on street corners and bemoaning the failures of their lives and the general lack of justice, of petty thieves and burglaries and drunkenness and casual acts of violence, the swift arc of a razor, the violent flick of a sharpened steel comb. It was a million fucking miles in his wake and he was never going back that way again, and if Twiddie and his brain-dead crumpet menaced his pleasant little world in any little way, they were history.

Eventually the streets thinned out and he entered an industrial estate, one that was clearly not thriving. FOR RENT signs hung outside hangar-sized buildings. Companies long defunct had had their names whited out but sometimes you could discern a spectral impression in faded paint of these former tenants, THOMAS BAILEY & SON, WELDERS. Or half a name might still survive in rust-coloured letters, like an enigma to be solved: GR SON EXP S D S V CE.

Haggs parked outside a small brick building that he owned for various purposes. A car he was obliged to stash, a shipment of this or that passing through. A meeting he wanted to hold in total privacy. The building was functional, the roof metal. The sign outside said GLENLORA RENTALS, although there was no indication of whatever might be available for rent. Haggs unlocked the door and went inside. He turned on the light because there were no windows. A sink was situated in a corner. There was a rudimentary crapper behind a partition. The air smelled dead. The space was hot with the day's trapped warmth.

Haggs shut the door and walked to the middle of the room and stood with his hands in his pockets and thought of burning vans and amateur arsonists and diddies in general who endangered your way of life. And that fucking Jew was no dummy. You could practically hear him calculate. He couldn't have Perlman strutting inside his golf club. He couldn't live with that.

Haggs walked in circles. He jingled his car keys in his pocket. That bloody wallet. How could they have overlooked that? They hadn't checked the van before they tried to torch it. It was elementary shite.

He heard a sound from outside. The slam of a car door.

He heard John Twiddie's voice. Then Twiddie and the Bucket-Faced Girlfriend entered the building. Rita was all pins, jaggy protrusions, things like miniature knitting needles sticking out of her piled-up hair or dangling from her earlobes. There was some sharp object lanced through her lower lip and a shiny stud in an eyebrow.

She wouldn't want to be outdoors in an electric storm, Haggs thought. He listened to the way her black leather trousers creaked as she moved. Twiddie, besuited in his counterfeit couture, wore a white slim-jim tie and a black shirt, what he considered gangster chic.

Haggs said, 'You're wondering why you're here.'

Rita said, 'Aye. It's a long way to come.'

'Oh, you're inconvenienced. I'm dead sorry. Note to self: do not inconvenience Rita in future.'

'So, eh,' Twiddie said. 'What's the score?'

Rita sniffed the air. 'Stinks a bit in here.'

'Only since you arrived,' Haggs said.

'Cheek,' Rita said.

Twiddie smiled. He understood the insult, and saw the need to defend Rita, but Haggs was the boss, and even if you despised Long Roddy his money kept you in cigarettes and clothes and food. He wasn't a man you crossed. So Twiddie's dilemma was resolved in a pallid smile.

'Fuck you grinning at, Twiddie?'

'I don't know,' Twiddie said.

'Fucking stupid grinning at nothing.' Haggs tugged Twiddie's tie out from his jacket and tossed the end of it over Twiddie's shoulder.

'Here,' Twiddie said.

Rita said, 'Leave him alone.'

'Don't you ever tell me what to do, bitch. Don't you open your mouth unless you're spoken to.'

'Fuck you,' Rita said.

Quickly, Haggs plucked a long needle from her hair and jabbed her face with it. He drew blood instantly. The girl yelped.

'I'm wounded. You've wounded me, Haggs.'

Twiddie said, 'You all right, love?'

Haggs said, 'She's not all right. You're not all right. You're both up shit creek. Pair of you. You couldn't burn that fucking van. Which would be bad enough. But you go one better. You overlook the old bastard's fucking wallet in the back of the fucking van.'

'Wallet? We didn't see the wallet,' Twiddie said.

'And your matches were damp as well, I suppose.'

'Some fires don't take,' Rita said.

Haggs's anger had the propulsion of a moon-shot. 'I've built myself a life. I like it. I like it an awful lot. I can't have it jeopardized by two completely worthless wankers like you pair. Do you understand that?'

'So, eh, what do you, ah, propose?' Twiddie said.

'I'd dearly like to torture you for a while, maybe a day or two, and then snuff you out.'

Twiddie laughed. Rita didn't. She said, 'Talk's cheap.'

Haggs cracked his knuckles. How in God's name had he ever become associated with this couple? There were moments of pleasure at times, sure, driving the dark streets, the sheer buzz of hands-on brutality, dancing with menace. But when you had Perlman in your own clubhouse right in your bloody face, when you smelled a bad tide swirling in your direction, then it was time for serious changes.

'You'll leave Glasgow,' he said.

'Is zat so?' Rita asked.

'You'll go to London. From London you'll catch a train to Holland, Germany, wherever, I don't give a fuck.'

'Wait a minute,' Rita said. 'I like Glasgow. I don't see why I should leave. My friends are here.'

Haggs said, 'You're not getting the picture, Rita. You

don't have a choice. Either you leave the country . . . or some more permanent location is found for you.'

'You're talking about . . .' Twiddie paused.

'I'm talking about closing time, Twiddie. You know, when the barman says drink up and leave, and he flicks the lights, and you're out on the street? I'm talking about that kind of situation. Only there's no tomorrow, see. You don't go back to the pub next day because for you there is no next day.'

'You've arranged this?' Rita asked.

Haggs said, 'It only takes one phone call.'

'So we bugger off and live in poverty with a buncha krauts and you go on enjoying the good life. Fuck that for a lark.'

'You'll receive compensation,' Haggs said. 'Which is bloody generous of me, considering I have that other option I just mentioned.'

'I want fifty grand, Haggs,' Rita said.

Haggs said, 'I split my sides.'

'What's your figure?' she asked.

'Five K each max. No haggling.'

'Har,' Twiddie said.

'Take it, leave it.' Haggs shrugged. 'One way or another, you don't live in this city any more. I want you gone by tonight.'

'Tonight?' Rita asked.

Twiddie said, 'Can't be done.'

'No choice,' Haggs said. 'Life's like that. In the immortal words of a certain M. Jagger, Twid, you can't always get what you want. Remember that.'

56

Eddie let himself into Joyce's flat. He felt weak, liquid-headed. The sun was dying and twilight gathered slowly in the city. He slipped off his damp T-shirt, took a fresh white linen shirt from his bag. He buttoned the shirt then pulled his dark suit, the one he'd wear at the funeral, from the bottom of the bag. He laid it on a chair, smoothed it with his hands. It made little difference, but so what? A crumpled suit: small potatoes in the scheme of things.

The day came rushing back at him. The train to Largs. The great bright promise of the sea at Saltcoats and the happy faces of the kids at the carriage windows. Ice cream and candy floss and gulls and innocence.

How it changed.

McWhinnie dying. Charlie in blood. The day framed in blood.

And then Joyce. Hotel rooms with Caskie, the child and the man, crushed sheets and skewed pillows. Why did he imagine rain sweeping hard across a dreary car park and battering the window of a tiny hotel room where Caskie had drawn the curtains and Joyce was undressing by the light of the bedside lamp?

He heard the doorbell ring. He went down the hallway to answer. Lou Perlman, stooped, hands behind his back, stood in shadow.

Perlman said, 'Invite me in.'

Eddie stepped aside, Perlman entered. Eddie shut the door and led Perlman into the living room.

Perlman lit a cigarette and said, 'SUNY. State University of New York. Right?'

'Right –'

'And Stony Brook is a campus in the system. You had it on your T-shirt earlier today. And yesterday when we met.'

'You saw me today?' Eddie asked.

'Me, no. Some other people did. At Central Station with Charlie. So tell me this – why were you with Charlie and what did the pair of you have in common?'

Eddie looked at the brown suit and the soiled tie and the shirt with the collar tips slightly upturned. He wasn't sure why, but he'd always felt at ease with Perlman. Probably the man's lack of affectation, the fact he made no concessions to modify his accent for the untrained ear: this is me, Lou Perlman, and I don't come in any other wrapping.

Eddie said, 'McWhinnie was helping me chase Gurk.'

'AKA Tommy G. See, I remembered to check the computer.' He dragged on his cigarette so deeply his cheeks hollowed. 'You and Charlie were working together? He never said.'

'He didn't have time to say. It happened suddenly. He liked a taste of action, I guess. He was sick of working for Caskie.'

'He wasn't the happiest young man I ever met, I'll say that,' Perlman remarked. 'So you and Charlie were in hot pursuit of Gurk. Charlie caught up with Gurk in the crowd. A struggle, then . . .'

'I went after Gurk, but he'd gone. I walked the streets for a time. I don't remember which ones. Just streets.' He pictured McWhinnie, and felt as if he'd had all the air kicked out of him. There was that ache in his neck again, resurgent. His thoughts, darkening and gloomy, drifted back to Joyce, and how she'd appeared on the staircase in Caskie's house, and then he remembered his conversation with Caskie just before Joyce had materialized out of shadow. *You set my father up.*

Surmise, Caskie had said.

Eddie shut his eyes. Surmise, no. It wasn't surmise that had killed Charlie McWhinnie. Caskie's face formed in his head, that smug little beard, that look of self-assurance, and he was filled suddenly with an anger so deep that it depressed him he could feel such a disagreeable emotion with this *intensity*.

He looked at Perlman and said, 'What do you think of Caskie, Lou? What do you *really* think of him?'

'Really? Not much. He's a class-act shite. He's a *keech* in a good suit. Fortunately he's about to retire, so he won't be occupying my thoughts much longer.'

'He just walks off into the sunset,' Eddie said. And maybe Joyce walks with him, he thought. 'It's more than he fucking deserves, Lou.'

'And what precisely does he deserve, Eddie?'

'What usually happens when you're an accessory before and after the fact of a murder. Jail, right?'

'Hold on. Put your foot on the brake. *Murder*, you say?' Perlman turned his head sharply and his glasses slipped down his nose. He caught them before they slid from his face.

Eddie said, 'Murder. The killing of my father. Caskie pulled strings in the background.'

'Murder's very rich gravy,' Perlman said, and focused his good eye hard on Eddie. 'Can you make it stick to the wall, son?'

Eddie, gazing at the high ceiling, saw a spider's web in which a couple of dead flies hung. *Make it stick to the wall*. He heard himself talk about the safe house, and how McWhinnie had escorted Bones there, and how Caskie must have participated in the killing of Jackie Mallon in some way, and Haggs's role in the scheme of things, and the words tumbled out of him, and they kept coming, colliding one with another until his throat was dry and he was rambling, and he'd begun to repeat himself. He wondered how he sounded to Perlman. Deranged? The victim of delusion?

He fell silent.

Perlman ran a hand through his bristle of hair. 'It's great gravy, son, and my appetite is well and truly whetted, and if you think you see me drooling, you're dead fucking right – but it's still not sticking.'

Eddie said, 'Bones could have provided the glue, but God knows where he went. And McWhinnie knew some of Caskie's machinations, but that poor bastard isn't coming back to tell us. So . . .'

'So I hear you howling in the wind, Eddie. Unless . . .'

'Unless what?'

'Unless I can make Haggs talk. Problem is, he's a stone, and it's damned hard to squeeze blood out of something that has none.'

'You can try,' Eddie said.

'Oh, I'd love to try, I'd *love* it,' Perlman said. He plucked at his eyepatch and rubbed his hands together briskly as if he were pleased. 'Call a taxi, Eddie.'

They rode in a black cab through the south of the city. Eddie recognized a couple of landmarks when they were in the vicinity of Haggs's neighbourhood. The big roundabout. Rouken Glen. Langtree Avenue and the house called Drumpellier. Lou Perlman didn't get out of the cab at once. He gazed in the direction of the house.

'I'll go in alone, Eddie. Me and him, we talk the same talk.'

'You've thought how you'll approach this?'

'I wing shit all the time, son.' Perlman winked. 'Maybe I'll hint we've got some truly damning evidence, then see what happens. Or I'll say Caskie confessed to everything. Who knows? I'm a man of great invention when I need to be.'

'He'll call his lawyer immediately.'

Perlman said, 'We'll see.'

Eddie stayed in the cab. He watched Perlman push through the front gate. He moved with a quiet confidence, like an insurance salesman certain of a client's signature on a policy. Eddie waited. The driver listened to a talk show on the radio. Eddie gazed at the house. He heard a sound of breaking glass – a swift crack – then he saw Perlman come back. He'd been gone little more than a minute.

'Nobody's home,' Perlman said.

'What was that noise?'

'Noise?'

'Glass breaking.'

'Oh, that.' Perlman looked slyly pleased. 'Those bloody

security cameras depress me, Eddie. I mean, here's this thing on a fucking stalk peering into your face without permission. I'm a Luddite, son. So I took a fine stout branch to it. Whackety-whack.'

'You vandalized it,' Eddie said.

'I *pulverized* it.'

'Now what?'

Perlman settled in the back of the cab and looked thoughtful. 'Haggs could be almost anywhere. One of his favourite restaurants, say. His golf club maybe . . . Or.'

'Or what?'

'He's got this run-down place he sometimes goes when he needs privacy. He thinks it's his secret rendezvous, and nobody else knows about it. He hasn't got a bloody clue I've clocked the place more than a few times and I've seen him come and go. Great fun to watch somebody who doesn't know he's being watched. This is worth a try.'

Perlman leaned forward to instruct the cab driver.

57

'Wotcher, mates.'

Haggs turned towards the door. He hadn't heard it open.

The man who stepped in kicked the door shut behind him, and smiled a big white-toothed smile. His bald brown scalp shone under the electric light and he carried himself in an easy manner, as if he had the ability to slough off all life's problems.

'Who the *fuck* are you?' Haggs asked.

'Tommy Gurk.'

'Gurk?' Haggs asked.

'Got it in one. Pardon my bad manners, if you will, but I been eavesdropping your conversation. It seems to me I can save you all kinds of problems, providing you do everything my way.'

'And what way is that?' Haggs asked.

Gurk had a gun in his hand. Out of nowhere, conjured up like a magician's prop, there it was, steel enclosed in a firm brown hand.

Twiddie said, 'He's fucking armed.'

'Bright boy,' Gurk said.

'You're not going to use that,' Rita said.

'It all depends, my beauty,' Gurk said.

'Depends on what?' Haggs asked.

'What do you know about my business with Jackie Mallon?'

'Sweet fuck all,' Haggs said.

Without expression, Gurk turned away from Haggs and shot Twiddie in the head. It was done so quickly, so casually, it was seconds before Haggs or Rita registered the fact that a gun had been fired and Twiddie had buckled like a beast shot in a slaughterhouse and lay sideways on the floor, and blood was flowing in little streams around his skull. Rita slumped to her knees beside Twiddie and covered her open mouth with her hand. She was terrifyingly mute.

'Now,' Gurk said. 'Have I got your attention?'

Haggs had a falling sensation, as if his internal organs had slipped inches inside him. He wondered if Billy McQueen had felt like this on the high-rise when he looked down the dark shaft. 'Very definitely. What do you want to know?'

'I hear you're looking for a certain cargo that was the basis of a business agreement involving the late Jackie Mallon, the just as late Billy McQueen and my good self.'

'I expressed an interest,' Haggs said. 'Mallon wouldn't give me the time of day.'

'And so you had him snuffed. And then you had Billy the Stump snuffed as well because he couldn't tell you jack shit.'

'Let's say there was, ah, a breakdown in communication.'

'But you're still looking to get in, aintcha?' Gurk asked.

Haggs said, 'Aye, but I'm tired banging my head

against a shithouse wall.' Was there a way out of this? he wondered. Could he ever walk away from this building and get in his car and go home? He was conscious of Rita bent over the dead Twiddie, and how she'd started to sob, and he imagined his life flushed down a toilet and swirling away, all the good things he'd accumulated sucked into sewers. He wanted to say *Spare me*. But he'd never begged in his life and he wasn't about to begin now. Note to self: Never ask for mercy. It lacks dignity.

Gurk looked at Rita and said, 'Here, love. Stifle that snivelling, eh? It's giving me the willies.'

Rita looked up at Gurk. Mascara ran down her face like ink spilled carelessly. Her hands were locked in upraised fists. 'You fucking *killed* him, you fucking pig, you fucking *cunt*.'

'Well, yeh. I did. I can hardly deny it, can I? So now you're lonely, is that it? Horrible being on your tod. Tell you what, love, I'll fix it for you. Cheerio, dear.' Gurk smiled and fired the gun and Haggs saw Rita's head split open like a squash that had dropped from the back of a vegetable lorry screaming down the motorway, and, sickened, he looked away from the sight.

Gurk said, 'You were saying, Haggsy.'

Haggs had a hard time regulating his voice. 'I was saying Mallon told me nothing.'

'He didn't mention the whereabouts or the nature of the cargo?'

'He never discussed any of that,' Haggs said. He might have had an old sock stuffed in his throat, so thick did his voice sound. He stared at Gurk's gun until it expanded and filled his vision entirely and then beyond even that. It was bigger than the world. His hearing had somehow been heightened – a tap dripped once every thirty seconds into the sink, a moth trapped and dying beat quietly at the metal roof, and something wet slid down the wall behind Rita but he didn't want to look.

'We weren't close, you know. We weren't friends.'

'Business involves trust, and me and my associates don't trust you, Haggsy. We don't like the idea of you looking under stones trying to find our property. We don't like you swanning around this dandy old city looking for something that isn't yours. I mean, what if you was to stumble over it, eh? You'd tell us, right? Yeh, sure, and I shit gold bricks. It would be gone in a flash, pal. And where would that leave me and my colleagues, eh? Out of pocket and no chance of recovering our goods.'

Haggs said, 'Look, I'd like to help, honest –'

'Oh, I'd like that too.' Gurk glanced at the gun in his hand. 'But my associates feel you've trespassed on their territory. You've been too fucking eager to muscle in on something that's got nothing to do with you. In short, you're out of fucking control, jack.'

'I can make inquiries on your behalf,' Haggs said. 'I know people, I can ask questions –'

'You been busy asking questions already, Haggsy. And it hasn't worked out very well. We're left with no cargo, and two dead associates. That's not kosher, is it? We can't have you giving us grief, squire.'

Haggs said, 'Maybe I can help. I know my way round this city, I know people who knew Jackie, the guys that worked for him in his warehouse in Bluevale Street, aye, you could ask them, or you could talk to the people he drank with, they might know something. Then there's his son Eddie –' *I'm begging*, he thought. *And I swore I never would.*

'Look at it this way,' Gurk said. 'This life is just a stage you're passing through. Shadows on walls, mate. Everything is appearance. You'll be back in some other form.'

'Once around the block is enough for me,' Haggs said. He couldn't think of anything else to say, any plea he might enter on his own behalf that would persuade this cold smiling brown man he was worth sparing. He took one step back and Gurk, who defined the past, present and future of Roddy Haggs, popped off a shot which Haggs heard only for as long as it takes an eye to blink.

'Fucking carnage,' Gurk said, and wondered how badly he'd dented the thin brass-plating of his karma. Very badly, he imagined. In his next incarnation he'd be a bleeding aphid with a lifespan of about forty-five minutes. He surveyed the bodies and stuffed the gun in his waistband and went outside just as a black cab came into the parking area.

A man got out of the taxi. That fucker from the hotel in Largs, Gurk thought. The one who'd chased him through the train station. Gurk moved quickly towards his car.

The man shouted, 'Gurk!'

Gurk fired off a single shot and it struck the door of the taxi and the man threw himself to the ground. Gurk opened the door of his green Fiat and got behind the wheel, aware of a second figure stepping out of the cab now, an older man who crouched low and was half-hidden by the cab door. The cabby had vanished, ducked down behind his wheel.

I finish them all off or I get the hell out of here, Gurk thought.

Did aphids fuck or did they procreate in some other way he knew nothing about? If he didn't jump out of the Fiat and shoot these people maybe he'd get a break on the karmic ladder, skipping the fruit-fly step and coming back a few levels up, a bee, say, buzzing from flower to flower, or a snail sliming along some damp basement.

Or a lawyer, he thought.

He drove quickly past the taxi. The guy from the train station was down on his knees, shouting something. Gurk couldn't hear what. The older fellow stood behind the open door, staring at the Fiat's plate, memorizing it. Fat lot of good that's going to do, Gurk thought. The registration was fake, no two ways, the car probably stolen. Gurk drove, tyres squealing, air dense with exhaust pall, through the streets of the industrial estate.

He didn't look back.

Perlman helped Eddie to his feet. The taxi driver, a chubby man with a liver-coloured birthmark on his neck, stumbled out of the cab.

'Fucking hell,' the cabby said. He examined the hole left by the bullet in the side door. 'Fucking hell,' and he said it several times in amazement.

Perlman showed him his police ID, as if this might mollify him. 'I'm sorry. That was unexpected.'

'Why the hell are you bastards riding about in taxis anyway? I thought you had souped-up squad cars,' the driver said. 'And don't even *think* about asking me to follow him, because I'm having none of that lark. Look at my hands, man. I'm shaking like a leaf. It's a Valium I need,' and he stepped back inside the cab and slumped chalk-faced behind the wheel. 'Fucking hell,' on and on, an incantation.

Perlman said, 'It's not worth chasing him. He'll dump

the car first alley he comes to,' and he mentioned something vague and apologetic about reimbursement and repairs, then he walked towards the building. Eddie followed. He thought of the bullet that had slammed into the cab door, and Gurk's face which, with dreadlocks gone, looked intense and luminously determined.

It was hot in the building and the air smelled of blood. Flies buzzed.

Eddie stood over Haggs, who lay face down, one eye gone, the other wide and open and blind. In death he seemed a few inches shorter than in life, as if he were dwindling.

Perlman sighed. 'I wanted him. But not like this. No way.'

Eddie looked at the other two bodies. Violent death always unsettled him. He'd never quite developed the protective carapace he found so common among his colleagues.

Perlman said, 'Allow me to introduce you, Eddie. The woman is – *was* – Rita Wright. Rita Wrong would've been more accurate. The other's John Twiddie, something of an enforcer for our Roddy, and very very nasty. Rita was Twiddie's helper and lover. They were not nice people, Eddie.'

Eddie gazed at the girl, and had an impression of safety pins and metallic studs and steely clasps covered with blood. There was nothing left that resembled a face. He turned to look at Twiddie. Bare bone was visible where flesh had been blown from the side of the skull.

'Right piece of work, our Twiddie,' Perlman said.

Eddie was shocked to hear a slight expulsion of air from Twiddie's open mouth. He went down on his knees and listened. 'Jesus, he's still breathing, Lou.'

Perlman came closer. 'Only just.'

Twiddie suddenly raised a hand and with enormous effort clutched Eddie's arm. He whispered so quietly Eddie was obliged to bring his face level with the man's mouth.

'You . . . eh, a priest . . . ?'

A priest. Eddie said nothing. Twiddie was functioning at a level where it was doubtful he'd have understood a response. How he'd managed to survive the wound to his head was one of those freak occurrences that depend on such circumstances as the trajectory of bullet or hardness of bone, or even something as unquantifiable as the sheer will to linger in the world a little longer. Eddie had seen shotgun victims survive bullets to the brain and stabbing casualties whose cerebra had been pierced without fatal effect.

'I've done bad things, Father . . . I want to confess.'

Eddie looked into the man's eyes. The glazed blue light was dulling rapidly and the pupils were tiny. 'What bad things?'

Twiddie tried to focus on Eddie's face. His eyes lacked coordination and his body convulsed. His hand slid from Eddie's arm, leaving a streak of blood.

Twiddie spoke again, voice almost inaudible. 'Rita . . . where are you, doll . . . doll, you there . . .' And then he was silent and his dead eyes stared directly into Eddie's face.

Perlman fingered Twiddie's pulse. 'He's gone. Christ knows where a soul like Twiddie's finds sanctuary. Look, get the cabby to drive you back to your sister's place, Eddie. I'm going to have to call Tay and I don't want you here when the heavy boys arrive. Tay'll ask too many questions, and you don't need to be involved.' He took his cellphone from his jacket.

Eddie walked outside. He heard Perlman talk on his phone. The cab driver was still slumped behind the wheel.

'Dennistoun,' Eddie said.

'You mind if we drive really slow?'

'Drive any way you like.'

Eddie climbed into the back seat and looked at John Twiddie's blood on his arm.

Twiddie, the enforcer. *I've done bad things . . .*

I want to confess . . .

Confess what? He wondered if it had been Twiddie who'd pulled the trigger on Jackie. If Haggs had ordered the slaying. Do the old man, Twiddie. Do it right.

He let the thought drift and stared out at the lamplit city and recognized nothing, street names, storefronts, bars. It was strange to him, and he had the feeling it always would be, a city he'd remember now and then, with diminishing clarity, when he was home in Queens.

58

In Joyce's flat Eddie sat on the sofa. Joyce wasn't home. He assumed she was with Caskie. He rang his home number, and heard Claire's melodic voice on the answering machine. *'We can't come to the phone right now. Please leave a message. Thanks.'* Fuck it, he felt lonely. He wandered through the small flat, drank tap water in the kitchen, looked out at the backs of the surrounding tenements. Laundry, lit by electric light from windows, hung motionless on lines below.

He ran cold water over his arm and rinsed Twiddie's blood off his skin, then he went back to the sofa and lay down, closing his eyes: a dark rolled across him and he dozed briefly. In his sleep he felt John Twiddie's hand circling his wrist. He woke, startled, trembling, half-expecting to see Twiddie stand above him, resurrected and murderous. He sat upright, clenched his hands together. I need alcohol, he thought, a shot for the nerves. He found a bottle of brandy in the kitchen and drank from it and he thought about Twiddie in the back of Jackie's car, waiting with gun in hand. Anticipating the moment. He thought of a twilight street and a half-acre of wasteland and Jackie getting into the Mazda and maybe he was humming a tune under his breath and Twiddie changed the whole picture into nightmare. He closed the brandy and set the bottle down and heard the sound of Perlman's voice in the hallway.

'Careless, Eddie. You didn't shut the door properly.'

Eddie couldn't remember getting out of the cab and climbing the stairs and returning to the flat. All blank. A kind of blackout. Going through motions. He went to the kitchen doorway. Perlman was smoking a cigarette in his avid manner.

'How did it go?' Eddie asked.

'Tay took total control. He likes to run his own show. He's excited, although you'd need an electron microscope to see any change in his expression. You'll be seeing Gurk's face, or a likeness thereof, on your TV screens before the night's out. Buzz buzz. The city's being turned over like a fucking pancake . . . You were never near the place, you understand. You never saw any corpses.'

'What about the cab driver?'

'I've spoken to him. He never saw you either. In fact, he saw nothing and he prefers it that way.'

Eddie was quiet a second before he came back to the inevitable and said, 'Caskie.'

'What can I say about him, Eddie? We've got nothing on him. The voices that might have spoken out – they're all silent. He just fades away into retirement, and that's the last of him.' He cleared his throat a few times. 'I need some night air. It's lovely out there. Crime to waste this kind of weather. You fancy keeping me company?'

'I'd like that.' The last of Caskie, Eddie thought. Not where Joyce was concerned. What did she see in the future? Herself and Chris yachting away on fresh tides? Love, albeit one constructed on lies and old subterfuges, prevailing? Why not. Maybe she deserved to believe in love.

Don't we all, he thought.

Perlman wandered towards the door. Eddie followed him down the stairs and outside. The air was curiously sweet; a hint of new-mown grass suffused the dark. They walked towards Whitehill Street, then turned left to Duke Street. Perlman was a slow stroller, pausing now and again when he heard a strain of music from a tenement flat or the sound of a cat or somebody's voice upraised in domestic dispute. Along Duke Street the smell of deep-fried food hung in the air. Streetlamps glowed. A moon almost full sailed over the city. Perlman stopped outside a fish and chip shop. 'I need some grease to keep my strength up. Fancy anything?'

Eddie wasn't hungry, but he went inside the shop anyway with Perlman, who ordered fish and chips. The counterman dumped the food into a cardboard tray which he then tucked inside a paper bag. Perlman carried the bag outside.

'They used to wrap it in old newspapers,' he said. 'You could read the sports pages while you stuffed your face,' and he fingered a chunk of fish into his mouth as he strolled. He belched very slightly. Eddie looked up at the lights in tenements. A birdcage hung in a third-floor window. A woman reached up to drape a cover over the cage. From somewhere else in the city came the sound of cop cars, harsh and unrelenting.

Both men crossed Duke Street.

'The city feels different,' Perlman said. 'I like to think I'm tuned into the wavelength of Glasgow, and when there's interference, I can hear it. Murder interferes with my reception. There's static.'

Eddie said nothing. He was seeing Charlie McWhinnie dropping to the ground and the crowd parting to create a space, and he was imagining Tommy Gurk, comedian, shooting Roddy Haggs; Gurk, wanted man, out there somewhere in the night.

They reached the corner of Bluevale Street, where Eddie said, 'I'd like to stroll down to the warehouse. I might never get another chance to look at it.'

'Planning to stay away for good? Don't like the city, eh?'

'Maybe I've been gone too long, and the drift's too wide.'

'Glasgow's an acquired taste,' Perlman said. He dumped the leftovers of his fish and chips in a dustbin.

They walked down Bluevale Street. When they reached the high wire fence that surrounded the yard, a huge dog reared barking inside, a snarling flurry of fur and claws and bared teeth. Beyond, a subdued light was lit in the warehouse window, and it cast a rectangle of illumination across the yard. Inside the building somebody was playing 'Red River Valley' very softly on a harmonica. Eddie was reminded of old black-and-white prison movies, the condemned man shuffling along Death Row to the chair and some sad-eyed inmate playing a harmonica in the background.

The dog's eyes gleamed, and piles of old brick and sinks and cisterns became dim forms piled willy-nilly. The dog kept growling, throwing itself at the wire. The harmonica stopped.

'Shut up, Chet,' Eddie said. 'Cool it.'

The dog appeared puzzled hearing the sound of his own name and withdrew a moment and then, triggered by his training, he dashed himself again at the fence.

A door opened somewhere in the darkness and a voice called out, 'Who's there?'

'Eddie Mallon.'

Joe Wilkie appeared at the fence. 'This is a surprise, Eddie. I wasn't expecting company at this time of night.'

'Joe, you remember Detective-Sergeant Perlman?'

'Sure I do,' Joe Wilkie said. 'We talked already.'

'Indeed we did,' Perlman said.

Silence a moment. Chet backed off, walking in anxious circles. Joe Wilkie fingered the rims of his glasses and coughed.

Eddie said, 'I just wanted a last look at the old place. Can we come inside?'

'Now?'

'Is it inconvenient for you?'

'No, no problem,' Joe Wilkie said. He rubbed his jaw, a small gesture of uncertainty, then unlocked the door in the fence and allowed Eddie and Perlman to come through. He shut the door with one hand while he restrained the dog with the other. 'We were just doing some stocktaking.'

'At this hour?' Eddie asked.

'Jackie was never tidy. It always got on my wick the way he did things. I like to keep an accurate record of stock. You want to know what you've got, what's of any value and what's junk you can just toss. Jackie hoarded like an effing jackdaw.'

They went inside the warehouse. The door to Jackie's office was open a few inches. A light burned in there. Eddie surveyed the warehouse; here and there dim overhead lamps were lit. Stone columns and statues, piles of rusted scaffolding that looked like the bones of prototype robots that had failed, quarry slates in great haphazard

412

stacks, chimneypots. It's weird, Eddie thought. Here was his childhood and suddenly he couldn't relate to it, not the way he'd done before in this place. The past was receding.

Joe Wilkie, cleaning his glasses against his sleeve, was emitting tension: was it because he didn't like being interrupted at work?

Perlman sniffed the air in the manner of a wine buff. 'You know, the smell in here reminds me a wee bit of the old subway system. That lovely underground damp and the scent of old oil.'

'Aye, I noticed that a few times.'

Ray Wilkie materialized from behind the stack of slates. He held a harmonica in one hand. He wore a warehouse-man's grey coat, exactly like Joe's. He nodded and tapped the harmonica in his palm.

'So this is the musician,' Perlman said. 'Sweet stuff, son.'

'I just blow a few notes now and then,' Ray Wilkie said.

'He's modest as hell.' Joe Wilkie laughed. 'You should hear him when he really gets going. He's a wizard. Play some jazz, Ray. Play that Cole Porter thing. "Love for Sale."'

'Da, I don't feel like it.'

'Never hide your light under a bushel,' Joe Wilkie said. 'Make with the music, Ray.'

Ray Wilkie frowned at his father and then raised the harmonica reluctantly to his mouth and blew. Eddie recognized the tune at once, but Ray hurried through the melody and into an area of improvisation that rendered the piece unrecognizable.

'Boy's good,' Perlman said.

'He's as good as yon fella, Larry Adler,' Joe Wilkie said with pride.

Eddie listened as he walked around the warehouse. A rat scuttled out from below a heap of old tarps. Above, pigeons stirred on metal beams. He stopped beside a headless statue whose shoulders were thick with years of bird droppings, and he looked across the room. The big aluminium door leading to the yard lay open; directly outside, both rear doors of the Mercedes van were wide.

Eddie was conscious of Joe Wilkie watching him. 'Isn't he something, eh, Eddie? Isn't the boy a bloody marvel?'

Without turning, Eddie said yeah, Joe, Ray was really something all right.

'Come back and listen,' Joe Wilkie said.

'In a minute.'

What looked to Eddie like a stack of unwanted items had been piled inside the big Merc. Stocktaking. Discard the worthless. Busted lamps, formica-top tables and broken-legged chairs all in a tangle, stacked rolls of old linoleum. 'Love for Sale.' Ray Wilkie segued into another familiar old song, 'Dream A Little Dream', and Perlman laughed in a delighted way.

Eddie drifted to the open door and looked at the Mercedes. He stepped out into the yard and peered at the junk heaped inside the vehicle. The dog appeared and growled, standing between Eddie and the van. Eddie shushed it, calmed it, carefully ran a hand over the animal's great powerful head.

Joe Wilkie called out, 'You can't hear the music properly from there, Eddie. Come back inside.'

Eddie didn't answer. *Joe doesn't want me near the vehicle. I wonder why.* 'Dream A Little Dream' took off down musical highways Eddie had never travelled before. Ray's playing became frantic. The tune changed mood, darkening suddenly, its inherent tenderness altered.

Perlman clapped his hands and said, 'Oh, he's the goods, he's the goods all right.'

'He's got the juice,' Joe Wilkie said.

'God-given,' Perlman said.

Eddie was drawn to the jumble-sale items in the van. He stared at the rubbish, and realized that between the arrangement of unwanted goods and the front of the van was a space which seemingly contained nothing, nothing he could see, as if the broken-down furniture had been deliberately arranged to create an impediment to viewing the deep interior of the Mercedes, but that was a stray thought, a gatecrasher, and Eddie was about to let it drift out of his mind when something caught his eye and he peered through a tunnel in the clutter of crap and caught a certain smell, a whiff of lubricant familiar to him – and then he turned away, tense, a pulse in his throat, hoping he hadn't been noticed, sticking his hands in his pockets, 'Dream A Little Dream'.

He heard Perlman clap his hands and say, 'Brilliant, bloody brilliant,' and the kid stopped playing and Joe Wilkie came to the doorway and asked, 'Jazz not your thing, Eddie?'

'Sometimes. It depends.'

Joe moved past Eddie and shut the doors of the Mercedes.

It's too late, Joe. I've seen. I didn't want to. I wish to Christ I hadn't.

He stepped back inside the warehouse and Wilkie followed him. Perlman was lighting a cigarette and talking in a quiet voice to young Ray, who was showing the cop his harmonica. Two jazz freaks, they could probably talk for hours.

Eddie saw the door of Jackie's old office open and Senga appeared there in a pair of dark blue jeans and a pale blue sweater. Her hair, unpinned, hung to her shoulders.

'Well, *Eddie*,' she said. She came towards him, embraced him. 'Why did you not tell me Eddie was here, Joe?'

'You were busy with the books,' Wilkie said.

'I was bored to hell, so I was.' Senga linked her arm through Eddie's. That overwhelming warmth, that sense of inner strength: Eddie thought some magnetic force flowed from the woman.

'I heard the music and I assumed Ray was just tooting for his own fun the way he sometimes does, I had no idea you were here . . . Who's your friend, Eddie?'

'Detective-Sergeant Lou Perlman. He's been involved in the murder investigation.'

'Oh.' She smiled and held her hand out and shook Lou Perlman's. 'Nice hands, Lou. You shouldn't bite your nails.'

'Bad habit,' Perlman said. 'I'm full of bad habits. You wouldn't believe.'

'I'd believe,' Senga said.

Eddie gestured round the warehouse. He felt he had to explain his presence. He cleared his throat. He was hoarse, dry. 'An exercise in nostalgia coming here.'

'It has a few good memories for Eddie,' Joe Wilkie said to Perlman. 'He was always in and out of here when he was a wee nipper. Right, Eddie?'

'Long before I knew him,' Senga said.

Eddie nodded. An awkward, fragile moment: something hung in the balance. *I saw what I wasn't supposed to see.* He was aware of Joe Wilkie running the back of his hand across his lips and Senga taking a cigarette out of a packet and Perlman, a gentleman, lighting it for her, and he was thinking of the van and the jumble of objects in back, and an old Scottish word came back to him that Granny Mallon had used to describe a mess, a *heelie-goleerie*, an expression he hadn't thought of in years. *This is a right heelie-goleerie*, she'd say when dirty dishes had been stacked in the sink or clothes lay about the bedroom floor.

'Let's call it a night,' Senga said. 'We can finish up the day after the funeral. I'm bone-tired.'

Eddie looked at her face. Without her usual make-up she appeared a little pale. Stocktaking on the night before the funeral service.

No, it's not that, not that at all.

Perlman said, 'I'm going back to the office. I've got some stuff to deal with.'

'The law never sleeps, eh?' Senga said.

'Only when criminals do.'

Eddie realized Perlman was flirting mildly with Senga. His body language was different, the stoop was gone, he was alert and smiling and his voice was less of a growl. They went out into the yard. Joe Wilkie locked the warehouse door. Ray made sure the van was secure, trying the back handles. The dog whined and whooped, knowing it was about to be abandoned for the night.

They walked into the street, all five of them, and Perlman said, 'I'll find a taxi.'

Joe Wilkie padlocked the gate. 'Taxi my arse. I've got my car right here,' and he indicated an old Honda. 'Not the most comfy ride in the world, but it'll take you anywhere you want to go and it won't cost you a penny.'

'I don't want to inconvenience you,' Perlman said.

'Come on, get in, I insist.' Wilkie unlocked the car. Ray climbed into the back seat, Perlman sat in front and looked cramped.

Joe Wilkie slid behind the wheel. 'What about you, Senga?'

'I'll walk home,' she said. 'I need the air and it's a nice night, and I've got Eddie for company. He and I can have a chat just between ourselves.'

Perlman said, 'I'll call you, Eddie.'

The Honda drew away in a stuttering burst of smoke, and Eddie stood without moving. Senga's arm was hooked through his. He was reluctant to move, as if by taking a step away from the warehouse he was abandoning his childhood for all time. When he moved, he didn't look back.

He walked up Bluevale Street to Duke Street, Senga attached to him. Neither spoke for a couple of blocks. When they'd crossed Duke Street and were heading up Whitehill, Eddie said, 'Tell me, Senga.'

'Don't ask.'

'Just tell me the truth.'

'The truth?'

'It would be a real nice change to hear it.'

Senga said, 'It's a rare commodity.'

'Practically extinct.'

'And you found it in the back of a big Mercedes van, didn't you?'

'It's a funny thing how hard you can look and how many people you can question,' Eddie said, 'but sometimes you find the truth by pure goddam chance.'

59

Gurk waited until the group had dispersed and the street was empty, then he crossed to the wire fence and looked at the sign: J MALLON, TRADER. This place was worth a look, he thought. Christ knows, he didn't have a whole lot of options. Earlier, while he'd been lurking in shadow, he'd heard the dog. A deep bark, trained guard dog probably, maybe a Doberman, maybe an Alsatian. It didn't matter. He had a way with animals. They sensed a oneness with him.

He took a run at the fence, which was twelve feet high. He caught the wire at around eight feet and hung there, gaining a toehold and raising his hands to the top. He'd haul himself up and over, one last effort, deep breath, easy-peasy.

The dog was going mental beneath him, snarling, barking, jumping at the fence.

Gurk said, 'Calm, boy, calm calm.'

The dog raged, curled, sprang. The stench of fur was strong. The teeth shone in what little light fell from a nearby streetlamp. Gurk caught the upper part of the fence: but in the poor light he hadn't seen the fucking barbed *wire*, compacted into wicked rolls and bolted along the top of the fence, that lacerated the palms of his hands. Jesus. *Ohhhh*. This world of pain. This world of mace and crucifixion on barbed wire.

He yelped, and dropped into the yard, and the dog streaked at his ankle and bit deep through cloth and flesh and muscle to the bone, and now blood flowed from Gurk's hands as well as his ankle. He kicked the dog hard and the creature squealed and came back at him, springing at his stomach, digging its teeth through the material of his shirt and locking on to his belly, and Gurk karate-chopped the beast with a vicious downward thrust, but the animal – enraged – continued to cling.

My gun, Gurk thought, I'll end this *now*.

The weapon was in the left-hand pocket of his jacket and it was his left hand that had been spiked by barbed wire and he couldn't grasp the gun. He twisted, tried to reach across himself and the snarling head of the dog to get the gun out of the pocket with his right hand, but the dog, sensing menace, dug fangs into the moving hand and burst the skin and veins and Gurk thought his right hand had been thrust inside an incinerator.

Right hand, left hand, stomach, he was bleeding from various punctures and wounds. How much fucking blood had he lost? He clubbed the dog with the side of his left hand – *aieee*, the pain of it – but the animal came at him again and this time Gurk got the gun out just before the beast launched itself in flight, but pain had slowed him and the dog bounded with such ferocity that the gun went spinning out of Gurk's hand and clanked to the ground somewhere close but dark.

He'd never find it.

He was leaking blood and he had no gun and no safe crawl space and the animal was *insatiably* violent.

It circled, sprang again, battered his shoulder, and he lost balance and fell over into a pile of bricks, sharp-edged motherfuckers that pierced his skin. A bed of goddammed stone.

He crawled, hands soaked with blood, brick grinding into palms and knees, and the dog came after him and caught his cheek in its teeth and he imagined fangs penetrating flesh right to the teeth and through that to the soft roots inside the gum, and I am going to black out pretty fucking soon if I don't get this monster, this remorseless thing from hell, away from me –

Easy boy easy now –

His voice enraged the dog. It bolted up on to his spine and bit the back of his neck and held on and Gurk turned this way and that, locked in a struggle with the beast, smelling its vile breath and the stink of its fur and all the while aware that blood was flowing out of him at a rate he couldn't afford, because before long he'd be light-headed and pass out. He fumbled for a slab of brick and brought it down on the dog's head and the animal, perplexed, yapped and drew back, but Gurk knew it was a momentary relief, the dog was gathering forces, regrouping to come again, and this time Gurk didn't think he could beat the animal off. He crawled over brick and rubble and planks of wood.

The Zone. Enter the Zone. Fuck the Zone. There is no Zone.

He saw the white van a few yards away. If he could get inside the vehicle and slam the door.

The dog was barking, ready to fight again.

Gurk tried to open the back of the van. *Bastard was locked*. Sometimes fate doesn't have a kind word for you. You're fucked no matter what.

He slammed a lump of brick against the handles again and again, bang bang – yield, you bastard, open up, let me inside, gimme haven. The dog raced towards him and he swung, lashing out with the brick, catching the animal at the side of its head, and it fell over dazed, but Gurk knew it would come again and if he didn't find a hiding place he was mincemeat ready to be dropped on the sizzling hot coals, barbecued Gurk on a bun. Karmaburger.

The animal, vast in bad light, shook itself, recovered its senses, and soared at him, crossing space with a lethal grace that in other circumstances Gurk might have admired. Sleek flesh, density of muscle, defiance of gravity such as that possessed by a hawk on the wing, and those teeth, those precise surgical instruments. He stepped back, stumbled against the van. The dog came zooming in and caught him low on the thigh and the teeth went through his flesh and this time Gurk screamed because so much pain couldn't be contained in silence. Screamed, then grunted, then went down on all fours, face to face with the beast. They eyeballed one another, the dog's snout a few inches from Gurk's nose: in that cold canine eye Gurk saw no mercy. He crawled back, the dog watched him, waited, cocked a head to one side, growled softly. With his spine pressed to the rear doors of the van, Gurk wondered, could I make a run for it, a beeline for the fence, did I have the strength to get over that wire? He was lathered in his own blood. He was weak.

He watched the dog, listened to the throaty growl and wondered if maybe the beast was offering a truce –

But no. Dogs didn't do truces. They didn't understand the concept.

The animal came at him and knocked him down and he banged his skull against the van as he fell, and what he saw was the full moon in wayward flight across the sky and all the stars above the city opening like ripe silver flowers and he raised a hand wearily as if he might push the dog away, but the animal yanked off a finger between its teeth and Gurk felt the horrible tearing of his flesh. He'd never known a sensation like that before: a bit of his body just ripped off. Like that. Gone. In shock he struggled to his feet while the dog played with the finger. Shoulders slumped, he caught the handles of the van doors with his intact hand and suddenly metal snapped from the face of the door – luck *luck* – and Gurk eased the door open and a cascade of household furniture clattered down on him, tables and chairs and lamps, a crash of trash.

The leg of a chair poked him directly in the mouth and he heard a tooth break. He spat blood. He thought, I fall to pieces, and he hauled himself into the back of the van and lay among the disarray of formica tables and pleated lampshades. He drew the doors closed. He knew he couldn't get out. He was a prisoner. The upside of this was that the dog couldn't get in. He listened to it bark and bark and bark, and he heard it prowl round the vehicle, and then there was silence. Or maybe he was faint and the world outside fading.

He crawled to the back of the van and his hands encountered objects he recognized at once and he thought, Jesus Christ in heaven, I know what these are, but before he had a chance to appreciate the dumb irony of his situation he went out like a meteor striking some lonely tundra, and his blood flowed and he didn't hear the dog sit in the dark growling every now and then as it waited.

60

The place where the school had once stood, that vacant lot of nettle and dock leaf, seemed hostile in the dark. Eddie ran a hand along the railings as he walked. Senga still held his arm.

'You shouldn't have looked,' she said. 'Very naughty of you, Eddie. Spying like that.'

Eddie thought the night had an emptiness about it, as if the pulses of the city had been stilled. The street was quiet.

'So, Eddie. What will you do?'

He hadn't thought. He hadn't had a chance to think.

Senga took her arm away from him and stopped, turning to face him. 'Your father did it for me, Eddie. I asked him. I told him what our people needed, and he found it.'

'Our people?'

Senga said, 'Our people, my people. It's in the blood, Eddie. You can't just squeeze it out of your system. Our people over there need the weapons.'

'There's never an end,' Eddie said. 'It goes on and on.'

'What do you imagine – that everybody buys all this

disarmament shite? Come, we'll open our arms dumps and you can take a look and see how cooperative we really are. Fucking hell, Eddie, you can talk peace and coexistence until you've got steam coming out your ears, and the politicians can huff and puff about how bloody brilliant they are – oh, aren't we wonderful, we've brought peace – but at the end of the day you've got people who'll never trust each other, because there's been too much blood for forgiveness, and too much hate. There's no peace, Eddie. Only PR. Only the image. The shadow on the wall. No substance. Not where it counts,' and she laid a hand on his arm. 'We can never trust the other side. Understand that. We may fight among ourselves now and again, we may squabble furiously, but when it comes right down to it, we're united against the enemy.'

The enemy. Eddie stared into the haunted darkness of the school grounds. He imagined cigarette smoke drifting from the boys' lavatory and the sound of kids playing football in the field beyond the bicycle shed, that space where annexe buildings, skimpy in their impermanence, had been erected to absorb an overflow of students. He grasped the railings and felt he was looking at the last resting place of innocence.

They strolled a few more yards. This time Senga walked a couple of feet away from him. She isn't touching me now, he thought. The intimacy has been abandoned.

'How did it work?' he asked.

'Jackie paid half the money upfront to Gurk in Largs, McQueen brokered the deal and got his share, and the cargo was duly collected by Joe Wilkie from a drop on the outskirts of a place called Port Glasgow. The other half of the money was due when Joe returned with the goods.

But then that arsehole Haggs stepped into the picture and he brought disaster – so who pays up when Jackie is dead?'

'Somebody has to,' Eddie said.

'But who? I don't have the three hundred thousand plus, or whatever Jackie owed.'

'Jackie must have had it,' Eddie said. 'He intended to pay, didn't he?'

'Jackie always squared his debts, Eddie. I have no doubt he had the cash somewhere. Finding where – that would be the real problem. Where did he stash it? There must be a thousand places, eh?'

She knows where Jackie hid his cash, Eddie thought. She knows.

He said, 'The cargo leaves Glasgow soon, I'd guess.'

Senga didn't answer this question. She said, 'Our people are waiting for it at the other end. They'll pay well for it. That's where Jackie made his profit.'

'But you won't use that money to settle the debt with the original supplier, will you?'

'Me? That was all Jackie's business. I don't know anything about these weapons or where they came from, do I? Look at me, Eddie, and you see a woman who just liked a few drinks and listening to the Eagles and keeping my man happy. An ordinary soul.'

'A nice façade,' Eddie said.

'And I played it well,' Senga said.

She's screwing with Kaminsky and his operation, Eddie thought. A dangerous line to walk. If Gurk couldn't get the cash or the return of the goods, somebody else would be despatched. And after that, if need be, somebody else. And on. Kaminsky would send his minions and emissaries into Ulster and Glasgow until he found out

426

what had happened to his consignment. It was business, and he couldn't be perceived as soft.

Senga, locked inside an airtight old dream of Protestant ascendancy in Ulster, didn't seem to get this. People obsessed with ancient causes were blind to reality and change. Eddie thought of the van and the clapped-out furniture and the cargo that lay hidden in the space beyond the tables and chairs, and he realized that he and Perlman had interrupted work in progress, that Senga and Joe and Ray must have intended to conceal the cargo under tarps, inside boxes, whatever.

I shouldn't have looked but I did.

He said, 'Jackie wasn't a fucking bigot.'

'Bigot? Where did you dig that one up, Eddie? We're not talking about bigotry. I believe in what I'm doing. I was born believing in it. That hasn't changed. That doesn't make me a bigot.'

'Okay. What word do you prefer? Patriot? Jackie didn't support this decrepit cause of yours.'

'Did he ever tell you that?'

'When I was a kid, I remember –' He paused, bringing back to mind that night when Jackie and his cronies had sung Orange songs in the living room, and the air smelled of smoke and spilled beer, and he fell into a silence that was oppressive.

'Somebody should point out that it's years since you've been a kid, Eddie.'

'I remember he said there was no difference between people, no matter their religion.' No, those hadn't been his words exactly, he'd phrased it some other way, and Eddie, foundering in the shallows of memory, troubled by this whole situation, couldn't bring back the precise sentences. I've lost my way, he thought.

'He was kidding you, Eddie. He was always a great kidder.'

'No, you must have changed him, you must have influenced his way of thinking –'

'He liked to think for himself, Eddie. He knew where his sympathies lay. They weren't quite so strong as mine, but he knew.'

They'd reached the corner of Onslow Drive. Eddie saw a lamp go on and off in one of the terraced houses. In the brief illumination a middle-aged woman appeared in a window, then vanished, like a figure in the abrupt pop of a flashlight. He thought of Jackie Mallon disappearing in sudden darkness, slipping away, indefinable. *Dad*, he thought. *Just come back for a moment and defend yourself, make your position absolutely clear.*

'I'll report this to the cops,' he said.

She shrugged. 'I don't think you'll go to the police, Eddie.'

'What's stopping me?'

'Let me put it this way, Eddie. We have friends all over the world, Eddie. Sympathizers who see a way of life threatened, and they don't like it. They feel they're being forced into peace on terms they don't want. They see their traditions undermined and the tide's turning against them, and they're in no mood for going under. They don't want to share power with some people whose hands are very very bloody. These friends are serious people.'

He saw it immediately: Claire and Mark. A dark night. A morning at dawn. A new mailman delivering a package. A man pretending there was a fault on the phone line or a gas leak, anything. Claire's car exploding as she turned the key. Mark struck by a hit-and-run driver while he cycled to school. He imagined empty rooms. Where a wife had been, or a kid, absences. His heart twisted in his chest.

He said, 'I don't believe what you're telling me.'

'I don't have to spell it out, Eddie. I like you. I'm fond of you. We're family, just about. Believe what I'm telling you, that's all I ask.'

'I fucking hate being threatened,' he said.

'Threatened? I was merely mentioning certain possibilities, love.'

He thought of the Mercedes. Automatic weapons in layers darkly shining at the front of the big van, some covered by tarp, a few visible. He had no idea how many. Hundreds of AK-47s or some similar automatic weapon, it was impossible to estimate the number of guns or the diversity of the consignment – there could have been thousands of rounds of ammunition, packs of plastic explosives, scores of grenades, and handguns. Without going back and checking the contents of the van, how could he know?

He gazed the length of Onslow Drive. *Our Orange friends need some hardware, what can you do for us, love?* And Jackie smelled the spoor of profit even as he heard the beating wings of the angels of Protestant righteousness. He'd buy the guns and sell them to Ulster connections at a hefty profit. Guns in oilskins, boxed and buried in fields, hidden in the outbuildings of lonely farmhouses, sunken in pits, concealed and ready for use when the time came.

He looked directly at Senga. *She'd threatened his family.* The full force of that struck him, and he was angry. 'Christ, you're such goddam neanderthals,' he said. 'You and all the people like you. Your marches and your tribal songs and your fucking banners. All right, Glasgow might be more superficially sophisticated these days and you might be better dressed and wear more fashionable clothes and maybe you visit your hairdresser once a week and get your fucking nails done, but the poison is the same as it always was. You're living in the past, and it's barbaric.'

'Believe me, I wish it was different, Eddie. I wish there was trust and peace and happy wee children from both sides of the divide holding hands and singing, believe me. But it's a barbaric world, and you're a part of it as well, so don't criticize me,' Senga said. 'Where the hell do you think the other side get their money and arms from? Smack in the heart of where you live your little bit of the American dream, Eddie Mallon. New York. Boston. Chicago. The money rolls in every time somebody sings "Danny Boy" in an Irish pub. Pass the coinbox. Let me make a contribution to the boyos. Well, we have to defend ourselves against all that cash rolling across the Atlantic into Ulster, Eddie, and there's not a damn thing you can do about it.'

'Now give me the speech about how the weapons are for defensive purposes only,' Eddie said.

'Of course they are, dear,' Senga replied. 'We're a peaceful people. But we're not weak.'

'You'll only shoot if you're shot at, right?'

'Naturally.'

Eddie shook his head: and I was born yesterday. 'What did you and Jackie see in one another, Senga?'

'We loved. We loved a lot.'

'And the Cause,' Eddie hated the sound of the word. 'Was that something you had in common, huh?'

'Oh, we had more in common than that, pet. But love's

430

a deep mystery. All kinds of people fall for one another and you never know why. Right?'

He looked at her face in lamplight. She was going somewhere with this, and he felt it, and he wanted to kill the conversation, but he waited, fascinated even as he sensed dread.

'Take . . .' She paused. She looked up at the streetlamp, concentrating on the torrent of moths, as if she were trying to count the numbers.

I know what she's going to say, he thought. I feel it coming.

'For instance, your sister,' Senga said. 'What does she see in Caskie? Makes you wonder.'

'You knew about that,' Eddie said.

Senga laughed. 'Oh, for years.'

Eddie sensed the light from the overhead lamp dwindle to little more than a faraway star. 'What about Jackie?' he said.

Don't tell me, he thought.

'Jackie knew from the beginning, Eddie. Jackie knew from the minute the stalls sprang open and Joyce was off and running into Caskie's bed.'

'She was *twelve*, for Christ's sake,' Eddie said.

'Mature for her years,' Senga remarked.

'I can't believe Jackie –'

'Oh, grow up, Eddie. He not only *knew*, he *encouraged* it.'

'I don't *believe*,' Eddie said.

'No skin off my nose,' she said. 'But Jackie wanted his own tame policeman. He thought Caskie might come in handy along the way somehow. So Joyce was deliciously sweet bait. Ripe and fresh, straight off the tree. And Caskie – poor love – he fell so hard it was almost comical.

And seeing him try to hide his feelings around Jackie, God, it was farcical.'

Caskie had been handcuffed by Haggs; but Jackie was the one who'd been the original jailer.

Chris Caskie, tame house-broken policeman.

'You might say Jackie pimped his own daughter,' Senga said.

'*Might* say? Is there another expression?'

'I prefer to think of it as a strategic manoeuvre, Eddie. Nightcap?'

Eddie refused. He felt cold. Despite the warmth.

Senga said, 'Another time then. Goodnight.'

He watched her walk away, tall and loose in her movements, and he thought about going after her to dispute her version of events, then he decided no, why should he, he'd come to the end of the road. Like every other time he'd tried to exculpate his father, it would be energy wasted and another scar across his heart. There was a limit to the search for excuses: nothing about Jackie Mallon merited tolerance. He deserved to have been shot in the back seat of a car parked on a piece of waste ground on a Glasgow street at twilight, with a whiff of scotch on his breath and his face blown off.

He fucking deserved that kind of ending.

His life had been a bankrupt affair.

Eddie turned and moved slowly down the street in the direction of Joyce's flat. He let himself into the building and climbed the stairs. Bone-weary. Sweating. A man at the end of revelations too heavy to carry. He was dragging his body through time until the moment of departure. He thought about the guns. He thought about Jackie negotiating in Largs with Tommy Gurk. He thought about Caskie and Joyce, and how Jackie had brought them together in the event that he might gain something from that illicit relationship. The cunning and brute insensitivity of it.

Yes, Jackie, fuck you, you deserved your execution.

He unlocked the door of the flat and went inside.

Joyce sat on the sofa with a glass of wine in her hand.

'It's late,' she said.

'And I'm tired.' *You never knew you were used, did you, Joyce?*

She got up from the sofa. 'I heard about McWhinnie and those other killings . . . Chris says the police are turning the city upside down. It's awful to think . . .'

Everything was receding already, Eddie thought. The tenements, the streets, the names of the living and the dead. Joyce put her arms round him. *Yes, dear Joyce, it's awful to think.* He smoothed a strand of hair from her forehead with a gentle gesture. You love Caskie, he thought. You've made a settlement with your emotions.

And you never knew Jackie played the role of a dark cupid, a gargoyle. And Caskie didn't know either.

'I'm sorry I upset you before,' she said.

'I'm over it, Joyce.'

'Are you?'

He nodded. 'I hope it all works out for you. I hope it happens the way you want it to happen.'

'Is that your blessing, Eddie?'

'Bestowed,' he said.

'In a half-hearted way.'

'You expect more?'

'I don't know what I expect,' she said. 'I wish you liked him.'

Eddie said, 'Bad chemistry.'

'No. More than that. Those accusations you made.'

433

'Let them go, Joyce.' He lay down. The room seemed fuzzy. 'Early rise in the morning.'

She leaned over him, kissed his forehead, and he wanted to cry suddenly. He felt a sadness as black as night in the city. There was the ache of dead hopes inside him.

'Big day,' she said. 'Hard to believe he's gone.'

'Yes.' They held one another tightly for a long time and Eddie remembered the cab that had taken him and Flora away so many years ago, and all the wreckage since, lies, crimes, love misguided, love abused.

61

A hot stillness lay across the city. TV weather maps showed an infinity of clear skies. Forecast: brilliant. More of the same. Eddie sat in his dark suit in the back of a small limo. Joyce, subdued in a black suit, wore sunglasses. And Senga, a small black lace scarf covering her face, sat next to Joyce in silence. She reminded Eddie of a grieving dowager, imposing and dignified in her well-tailored clothes of grief.

The limo travelled east in the direction of Daldowie Crematorium; the car carrying Jackie's coffin was scheduled to arrive at the crematorium at the same time as the limo. The funeral service would begin at 10:30.

Eddie hadn't slept. He'd lain a long time in the dark, too fatigued to sleep. At one point he drank a glass of Joyce's wine but it hadn't helped him over the edge. He called Claire and spoke quietly to her, nothing words, just touching base – everything okay back there? Mark staying out of mischief? He loved the sound of her voice, her calm, the way she had of putting a favourable light on dark circumstances. *Yeah, but how would she deal, say, with letter bombs?* He imagined limbs blown off. His head was filled with images of destruction. He lay staring into the unlit sitting room, and the busts, outlined by a faint light from a streetlamp, seemed to be watching him like the members of a judiciary committee.

Do you really want to put your family in danger?

No, of course I don't.

Then will you say nothing about the armaments?

I can't stay silent. That would be –

What? Unprofessional? Dereliction of duty? Unethical?

All of the above –

And how do you find Jackie Mallon?

Guilty.

No mitigating circumstances?

I've looked hard.

None then?

None.

Bleary, he gazed from the limo into the sun and realized he was travelling deep into eastern regions of the city that were totally unfamiliar, ramshackle industrial buildings, used car lots, run-down housing. He had a sense that none of this was real, he was skirting the threadbare fringes of Glasgow, a man travelling inside a white-lit stereopticon. Something called Parkland. Then Carland. Then Zoo Park. McDonalds. St Peter's Cemetery. He wished he'd worn dark glasses.

He felt Joyce's hand on his own. He squeezed her fingers. He longed for sudden rain, more appropriate weather for funerals, mourners crowded under umbrellas, the miserable drip of water from trees, small puddles on the oiled wood surface of the coffin.

The limo entered the grounds of the crematorium and parked in front of the chapel. Eddie got out, helped Joyce from the car; she looked frail and unprepared for this. He glanced at Senga who raised her veil and smiled at him in a quiet way, and then dropped the veil back. *Remember, Eddie*, she was saying. *Keep in mind our talk.*

He scanned the place. Men in uniforms worked the memorial gardens, surrounded by rich-coloured roses. Here and there people sat on benches in contemplation, remembering their dead. Eddie found himself gazing at the green metal dome of the furnace above the chapel building; heatwaves shimmered from the dome, and the air became liquid. At what temperature did the human body combust? Infernal.

The motorway beyond the memorial grounds droned and droned. There could never be any tranquillity here. Trucks passed day and night, cars, buses.

Joyce took off her glasses. She had that look of bewilderment, a mourner's disbelief: *This can't be happening. We'll wake from this any moment now.* Eddie held her by the elbow and took a few steps with her towards the chapel. He recognized the man from the funeral home, Crichton, dark jacket and pin-striped trousers and an expression of discreet sympathy. He nodded at Eddie very slightly just as Eddie entered the chapel.

Fluorescent lights, cream walls, a ceiling of deep red. Jackie Mallon's coffin sat on a plinth behind which were brass doors. The coffin would slide through those doors and down into the furnace, into that fiery kiln where wood and flesh and bone imploded in hot ash.

He sat beside Joyce. He was aware of Chris Caskie, dark-suited, sitting in the row behind. He felt an odd little flutter of pity for the man. Joe Wilkie sat alongside Senga: conspirators. There were others Eddie had never seen before, neighbours probably, some of Jackie's old friends. At the back, close to the door, was Lou Perlman. He raised a hand in Eddie's direction, a small gesture.

Here we all are, Eddie thought, waiting for fire to begin its consummation.

Waiting for Jackie to burn.

A minister, dog-collared and pallid, stepped in front of the plinth. *We come to mourn our friend Jackie Mallon,* he said, and his voice was high-pitched and nasal, and Eddie, in a moment of irreverence, imagined him calling bingo numbers.

We come to remember him, and his kindnesses, and the goodness of his heart. We come to extend our condolences to his family members. He was a man much loved by his friends and held in high esteem within his community. He was a man who loved life.

Eddie glanced at Caskie. But Caskie, with a distant depressed expression, was looking up at the ceiling, as if he wanted no connection of eyes.

We come today to pray for his soul.

Yes, Eddie thought. Pray hard. If you can find the man's soul. Jackie had lost it long ago in the streets of this city. *Caskie's shagging my daughter and he doesn't know I know. It's a bit of a laugh, intit? Have another glass of cider, Senga, eh?*

Was it only late in life you felt some shame, Jackie?

But it was way too late by then.

Eddie lowered his head, stared at the floor. Don't talk about the weapons. Say nothing, keep them secret. But that went against his grain. Such neglect would come back years later to haunt him, and he'd open a newspaper and read about a fresh atrocity in Ulster, or see a bomb-wrecked house smoulder in a TV film, and what would he feel then? I could have helped. I could have helped just a little. If I don't lift a finger, how will I live with myself? How will I teach my kid anything about

438

truth? Okay, so I take extra security precautions, vigilance at all times, I live as if there's menace in everything, and if it comes right down to it we pick up and move and start all over: it was a lot to ask, a lot to expect. But what else could he demand of himself?

We come to pray that God takes Jackie into the heavenly masses.

Eddie held his sister's hand. She uttered a sob, raised a hand to cover her eyes. Caskie leaned forward and touched her shoulder to comfort her, and Senga, turning a little, observed these small movements from behind the mystery of her veil. Joe Wilkie blew his nose. Somebody else, situated at the back of the chapel, began to cry. Eddie expected he'd feel something, despite himself, maybe a reflex of grief, a spasm of sorrow, but no, he was beyond it now.

He remembered his hand in his father's and Jackie Mallon saying, *I was never a criminal, son. Remember that. If anybody says anything against me at school, learn to ignore it. I was the victim of spiteful men. That's the truth.*

You never knew what truth was, Dad.

Eddie realized music was playing through a sound system and that people around him were getting to their feet and singing 'What A Friend We Have in Jesus'.

I was never a criminal, son.

Eddie thought: You were worse than that.

Curtains closed in front of the coffin. Senga uttered a tiny cry and Joyce wept against Eddie's shoulder, and then he led her up the aisle and out of the chapel into the sun. He looked at the crematorium dome and the waves of heat rising from it, aware that Joyce had wandered away from him and was talking to Caskie, and that Senga, a cigarette in her hand, was surrounded by neighbours and acquaintances who wanted to offer a word of comfort, a hug, a kiss.

Perlman said, 'I like these things brief. Get to the point. I never believed in long-drawn-out funerals. I've been to some where I wished I'd brought a packed lunch and a bloody sleeping bag. Believe me.'

'It was good of you to come,' Eddie said.

'Everything I do has a concealed purpose, Eddie. I'm a cunning old bastard. I've been around the block more times than I can count. Never forget that. I've got my eye, and I mean that in the singular, on a certain person here.'

'Would he be a colleague of yours?'

Perlman said, 'Aye. A few wee problems have cropped up that I need to probe a little further.'

'Such as?'

'They concern poor Charlie McWhinnie and his relationship with Caskie.'

'Tell me.'

'It appears Charlie kept a small if somewhat cryptic personal notebook tucked away in his desk under paper clips and rubber bands,' Perlman said. 'A few entries are intriguing. Something about a safe house in Govan, and Matty Bones – which seem to verify your own suggestions. Also, it seems there were certain irregular orders he took from Caskie beyond the call of duty. Of course, it might just be Charlie's imagination working overtime. He was unhappy with his lot, after all, and unhappy men are sometimes driven to flights of utter fancy.'

'Sometimes,' Eddie said.

'But not in this case,' Perlman said.

'Right.' Eddie looked in the direction of Caskie, who returned the look and smiled a little nervously. Lou

Perlman lifted one hand, a lazy gesture of greeting at his colleague. Then Caskie stared away in the direction of men pruning roses.

Eddie watched his sister. Be strong, Joyce. And when things go wrong for you here, when the ground opens up and the plunge is a deep one, you know where I'll be, and you know I'll help. Then he gazed at Senga, tall and seemingly devastated by her grief, red hair tucked under her wide-brimmed black hat, holding court with friends and neighbours. She had a handkerchief in one hand and she stuck it under her veil to wipe her tears away. Eddie couldn't see her eyes, couldn't tell if she was looking at him.

He said, 'I don't see young Ray Wilkie anywhere.'

'Aye, right enough, he's missing,' Perlman said.

'I seem to remember I heard him say he had some overtime to do at the warehouse.'

'On the day of the funeral? Seems strange.' Perlman lit a cigarette and sucked smoke deep. 'There's an odd wee note in your voice, Eddie. Are you trying to tell me something?'

Eddie hesitated. But he knew where he was going and what he had to say. There wasn't a choice. There never had been. 'They had a load of quite fascinating crap inside that big Mercedes van, Lou. Maybe Ray's planning to dump it.'

'What crap?'

'Old tables and chairs, busted lamps, other stuff.'

'You sneaked a peek, did you?'

'I'm a nosy bastard.'

'And you think this van's worth me bothering about?'

Eddie said, 'Yeah. But you didn't hear it from me, Lou.'

'An anonymous tip.' Perlman sighed. 'We get a lot of them in this business.'

'Some good,' Eddie said.

'Others pure shite.'

'But you check them all anyway.'

'That's what we do,' Perlman said.

'No sign of Gurk?'

'Not yet. Ah, I daresay we'll find him soon enough.'

Eddie looked in the direction of the green dome and he thought, *You're burning, Jackie, you're ashes now*, and just for a moment he imagined his father hovering above this place, taking form in shifting patterns of light, a malign genie.

Burn, old man, float away, leave us. A father lost for all time.

But he'd always been lost. You only dreamed he might be found, Eddie.

There was a sudden breathless silence as if for a tiny fraction of time Jackie had taken all the sound of the world with him as he turned to flame, then Eddie heard people chattering on all sides of him, and someone crying, and the crinkle of plastic wrapped round a bunch of lilies held in somebody's arms, and Lou Perlman, activated by an anonymous tip, punching numbers into his cellphone.

Eddie felt sun hot on his face and heard the motorway buzzing like a machine fuelled to run for ever and he imagined the city spread out under a haze of heat, and light rise in shimmering films from the Clyde, and he thought: Welcome to Glasgow, and goodbye.